Stories From the Near-Future

Edited by
Andrew MacRae

DARKHOUSE
BOOKS

Anthology copyright © 2016 by Darkhouse Books
ISBN 978-1-945467-01-1
Published September, 2016
Published in the United States of America

Darkhouse Books
160 J Street, #2223
Niles, California 94539

Stories from the Near-Future

Introduction

by Andrew MacRae

The future has a sneaky way of creeping up on us, catlike, as the future is wont to do. We blink, and another technological wonder is achieved. Electric cars are commonplace, and rarely a day goes by that a self-driving car doesn't purr softly by – and politely stops and waits, should someone be in its path. Entry-level 3D printers have dropped enough in price to make them affordable for grade schools. The IOT (Internet Of Things) is ushering in a new class of connected, and sometimes chatty, appliances. We feel sorry for the robotic dog kicked by its inventor, and cheer for the robot who successfully stacks one box upon another, despite a human moving the boxes away, and trying to trip it.

Smart phones, smart cars, smart toasters, where can this lead? Will our new, interconnected life deliver on its Bellamyian prophesies, or will we find ourselves in an *Uber-tech*, Orwellian world?

Such is the nature of the stories in this anthology. We asked our authors for stories envisioning life in the *Near Future* – a future recognizably related to the world in which we live today, but a smattering of years from now, and extrapolated from our present.

Within this volume you will find cautionary tales that warn, satirical stories that bite, humorous horror stories and the reverse, and stories expressing an optimism for our future that is based, not on our tool-making skills, but upon on our species' indomitable will to persevere.

Andrew MacRae
September, 2016
Niles, California

We begin our anthology not with a bang, but a soft pop. It is a noise that heralds the dawn of a new age of travel. This story by Michael Chandos takes us to the time of its discovery – and introduces us to an enjoyable pair of protagonists.

Mr. Chandos has retired after a long career in the USAF Space Command and turned to writing. Readers of the Darkhouse Books anthology, Stories from The World of Tomorrow may remember his story, Master of the Underworld, from that volume.

Blynk

by Michael Chandos

"Jelly, your lab is a mess. Are you having a satellite junk sale?" Amber kept her lab spotless.

Cubesat components were piled into cardboard boxes on the floor. The large table in the middle of the lab was hidden under wires, solar cells and subassemblies of unknown utility. Even Kjell's 3D printer and CAD terminal were covered with discarded experimental parts and colorful failures from the printer. It wasn't dirty, just full. It was a typical small lab for a young PhD.

"Hi Amber. No, moving. My repair drone space experiment was a success, and NASA and the Dean are very happy. NASA is so happy, in fact, they've funded three more years to make a bigger and more capable space experiment, and that made the Dean so happy, he's given me a larger lab with a cleanroom, and several grad students."

Kjell looked around at his mess. "One of them will be back with the trolley in a minute and we'll take more boxes to the new lab. It's in the northeast corner, first floor. You can come and see it."

"Busy, busy, busy, huh?"

"Actually, the NASA money won't be here for a month or two, so the Dean strongly suggested I take a vacation."

"Oh? Where are we going, boyfriend? Vegas? Don't you go anywhere without me. I'm not staying behind like last year," she said, with a warning smile.

"Uh, well, I've been working on an independent project at home in my garage lab. I plan on giving it a couple weeks of concentrated work, but maybe then we can go somewhere." He wrung his hands and held his breath.

"I love you, Dr. Kjellgaard, and will follow you anywhere, especially when it involves a large pool, sunshine and endless buffets. Is what you're doing more important than taking your beautiful girlfriend to Las Vegas?"

"I'm, uh, turning my Ensign electric car into a spaceship." Kjell looked away. He was inventive and creative, but his garage, like his lab, was filled with imaginative but unfinished projects and bins of possibly useful materials of every description.

"Aw, what are you doing, Kjell? I like that little car. I always feel like Cinderella in her egg-shaped carriage. Is it broken?"

"Oh, no, not at all. Do you know that some guys in the Netherlands posted a video where they sealed up the doors in their Ensigns and they floated? One guy even made his submerge. A submarine is just a spaceship in water, you know."

"All you need now is a warp drive."

"Exactly!" Kjell stabbed at the air with an index finger.

"What?"

"I've got one. Made it myself. And I think it works."

"You have oxygen and a way to maneuver around and, just maybe, a way to get home alive?" said Amber. "Do I have to worry about you being hurt? Like when you went skydiving that time? I hate that feeling!"

Kjell only stared.

"This is pointless, isn't it?" Amber looked at him with satiric sadness and turned to leave. "My protein biosynthesis project calls me."

"No, Amber, it's not pointless." He followed her down the hall. "Come by tonight; I'll show you."

Kjell put a hand on her shoulder. Amber stopped, but didn't quite look at him. "I've built prototypes, and they've gone somewhere and they've returned. And not with magic crystals or Unobtainium 115, but just wires, electro magnets, battery power, and the right theory."

"They come back? By themselves?"

"I've made an automated inertial guidance and control system with accelerometers and gyros from cell phone parts."

She looked at Kjell. "Oh, Jelly. You actually plan to scale it up to send your car into space-knows-where? Soon?"

"Yep, almost done in fact. I'll do a few instrumented runs with the latest prototype for fine tuning and then send the Ensign off with the automated G&C."

"And then… get in yourself." Amber shook her head and resumed walking down the hall to the elevators. "I'll stop by tonight and I'll bring dinner. Please be there and not on the moon. Ok?"

"You'll be amazed, Amber," he yelled after her. "And so proud of me, dear Amber," he said to himself.

Amber parked her Lux400 in Kjell's driveway and walked to the backyard. A detached garage sat behind the small two bedroom house with the door facing the alley behind. He had expanded the garage three years ago to turn it into a personal lab. Only a five foot strip of meager grass was left for a backyard. An open carport on the right side was where he kept his trusty mini-truck.

Amber had stopped at her apartment to change to jeans. The hot fried chicken in the paper bag she carried was intoxicating.

The Ensign electric car was just inside the garage door. Kjell bought it for the short drive to the campus; it was the right thing to do, he always said. But, almost as soon as he bought it, he began to tinker with it. He upgraded the motor's power, doubled the battery packs and installed a wireless hotspot. Everything was instrumented, with an internal wireless network for data communications, backed with a large solid-state recorder.

The car was royal blue, like a dark robin's egg, which the carbon-fiber molded shape resembled. The windows and doors continued the smooth shape, and a large solar panel was glassed into the roof. A twelve-inch tire with a short fender capped each corner. It looked silly to some, but it'd run forty-five miles per hour and it cost nearly nothing to drive.

Was Kjell here?

"Doctor Kjellgaard, are you here or on the moon? Your goddess has arrived and she has fried chicken offerings."

"Yo," shouted Kjell, from the floor. He got up, dusted plastic shavings from his coveralls and quickly cleared a space for dinner on the central worktable. He pulled up two chairs and set surprisingly clean dinnerware.

"Oh Lord, that smells good. Did you get macaroni and cheese or coleslaw? Actually, either is fine." Kjell could get absorbed by his projects and forget the time, especially dinnertime and bedtime.

"Let me show you what's new since you were here last. That shiny cylinder on the bookcase is the prototype for the repair drone we just tested in space. It saw life here first. The big white delta wing thing is a hand-launched communications relay drone that uses a hydrogen fuel cell I built myself, and a high-speed electric motor from an English carpet sweeper to drive a ducted fan. It can orbit over a forest fire and relay radio comms between the fire boss and all the deployed fire teams. It flies by itself for hours using GPS and it lands where it was launched when the fuel cell runs low."

He retrieved a large glass jar that had a mangled collection of wires, batteries and unidentifiable wreckage.

"This is the most important one," he said with reverence.

"I guess it wasn't successful."

"Well, first tries seldom are, but it was the start of my warp drive, or interdimensional drive. I don't know what to call it because I'm not exactly sure what it does.

"My man in the wilderness." Amber made herself comfortable on a lab stool. "Okay, give me the lecture."

"I shall explain. I came across an academic paper by a Professor Pyotr Dyatov, a Russian theoretical mathematician who was analyzing Maxwell's equations of electromagnetism. Now, we know the equations work. They govern almost everything we do from electric motors and televisions to generating electricity in the first place. We also know they are approximations, especially when photons are involved. Quantum Electrodynamics is more precise."

Amber rolled her eyes. "I have a Doctorate in Biophysics. I think I know this."

"Well, Dyatov wasn't a physicist, so I don't think he realized the physical consequences of his analyses. His derivations, with Gauss' Law as a backdrop, point at magnetic monopoles and a source for propulsive power of a special kind. My extensions to Maxwell with Dyatov's variations can be scaled to transport any defined space to almost any range with repeatable accuracy."

"I presume the stuff in the jar is proof of your theories?"

"That was just the first experiment; I'm on number six now. I didn't understand fully how the applied electrical power affected propulsive forces. Turns out, the system is really efficient and it needs remarkably little power. The secret is in the coils and the oscillator. On the first flight, I accumulated power in a big capacitor, pulsed it through the coil in a special way, and blamo! The thing flew into pieces. Scorched the table a bit too."

"Did you try again, Doctor Tesla?"

"I did. The next two tries were less destructive. I developed an electrical power to propulsive power balancing algorithm and the fourth one just… disappeared."

Amber began to clear the table while Kjell to explain.

"I wanted it to come back, so using cell phone parts again, I built the next one with a timer and a computer to automatically reverse the settings and repeat the pulse. I included a cell phone camera and some memory, and put it all in a thermos bottle. I figured space was cold. It came back in the three minutes I had programmed it for, but it sorta bounced off the table hard and

11

things broke again. The camera worked but I guess the prototype had been spinning so all I saw was a spiral of lights. The current model has a control moment gyro and accelerometer made from my phablet and three cameras with wide-angle lenses. It's ready to go tonight."

"Oh. No TV tonight, I guess. Actually, I'd like to see it work."

"That's it on the table. Bet you didn't notice it. I bought a much larger thermos since there's more electronics to fit inside. The cameras are those hardened glass blisters and the rubber rings made from instrument packing material will help cushion the landing, I think. I've developed a power to distance algorithm and a relative coordinate system for the computer to use to jump back with more precision. It's been on the charger for a while. Should be ready."

"Is it safe to set it off inside, Jelly?"

"It seems so. It doesn't physically 'move' from here to the coordinates I set, not through what we consider normal space. Haven't punched any holes in the ceiling. I think it moves almost instantaneously, either between dimensions, within another dimension or across warped and folded space. I hope the video gives me a clue"

"Ok. Where do you want me to sit?"

"How about we both stand behind the heavy equipment in the power rack, just in case? I've set the algorithm at five thousand kilometers straight up with a return in three hundred seconds. I'd let it fly longer but I haven't figured out how to compensate for the rotation of the Earth and a longer flight might have it land inside the wall or next door."

Kjell unrolled his tablet and entered a few instructions and numbers into the mission planning screen, and then pulled the power and data cables from the thermos. He picked the cylinder up and hooked it to fishing line hanging from the ceiling.

"I started hanging the prototypes from fishing line after the table got scorched."

"Why does it say Blynk 6 on the side?"

"You'll see when it goes. Anyway, it's the sixth model and I think the Y is sexy."

"Maybe I should change my name."

"Keep Amber. You're sexy enough as it is. Ready?"

They moved behind the humming power tower and Kjell turned off the lights in the room except for two LED floods for the lab cameras.

"Three, two, one, go." Kjell pressed a key on his tablet. There was a brief medium-blue glow around the thermos and then it vanished with a slight pop.

"Not very dramatic, huh? Blink and you'd miss it, right? Now we count down the time. I suggest we stay behind the tower." He put on heavy leather gloves.

The three hundred seconds dragged by. Amber startled when a monitor came on to count down the last five seconds. The thermos blinked into existence just above the table and plopped down on its rubber rings. It began to emit vapor like super-cold carbon dioxide fog.

Kjell hurried to the workbench and plugged in the data cable. "Space is well under minus one hundred degrees Celsius and the outside of the thermos is pretty cold when it comes back. That's water vapor turning into an ice cloud." Kjell twisted off the cap, took off his right glove and reached into the thermos.

"There's no active heating inside, but it only feels a little cooler than room temperature. The cargo is fine, too."

In his hand was a field mouse lightly strapped down with a thin gauze wrap to a small platform. He removed the gauze and put the mouse into a cage.

"I want to watch the mouse for a couple days to see if there are any ill effects. You could help with that, Amber."

"It's not my usual white lab mouse, but… It looks pretty hardy so far. Poor mousie."

"It's my first passenger. Let's take a look at the data on the mini-super."

The mini-super was a massive parallel processing computer about the size of a floor woofer. It could handle numerous parallel data streams and their analysis programs at the same time and it was packed with terabytes of memory. The monitor was at least a meter wide. Various graphs and columns of numbers appeared on the screen in segmented windows.

"The trip was pretty gentle. The mouse experienced more G's landing on the table than in the voyage itself. Camera one and two don't show much, dots, presumably stars. It's nice to see a very low rotation rate. The best camera looks along the minus Z axis, or behind. I'm hoping to see the sun or maybe even… oh my gosh." The window representing the rear camera showed a large, over-exposed circle slowly moving across the screen. "I think that's the Earth from five thousand kilometers. I need to tweak the auto-exposure."

"The mouse is nibbling on the seed log. I think he looks ok," said Amber. "I wish he could tell us what it felt like."

"Yeah. I wonder too."

"Are you at work tomorrow?"

"No. My two graduate assistants will move stuff into the new lab and try to make some logical sense of all my crap for a couple days. I'll go in for a day next week and help organize things and set up the NASA follow-on task. I'll be here otherwise. Maybe I'll look up hotel prices in Vegas."

"You'd better. I have to work tomorrow, so I'm off to bed." Amber gathered her stuff. "Don't forget to water and feed the mouse and log everything he does. See you later. I'll call. This was fantastic, Kjell." She kissed him and hurried out the door.

Kjell tested Blynk 6 three more times over the next four days. Each trip was longer and went much further out as he was concerned low Earth orbit tests risked being hit by debris. The mouse went on the first two. Other than protesting the gauze wrap, he came back intact. The last flight included an Earth rotation compensator and went out to two million kilometers and twenty minutes. Kjell included a battery-run heater and instrumentation for cosmic rays and other radiation. The mouse, Kjell named it Kal-Mouse, stayed home for that one.

Kjell still wondered how it felt.

———————————

Amber opened the garage door, looking for Kjell, since he didn't seem to be in the house. "Jelly, are you in here?" Nothing. She checked on the mouse; its water and food were ok.

As she turned to leave, she found Kjell in the Ensign. He wasn't moving, just sitting on the driver's side, staring. Maybe he hadn't noticed her yet.

He had coated the outside of the Ensign with what looked like tough truck bed-liner material. The windows and the small oval hatchback had a second layer of Lexan carefully sealed over with molecular glue. Blisters containing cameras were installed at strategic points. Black squares were attached to the sides, top, front and back. The robin's egg had been ruggedized and prepped for space.

Behind the front seats Amber could see Kjell's drive coil, a dodecahedron-shaped web of evenly wound copper wires. A thick braided steel cable fed power from the battery packs. Colored wire bundles ran from the drive assembly to all corners of the tiny car, doing what she couldn't tell. She tapped on the passenger-side window.

Kjell looked like he'd been awakened from a deep trance. When he saw Amber, he blinked and opened his door. "Oh Amber, I'm sorry. Have you been here long?"

"I was afraid you would take a trip into space in this thing and leave me a premarital widow. I didn't think you'd trip out mentally, too. Have you slept and eaten? Recently?"

"Uh yeah. Got up just an hour ago. Always got up early on Saturdays, even as a kid. Had to catch my favorite cartoons. Still do it, no matter how late I was up Friday night."

"I brought breakfast. Let's eat and you tell me what's happening." She placed paper-wrapped food on the table.

"I sent the big thermos out for a two million kilometer, twenty minute test. It came back as expected, but it slammed into the table. It's flying days are over."

"I see the mouse made it through the crash."

"He wasn't aboard for that test because I needed room for more instrumentation. It was tumbling rapidly when it came back and it bounced around the room a few times. Took over a hundred gee's, so it's just as well the mouse wasn't aboard."

"What happened?"

"Natural forces two million klicks out are small, but after twenty minutes floating in space they were enough to spin it up, a complex three-axis spin. To help the Ensign stay stable I've attached microfluidic electrodynamic thrusters to all six axes, those black squares you see. They will afford enough control for basic stability. I'm gonna send Kal-Mouse out in the Ensign this morning."

"Kal-Mouse?"

"Oh, yeah. I guess I was getting tired and punchy yesterday. He needed a name, so I made up Kal-Mouse, like Kal-El, Superman's real Kryptonian name when he was a baby and escaped the planet's destruction in his father's rocket. Could you wrap him in his gauze? We'll test the Ensign."

Amber carefully wrapped the mouse on to his platform and placed him on the Ensign passenger seat. Two small shock cords held it down. Kjell was busy with mission planning on his tablet.

"This will be a quick one, seventy-five thousand kilometers to get above the Van Allen radiation belts and just five minutes duration. I've programmed in a one hundred and eighty degree maneuver to test the thrusters so we should see the car pointing the other way when it comes back."

Kjell set the lights and cameras, and both of them retreated to the far corner of the garage behind a bank of file cabinets.

"Ready? Three, two, one, go." The Ensign flashed blue and blinked out with a somewhat louder 'bloop' than the thermos, something like dropping a heavy book onto a carpet from ten centimeters. They stood close to each other, but without moving or talking. The monitor flashed the final seconds and the Ensign popped back pointing one hundred and eighty around, bouncing lightly on its tires.

Kjell released the doors and started to analyze the streaming data download. Amber reached in for Kal-Mouse. The wrapping had loosened in zero gee. The mouse leaped out of the door and disappeared into the next room.

"Oh, damn. I'm sorry, Jelly."

"No problem; he has served bravely and was due to be released anyway. There are seat belts for human passengers." At that thought, Kjell quickly looked at Amber. She was staring back. Her face reddened and she looked away.

"That's the whole point. I have to go myself. At work I design and build space sensors and systems, and even free-flying satellites. Inside it all is my desire to go myself."

"I know." Amber, arms folded, walked to the main lab room.

Kjell followed. "The Ensign will work and it will come back."

Amber was at the empty mouse cage. She turned to Kjell. "Oh? Can you survive a hundred gees's?"

"I think I've solved that problem."

"One success might just be luck. You should test it many times, under stress, to make sure everything works before sending people. Promise me you'll test it properly." Amber searched Kjell's face. "No, don't say anything. When I leave to go home you'll try it anyway, and I'll have to scrape you off the garage floor with a shovel."

Kjell couldn't move.

Amber walked to the Ensign and stopped, one hand to her forehead. She closed her eyes, and then opened them as her head came up.

"Ok, Jelly, what should we take with us?"

Kjell's eyes widened. He started to smile, then his brain kicked in. "The data download from the first flight doesn't show any dangerous problems, although the cameras still need more dynamic range. Let's wear winter coats and bring sunglasses, even though it's a quick flight. The Ensign is insulated and has a heater, but you never know, and the sun will be bright." Kjell consulted his linked tablet. "The video and data memories have been cleared and reinitialized, and the internal network shows green on all inputs. I've already prepared a spares and tools kit. There's a bottle of pure oxygen available if the air gets stale. We just need to hit the bathroom, get in, and run the short checklist. I'll set it for the same as the first flight, seventy-five thousand and five."

"Ok, fine." Amber gave him a quick hug and did her prep. "I'll wear a small blood pressure and temperature monitor. It has its own memory and power." Amber, the scientist, was calm.

The Ensign was small. In their winter coats, their shoulders touched and they had to take turns fastening their seat belts. Kjell locked the doors electronically and set mechanical over-center latches to ensure they stayed sealed. He checked the power system and monitored the capacitor loading. The charging system whined a little; there was no vibration. The thrusters heated up and the video and data recorders started.

"Ready?"

Amber took a deep breath. "Yes."

"Three, two, one, go!"

BLYNK

There are unsavory undersides to all technologies, and some can be quite profitable, if you don't mind the moral ambiguities. The toll-takers of our next story demonstrably do not. The sight of them gliding up in their air cars is the last thing anyone wants to see—and for some—it is the last thing they see.

Mr. Gibbs is a double threat, both a professional musician and a professional writer, with over two-dozen stories published in the last few years. His turn toward the shadows came early in the third grade, when a macabre story he wrote prompted a parent-teacher conference.

Toll Takers

by David J. Gibbs

Winter nights were always quick and cold. The city was unforgiving in that respect. Dirty buildings were a constant audience outside his sparsely furnished apartment. Peeling paint fell from the ceiling, an almost constant bit of habitual dandruff he flecked off his belongings daily. The curtains, discolored and frayed, were from five or six tenants ago, as was the coffee table and the dinette set with the one heavily-duct taped leg.

Other than sleeping, he didn't spend much time in his apartment, and the thought of spending money on such things, much less having to shop for them, seemed tedious and unnecessary. He realized if his mother knew the squalor he lived in, she would have been livid. Thankfully, she knew nothing more than he was gainfully employed with the League and she believed he was doing well.

The freezing rain that had lulled him to sleep a few hours ago, still tapped out its uneven song against the window. The hand held

ARC glowed bright blue across its oval base, the shrill chirping still grated on his nerves. That's what woke him up.

It didn't matter what the weather was like, when the call came, he had to answer it. He knew that, despite his scowl at the sound of the freezing rain. After midnight and before dawn was the sweet spot when most of his calls came through. Most of the other Toll Men he worked with despised the late hours and the darkness that tainted these calls. For him, it had been a perfect match. It was the perfect job for an insomniac with a need to keep busy.

The small screen on the ARC's face filled with the details of the call, including diagrams, pictures and victims involved. It made responding to the calls so much easier than it used to be.

Martin Newcomb sat up and rubbed his hand through thick brown hair. He grabbed the handheld ARC and read the screen, squinted against its glare and exhaled tiredly. It was his third of the night. Granted that wasn't close to his record which was eleven calls in one night, but then again, that was in the stiff and unrelenting heat of August when the annual drought was upon the city, not the dead of winter.

"Not again," Marty groaned realizing that the call was from the West End District.

That was one of the more violent districts, and despite the city's best efforts it remained that way. One of his friends had been attacked while responding to a call just a few weeks ago, and it had put everyone on edge downtown. He wasn't looking forward to heading out, but knew he had to.

Marty dressed quickly, donning his uniform of black pants, tall boots, and bowler hat. They were all that remained from the early days of the League of Toll Men. He grabbed his bag and went to the garage, where an Air-Hearse waited."

He disconnected the Air-fill hose and put it back into the Hydrogen slot on the tank with a satisfying rattle. He paused a moment, checking the digital display panel beside the fill port of the hearse, determining it was full enough for his needs. Brushing his thumb across the pad, the door opened with a dusty rush of air from the pneumatics.

He left the steep hills of his neighborhood for the dark, towering heart of Downtown, the hearse gliding a bit closer to the ground than regulation allowed, because he hadn't time to get the right rear cushioner replaced. He wasn't worried, Marty knew the roads were paved and leveled regularly, otherwise he wouldn't risk it. The hum of the Hydrogen saturated air engine sped him along the outer edge of the city before cutting a bit south. It didn't take him long to arrive at his destination.

"We're here Marty. One hundred and six feet to the north. Three victims."

"Thanks Edith," Marty said, smiling at the sound of his long dead grandmother's mimicked voice coming through the AI navigation module of the Air-Hearse.

He swiped his thumb across the inner security panel of the hearse. The car's hum quieted as it settled down to the ground.

"Marty," said someone from the open window on the other side of his hearse.

"Joe," he said, slipping out of his car and looking across the roof. "How'd you get stuck with this one?"

"Hank is out with Titan Flu and Margaret is already on a call in District South."

"Titan Flu?"

"Yeah I know. I got the vaccine, but it was out of pocket, so a lotta the department opted out."

"I don't blame them. I didn't get it either," Marty said, shaking his head.

"Then I guess you better not be kissing Hank then, huh?" joked Joe.

Marty chuckled and said, "Well not so you'd know."

Marty headed toward the accident site, bits of plasticone and fiberglass crunching under his boots. It was an Air-Cycle, one of the newer ones, a model that was known to have a few control problems, and an older model Pillar Van powered by a copper wrapped ion turbine. Marty signed heavily, it would've been like a missile hitting a turtle. There was no hope for any of the victims.

He took off his bowler so he could get a closer look at the first victim. She was a young girl named Vivian Fitzgerald, her twisted and broken form sprawled out on the pavement. She was too small for anyone on his current client list. He would have to hope the other victims were adults.

Marty was in luck.

"Well look what we have here, the Vulture Culture King. Don't you get tired of all this bullshit Marty? Chewing apart all of these poor people the way you do. Doesn't that get to you?"

"Hey Jefferson. Don't you get tired of always being an ass-hole?" Marty asked not bothering to turn around. He recognized the officer's voice and wasn't going to give him the satisfaction of looking at him.

"That's all you got?" asked Jefferson, shaking his head.

"Hey I can't help it if HQ knows you weren't right for this gig."

Jefferson spit sharply to one side and said, "I didn't want the damn job, you idiot."

"Then why'd you put in for it, Jefferson?" Marty asked.

He knew he had him. There was a stretch of silence that was finally broken by "You know, I might have to report you New-comb."

"Feel free. You know that since they declared Toll Men legal guardians over all victims, you don't stand a chance. But if you've got the time to waste then, by all means, please bring it."

He came to the second victim and smiled. She would do nicely. Putting down his hard-sided case, he opened it and began readying his tools. The Coupler began warming up, the orange glow pulsing as it heated the coil cutter encased in both ends of the hollow machine. Marty pushed several buttons on the panel of the side of the Coupler. It opened up with squeak of hydraulics.

His headset clicked behind his ears, as he indicated that he was ready for his first toll of the night. The implant was cinched to connective tissue and allowed him to have direct contact with The Booth, which was the central office. Even though it was required gear for all Toll Men, Marty didn't care for the metallic implant connectors.

He checked his list and smiled. He had been right, the adult female would help him with at least one of his clients. Placing her arm into the open sleeve of the coupler, he pressed several buttons and watched as it automatically closed. He was able to see an interior digital rendering of her arm from just above the wrist all the way to the shoulder through his helmet's interface. Everything appeared intact. He nodded and pressed the synch button.

With surgical precision, the Coupler's coils cut the arm precisely where he had set it. Once the cut was made, the Coupler moved the limb to a lower storage section where it could be sealed in plastic and chilled to the appropriate twenty-nine degrees Fahrenheit. As the storage process finished, the Coupler quickly created a replica arm from high-tension foam.

He shook his head. The only reason that the government sanctioned the Toll Men was that whatever parts they took as a Toll, they replaced with replica parts so that families could still have memorial viewings without their loved ones missing anything. He thought it was a little ridiculous, but then again, he didn't much care as long as it didn't keep him from doing his job.

He pulled the Ocular Weevil from a pocket and placed it over the eye socket, and pushed the raised red button. The Weevil made a whining noise before it began to sever the optic nerve. He needed just one of the eyes to clean code two of his clients.

It was early and he was already half way through his client list. He wasn't foolish enough to believe that it was a good sign of things to come, or that his shift would go quickly and he could clean code his entire list, but he could still hope.

"Are you planning on taking the entire night to code the scene? I mean I can go home and sleep for a few hours and be back if you're going to be awhile, Cupcake."

He put on his bowler, stood up, and watched Jefferson walk over. The large man had hooked his thumbs into the waistband of his uniformed pants.

"I marvel every day at why they haven't made you a lieutenant, Jefferson."

"I know, right? I figure I got it coming, though."

"Oh you do, all right," muttered Marty.

"Smart mouth there, Marty. Better check that."

"Or what Jefferson? You know you can't touch me. This bowler and this ARC make me out of reach. You're the one that needs to check that."

The big man's thumbs came free of his belt as he pointed at Marty and said, "Listen here, you spoiled little snot."

"The scene is coded. Clean it up," he said evenly, noting the anger seething behind the bigger man's eyes. Not that it mattered. Jefferson knew he was stuck. He knew his place. The Toll Men were at the top of the food chain.

He didn't wait to see the man's reaction. Instead, he stooped and put his gear back into his bag and headed back to his car. Marty nodded to his friend Joe, before dipping his head to step into the Air-Hearse. The door shut quietly and sealed out the night and all of its sounds. Taking a deep breath, his thumb swiped the dash and the car lifted with an almost silent whisper of air. Marty didn't bother looking back at the scene as he sped away.

He stopped for a quick bite, and afterward leaned against the hearse and finished drinking a can of Quantum Soda. After stopping for a quick bite, he leaned against the hearse and finished his drink. Tossing the crumpled cup into the can, his ARC alerted him to another call. Marty sighed. He wanted to finish his client list, but he also wanted to get some much-needed sleep. Marty knew that if he didn't respond and it turned out to be a victim with some viable parts to supply a client, he would be reprimanded. He already had two in the last year and knew a third would mean a suspension.

Jefferson would just love that.

Rubbing his eyes, bowler perched atop his head, Marty sped to the scene in his Air-Hearse. He was thankful that there wasn't much traffic at this late hour. Marty cut across the viaduct into Downtown. He directed his vehicle around the long curve that bordered Over-The-Rhine to the south, knowing that the Automated Construction Corps were working on the southbound lanes.

What he hadn't counted on however, was uneven pavement in the northbound lanes, and as he tried to slow down using the bracing jets, the right rear cushioner couldn't keep the back of the Air-Hearse from catching on the lip of the pavement. As the rear of the streamlined hearse bounced harshly from the broken and uneven roadway, the front dipped and the curb violently grabbed at it, tossing the vehicle end over end through barrier.

In a whitewash of light and horrendous tearing sounds of rending plasticone and fiberstone, he realized he was in some serious trouble.

"You're in some serious trouble sport," the voice said, cutting through the haze of pain and consciousness.

Something was wrong with his legs and his right arm wasn't moving. Blinking several times, his head pounded with sharp pain. A slick wetness dripped down the back of his shirt. He tried to raise his head again.

"Oh I wouldn't do that if I were you. That's gotta hurt."

Someone was kneeling next to him and he struggled to focus his eyes on them. He couldn't take deep breaths, his chest churning with a steady bright pain. Marty tried to get the ARC from his pocket so the person beside him could radio for help.

"You're looking for your ARC?"

How did they know what he was looking for?

"It's smashed. I smashed it. Didn't you say that made you above me or something earlier? Funny how things change, huh Marty?"

That brought him back to consciousness and the finger of a different kind of fear danced around his heart making him shudder. He tried to talk, but couldn't form the words. His hand moved up to his mouth and he realized his lower jaw was gone.

"Yeah you're a mess. Nothing really left to harvest from you. No Vulture Culture for this scene. It'll be cleaned and coded quickly I imagine."

His mind finally put it together. It was Jefferson kneeling beside him.

"Well nothing left that is, except your eyes."

Marty heard the familiar whine of the Ocular-Weevil and tried to scream as Jefferson fitted it against his eye socket. He could only manage a wet gargling sound.

"Guess we know who had it coming now, don't we Marty?"

Bud Sparhawk has been successfully publishing fiction since shortly after the earth cooled and continents formed. More information about Mr. Sparhawk, including a complete bibliography, may be found at his web site, www. budsparhawk.com. This story was previously published.

He tells us that this story was inspired by reading of advances in smart fabrics and micro-detectors that will allow the commercial goods we buy and wear keep a close eye on us.

The Suit

by Bud Sparhawk

My morning did not get off to a great start.

You did not pick up yesterday's milk order, the fridge chided over my house link. I looked in my to-do and couldn't find the order. Once again, my unpatched suit hadn't picked up the fridge's message, but just try explaining that to an irate icebox at too-damn-early on a dismal November morning when you're standing around in the bath wearing nothing but your earbud.

After cursing the engineers who had bestowed that Pandora's box of a modern appliance on me, I added "Get milk" to my to-do and resigned myself to a milkless breakfast of dry VegeCrunchies and the electrolyte-supplemented juice my ever-solicitous toilet had recommended in its prim schoolmarm voice after analyzing my morning pee and dump.

I wanted to follow my breakfast with a chocolate dough-nut and a hot cup of coffee, but the kitchen overseer insisted I eat one of Merck's enhanced biomedical apples to go with the stove's selection of an invigorating organic herbal tea. *Flu season is approaching*, it warned me as I took the apple from the tray. *You do not need additional stimulation*, it added as I sipped the vile, decaffeinated brew that it had dribbled into my commuter's cup.

For a moment, the thought crossed my mind that the whole kitchen was pissed at me for forgetting the milk. I took a bite of the apple, mindful of my toilet's warning about restricting my sugar levels and wondered, as I dumped the apple's core into the disposal, how my ancestors had managed to survive without smart appliances ensuring their continued health.

But a part of me wished I could find out.

The closet wanted to know what I wanted to wear to the office but, without the coffee and doughnut I was too sleep-fogged and sugar-deprived to think. Instead I grabbed the dark blue, double-breasted Lauren I'd worn yesterday. I really liked that suit, even though it was running a buggy version of e-suitware.

I stopped upgrading and patching that suit's software when I heard Lauren was about to release version 7.0. I generally avoid buying the first version of any release, but for Lauren suitware, I'll always make an exception.

With Lauren about to release, it was certain that the other major lines would quickly follow with upgrades of their own. Everyone in the dog-eat-dog world of e-Fashion industry was anxious that no rival gained more than a microsecond's advantage.

For a moment I considered wearing the Armani, just for variety. I'd gotten that suit for a semi-formal dinner party two months ago. It was nice-looking, fit me well in fact, but, like most of that line's strict protocols, refused to link with those suits that had been crafted by an "inferior clothier." The suit was gorgeous but was only useful in those circles where its e-snobbery was acceptable, if not expected.

The Armani's haughty incompatibility hadn't saved me from the clutches of a woman who had been wearing an Eddo gown. I later learned too late, and much to my embarrassment, that she'd set her e-jewelry to autoblog a continual stream of everything she was doing, both clothed and otherwise. That was a little too much disclosure for my taste, especially since it reflected poorly on my, how shall we say, performance.

So I put on the six-months-old Lauren, whose timeless cut was still fashionable. That's the value of classic cut and fabric.

Even with its occasional problem, the buggy v6.3 suitware was adequate for my work a day needs. The software kept a close watch on my health, maintained my appointment calendar in real time, and knew when to adapt to the sudden changes in temperature as I moved from frigid conference rooms to over-heated offices, cold washrooms, or even into the intense heat of Dallas's summer afternoons. I could put up with the occasional communications bug for a few more days, I thought.

Lauren had announced that the new suitware would have not only all the functionality of v6.3, but would maintain active links to the local environment, perhaps alerting the owner when their favorite restaurant was featuring something they liked or discovering where new shows were opening nearby. It even had a flash advertising suppression feature, which was skirting on the illegal but, so long as the suppression remained on less than ten minutes, it was permissible. That was a small price to pay to keep the suit network viable.

The suit's bug sometimes made meetings awkward. The automatic exchange that was part of the communications package sometimes locked up. When that happened I had to go through an awkward suit-to-suit request-permit-acknowledge routine that wasted precious seconds and made me look like a novice e-suiter.

The new version supposedly prevented that sort of gaffe and, in addition, promised to grab name, title, business names, web URLs, addresses, cell and other phones, suit numbers, email, personal web sites, blogs, registered biases or proclivities that were legally required or that demanded a degree of discretion, and any allergies or medical conditions of which I should be aware, all within one microsecond. Acquiring that much richer data set would place me at a definite advantage when it came to office schmoozing, or even measuring up a client. The first one with any advanced e-suit features always got a leg up on the competition.

You have gained two pounds over your ideal weight, my shoes announced as I slipped them on. I already suspected that from the way my underwear had tightened my waistband and how my SmartShirt had loosened the fit around my stomach.

Watch your blood pressure, my tie warned me as it clicked into place against my neck and synchronized with the shirt, suit, underwear, and shoes.

Thankfully, my suit had nothing to say as I slipped on the jacket. I suppose it was just happy to be worn.

Don't forget the milk, the fridge reminded me on the way out. *Watch those calories*, the kitchen reminded me. *Have a nice day*, said the door.

The morning went quite smoothly as my suit and I swam through the tsunami of junk calls, messages from assorted clients and vendors, competing text, cell, and phone calls, and requests from all the office machines, all anxious to perform some task for me. None of them gave rise to the appearance of the bug.

At the same time I was trying to keep up with the office's suit-to-suit banter, news, and the continuing arguments about football, baseball, soccer, and damn near every other sport I never watched. From the reactions of others my suit was probably missing half of what was being transmitted. Bugs. Sometimes I was grateful for them.

By the time my lunch break arrived I was fed up with the cascade of missed jokes, partial gossip, and tiny, tantalizing snippets of someone's previous night's adventures. I think there was a futile attempt to organize another disastrous office kick-ball league, but it might have been another sports discussion. Hard to tell when you can't monitor the entire string. Although I love my job, lunch gave me an opportunity to get away from the confusing din.

Dallas's downtown was teeming with the hustle and bustle of the workaday crowds and the buzz of a million advertisements shouting on every channel of my suit as I strolled along.

Despite the commercial and political cacophony, I loved walking around downtown and watching people in their endless variety: a stagger of joggers churning legs at a stoplight, the gabble of women carrying on a six-way vocal and electronic conversation, a fat man gesturing wildly as he shouted into his earbud, and two rich ranchers in suppression coats, dumb canvas pants, and unsubsidized leather boots ambling along and laughing, deaf to the electronic cries from storefronts, street vendors, and sidewalk kiosks. I resented them for flaunting their wealth so brazenly in public as if nothing mattered to them but what they heard and saw through their naked ears and eyes.

A moment later, my resentment evaporated as I passed by Giorgio's and saw that they were featuring orange blossom salad, my favorite, as a luncheon special. I queried the menu and, since its response didn't produce a stern warning from my briefs, I figured either the salad's labeled sugar content was acceptable or that not having that chocolate doughnut had kept my blood sugar levels at an acceptable level.

After a delicious lunch I wandered across the street to Dankers to see if they had the new Lauren in stock. I rarely came away from there without buying something, even if it was only an expensive pair of dumb, unsubsidized socks.

The atmosphere inside the store was a welcome relief. Even in autumn, Dallas' afternoon heat can be oppressive. My suit adjusted the weave to let the cool air flow over my skin and, at the same time, dumped the heat into my soles, where the cool Mexican tiles would absorb it.

"Good afternoon, Mr. Dwight," an obsequious sales robot said. "Dankers has a nice line of winter wear that just arrived. There are four models that would be a fine addition to your wardrobe." It flashed an image on its screen. "Note the fine attention to detail, the delicate stitching on the lapels, the…"

I interrupted, not wanting to hear the store's spiel. "What are your latest versions of suitware?"

"We have a gorgeous double-breasted Julian running Microsoft's SW6.6," the robot responded immediately. "Version 6.6 offers several features that will allow you to…"

"How about the new Lauren that's been announced?"

The robot blinked to check inventory. "I'm sorry, sir, but their suitware won't be in stock for several days. Can I interest you in anything else?"

I was disappointed that I'd have to wait, but I didn't want to waste the trip. I needed something more casual than suits. "What have you got in sport jackets and slacks?"

"We have some excellent GTC coats in your preferred color range," the robot continued smoothly as it displayed a selection of coats fabricated by the General Threads Consortium. I watched with some excitement as it paged through the selections just slowly enough for me to appreciate the details of cut and fabric.

I spotted a nice Harris Tweed with cinched belt. "It comes with the latest Apple suitware," the robot whispered when it detected my interest. "The fabric is completely waterproof, stain-resistant, and temperature-compliant. In addition, the suitware can handle up to sixteen suit-to-suit interactions simultaneously. What's more," it added softly as if to convey a great secret, "it is on sale at a price you can afford."

For the tenth time in as many days I regretted not restricting disclosure of my account balances to commercial inquiries. Sure, making my financial health available to authorized stores made shopping more convenient and efficient, but still, it rankled that my finances should be so transparent.

"I'll take it," I said, deciding, after a moment's consideration that the price was eminently affordable. "I'd like a new pair of shoes as well," I added, hoping that I could find a pair that wouldn't be so critical about my weight.

"Of course, sir. Would you like them in brown, cordovan, or black? Would you like loafer, or laced, boot or moccasin style, leather or…?"

I stopped the robot, not wanting to hear every option the store might offer. "I think a pair of leather loafers would be nice." A simple, understated pair would go well with the tweed jacket.

The robot blinked again. "We have two hundred and fifty-three possible variations of leather loafers in our inventory," it said. "Shall I display them?"

I knew that the only way to find a pair I liked was to plow through the list. "Let's begin," I said with a sigh.

The robot brought a dozen pair of shoes into its display. I admired the handsome leathers, the fine stitching, and the exquisite polish that seemed inches deep. The pair with a lustrous pearl color and pink highlights was particularly beautiful. There was only one problem. "These are all women's pumps," I exclaimed.

The robot blinked again. "But you requested…" it began and then switched to "Of course, sir. My mistake," and displayed a selection of more appropriate loafers.

"No tassels, please," I insisted, which dropped the number of possible styles to a mere one hundred. We proceeded merrily along until a collection of woman's red heels appeared on the screen. They were elegant, more suitable for an evening out, I thought, than a business office.

"Those are lovely," a husky voice announced from behind me. "I admire your taste. I'll bet your wife or girlfriend would be very happy with any of those." I turned to find myself facing an attractive redhead. "Unless they are for you?" she added.

"First," I corrected her, "I am not shopping for anyone, and, I should add, there is no way I would wear *these*," I pointed at one pair of highly decorated four-inch heels, "under any circumstances."

She tilted her head to one side, put a finger to her cheek, and looked me over. "I don't know," she grinned. "You'd probably look cute with those—taller, for sure."

"They'd probably look better on you," I replied and returned the smile, thankful for that extra tuck on the waistband. She was awfully cute.

Before she had a chance to answer, her obviously distraught robot interrupted as it rolled up. "Madam," it declared obsequiously. "Your selection, please." Its screen was displaying an array of cordovan, tassel-free, men's loafers.

She glanced over her shoulder and then at me. "I was shopping for a pair of evening shoes. In fact, those." She pointed to one pair on my robot's display panel. "Apparently the store has gotten our accounts confused."

The robots insisted, but slightly out of synch, to each of us. "Aren't-t these-se what-t you-ou requested-ed?"

There was quite obviously a serious glitch in the store's inventory software. Instead of continuing to argue with the witless robots, I said as plainly as possible. "I'll take those cordovans," and pointed at a pair on the woman's display. "I'm sure those red shoes will look great," I added in an aside.

"Perhaps, but only with the right dress," she replied. My suit alerted me to a download request for my profile. Flattered, I responded with a request of my own. A man two aisles over smiled and waved for no obvious reason.

"Any dress would look great on you," I answered gallantly, hoping I was not overstepping the bounds. Flirting had gotten less perilous of late, but the threat of a harassment charge still loomed large. For some reason her data wasn't coming across.

She clapped her hands and called up a green dress on her robot's display. "This is the one I already picked. It comes with the latest e-dress upgrade too."

"A beautiful dress," I said, struggling to keep a smile on my face as I tried to force the damned suit to link to hers.

"Since you agree, that's what I'll get." She leaned toward my robot and said, "I'll take those red heels with the strap," and touched the pair she wanted.

While our robots negotiated with our clothing over the billing, I smiled and got a nice one in reply. Who knew what this could lead to if only my suit would establish that damned link? Were beads of sweat forming on my forehead? In desperation I turned off the comm feature entirely.

Her face became expressionless, the usual sign that someone is turning their attention inward. Her face lost the smile. "Look, I'm sorry," she said quickly as she came out of the call and stepped backwards. "But I have to rush. Nice meeting you and all that," she shouted over her shoulder as she practically ran from the store.

Had it been something she got from my suit?

I tried to access the data my suit had downloaded as I walked back to the office but there were nothing but blank fields. Had she refused to send her data or was it the buggy suitware acting up again? Damn, and here I thought we were making a real connection, more than just casual conversation, at any rate. Had I read the situation wrong? Was there something about my data that had caused her to rush away? Had a serial killer or potential rapist hacked my suitware? No, that couldn't be. A moment's check told me there was nothing untoward in my files. In fact, there was nothing in my files whatsoever and the suit insisted I was named Susan.

A quick reset restored the suit as of the last backup, which was fifteen minutes before I ate that delightful salad. Sadly, I had no record whatever of anything that had happened while I was in Dankers.

I had to assume that the redhead simply did not like whatever my suit had downloaded to her. The more I considered that possibility the more despondent I became. Why had I ever chosen to wear a suit that wasn't functioning properly? Stupid, stupid, stupid, I cursed.

I needed something to make me feel better so I instructed my suit to call in an order for a pint of chocolate chip ice cream from an automated kiosk near my apartment. I knew that the pleasure of tasting those chill chunks of chocolate surrounded by creamy vanilla would bring my wounded emotions back into balance.

"*You should not indulge in ice cream,*" my underwear informed me. I ignored the warning. The ice cream wasn't about weight, calories, or blood sugar levels and I damn sure wasn't going to let a pair of nagging briefs tell me what I needed to fill the emotional void that had suddenly opened.

Did you get the milk? The fridge demanded as I opened the door. I glanced at the yawning emptiness where the milk jug should be and realized I had missed the reminder once again. Was that my fault or was this yet another manifestation of the suit's problems? I'd have to check later.

I'd scheduled the artificial sashimi tuna with wasabi, but the freezer had thawed out a vegetarian medley instead. I stared at the low-cal dinner choice, wondering if this was the fridge's punishment for forgetting the milk. A second's thought made me realize that the kitchen must have learned about my ice cream order and adjusted the dinner choice. Damn, it's really rough when your clothes and appliances conspire against you. "Traitors," I hissed at them as I picked up my ration of squash and corn, asparagus and potatoes, and tomatoes and onions, all afloat in some sort of undoubtedly nutritious and vitamin-fortified sauce.

The package from Danker's arrived and begged to be opened as I munched my way through my obscenely healthy dinner. Despite their pleas, I finished my plate and dumped the dirty dish and tableware into the washer. *Thank you*, it said, no doubt grateful for the small bit of attention it got from me twice a day.

I opened the shoebox that should have held my loafers but, instead, I beheld the redhead's three-inch heels. It didn't take a genius to figure what must have happened: I'd ordered my shoes from her screen and she from mine. The perplexed store software must have confused our orders. The mix-up wasn't that big a problem. I'd just send them back with a note. Sure, and she'd probably do the same with the loafers she got, and that would be the end of it.

Before I could open the other box, my cell chirped. "You must have my heels," an obviously distraught female voice proclaimed before I could say hello. "I needed those for tonight, damn it."

"How did you..." I began and then remembered that she'd accepted my profile and had my number. This was an opportunity not to be missed. I thought quickly, wondering how I could take advantage of this chance. "I can bring them to you," I suggested. If I could arrange a meeting, perhaps she'd clarify how my profile had offended her.

"Great," she quickly replied. "We don't live that far from each other. Bring them over." The phone clicked without another word from her.

That would have been great if I had her address. Not knowing where she lived left me somewhat embarrassed, frustrated, and wondering if suitware could be jailed for mismanagement of a person's files. I tried to redial her number, but the suit had already deleted it, along with the reminder about the damned milk.

Wait a minute! Didn't she say we didn't live that far apart? She had to be within walking distance. All I had to do was wander around and hope she would spot me. What else could I do? Maybe she'd call again, I hoped.

I pulled on a dumb pair of jeans with a decent communications link and slipped on a pair of running shoes. *You need to run at aerobic speed for twenty-four point five minutes*, the shoes said as soon as I fastened them. *You need to lose weight.*

Obviously it had been talking to the kitchen about my lunchtime orange blossom salad containing excess calories. Hadn't I burned enough calories, despite eating the vegetarian medley, or did they just want a nice run? Regardless of the reason, it was obvious that the household conspiracy was growing and the other gadgets had recruited my running shoes.

The shoes began playing the opening riff of Jackson's *Apple Downbeat Rag* as I headed out. *Pick up the pace* one said every twenty steps. *Pick up the pace.* I ignored it as I set out on my search with her shoebox under my arm.

The area where I live is pockmarked with redevelopments—industrial sites, shops, and storage buildings converted to apartments, condominiums, and multi-family homes. The only way you could tell was that most of the converted ones had awnings over the main doors. The doormen all gazed suspiciously at me as I walked slowly past with uplifted eyes, as if I were casing their posts. Their gazes grew steadily more suspicious every time I passed. I ignored them and prayed that she would spot me as I continued to jog along to alternate exhortations to *pick up the pace* and bits of new jazz at an aerobic tempo.

After the third repetition of my circular trek I started to doubt that my lovely redhead would be glancing out her window in anticipation of the arriving pumps. What reason would she have? She probably thought that I, like ninety-nine percent of the population over five years of age, had captured her address during our exchange, just as she had captured mine.

But I hadn't. I was the idiot who decided to wear unpatched suitware and was now suffering for his sins. This wasn't going to work. There was no chance that I would find her among the hundreds who occupied the densely populated area. She would never get her shoes, miss her party tonight, and probably hate me forever. Even if I eventually ran into her somewhere else I'd still be the jerk who ruined her evening by wearing unpatched suitware.

Finally, concluding that this wasn't going to work and much to the relief of numerous nervous doormen, I headed for the kiosk to pick up my ice cream. Maybe that would console me for my loss.

"I ordered chocolate chip," I keyed to the machine.

Error. Your order was a pint of low-fat chocolate chunk pistachio, the ice cream kiosk disagreed with all the weigh of authority vested in it by its software.

I checked my to-do and found that damned milk reminder I had missed earlier. Where was the… there, I had it: one order for low-fat chocolate chunk pistachio, just as the machine claimed. Obviously the dietary conspiracy had changed my order. It wasn't the kiosk that screwed up, it was those damned appliances.

"I'm changing the order. Give me a pint of chocolate-chip," I keyed.

You have not burned sufficient calories, my shoes said in rhythm to its aerobic background beat. There was a twitter of interchange from my briefs.

Confirming, the machine acknowledged as a pint clunked into the delivery chute. *Have a nice day.*

I looked at the container. It was a pint of low-fat, chocolate chunk pistachio. I looked around but there was no one I could complain to. It seemed that all my software were now part of the conspiracy.

Slowly I slouched away from the kiosk. Nothing, not a damn thing was going right today. I couldn't eat the food I wanted, couldn't find a freaking address I needed, and I'd never get to find out why the redhead had run away from me.

Then the phone rang. "This is Viola, Jeff. Where are you? Did something happen?" It was a reprieve, a breath of fresh air, an awakening of possibility once again. Life was suddenly good.

"I didn't get your address," I blurted. "My suitware has a bug that…"

"Never mind," she replied before I could finish. "I'll bring your stuff over and take a cab. I'm late already."

I beat her to my flat by three minutes, threw the pint on the table and barely had time to grab the other package when she rang the bell.

She was as breathless as I. She had a makeup case and two packages under her arms. "I got here as fast as I could," she said and pointed at the larger package in my hands. "Is that my dress?" I nodded dumbly. "Now, where can I change?"

"The bath's over there," I pointed at the door. "The other door's my closet." Stupid thing to say, I realized as she took her packages and disappeared into the bathroom. I prayed she didn't get too chummy with my toilet. As it had with previous women, and notably with my mother, it would lecture her on the dangers of unprotected sex, the evils of excess sugar, and the need to remain hydrated.

I slipped off my running shoes. *You did not exercise sufficiently*, the shoes said in their drill sergeant manner as soon as my fingers touched the straps. *Your aerobic heartbeat has not been raised suffiently for good cardiac health.*

"Screw you," I said as I threw them across the room. I opened the box with the new loafers. They looked as nice as I imagined they would. *Searching for data* was all they murmured in a refined voice as I slipped them on. I was admiring the look and feel of the new jacket when the bathroom door opened and a vision in green stepped out.

Viola had done something with her hair and makeup that took my breath away. Her eyes looked larger, her lips more full, and her figure in that green evening dress was breathtaking. I barely noticed the tips of her red shoes as she stepped daintily forward.

The tweed's link was going insane from the downloads her dress was throwing at me. Music, images, lists of favorite topics, foods, colors, and a plethora of possible conversational gambits. I stood there, mouth agape, not knowing how to deal with this tsunami of information. I hadn't had time to set the filters on the defaults. The tweed was having fits trying to access the apartment's databanks, find my personal profiles, and respond in kind.

Viola looked as confused as I and was fumbling at her waist. "Sorry," she said. "I forgot to adjust the dress. The default's *Cocktail Party*."

I was struggling to gain control of the tweed, which was merrily downloading my entire music library, to shut off the gushing flood of unwanted data. On top of running buggy suitware I now looked like someone who couldn't control their own clothes.

"Think what a crowded room must be like with everyone's clothes throwing out that much information," I laughed as I tried to access the tweed's menu.

"It probably wouldn't matter in the general din at most of those affairs," she replied as she continued to flail at her dress. "Why do they set the damn defaults like this?"

I tore the jacket off and threw it down, breaking the circuit and hopefully silencing the stream of too much information.

"I think it's stuck," Viola cursed as she beat at her waistline. "Oh, crap." She ran back into the bathroom as my briefs beeped for attention.

You are under stress, they said. *Lie down and breathe slowly. Your heartrate is exceeding normal limits,* my new loafers said. *Did you get the milk?* asked the refrigerator.

Viola emerged from the bathroom, a dripping dress in one hand. "I had to drown it to shut it off," she said. "Your toilet is very upset with me."

"I ought to shut everything down," I said. "I don't think I can take it any more." When she gave me a perplexed look there was nothing else to do than explain how my day had gone: my issues with the kitchen; my choosing to wear buggy suitware; the screw-up in Dankers; the argument with the kiosk; not being able to find her apartment; and the desolation that I felt that I would never again see this attractive, intelligent, wonderful woman I'd met as a result. If I had less self-control I would have cried at that point. "I'm almost at the point where I want to just shut down my links and cut myself off from everything."

"I sometimes feel the same way," she admitted. "But I can't imagine what it would be like to be unlinked. Oh, did you know that your ice cream is melting?"

I had forgotten the pint of fat-free I had absent-mindedly set aside, a container that was now leaking a bilious green flow across my coffee table and spilling onto the rug. I turned, scooped up the container and tossed it into the fridge.

You should eat no more than an eighth of a pint, the fridge chided as I dropped into the freezer slot.

"I'll never eat any of that low-fat crap," I remarked as I slammed the door on the fridge's dietary advice.

"I guess I can forget going anywhere else this evening," Viola said sadly. She was looking at the sodden dress.

"Maybe I can make it up to you," I suggested tentatively. "We could go somewhere we don't have to dress up." There was no way I was going to risk wearing a suit this time.

She glanced at the refrigerator. "That would be nice. I doubt I have anything to fear from someone named Susan who's never even gotten a traffic ticket."

When I saw her inviting smile I felt as if I had won the lottery. "Do you like chocolate chip ice cream?" I ventured.

"The only thing better is Rocky Road," she replied with a wistful expression. "Or maybe Tin Roof." Then her face fell. "But my dressware won't let me have it."

We looked at each other for a moment, nodded, smiled, unlinked, and shut off the world to everything but each other.

Names are tricky things. A real person named Patti Smith, who lives in Ann Arbor, Michigan, won a charity auction. Her prize was her name used as the main character in a story in which she saves Ann Arbor.

Ken MacGregor's stories have been published widely, and a collection, An Aberrant Mind, is available online and in select bookstores. He also edits an annual horror-themed anthology for the Great Lakes Association of Horror Writers. Mr. MacGregor lives in Michigan with his family and two cats, one of whom is dead but still haunts them, as cats will. This story originally appeared in 2013 in Silverthought Online

Patti Smith Saves Ann Arbor

by Ken MacGregor

It was a Thursday and Bill's Beer Garden was sparsely populated. Though it was 8:30PM, the sun still hovered well above the western horizon. Unlike the ear-numbing hum of the big Saturday crowds, individual conversations could be picked out.

Patti Smith sipped an IPA and leaned back in her chair. Across the street, well-heeled couples of varying genders came and went from the Old Town. She reflected that people had been doing that for over four decades. The bar had been there that long.

At the next table, a young man, a boy really, slid a cigarette between his lips and popped the lid off his Zippo with a metallic *ping*. He put his thumb against the striking wheel and Patti cleared her throat. He looked over, moving just his eyes. He had very long lashes. She smiled at him.

"You can't really smoke in here."

He looked around deliberately and then up at the sky. He met her gaze again and spoke around the filter.

43

"We're outside."

She nodded as though this was perfectly reasonable.

"Mm-hmm. But, this is a dining establishment and as such is a non-smoking zone according to the law. You may have been unaware of that."

The sharp tang of lighter fluid drifted to her nose. She wrinkled it involuntarily. The boy snapped the lid shut. Maintaining eye contact with her the whole time, he put the cigarette back in the case.

"Happy?"

She nodded.

"Yes, thank you." She took a sip of her beer. "What are you drinking?"

Glancing at the glass, the boy met her eyes again.

"Bollywood Blonde."

Patti nodded.

"Good choice. Let me get the next one. To, you know, make up for kind of being a dick about the smoking thing."

"Yeah? All right. Thanks."

It wasn't long before the waiter came around again. The sleeve of his T-shirt was rolled up around a cigarette pack. It complemented his hair, slicked back into a Duck's Ass. None of the other servers here seemed to be going for a fifties theme, though many sported their own tattoos and several wore jewelry sticking through various parts of their faces. She ordered another Buzzsaw and a Blonde for the boy.

On the sidewalk, a woman wearing yoga pants and a tank top walked a Pekingese on a red vinyl leash that spooled out of a plastic handle with a trigger to rein the dog back in. She and the dog dodged to the side as an Ambassador zinged past on its Segway. Like all Ambassadors, its eyes were covered by mirrored lenses and its blinding white smile stretched permanently into its cheeks. The Pekingese trembled slightly and dropped tiny turds on the sidewalk.

The Segway's wheels stopped. The Ambassador's head turned with a series of barely audible clicks. The speaker in its chest gave a single, sharp pop before it spoke.

"Please clean up after your animal." The head clicked towards where Patti sat. "And you folks drink responsibly. Make sure you are sober before you drive home. All citizens' lives are precious."

The hum of the retreating Segway faded. The woman used an inverted plastic baggie to clean up after her dog and moved on. Patti caught the boy's eye over her beer. He shook his head.

"I hate those things."

She nodded. Everybody hated them. Even before they had replaced the human Ambassadors with robots, she had been against the idea. It was almost like the city officials thought Ann Arbor's citizens were incapable of getting along without help. In some ways, of course, the human Ambassadors had been worse. At least the robots did what they were programmed to do. There had been *incidents* with the humans.

The boy spoke, scattering her thoughts.

"Hey, lady? Keep an eye on my beer for minute? I'm gonna go down the street a little to smoke."

She nodded and watched his table. No one molested his beer. By the time he got back, it was nearly dark. She swallowed the last of the IPA and stood.

"Takin' off?"

She told the boy she was.

"Okay. Thanks for the beer. You're all right. Be cool."

Patti "shot" him with a forefinger.

"I'm always cool."

The effect was somewhat spoiled when the boy rolled his eyes.

She only lived a few blocks from downtown, but on the walk, Patti passed two more Ambassadors. Their mirrored gazes and maniac smiles swept over her like judgment. Buzzsaw IPA had a pretty substantial alcohol content by volume, and she had put away three pints. She told herself the beer was making her paranoid.

The key sank in the lock on the second try and she swept through the open door, closing it as soon as possible. Only then did she relax. For a long moment she stood in the dark, leaning against the door. Her stomach rumbled, propelling her toward the

45

kitchen. She microwaved a plate of nachos with cheddar cheese. It was the perfect thing to go with a belly-full of beer.

———————

The Ann Arbor Farmer's Market was a weekly open-air extravaganza that was not to be missed. Fresh produce from outlying farms, handmade crafts, honey from local bees and roasted nuts. There was even a guy with a popcorn maker who gave small bags to kids, for free.

,A woman had been selling super-sturdy hemp bags with handles a couple years back. She had made them by hand and dyed them all the colors of the rainbow. Patti moved through the market throngs, buying potatoes, radishes, beets, broccoli and tomatoes and carefully arranging them in one of those bags. Hers was the blue green of the Atlantic off the northeast coast.

Several faces she had seen before. She didn't know their names, but often entertained fantasies about who they might be. What is her day job? Is he having an affair? Do they cheat on their taxes? Is she a Russian spy? It was her favorite game, imagining the secret lives of the nameless faces in the crowd.

Shouting shook her from her reverie. On Detroit Street, a man, forty-something, bald, was being pulled from the sidewalk against his will. He struggled to break the Ambassador's grip but could not. He spat curses at the Segway-riding, sunglass-sporting, grinning automaton. When that didn't work, the man slapped the Ambassador in the face hard enough that the whole market when quiet from the sound.

The Ambassador paused, turning its head with a series of clicks. Nobody moved. The Segway wheels kicked to life and the man stumbled, caught his balance and trip-stepped forward. Once they got to the market side, the Ambassador let him go. The voice from his chest blared into the silent crowd.

"Crossing the streets when there is no traffic is important. Have a safe and happy day."

It turned and left. By degrees, the market started back up. Patti watched the Ambassador until it was out of sight. She realized she was clenching her jaw and forced herself to stop. A high school girl with multiple earrings and shredded clothing put her hand on the bald man's arm.

"You okay, bro?"

The bald man nodded.

"Man, fuck those things."

The man nodded again. He focused at the girl.

"What happened to your shirt?"

Her eyes, deeply outlined in a vivid green liner, widened. She leaned in and her voice dropped into a stage whisper.

"Tiger attack. Had about eight hundred stitches that are now covered in skin grafts. They took the skin from my thighs and my butt."

"Oh. Were you in India or something?"

"Nope. Downtown Detroit. Craziest thing."

"Huh."

The man glanced back at the street, paused, shook his head and wandered deeper into the market. Patti caught the girl's eye.

"Tiger attack, huh?"

"Always lie to bald guys. It's one of my rules."

"It's random. I like it."

The girl smiled and walked away, tossing a look over her shoulder.

"Peace."

Patti flashed two fingers in a "V". An old guy saw it and grinned at her. His hair started behind his ears and hung, white and thin down his back.

"Old school," he said, flashing his own peace sign.

I love this town, she thought and scurried to get the other things she needed before they were all snatched up.

Patti wore her favorite green dress, the one with the plunging neckline. Her husband, Ken, actually wore a tie. They were super-fancy tonight for a show at The Ark, Ann Arbor's coolest little concert venue. Roger Waters was in town, doing an acoustic set and the line to get in wrapped around the block. She looked at Ken.

"This is gonna be awesome. You know that, right?"

He nodded.

"I mean, *Roger Waters*? Live? At The Ark? The very heart of Pink Floyd since *Dark Side of the Moon*? It's off the hook."

"Completely hook-free."

She laughed. "Hookless."

Ken smiled. "Not a hooker in sight."

"You went there."

He nodded again. "I did."

They were still about thirty people away from getting inside when she saw the man with the limp. He angled across the street toward the crowd, wearing a winter coat despite the warmth. Mud caked the cuffs of his burgundy, corduroy pants. His hair was plastered to one side of his head and he was several days late for a shave.

He worked the crowd, asking for change. Most people avoided his eyes and mumbled something noncommittal. A man in a black bowler gave him a dollar.

From near the end of the line, around the corner, Patti heard a whirring, clicking sound. Everyone in line turned to look, too. The Segway navigated the narrow space between the people in line and the parking meters by the curb. It zipped along until the Ambassador stopped in front of the man in the grungy clothes.

"Panhandling is against the law. You are in violation of the law. You will come with me now."

"I will not, fascist pig-fuck machine."

The Ambassador clamped a hand on the man's arm. The man cried out.

"Profanity offends these citizens' ears. I will remove you from their presence."

Patti held up her hand.

"It doesn't offend mine. Really. I don't give a shit."

Click, click, click. It turned its head toward her.

"This unit is capable of removing more than one offensive individual at a time."

Her mouth opened, a stream of invectives perched on her lips. Ken put a hand on her arm and shook his head, his eyes pleading with her.

She glared at him. Very quietly, he spoke.

"Roger Waters. We've been waiting months for this. Please don't get arrested."

"They can't arrest me. They're not police. But, fine. I'll keep my mouth shut. For now."

The Ambassador returned its attention to the man it still held. He struggled against the thing's grip. It was a losing battle. In the end, it lifted him off the ground by his arm and carried him away. Patti could hear him curse the thing as they left.

"I should have fought back."

Ken nodded.

"Yeah. I get that. But, how would it help that guy for you to get hauled along with him?"

"I don't know. Damn it."

They were almost to the door. Ken grinned at her and nudged her in the ribs.

"Maybe he'll play 'Not Now, John.'"

She grinned back. "If he does, I'm totally singing along. If for no other reason than I have a sudden burning desire to say 'fuck' a lot."

She glanced over her shoulder, but there was just the line. All human. No Segways. No Ambassadors.

After the show, Patti and Ken stopped at the Grizzly Peak for a bite to eat and a couple of beers. They turned their phones back on and the local news app popped up on Patti's

"Oh. Oh no. My god."

Ken leaned in to look.

"What happened? Hello? What's up?"

She turned the phone toward him so he could see. The headline read "homeless man found beaten to death." There was a picture. In it, all you could see were the legs. The dirty, burgundy corduroy pants.

"That guy? From outside The Ark? He's dead?"

She nodded.

"You think the Ambassador left him somewhere and he got jumped?"

She shrugged and took a long pull from her beer.

"Either that, or the Ambassador killed him."

Their food steamed on the plates between them. It smelled fantastic, but Patti felt like she had a dead raccoon in her belly.

Finally, hunger won out and they ate. In mid-bite, movement outside caught Patti's eye. She glanced over at the window by the next table. The head and shoulders of an Ambassador was framed in the glass. It was sitting there, on the sidewalk, facing left. Its head slowly turned toward her. She couldn't hear the clicking over the noise in the bar, but she heard it in her head. The mirrored shades and insane, gleaming grin faced her. The burger sat in her hands forgotten.

She leaned forward, squinting. *There*. Spatters of red on its plastic cheek. Blood. She jerked back, slamming into the chair. Ken looked up from his food.

"What's wrong?"

She pointed outside, but the Ambassador was gone.

She let out the breath she had been holding.

"Jesus."

In the warm light of the morning sun, the thoughts running through her head seemed paranoid and ludicrous. She didn't care. Patti hunched over her laptop, digging, delving. She would turn over every rock, exposing every grub and nasty, crawling thing until she found what she wanted. An hour after lunch, she found it.

"*Ha*. Gotcha."

Ken poked his head in from the kitchen where he was rinsing dishes.

"What'd you get?"

"They're centrally controlled. At least, they were. And, and… this is the best part: they installed a kill switch."

Ken nodded, frowned and shook his head.

"I have no idea what you're talking about."

"The Ambassadors, dummy. The rogue robots. Try to keep up."

"Oh right. I hate those things."

She closed the laptop, grabbed her bag and pulled on some comfy walking shoes.

"Don't wait for me. I might be late. Hopefully not in the morbid sense of the word."

"Yeah. Try not to die. I would really not be okay with that."

"Gotcha. Do my best."

She kissed him. She took her time and enjoyed it, just in case. "Bye, dude."

———————

On a day like today, one could expect to see parents pushing strollers, cyclists every other block and hundreds of pedestrians walking, shopping and enjoying downtown Ann Arbor.

Hardly anyone was out. The few people she did see ducked furtively out stores, clutching their bags. They shot quick glances around and jumped in their cars, locking the doors and pulling away.

There were others on the sidewalk besides her, but for the most part they wore mirror shades and rode Segways.

No wonder no one is on the streets.

Passing Bill's Beer Garden, she paused. One table had two women at it, sitting quietly over their glasses of beer. A server stood in the shadow of a tree, keeping an eye on them.

"Hey."

Patti jumped and whirled around. It was the boy from the other day. He was smoking.

"You scared the crap out of me, man."

"Sorry."

She scoffed and shrugged.

"Whatever. I'm on edge as hell today. Where is everybody?"

The boy glanced around and leaned close.

"It's the Ambassadors. They're hauling people away left and right. It's like they declared martial law or something. Confidentially, they fucking terrify me."

She nodded. The hum of a Segway made them both turn. The mirrored shades regarded them silently from a few feet away. The boy inhaled deeply from his cigarette and let the smoke out of his nostrils.

"What? Huh? What are we doing wrong, pal?"

The machine didn't move. The boy shook his head.

"Asshole," he mumbled. He flicked his cigarette at the thing. The butt bounced off its plastic chin and hit the sidewalk.

Its wheels engaged and it shot forward. With one hand, it clamped on the boy's throat. He reached up with both hands, but couldn't pry it loose.

"Littering," the speaker crackled, "is a crime."

The boy's face purpled. He kicked the Ambassador with both feet, pushing the wheels back a few inches.

Patti was shocked into inaction. Her hands hung at her sides and her jaw dropped.

The boy stopped thrashing.

The Ambassador's neck click-turned toward Patti, who backed up a step. Its mechanical arm shot to the left and she could hear the bones of the boys neck snap. The hand shot to the right with a wet, tearing sound.

She took another step away.

The Ambassador whipped its arm at propeller speed: left, right, left. The boy's body crumpled to the ground. It still held his head.

"The criminal has been dealt with, citizen. Have a nice day."

Patti swallowed hard. She reluctantly turned her back on the thing and walked fast, clutching her purse to her side.

A few blocks later another Ambassador cut her off. It stood silently before her. Suppressing her recent horror, she smiled at it pleasantly.

"Something I can help you with?"

The speaker popped.

"State your business, citizen."

"Why, I'm going for a walk. It's a lovely day and I am out enjoying it. That's okay, isn't it?"

It was quiet for a moment. Patti imagined gears whirling inside its head.

"Exercise is proven to be good for citizens. Sunshine, in moderation can provide vitamin D. Be cautious not to burn. Have a nice day."

It spun aside and she walked on. She kept her chin up and hummed "Another Brick in the Wall, Part 2". The other Ambassadors ignored her and she arrived unmolested at her destination.

The Bell Tower.

It was one of Ann Arbor's iconic buildings, standing proud above U of M's central campus. The attached hotel was one of the area's finest. It was one of her favorite landmarks.

Instead of valet parking attendants out front, five Ambassadors stood sentry before the door. She walked up like she belonged. Two of them moved to block her. She made an indignant face at them.

"Excuse me. I am meeting a client in the lobby and you are quite rudely blocking my path."

One's head clicked to face her. Its speaker crackled.

"We are unfailingly polite."

"Clearly, you are not."

For a moment, no one moved or spoke. Finally, the one who had spoken faced her again.

"Please forgive our breach of etiquette. These are... trying times."

She smiled hugely.

"Think nothing of it. Have a safe and happy day."

She squeezed into the gap they provided and nearly pranced through the doors. Several Ambassadors turned to watch her, but none interfered. She strode across the lobby, casting her gaze about as if seeking someone. But, when she got to the stairs, she abruptly started up.

Behind her, Segway wheels sped across carpet.

"Stop. That is an unauthorized area. Return to the lobby, citizen."

She stopped on the first landing. Turning around, she faced the Ambassadors. More than twenty gazed up at her. A slow smile twitched its way across her mouth.

"Hmm. Well, you see, it's like this. Go fuck yourselves, you fucking junk pile fucks."

She raced up the stairs, taking two at a time. By the time she hit the fourth floor, she was sweating, panting and holding her side.

"Oh man. Getting too old for this kind of thing. Better walk the rest of the way."

Several minutes later, she reached the top floor of the hotel. She paused to catch her breath, hands on her knees.

The elevator *dinged*.

"Uh oh."

The ornate doors slid open and six Ambassadors slid out on their Segways. They made a beeline for Patti.

"Shit."

She turned and ran. Reaching into her purse, she yanked out the bolt cutters she'd brought. Positioning them as fast as she could, she snapped the chain on the door marked "No Admittance. Staff Only." The chain fell loudly to the floor and she grabbed the handle, yanking open the door.

Running up six steps, she turned around. The Ambassadors clustered in the doorway on their Segways. She pointed at them.

"No elevator to the top, bitches."

She turned to keep climbing but stopped at the sound behind her. Looking back over her shoulder, she gasped. An Ambassador lifted a heavy metal foot off the Segway. It slowly moved it to the side and put it on the floor. The other foot followed and thumped down next to the first.

The other Ambassadors watched this happen. As one, they lifted their left feet and put it on the floor.

Patti closed her mouth and ran up the stairs. Less than a minute later, six Segways sat empty outside the door with the severed chain. The metal feet on metal stairs was nearly deafening in the narrow space. It was the sound of hammers on anvils, forging doom.

Breathless, she reached the door at the top. It was unlocked. *Small favors.* Once through, she pushed it closed and pulled the heavy padlock from her purse. Sliding through the steel ring made for that purpose, she clicked it shut.

"That ought to buy me a few seconds."

She had never been up here. The bells were much bigger than she realized. Even the smallest one was twice the size of her head. An elaborate system of pulleys hung above them and ropes disappeared through the floor below.

The footfalls were getting close. She ran around on the catwalk. She had almost made a complete circuit when she found what she came for.

"Ah. There you are. Let's do this."

An unpainted metal box, hinged at the top, sat on a wooden table that was built into the wall. It had a *caution: electricity* sticker and a tiny padlock holding it shut. The bolt cutters snapped shut on it and the lock fell away. Flipping open the lid, Patti scanned the inside. *There.*

She yanked the printed pages from her purse, the ones detailing this electronic "brain". She hadn't time to study them before leaving, so was trying to figure out how to do this on the fly.

The stairway was quiet. After the constant heavy tread, the silence was startling. She looked at the door. It shook with impact.

"Shit."

Back to the pages. She examined the diagrams. Wires everywhere, connections to here and there and all over the place. This was way more complicated than she realized.

"Come on, come on. You're almost there. You can do this."

The door bent in the middle. The Ambassadors pounded harder.

She flipped through the pages, trying to find the one that showed how to reprogram them.

"Where are you, damn it?"

The door leaned in at the top. Light from the other side spilled into the belfry. She flipped the pages faster.

"Where *is* it?"

The pages slipped through her fingers. They scattered across the floor. A single, loud sob escaped her throat. She bent to pick them up.

The door crashed inward. One at a time, the Ambassadors stomped slowly onto the catwalk. Their mirrored sunglasses pointed at her. Their white, white grins seemed predatory.

"Oh, the hell with it."

She reached into the box, grabbed a handful of wires and yanked them out. The Ambassadors paused, faltered. She grabbed two more handfuls and pulled them out. She went back for more.

When all the wires were pulled out, she hefted the bolt cutters, bringing down the metal end hard, smashing the circuit boards and tiny components.

The robots weren't moving. They were as still as statues.

"Yeah. I'm not really buying it, fellas."

She pulled two of the last three things from her purse. She squirted the lighter fluid into the box, coating the whole thing. Then, she fired up the Zippo. She tossed the flaming lighter in the box and it went up with a *fwoosh*. The electronics melted into unrecognizable slag.

The Ambassadors still stood, but each one's head fell forward, chins clunking against metal chests.

Patti brushed off her hands.

"Score one for the humans."

On an unseasonably warm Halloween night, Patti sat on her front porch. She was dressed as a mummy who had been in a car accident. She had painted tire tracks on her bandages. Everyone had said they loved it.

She sipped beer and gave out candy to the few kids who trick-or-treated by her house.

One boy, maybe seven or eight, was dressed in mirrored sunglasses. He had a huge, white smile. At his feet were the wheels of a fake Segway.

"Wow. That's the scariest costume I've seen all night, buddy."

He pulled the fake smile away. It was held in his teeth by a piece of plastic.

"Trick or treat."

She held out the basket.

"Here. Take a handful. You've earned it. Now get out of my sight, kid. I hate those things."

Science fiction can allow us to occupy, if only for the length of a story, a world made better through technology. Of course, better is subjective, and it is possible the men inhabiting Tara Campbell's future might disagree. This story was previously published in Silver Thought, in 2013.

Ms. Campbell informs us that speculating on how the modern dating scene could be improved led to this story. She is an assistant fiction editor with a publisher in Washington, DC.

The Bar Exam

by Tara Campbell

Diana frowned as she peeled the electrodes from her client's temples. "You know, you can't start sleeping with both sisters at the same time. I mean, unless they're okay with it, which in this case they weren't."

The client looked at her drowsily and rubbed the spots where the electrodes had been. Sometimes it took men a moment to fully come to after a simulation, especially when they were new to the process.

"You realize," Diana continued, "this was an entry-level situation."

"Uh, yeah, sorry."

"Did you read the manual?" The answer was usually "no," but she still had not given up hope that someone actually *would* review the material before coming in for a screening.

Her client's silence confirmed that he was not that person.

"Look," said Diana, "I want to help you, but you really have to take this a little more seriously if you want to start dating." As long as this process had been in place, she couldn't believe how many men continued to think they could just wing it. Of course, that type of thinking was probably why the whole system was started in the first place.

"Yeah, okay, sorry," he mumbled.

As a caseworker, she'd learned how to read the look in someone's eyes. She could tell this guy had learned his lesson and was actually going to do the work. "All right, then," she said, folding her hands onto her lap, "let's go over again what you *should* do when you meet your girlfriend's sister…"

Diana wrapped up the appointment and took a break before her next client was due. In the restroom she lingered at the sink for a moment, looking into the mirror. Her eyes were a nice shade of blue, she thought, and weren't yet ringed by excessive bags or crow's feet. Her mouth, while not exactly full, wasn't flanked by lines. She tucked a few gray strands back down into the waves of her shoulder-length, brown hair. She always felt a bit relieved to see that, even in the unflattering lighting of the office bathroom, she didn't look as ancient as this place could make her feel.

At thirty-three, she was older than most of her coworkers. She'd been a Senior Caseworker for about five years, and her higher-ups were encouraging her to apply for a supervisory position or something in the policy or public affairs divisions of the Agency. She was continually held up as a role model to other staffers, but she knew that more than a few of them actually regarded her as a cautionary tale. Despite a series of promising relationships, she'd never been married, and because of this she seemed to occupy a space outside the comfort zone of her married, divorced, or twenty-something coworkers.

As if on cue, one of her younger colleagues entered the bathroom and smiled hello. Diana smiled back and pretended to finish checking her makeup before heading back to meet Roger Henderson, her next client.

She walked down the hall trying not to think about his honey-brown eyes, fringed in long, dark lashes that made her jealous and weak in the knees all at once. She didn't think men should be allowed to have lashes like that…

Dammit, Diana, get a grip! She'd always disapproved of caseworkers who let themselves develop crushes on clients, and now here she was, vying for the title of Ms. Unprofessional.

Diana rounded the corner into the reception area that lay between the restrooms and her office. She knew he would be there, and yet she was never quite prepared to see him leaning back in one of the waiting-room chairs.

He was reading, as usual, while other men fidgeted or dozed or watched TV. Sometimes Diana would catch a glimpse of the screen before he turned off his reader. She wished people still read things on paper so she would at least be able to see the cover. She wondered if people used to change their reading material depending on where they went, like an outfit. She asked herself what kind of book Roger would wear to a screening.

"Hello, Roger."

He looked up from his reader and smiled pleasantly. "Hello, Ms. Kirkwood."

She tried not to let his dimples distract her. This was not the time to be thinking about running her fingers through his dark brown curls.

"Daphne," she said to the receptionist, "as long as I'm here, I'll go ahead and take Roger back."

Daphne raised a discreet eyebrow. It was standard practice for the receptionist to call back to the caseworker to announce a client, yet Diana always happened to be just coming back from the restroom before Roger's appointments. Whatever was going on, Daphne was smart enough to stay out of it.

But Daphne had to admit, Diana's new dresses *were* pretty cute.

———

Roger Henderson settled into the recliner and prepared for the last of his introductory simulations.

"All right," said Diana, "you know what happens if you don't pass this time."

"Yes, Ms. Kirkwood, I know."

"Okay, because I really want this to work out for you."

"Me too," he smiled. "Here goes."

Diana made a final check of the electrodes and sat down at the monitoring station. She wished he would stop calling her "Ms. Kirkwood." She knew the technique, client trying to curry favor with the caseworker. Some of her colleagues seemed to like the show of subservience, but the "Ms." treatment just made Diana feel like an old schoolmarm.

"Are you ready, Roger?"

He nodded. She flicked a switch to dim the lights and told him to clear his mind.

Diana scrolled through the training scenarios. He'd already been through the basics: the wasted girl at the bar, the girlfriend's hot sister, the booty call from an ex when you've just started sleeping with someone else. He'd been passing, but not without testing the limits of her judgment—after all, how much flirting *was* acceptable at a funeral? How long after a breakup *should* a guy wait before calling his ex's best friend?

Now he'd come to the part of the training where there was no more time to fool around. If he didn't get this right he wouldn't qualify for the chits he needed to enter the pairing bars and cafés, which were the only places men could meet real women. Even though men were free to choose if and when to go through screening, Diana knew her clients didn't really have a choice. She'd seen women at the non-pairing bars; she'd heard the stories. If a man wanted to meet a woman who wasn't either completely insane or looking for paying customers, he'd have to come to the Agency for screening.

She tapped on her screen to call up the last scenario for Stage 1: driving the babysitter home on a summer night after years of marital ennui. As she fine-tuned the reception on Roger's thought patterns, she could hear that he was already planning where to go once he passed. "Bar Nonna, huh? Nothing but the best," she murmured, tapping through the sequence of screens that would bring him into the simulation. "Not everyone can afford the drinks there, pal. Why not give the rest of us a chance?"

Still, she had to smile.

A little while later, Roger stretched and rubbed his eyes as he came out of the simulation. He looked over at Diana, and then shot up in his recliner.

"How'd I do, Ms. Kirkwood, did I pass?"

Diana looked at him intently. She walked over to his chair and pressed a single chit into his hand. "Meet me at the Starbucks at Seventh and Main tomorrow night and we'll talk about it." She clasped her hands together to steady them. "And from now on, just call me Diana."

Diana stood in her kitchen staring at the oven as it reconstituted her dinner. The glass of wine she'd intended to have with her meal was already empty, so she refilled it. She took a bowl from the cupboard just as the oven "pinged," and carefully transferred the pouch of steaming noodles into it. Just because she was taking a quikmeal again, that didn't mean she had to gulp it down in pill form like a…

Like a what? Like a sad, lonely, single woman?

So there it was, this is what had turned her into the degenerate lawbreaker she'd become: the prospect of another night alone on her couch with a bowl of reconstituted quikmeal on her lap.

Perhaps "degenerate" was a bit extreme, but "lawbreaker" was probably not far off. At the very least, she'd exhibited highly questionable professional behavior. She'd probably lose her job if anyone found out. Encouraging a client was one thing, but actually messing around with simulation results was pretty serious. She'd never known anyone who'd done that.

That's probably the point, she told herself, stabbing at her noodles with a fork, *the Agency doesn't keep them around.*

She exhaled, not realizing until then that she'd been holding her breath. "Think, think, think." She grabbed her dinner and wine and headed for the couch.

She hadn't actually done that much, really. She hadn't manipulated the testing scenarios, hadn't prodded or prepped him. All she'd done was start to like this guy, maybe root for him a bit more than was professionally called for. All she'd wanted was a little more time with him before releasing him into the dating-eligible population.

All she'd really done was postpone the debrief—and move it to a completely inappropriate location.

She was supposed to do debriefs right then and there in the office, go through the scenarios with clients while they were still fresh and give them insight as to why their instincts were so utterly wrong. Well, at least that's how most of the sessions went. In her darker moments she felt like she was just part of a sham finishing school, not enlightening clients so much as teaching them how to more effectively mask their true natures. But she still hoped that little bits and pieces of her guidance would filter in and take root somewhere.

Even if she couldn't teach men how to truly understand women's needs, she could at least make women's lives easier through the effective training of men. Even the least intuitive client could be taught that a woman telling you she's "independent" does not necessarily mean, "sleep with as many other women as you like." Through simulation technology, Diana could spare women the pain of going through these scenarios in real life while men learned proper interaction techniques.

If only there were a training scenario for screening fraud, Diana mused. Her dinner grew cold on her lap as she wondered what she was going to say to Roger the next evening.

Roger walked with his hands in his pockets in an effort to appear relaxed. This out-of-office debrief he was headed to couldn't be normal.

He fingered the single one-chit token in his pocket. Usually they gave you a five—or ten-pack after your last simulation, depending on how well you'd done. Then you'd keep meeting your caseworker for refills, and after a while, if it had been established that you weren't a complete slime bag, you worked your way up to the card. But he hadn't even rated a five pack? Something was wrong here.

And what if he was right, what if Kirkwood were going rogue? Should he just report it to the Agency—or was there something else he should be looking to gain? He knew some of his buddies would view this as a golden opportunity to shake down a caseworker. Roger didn't have the stomach for extortion, but maybe if he could expose an out-of-control caseworker—if in fact that's where she was heading—that might be a reason to reopen the whole debate on screening.

Of course, with a majority female congress and woman president, there was little chance the Screening Act would be repealed anytime soon. And it would be a shame to get Diana into trouble, because she was kind of cute.

Roger had walked half a block past the Starbucks before he thought to look up. He circled back to the entrance and the doors slid open. A tall, muscular man in a dark suit approached Roger as he stepped inside and scanned the room.

"Sir?"

Roger stared at him blankly, then noticed the hand extended, palm up, in his direction. Of course, his token. His one chit.

He took it out of his pocket, dropped it into the bouncer's hand, and walked into the café.

———

Diana fidgeted with the cup of coffee she'd ordered on autopilot. There was no way she needed the caffeine sitting in front of her. The fear of losing her job was going to be enough to keep her up all night.

She slipped a hand into her purse to check again for the rest of the five-pack she should have given him back at the office. It wasn't too late to fix this; she would tell him he'd passed, and that she was just there to take him through his first visit to a pairing locale. No one could fault a caseworker for going the extra mile for a client, could they?

Diana saw Roger at the door with the bouncer. Her hand shot out of her purse to motion to him, sending the tokens flying across the table. Cursing under her breath, she scrambled to scoop them back into her bag.

She looked up again and pasted a serene, slightly detached smile on her face, hoping it would counteract the flush she felt rising to her cheeks. Roger had seen her and was heading her way. He seemed to be savoring his first visit, walking slowly and looking around as he moved through the room. In all her years as a caseworker, she'd never really thought about what it was like for a man on his first visit to an actual pairing locale.

Okay, she said to herself, *time to take care of this.* She stood up briskly and waved him over to a seat at her table.

"Hello Roger," she said, careful to make her smile welcoming but professional. She noted that he was still scanning the room from his seat, and hoped it was just due to the novelty of being in a pairing café. Surely he couldn't be looking at other women when he'd come there to meet her. But then again, that was her job, to help men become eligible to meet other women. He was just coming to get the rest of his chits.

"Hi." Roger's voice snapped Diana back to attention, and she realized that he was looking directly at her. The heat in her cheeks intensified.

"Yes, hello," she said, tapping the table twice to activate the menu. "Would you like something to drink?"

"Um, no thanks." He sat ramrod straight with his hands on his knees. How had she ever thought this was going to go anywhere?

"So, welcome to Starbucks."

"Thank you."

"Your first pairing café."

"Yes, yes it is…"

Diana understood loud and clear. It would be best for everyone if she just gave him the rest of his chits and went home. She opened her purse again and fished for the tokens. She'd write a memo to get him reassigned to another caseworker tomorrow.

"…and," continued Roger, "it's kind of nice to see you outside of the training center."

Her hand froze inside her bag.

"Maybe I will have something," he said, leaning forward to scan the menu.

"The lattes are good." Diana noted the way the café lighting brought out little highlights in his hair and accentuated the fullness of his lips.

Roger nodded and tapped in his order. He leaned back in his seat and ventured a smile.

Diana looked into his honey-brown eyes. She closed her purse and smiled back.

Louie's was one of the few non-pairing locales trendy enough for a guy to be seen in without feeling like a loser. It was the perfect place for buddies with mixed dating clearances to meet up.

Roger was sitting at a high-top table with a beer when his friend Jared walked in. He strode over to Roger with casual authority. Tall and trim with chiseled features and perfect teeth, he was the kind of guy even other guys had to admit was good looking. If anyone was in a position to give dating advice, it was Jared.

Jared had taken the whole process pretty seriously, plugging into his network of female acquaintances for feedback, and leaping at any opportunity to share his wisdom with others. "You just have to listen, man," he would tell them, "really try to understand *why* they're saying what they're saying. It's actually pretty interesting once you stop to listen."

And of course Jared's female friends had loved being consulted. They'd fallen for that big time. By the time he'd asked for their advice, listened intently and considered their various points of view, the actual test was pretty much a technicality—Jared had a bevy of women who couldn't wait until he could start dating. Strictly speaking, they didn't have to wait, but none of them wanted to be like those women at the other, non-pairing bars. So they were all content to let the process run its course, each woman thinking her long talks with Jared would give her the inside edge once he was cleared for the pairing locales.

Roger had to hand it to him; he knew how to work it. But sometimes he couldn't tell if Jared was still playing the system or if he had really drunk the Kool-Aid. Whenever Roger complained about screening, Jared would remind him that it was all opt-in; no one was forcing him to do it. Jared couldn't be for real—didn't he chafe under the manipulation? Or was he just a Zen-master of the process?

Jared smiled and clapped Roger on the shoulder. "Hey, man, good to see you."

"Hey."

"So," said Jared, settling onto a stool. "What's up? How'd your screening go?" He pulled up the tabletop menu and ordered a martini.

"Well, it's weird, man. I think I just went on a date with my caseworker."

Jared gaped. Roger briefed him on the events of the past few days, feeling a rush of pride at being able to surprise Jared with something related to the screening process.

"...so she gives me the rest of the tokens at the end of our—meeting, date, whatever it was."

"Whatd'ya get, 5-pack? 10-pack?"

"5-pack. Which by then was a 4-pack."

"Well, see, if you hadn't I screwed up the young widow at the funeral scenario..."

"I didn't screw up the—look, that's not the point. So she hands me the tokens and says, now that she's shown me a pairing café, she should take me to my first pairing *bar* too."

"Wait, wait, wait, she can't do that!"

Roger laughed and waved his hand dismissively. "Oh, it's okay, I don't mind meeting up with her."

"No, man, that's crazy. I've never heard of that. There have to be some kind of guidelines for this." Jared pulled out his phone and started a search.

"Don't worry about it, I don't want to make a big deal out of it."

"So you don't even care that she's using up your chits? Think about it, how are you supposed to meet anyone with your case-worker hanging around?"

"I don't know," said Roger with a shrug, "she's kind of hot herself."

Jared looked at Roger and shook his head. "All right, man," he said, putting his phone away. "But I can't help you out here. This is all uncharted territory."

"No worries, I'll handle it. And for once *I* get to tell *you* how things go."

Jared rubbed his chin thoughtfully. "You know, this is probably a pretty big risk for her."

"Probably."

"So what do you think she wants?"

"No idea, man."

"Well, what are you going to do?" asked Jared.

Roger shrugged again. The waiter brought their drinks to the table, and Roger lifted his glass. "To uncharted territory."

Client Progress Report
Client: *Roger Henderson*
Caseworker: *Diana Kirkwood*
Comments: *Client has been adjusting well to a variety of pairing locales. Has displayed respectful and responsible behavior toward female patrons in both daytime and evening settings. Use of alcohol has not impaired judgment beyond an acceptable degree. Client has successfully*

1.) Procured contact information from women in non-coercive manner

2.) Used contact information to initiate subsequent dates

3.) Embraced approach of cautious optimism regarding sex. Coercion, pleading, petulance not employed

Recommendation: *increase to 10-pack.*
References: …

Diana looked up from her monitor and leaned back in her chair. She was stuck at the references. She had to list at least one woman who could vouch for Roger's dating behavior out in the world. Problem was, Diana was the only reference he had.

She and Roger had burned through his first packet of tokens and had already started in on his 10-pack, so technically her report was already late. Of course, no one would notice; the paperwork was always running behind in this place. Besides, they all trusted her to get it done right. They trusted her—she'd been trying not to let that part get to her.

But then, who was actually getting hurt here? Roger obviously didn't mind. If he didn't want to go along with it, he could file a complaint tomorrow and be done with it. She wondered if this is how other girls at work had been finding their boyfriends and husbands. Maybe she should have been doing this all along.

So, which of her friends would least mind being Roger's reference? Not that it mattered; everyone's caseload went through a periodic review, but nobody actually called Diana's references anymore.

Her friend Natalie was a bit on the wild side, she wouldn't mind. She typed in Natalie's name with a random phone number and submitted the report.

"Just in time," she said, checking the time on her monitor. She didn't want to be late for dinner with Roger.

Natalie's mouth melted from a shocked "O" into a wolfish grin. She looked at Diana out of the corner of her eye. "Diana, you dog!"

"Come on, Natalie, this is serious."

"Okay, sorry, I'll focus. So, tell me more about this guy Roger. What's he like, how did we meet?"

Just two weeks after submitting Roger's Client Progress Report, Diana found herself prepping Natalie for the reference check the agency would be making any day now—the call Diana never thought would happen.

Diana's files were under review, everyone's were. She'd seen a number of investigations go down at the Agency—every time a well-placed woman went through a nasty breakup there were congressional inquiries into their screening methods. But this time it was the Vice President's daughter, and it was a very public, very broken engagement. These reviews were being conducted with a whole new level of thoroughness.

Diana had gained some time when the investigators had asked for a current phone number for Natalie. Somehow she'd thought a home-cooked dinner with bottomless wine would make coaching her friend for a fraudulent reference check seem a little less criminal. It didn't.

"Okay," said Diana, "we'll say you met him at a Starbucks…"

"Aw jeez, Diana, you know I hate Starbucks!"

"You've got to be kidding me, I'm about to lose my job, and you can't handle a visit to Starbucks?"

Natalie raised her hands in surrender. "All right, so I met him at Starbucks. What does he look like?"

"Well, he's really good looking…"

"That much I guessed."

"Curly dark hair, light brown eyes with nauseatingly long eyelashes." She and Natalie had the same objection to—and weakness for—female-length eyelashes on men. "He's about 5'8", nice and fit. He jogs. Outside."

"Hmmm."

"He's into astropunkhop. Not my taste in music, but you can't have everything, right?"

"Right. And what does he do?"

"He's a teacher. But it's not about the money," she added quickly. She almost wished he were a lawyer or something like that so she wouldn't come across as a gold-digger. Education sector salaries had jumped considerably since the Fair Pay Act, and superstar teachers like Roger could bring home bonuses that made moguls think about jumping ship from Wall Street.

"Diana, I've met your boyfriends, I know you're not all about money," Natalie said, taking another sip of wine. "Most importantly, is he any good in bed?"

Diana shook her head. "I mean, I don't know. It hasn't… we haven't." Normally she'd have had a guy over by this point, but this was not a normal situation. And maybe it was for the best anyway—having sex was usually the beginning of the end of her relationships. Except when declining sex was the beginning of the end.

"Well, if he wants to get anywhere," Natalie said with a wink, "it sounds like he's going to have to take me somewhere nice on our next date."

"Sure," said Diana flatly, "for the sake of authenticity." It was bad enough that she and Roger had already decided to curtail their dates until the scandal blew over; now she was going to have to set up a date between him and Natalie. She trusted Natalie, but Roger? He'd passed the screening and all, but it's not like he was getting objective follow-up.

She was just going to have to trust him too.

"Hey, Di, can you hear me?"

Diana turned the volume up and inched her own mic higher. "Yeah, I can hear you." She hated videochatting, but since the inquiry had started, it had been the best way to stay in touch with Roger without having to risk seeing him in public.

"Hey, how you doing?" he asked.

"Oh good. How was your date with Natalie?" she teased.

"Well, aside from the threat to disembowel me if I ever treated you like less than a queen, I'd say it went pretty well."

"That's my girl!" she laughed. "But I don't think you're going to have to spend any more chits on death threats. Hopefully this whole thing will blow over soon."

"Yeah, I hope so."

They launched into an easy conversation about how their days had been, what their students and clients had said, things that had struck them as funny or made them angry, and what had just made them sit and shake their heads.

Just when Diana thought the call was winding down, Roger cocked his head and asked, "So, what happens now?"

She cocked her head. "What do you mean?"

"Well, when do I see you again?"

Diana sighed. "It's not that simple."

"Sure it is, come over for dinner."

"I'll think about it."

"Come on, I'll throw down a rope you can climb up the back of the building. No one will see you!"

She rolled her eyes and laughed. "Okay, I'll think about it."

They said their goodbyes and she flipped the videochat off. She asked herself how long she could postpone the beginning of the end.

Diana kept going in to the office as usual, trying to look as concerned as the next person, not more, not less. Everyone walked around waiting for the other shoe to drop, hoping it would fall into someone else's office. She'd always known her files were on the network and could be reviewed at any time. But this time, for the first time, she knew there was something in those files that could come back to haunt her. She told herself to just keep her head and do her job, and tried not to think about how the whole thing could unravel.

By the end of the second week, things started to feel almost normal. The higher-ups were still nervous, but Natalie hadn't said anything about getting a call, and Diana was able to convince herself that her coworkers weren't really looking at her suspiciously.

And at last another week was over. Things had died down with the inquiry, and Diana thought she had gone long enough without seeing Roger. She messaged him before she had time to talk herself out of it and they arranged to meet up for a drink after work. If he invited her over later, she thought she might just be ready to go.

When her last client of the day canceled, she took it as a sign to take off a little early and freshen up. She was just logging off her computer when she heard a knock on her door. Cynthia, her supervisor, leaned in.

"Hey, Diana, do you have any more clients today?"

"Um… no."

"Oh good, I'd like to see you in my office for a minute, please."

"Sure, I'll just finish logging off here." She wondered how she could answer so calmly when all she could think was *ohmygodohmygodohmygod…* She stood up too fast, and the sound of blood rushing in her ears was almost overpowering as she followed Cynthia down the hall.

Cynthia waved Diana into a chair as they entered her office. She sat down behind her desk and folded her hands on top of it.

"Diana, you've been here for a while, you've seen how these inquiries play out. Everyone starts clamoring for accountability, so of course we have to start digging."

"Of course," said Diana, trying not to wring her hands. *Oh god, I'm getting fired.*

"And once we start digging, it's inevitable that all kinds of—issues—are uncovered with caseworkers across the agency."

"Yes, unfortunately." *Are they going to press charges? And what about Natalie?*

"And I know," said Cynthia, leaning closer, "you're used to seeing things patched up or papered over, but this time there's too much scrutiny for that. We can't just sweep things under the rug this time. And that's why I need to talk to you…"

———————

Diana arrived at the Starbucks at Seventh and Main, still trying to wrap her head around what had just happened. Roger was waiting for her in front.

"Sorry I'm late."

"No problem, I just wanted to be sure you could make it before I gave up my last token." He handed his chit over and they went inside to find a table.

They settled into a booth and he leaned in close. "So I guess I need to go in for a refill now. There's this woman I'd like to keep seeing." She couldn't help but notice how his eyes lingered on her lips.

"I wish I could help you, but it looks like this was my last week as your caseworker."

His playful smile disappeared. "So they're on to us. What did they say?"

Diana read Roger's reaction with her caseworker's eye. She was relieved to see he wasn't oozing fear or the will to flee. "Don't worry, they don't know anything. Natalie's very convincing."

"Uh, yeah, she convinced me she'd kill me if I ever cheated on you."

"You have a problem with that?"

Roger grinned and shook his head. "Come on, what's up? Why can't you be my caseworker anymore?"

Diana laughed. "Re-org. They want all the Senior Caseworkers to have more time for oversight, so they're reassigning some of our clients. I guess your file was so thin, it looked like it would be easy to hand off to someone junior."

Roger was speechless.

"That's not all. My boss said there's a position coming up that they really want me to apply for. Won't take no for an answer this time." She still couldn't believe this part. "They want me to be the next Head of Screening Oversight."

Diana could see surprise and relief in Roger's eyes, mixing with pride. Whether he was prouder of her promotion or at having pulled one over on the agency, she couldn't quite tell. But he was happy and, she noted, even more turned on than before.

So this was Roger Henderson, in person and unplugged: no case file, no electrodes, no control panel.

Diana smiled. She was looking forward to the ride.

The light from a trio of streetlights on a late-evening walk created three distinct shadows of Mr. Sproule, each going a different direction. Such was the genesis of our next story, which first appeared in 2013 in Psychedelia Gothique, a collection of his fiction.

Dale L. Sproule has published more than forty short stories over the past thirty years, as well co-publishing and co-editing TransVersions - Literature of the Fantastic.

Bad Copies

by Dale L. Sproule

In the intersecting light of the three street lamps, Floyd Sterling glanced at the sidewalk as he closed in on himself from both sides. The instant the three faint shadows merged into a single dark silhouette, Floyd's mind snapped back to the unpleasant task at hand.

He had been waiting across the street for less than an hour when the New Vista Home Renovations truck rumbled out of the long driveway beside the house. It was nine-thirty. He hadn't wanted to believe the clues that his best crew was getting sloppy, but this pretty much confirmed it. Leaving a job site this early on a conversion night was downright negligent.

The fresh dupes would still be sticky and couldn't be safely left alone until at least eleven. What if a friend or a relative dropped in unexpectedly? What if the matter wasn't dealt with promptly and thoroughly? And what if the half baked simulacra drew the attention of local law enforcement?

Floyd had hired Josh and Colin after they had stolen three prospective clients in a row with their snappy portfolio and hipster cred. Floyd kept an eye out and watched them go on to bilk each of those clients out of thousands and tens of thousands of dollars before they even needed to change their company name. When he offered them jobs, they weren't interested, until he waved the six figure salaries in their faces.

Josh scored a 35 on the PCL (Psychopathy Check List) Scale and Colin got 25, which was barely adequate but he was in Josh's thrall so it worked fine, at least for the first five months. But running this scam was a stressful gig. Despite the astronomical pay cheques and the fact that the actual victims were never physically harmed, the persuasion portion of the operation was truly tortuous for some and the deletion of the dupes at the end of the operation was murder for anybody without a flexible sense of morality. Even the toughest cookies could crack under the stress and Colin was anything but tough.

Floyd shouldn't have ignored the warning signs when the clean-up crew reported a lingering scent of dope in the truck cabin.

But he had cut them way too much slack and now it had come to this. Floyd shook his head while he ritualistically (and somewhat sensuously) squeezed the pistol through the satiny fabric of his jacket as he walked up the Henson's walkway. Slipping into the bathroom to put on the silencer would be far less conspicuous than walking in with a gun drawn.

When he rang the bell, Joy Henson answered. "Floyd. What's up? Your guys have already left."

"Yeah, I saw them go." He looked her right in the eye but could see no traces of prematurity—no red eye or strange swellings as a result of being ambulant before her bones had properly set and hardened. Her eyes were pale blue, but he thought he remembered that being their natural colour. "I saw the guys leaving. They were… scheduled to work late tonight."

"Well, they came in really early."

"Yeah?"

"Yeah. With Josh's wife having a baby we thought you'd be okay with that."

"Of course," Floyd scratched his head, utterly failing to hide his bemusement. As far as he knew, Josh didn't even have a girl-friend. This was clearly a premeditated absence! Given that the new Joy was clearly functional, they had at least covered their tracks well. Floyd's worry started to dissipate a bit. Maybe it wasn't as bad as it looked. Maybe he'd have to give the boys a dressing down, but if all they'd done was connived a way to leave early, he might not even have to fire them.

"You want to come in and see what they've done downstairs?" Joy stepped back and allowed Floyd to precede her down the hall. Her voice kept jabbering from behind him, just like the real Joy would have done. "They didn't actually need to stay *this* late for crying out loud. And we certainly didn't mind them leaving early. Did we Arn?"

Arnie Henson stuck his head out from the kitchen and stuck out his hand. "Hey Floyd! Come to check out the reno?"

Floyd had been forced to buy an insurance policy from Arnie before the Hensons had agreed to hire New Vista for the renovation in the basement. Home based entrepreneurs were usually easy marks but they could be such pains in the ass! Floyd had tired of Arnie's eager beaver attitude about five minutes after meeting him. Tonight, Arnie's handshake seemed forebodingly moist, until he said, "Sorry, just finishing up the dishes. You go on down, I'll be right behind you."

Joy led him downstairs to the rec room, where the windows had been boarded over for the basement upgrade. When she flicked on the light, Floyd jumped back in shock.

There was indeed a pair of melters in the house, but they weren't the ones Floyd was expecting. A skeletal version of Josh stood pointing at the printer. "It jammed just after lunch. And numbnuts here was so stoned he couldn't fix it himself." He pointed at the gooey foetal version of Colin who was curled up on the floor like a half-eaten sticky bun.

This was typical of dupes that had been removed from the cylinder too soon before the process was complete. Without the injections to gauge and adjust their skin elasticity, they would melt into puddles within hours.

Arnie came through the door behind Floyd and filled in some of the details. "First thing I remember is waking up in that cylinder in a standing position and looking down to see that kid kneeling on the floor with his head between my legs." He absently kicked at Colin, who simply mewled louder and curled tighter.

The thing that resembled Josh spoke in a slur that suggested his tongue was turning to jelly. "I sho…sho…shink…zo problemsh in zha feeder unit, sho I shen Colin to sheck. I din shee he hadj za door open for so long zhey regain consciouzzz…nezz."

"Just had to put my foot on the back of the kid's neck and push down. Smack! Out like a light," Arnie said. "First thing we're going to do when we take over your operation is enroll these boys in self-defence training."

"And rehab," added Joy.

"Well yeah. We don't want them making the same mistakes when they're working for us."

"Hey, i' wazh jush him!" said Josh, waving a three fingered hand at his co-worker. Proto-flesh dripped from it like molten wax.

Floyd slid his hand very slowly into his coat, but before he reached his gun, he heard a pop and felt a three inch spike pierce through the bone and cartilage of his elbow. As he screamed and spun, Joy Henson swung an eighteen-inch pry bar up hard under his chin.

By the time Floyd swam back to consciousness, the half baked copies of his crew had melted completely. The real Josh was looking into his eyes, looking larger than life somehow. His face was intact and his voice was clear and crisp. "He's awake!"

Working hard to concentrate despite the pain in his arm, and to talk despite the swelling in his mouth and throat, a question occurred to Floyd, and he struggled to ask it through the lingering effects of the knockout drug, "Who was driving the truck?"

"What?"

"Truck was driving away when I got here." His voice sounded like he'd been sucking on helium. That was an effect he'd never seen before. "If you weren't driving, who was?"

"That was the final set of dupes," said Josh. "There was a bunch of sets. Printer was *really* jammed."

"You let the preemies drive? What if they got pulled over?"

"I'm sure even my knockoff has some pretty mad motoring skills." Josh sounded offended. "But with the melty fingers they didn't have the manual dexterity to fix the printer." He wiggled his fingers demonstratively.

"They took the truck back to your yard," said Joy, looming into Floyd's blurry field of vision. "We worried they might melt down before you encountered them. But even then, we hoped you'd come over here looking for the machine. But we were pretty surprised when you just showed up like that."

Arnie snapped his fingers in her ear and she giggled and snapped hers. "Yeah. Like that!"

As Floyd stared at her, disconcerted by the ongoing distortion, he realized he was looking out through the copier cover.

With the hi-res duplication of brain chemistry that this particular printer model delivered, the dupes hardly ever realized they weren't originals. But this being his operation, Floyd knew from the get-go that he must be a facsimile. His original was probably still in the machine behind him.

Floyd touched his face and despite his injuries from the scuffle, found all of the musculature and skin in place. "You fixed the printer?" he asked Josh.

"Well, it's not fixed yet, "said Josh. "The compound feeder is partially plugged. But as long as I don't print at 100%, the replication is fine."

"You mean I'm not…"

Josh slid open the cover. "You're at 50%. And you're perfect."

He lifted Floyd out and set him on the floor. He looked up right into the camel toe of Joy's crotch in her tight beige stretch pants.

So much for the plan of surprising Joy and using her as a hostage to get his gun back from Arnie.

"50% is not fucking perfect," Floyd mumbled looking up in awe at the giant Joy and Arnie. Now that Arnie had Floyd's pistol, she had the nail gun.

Joy sighed happily, "We thought it might take you days to show up."

"You *wanted* me here?"

"How else are you going to sign the contract to sell us the printer?" asked Joy.

Aha. The tables were turned. They could do whatever they wanted to him and his original would have no memory of it.

"On very generous terms," Arnie clarified. "You didn't list the printer on your insurance policy, so you'll do much better this way than if it was accidentally damaged or destroyed. If you catch my drift."

"The machine is broken. Why would you buy a machine that only makes 50% copies?"

"Josh says he can have it fixed in an hour."

Josh shrugged when Floyd glared at him. Floyd felt like punching him in the kneecap.

"Printing you at 50% was the test that confirmed what was wrong," Josh explained. "When I explained to the Hensons, they were okay with it. They said you'd be more manageable this way."

"We've been looking for new business opportunities," Joy chirped. "So this was a gift! Now we get to go into the "printing" business, your employees get to stay employed and you get to walk away. Or at least the full size version of you." She nodded at the feeder tube that held the real Floyd. "It's a win-win-win, just like they teach us in business school."

"How do I know you're not gonna kill him...the real me... right after I sign?"

"The deal will seem much more legitimate if you're still kicking. And you'd have a hard time passing for him," laughed Arnie. He handed Floyd a pen as big as a porn stud's junk.

"I'm not signing anything," Floyd said pushing it away. He didn't see Joy coming at him with a yardstick until he heard the swish. "What the fuck!" he screamed.

He turned to see Joy slapping her palm with the thick wooden instrument. "I might just have to put you over my knee," she said.

Anger and pain mixed in equal parts in Floyd's brain. He knew martial arts! He had one good arm! He didn't have to put up with this crap!

Hearing the wooden blade whistling through the air again, Floyd hand shot out just in time for the yardstick to catch him on the backs of his knuckles, breaking at least one finger. Floyd screamed and lurched away, tripping over the compressor cord and falling face down. The pain in his left hand fingers and right elbow flared unimaginably as he tried to break his fall. That's when he discovered he was still too embryonic to bleed properly. His nose had snapped right over to the side. Joy grasped it between two fingers and twisted it back into position.

His hosts waited patiently until Floyd stopped squawking. When he was finally able to gather a coherent thought, he said, "That wasn't so bright, now how am I going to sign the contract?

Joy put him over her knee and whaled him to within an inch of his life.

When she put him back on the floor, he was still simpering so bad he couldn't talk for ten more minutes. Arnie kept talking like nothing had happened. "Your boys were saying this is what you always do to the facsimiles, torture them until they give what you need. Melt them down with a solvent injection and the originals wake up in the morning in their own beds with no idea the dupes had ever been made. But Josh said you never thought of reducing their size."

Floyd muttered, "You wouldn't thought of it either if he hadn't been forced to print me this size. I fell right in your lap." He gaze flickered fearfully to Joy's substantial lap, where he had been sprawled for the past ten minutes. "So to speak."

"You know, Floyd," said Arnie nodding his head amiably, "you may be right. Funny how you can miss things that are right in front of your face."

"I pioneered this scam," Floyd muttered.

"Worked out most of the angles." Arnie said admiringly.

"You know I'm never going to sell you the copier," Floyd stated.

"I think you will. Or the new Floyd we're cooking up right now will," said Arnie. "I wanted to go down to 25% but Josh said the copies started noticeably degrading at 35."

"At that size, there's a danger of accidentally squashing them," said Joy.

"But that's okay," added Arnie, "They're dry and ready to interrogate in just over two hours so we can do six batches."

Floyd stared at his doll sized replacement as Joy said, "I trust that seeing what we've done to you will convince him to sign."

Floyd's body stiffened as he heard the yardstick switch cut the air again and he surrendered.

As he authenticated his e-sig, he was admiring their business model. You could close a deal three times as fast, using a fraction of the raw materials and leave hardly any mess for the disposal guys. Maybe if he factored this into his next business plan he could get enough of a loan to buy a new machine. That's what he'd do! This would just be a temporary setback! He grinned, looking up just as the syringe plunged into his neck. Or at least that's what he *should* do, little Floyd realized, if his original had any way of knowing about it. Until then, he'd be just another mark.

Right around the time that 50% Floyd was turning into a puddle, the beep told them that the 35% copy was ready.

"Hey honey," said Joy. "We never actually talked about what we're going to do with the original Floyd."

"We're gonna let him go. Just like a regular client."

"Only they have no idea what happened. He does! He'll be dangerous. What if he comes after us?"

Arnie grimaced and ran one hand through his thinning hair. "What else are we gonna do?"

Joy turned to Josh. "What would happen if we enlarged this new copy by 400%. Would he be the same size as the original?"

"Yeah," Josh agreed. "But there'd be a ton of generation loss. It would be a really crappy copy.

"Would people be able to see it melting?"

"Probably not. He'd just be really porous."

"What would that do?" asked Arnie.

"Make him sweaty, uncoordinated, forgetful. And he might need a diaper."

"Sounds like my uncle after his stroke," said Joy.

"It would be just like that," Josh admitted.

"Perfect," said Joy. "And what would happen if you gave the original a shot of solvent?

"You want me to kill a real person?" said Josh shaking his head.

"You did say you scored a 35 on the PCL."

"But this is too risky."

"And the new cost efficiencies will allow us to double your take."

"Oh fine," said Josh ruefully.

After Floyd woke up, he allowed the clients to guide him up the stairs at their house, the man kept pressing the car keys into his hand while the woman said, "He's in no condition to drive. We should call a cab."

Why had he been drinking with them? He couldn't remember.

They poured him a glass of Scotch while they waited for the cab. It tasted wonderful but made him sweat even worse than before. He kept forgetting the woman's name…Grace or Gay or…Joy. That was it! Joy. And he couldn't help but feel that there was something even more important that he was forgetting.

When the driver came to the door they gave him Floyd's home address and voiced their regret about letting him drink so much. Floyd had been too embarrassed to ask if he was the one who left that mess on their new basement carpet. But that concern weighed on him now. While he considered going back to apologise, he saw his shadow on the sidewalk, separating into three shadows before fading away completely. It seemed eerily familiar and somehow profound.

The venerable Paris Opera House has featured in stories, novels, plays, and movies since its completion well over a century ago. Our next story takes up that tradition, with a decidedly modern twist.

Jonathan Shipley is a widely published author of fantasy, science fiction, and horror short stories, as well as a series of novels, who's story arc includes Nazis, vampires, and space opera.

Phantoms of the Opera

by Jonathan Shipley

Ydaire strode briskly down the winding Ile de Saint-Louis toward the bridge that connected with the Ile de la Cité and Notre Dame. Her wristcom tingled and she turned up her wrist to view the message:

GYPSYPRINCE to EMERALDSTORM: jst arrvd @ cafe. ? r u

She typed a single word back—*coming*—and picked up her pace, even though she wasn't late. He was atypically early. She crossed the bridge, rounded the last corner, and emerged on the busy square fronting the cathedral with its huge anti-UV canopy hovering over it like some monstrous transparent umbrella, and always surprising first-time visitors.

The cafe was to the right, one of a row of sidewalk cafés catering to Notre Dame tourists. Well, it couldn't be helped—everything on the square catered to tourists—and the food at this cafe was quite good, if overpriced. Another vibration:

GYPSYPRINCE to EMERALDSTORM: ? 2 eat. ordering nw

That was just annoying. She would think about food when she reached the cafe and not before. Ordering was not a task that needed pre-planning. She moved through the crowd of tourists… and there was the cafe and there was GypsyPrince himself at a sidewalk table.

She slowed, and it wasn't just the annoyance of him industriously chatting up the waitress. It had been a long time since their last face-to-face meeting and she wanted a good look at him.

It was definitely a new and improved Nikolai. He had filled out nicely in the last two years, something that didn't come across in their flashtexts to each other. Last time they met, he had been a lanky adolescent; now he was lean young man with broad shoulders and the hint of a mustache. And he seemed very comfortable with himself as he oozed charm at the waitress. None of the old awkwardness of adolescence.

"We'll order later—thank you," Ydaire said, walking over to the table and taking a seat. She caught a hint of trees and campfires. Yes, that same wonderful scent of woods she remembered from their childhood.

Nikolai looked up and his eyes lit as he recognized her. The waitress moved off, forgotten.

"Thanks for meeting me," Ydaire said. "It's been too long."

"EmeraldStorm texts the wandering GypsyPrince to rendezvous in Paris," he grinned. "How could I possibly refuse that?"

"I wasn't even sure we'd recognize each other."

He gave a snort. "Speak for yourself, Ydaire. It would take more than a couple years to fuzz my memories of you. You were beautiful then, but now—"

"—I'm just as impatient with empty phraseology as ever. Do these lines actually work on girls you meet?"

"Actually, yes," he nodded. "I don't have too much trouble in that department."

I suppose you wouldn't, she assessed silently. His gypsy coloring gave him a mysterious air with deep, smoldering Romany eyes.

Bedroom eyes, she had to admit. She'd always wondered what that phrase meant. Now she knew.

"I even remember the last thing you said two years ago when we parted," he continued. "You said, 'I'll never forget our time together this summer. It means a lot to have a friend like you'."

"No," she corrected, "My actual words were: 'I've enjoyed our time together this summer. Friendships like ours are—damn, is that the time? I've got to go.' Your version is your largely own creation."

He gave her a sour look. "Yes, thank you, Miss Perfect Memory for destroying a moment I held dear. You do know, don't you, that most people would consider a real photographic memory like yours very freaky?"

"I'm aware. I don't flaunt it to just anyone. Just very close friends."

He looked placated. "Why are we meeting *here*, by the way? Your Paris château is just around the corner, if I remember."

"It's a house, not a château, and I prefer—"

"Well, it's got a courtyard and a servants wing, so it's more than a townhouse."

"Are you in real estate now?" she asked pointedly. "I prefer not to meet on family property. It would only broadcast this reunion."

"Ah, reunion," he repeated archly. "Such potential in that word. Almost as good as rendezvous." Then he frowned. "What happened to EmeraldStorm's emerald eyes? They've turned more brownish… less spectacular."

"Tinted contacts. These days I routinely filter to a nondescript hazel. I'm trying to look less conspicuous."

He gave a laugh. "You need more than tinted contacts to be inconspicuous. Tall, blond, and beautiful is high profile in any crowd."

"Again with the empty phraseology." She tapped his arm in mock threat. "Don't force me to hurt you."

"Physical coercion is also high profile," he pointed out with a grin. "I think, Ydaire, you're doomed to be conspicuous all your days." Then he sighed and sat back in his chair. "I know you want something from me—you wouldn't ask me here if you didn't. And knowing you, it won't be anything easy."

"I do have a night escapade in mind," she said, leaning forward conspiratorially. "The same type of escapade we both delighted in as children. This involves old mysteries, secret passages, and an opera house."

"Could be interesting," he hedged. "So we're going to burgle an opera house?"

"It can't be burglary when there's no theft involved—just breaking and entering."

"Sounds beneath you," he grinned. "As long as you're in the mood for wild, why not break into the Louvre and steal the Mona Lisa? Now that's an act with substance. But an opera house? Who breaks in to an opera house?"

Ydaire tossed her head in annoyance. "I'm not doing this to be wild. I'm satisfying my curiosity by collecting information that's not virtualized anywhere. You've seen the *Phantom of the Opera*, haven't you?"

"The old 2014 gothvid?" he asked.

"No, the 1986 operetta by Lord Andrew Webber. It's the fortieth anniversary of the original London opening, and theaters across the world are staging productions of it, including the Palais Garnier, better known as the Paris Opera House. That in itself is special, but I thought we could celebrate by doing something far more special."

"By breaking into the Paris Opera?"

She shook her head. "Are you *trying* to be dense? The Paris Opera House is where the story takes place."

"So sue me—I don't do operettas."

"Then you're culturally deficit. In 1909, Gaston Leroux published a novel about a deformed man, thought to be a ghost, living in the catacombs beneath the Paris Opera. The book and its film and stage adaptations are all considered classics. The Webber operetta has been running on Broadway continuously since it opened.

"But here's the interesting part. In the operetta, the play, and the book, the Phantom survives by utilizing a series of secret passages and waterways beneath the opera house. While it is known that Old Paris is riddled with tunnels and catacombs, there is a curious lack of verification whether the Phantom's passageways actually exist. And if the passageways exist, it could mean the Phantom himself existed. We might even find a desiccated corpse and be the first to know the truth."

Nikolai have a short laugh. "Desiccated corpse—you make this sound so appealing. Most likely it's all collapsed over the years and there's nothing left."

"The last is unlikely," Ydaire pointed out. "I've checked building inspection records back to the early twentieth-century, and there's no mention of any foundation settling, which would happen if a sub-basement collapsed under it. So the field is clear for discovery. I've been comparing documentation. Everything currently on line says the Opera House has fifteen levels, ten above ground and five below."

"Five basements? What for?"

"Dressing rooms, green rooms, rehearsal space, but mainly storage. Supposedly there are acres of sets and props from almost a hundred and fifty years of productions since the Opera opened in 1875. The building was begun 1861, but construction took over a decade because of constant setbacks, one being a subterranean lake that had to be pumped out to lay the foundation. The lake is significant. All the modern databanks say five basement levels, but when I tracked all the way back to some old twentieth-century sources, I picked up references to *seven* basement levels. The seventh is supposedly flooded by the subterranean lake. These old sources indicated that no one was allowed to see the lake, even back then, and since that time, both Basement Seven and Basement Six seem to have disappeared from all documentation and floor plans. I find that well worth investigating."

"This is getting better, I have to admit," Nikolai nodded. "An indoor subterranean lake in the middle of Paris is actually pretty cool. I wouldn't mind seeing that."

"Glad to have you on board. Here's the plan. I'll enter through the front door as a ticketed patron to the *Phantom of the Opera* production, while you wait by the side emergency exit for me to let you in with the equipment."

"There's equipment?"

"Torches, metal detector, and the same type spatial scanner used for archaeological excavations. Not things a young opera-goer would have under her arm and much too awkward to sneak in under her skirt."

"Do you regularly sneak things in under your skirt?" he asked with a lift of his eyebrow.

"Why else do you think skirts were invented?" she countered, then forged onward. "I have all the equipment. All you have to do is transport it to location."

"In what?"

"I've rented a minicar for you. I'll let you in the emergency exit under the carriage ramp, and from then we have almost three hours until the opera ends, the building vacates, and they turn on internal sensors for the night."

He frowned. "Wait—we're doing this treasure hunt while the building is full of people? That's risky."

"But less risky than the sensor system. I've checked—it's a unified internal system. If it's off upstairs, it will also be off in the basements. The only disadvantage is the time deadline. But frankly, if I can't find these passages in three hours, then they probably don't exist."

"Three hours—really?" Nikolai repeated in mock surprise. "I would have thought fifteen minutes—twenty tops—for such a superior being as you."

"The three hours includes fifteen minutes for me to find the way, and two-and-a-half hours for you to get lost following me," she shot back. "And that's the plan. I'll have the trike and equipment ready for you at seven at the Pyramid."

"And thank goodness the plan is done," he said with an exaggerated roll of the eyes. "Can we now have a quiet, post-conspiracy coffee and just chat?"

Ydaire hadn't planned to stay, but there was no reason not to. All the props were ready for tonight. "Yes, actually," she said. "I'd enjoy that."

He sat back with a suspicious look. "Really?"

"Yes, really," she laughed. "I can enjoy a quiet chat when the mood strikes. And the mood strikes me now. So, an amaretto latte, please. And the cheese crepes here are truly excellent."

In the Paris twilight, a young man in dark jacket, jeans, and boots sauntered past the Pyramid in front of the Louvre. He paused at a bench and smiled an infectious smile. "Looking for a good time, pretty lady?"

Ydaire pulled herself from the bench where she had been impatiently waiting. "You're late. Apparently seven o'clock translates as seven-thirteen, Nikolai time."

Nikolai gave a sigh. "Don't be cross. You know I'm bad with time. The only mystery is why if you wanted true seven o'clock, you didn't tell me six-forty. Besides, you can't complain when *I'm* helping *you*."

"I can't complain? And you claim to know me?" But she let it go, even though it was incredibly sloppy on his part. She actually had built extra time into the schedule. She pointed to the curb where a single-person electrosol minicar stood parked. "There's your chariot. Two blocks down the rue de Rivoli and then a straight shot up the Avenue de l'Opéra. The emergency entrance is under the carriage ramp on the left side of the building. And you're off."

But he didn't go. "You look incredibly elegant tonight," he said, eying her outfit.

"Go," she repeated more forcefully and headed away from him. She hadn't scheduled that much extra time.

At the corner, she climbed into the larger three-wheeled cab that she'd kept waiting for the last half-hour. A glance back showed that Nikolai had finally taken the hint and was just pulling away from the curb. The cab passed him at the turn onto the Avenue de l'Opéra and kept increasing its lead. But that was fine. He didn't need to arrive until well after she did.

The huge Opera House sat directly at the end of the avenue like a gigantic wedding cake with carved and gilt decoration. Even at a distance, she could make out the lit dome with a gilded Apollo topping the whole confection of a building. Second Empire style was nothing if not grand, and even the umbrella-like UV shield above it couldn't take that grandness away. As they drew closer, she saw patrons making their way up the broad front steps to the foot entrance with its seven arched doors.

"Stop here," she called to the driver before he could pull around to the grand carriage entrance on the side of the building. "And I'll need to be picked up afterwards."

"Dispatcher always sends a whole fleet for afterward, *mam'selle*," he assured her as she thumbprinted the credit transfer and stepped out.

She joined the crowd marching up the steps, already catching the sweetish scent of mixed perfumes that she associated with Parisian social events. This foot entrance appealed to her more than the grander Emperor's Entrance with its carriage ramp because it offered the best display of the grand staircase, which if not the heart of the Opera House, was at least a kidney.

Just inside the foyer, she brushed a thumb against the ticket sensor to validate herself. At the moment, she was a perfectly legitimate patron, dressed in opera black, though her long skirt over boots was more utilitarian than elegant, despite Nikolai's opinion. But she compensated with a designer wrap of black silk and scattered silver sequins.

She crossed the foyer with the *Grand Escalier* straight ahead. She knew many castles and palaces and adjudged this grand staircase with its four tiers of overhanging balconies to be among the grandest. It had been designed as a theatrical backdrop for opera patrons to see and be seen and to this day, it functioned magnificently in that role. It was a visual feast in marble, onyx, and bronze, ascending one flight, then branching left and right.

She made the ascent and turned right at the landing toward her seat in one of the lower-tier boxes. She sat as the lights dimmed and the orchestra began the driving chords of the overture to *Phan-*

tom of the Opera. She listened all the way through with a knowing smile. Then as the curtain rose in the first scene, she slipped from her seat into the side corridors that flanked the auditorium. She'd planned the evening with a nicely symmetrical touch—to see the opening of the operetta, sneak below to wrest the secrets from the sub-basements, and be back in time for the closing scene of the production.

Reaching street level via one of the winding secondary staircases was not a problem. As she descended, she pulled off the expensive wrap and unzipped her long, flowing skirt to reveal dark trousers underneath. She avoided the main ways where the ushers still stood on duty and found the emergency exit tucked under the carriage ramp of the Emperor's Entrance. Quickly pulling on gloves to keep her DNA to herself, she produced a metal relay stud from her pocket and positioned her hand close to the one on the door frame. Internal sensors might be deactivated, but the door could still be alarmed. Slowly, she eased the door open, at the same time sliding her relay into place against the door frame to ensure that contact was never broken. To do it right took the better part of two minutes, but now the door was accessible for coming and going. She held it open and called softly, "Nikolai?"

When there was no answer, she added, "This had better not be another example of Nikolai time." Then she smelled evergreen.

He materialized from the shadows, dark hair, dark clothes, dark gloves, and very white teeth exposed in a wide grin. "It's not—but I had you wondering, didn't I?" He transferred two shoulder bags to her, accepted her clothing items in return, and went back to the minicar for the third bag.

When he returned, she let the door shut. It didn't close completely, but her temporary contact remained secure. There was a quick reshuffling of the load so that he had two bags and she only one, and then they were on their way down the side corridor, toward the back of the Opera House.

"Making the male carry the heavier load is very sexist, you know," Nikolai murmured as they walked.

"It's what testosterone is for," she replied absently, her attention on comparing the doorways in this section of the corridor to the floor plan in her head. "This one," she said, stopping beside a locked door and stepping to the side. "Would you?"

With a nod, he unslung his cargo and produced a slim kit from his pocket. It was an old-fashioned key lock but yielded quickly to his picks. She could have accomplished the same thing, but he was the faster lock-pick. Even as a boy, he'd had an impressive knack for it.

The door opened to a steep service staircase down to the first two basement levels. From here the way would get harder, she knew. The staircase locations were less predictable, the plans less accurate, and always the problem that these were not public areas. If seen, they would have no excuse for being there.

"So that's two basements down, five to go," Nikolai commented. "Or would that more accurately be all basements down."

"Don't attempt jokes," she said. "It's too painful. Access from here on down is going to be at the back of the building designed for crew use. The lower levels are mainly storage areas for sets and props. Supposedly, the lower the level, the older and more forgotten the props. And be aware there are dressing rooms on this level."

"I shall glide like a shadow, milady," he acknowledged in deep, sepulchral tones.

They continued the journey downward without incident. She found the doors; he picked the locks; they both glided like shadows. As they descended below the regularly accessed areas, they left ambient lighting behind and used heavy-duty chemical torches from one of Nikolai's bags. That grimmed the tone of the excursion instantly.

The reality of walking through endless storerooms of unusual items with minimal light was skin-crawling-eerie. Some of the props were not only unusual, but downright gruesome. She could make an association between a rack of severed plaster heads and a production of *Salome*, but huge coiled snakes and oversized dancing demons she had no context for. At least the air was good, surprisingly fresh for how deep they were. She mentally thanked Monsieur

Garnier for building adequate ventilation into his sub-basement design.

Her wristcom clicked softly. "Intermission," she said. "This is taking longer than I expected."

"Where are we now?" he asked. "I see demons, so this must be the Fifth Circle of Hell."

"It's the fifth basement—the last documented level. The seventh level is where the underground lake is said to be, and I have no idea what's on the sixth level. I could find no references at all. Consequently"—she unshouldered her bag to pull out the scanner—"no more easy staircases. We'll have to find our own way."

"Following the dust trails left by others?" he suggested.

"There's not much dust in a self-contained environment."

"Then what's this?" he asked, sweeping his torch beam over the floor.

She stepped over to look. "Not dust." She stooped down. "It's... blood. The air seemed suddenly much colder. She shivered.

Nikolai stepped closer, draping an arm over her shoulders. "The spatter seems to lead from the last staircase to somewhere," he said slowly. "And it's recent."

Her mouth tightened into a thin line. A blood trail in an unused sub-basement was considerably eerier than giant coiled snakes. "We may have squatters down here with us," she told Nikolai quietly. She was thinking, however, of desiccated corpses and phantoms never found.

He gave a dark look. "We have no idea what we're getting into, and it's starting to look bigger than an underground lake. If we go on, it has to be stealthy as a ghost."

If we go on—the words resonated with her own growing doubts. This was supposed to be an adventure, a fling, not a crime scene investigation. "I'm willing to take it another step," she finally said. "But maybe not much farther than that. I didn't come prepared for a serious encounter."

A knife blossomed suddenly in his palm. "I'm always prepared."

She managed a tense smile. Nikolai had definitely been the right choice of partners for tonight. His hunter's instincts had improved as much as the rest of him.

They moved over an aisle, following the blood spatter. When it seemed to dead-end into the west cellar wall, Ydaire brought out the spatial scanner and imaged sections of the wall before her. "The middle section has a cavity behind it," she said softly. "Hidden doors of the nineteenth century relied on mechanical linkages with manual releases, usually metal." She held out her hand. "Metal detector, if you please."

Nikolai pulled out the portable detector and handed it over. She panned her torch over the immediate area. The architect had used a great deal of steel throughout the structure, but this sub-basement seemed to be solidly stone construction. Metal light fixtures overheard—she could filter those out—and the props were mainly wood and plaster. A fairly good field for detecting the odd bit of metal.

She aimed and panned the device along first one edge of the suspect wall section, then the other. She detected a rod running up and down within the wall, connected to a metal lump under the stone footing. She calculated the exact location and clicked off the metal detector. "There's a pressure point under a stone to the left," she said, advancing. "I think this is the way down to the next level."

"Careful," Nikolai warned softly. "It's also where the blood leads. Don't break cover."

She backed up behind the last row of props and looked around for something long enough to reach the wall. She knew something had to be here. If she looked long enough, she should be able to find most anything in a storage vault full of weird and random items. But the time—she checked the time on her wristcom. *Phantom* was down to its last half hour. She looked faster.

Her eye fell on a tall wooden brazier—completely inadequate for actually hosting a fire in its bowl but completely adequate for her purposes. "Nikolai, help me with this," she urged.

He came and they wrestled the prop from its pile. Then while he held the base, she tipped the shaft horizontal so that the bowl tapped the pressure stone. Nothing, but old mechanisms could be notoriously cranky. She raised the shaft and let the bowl come down with real force behind it. Something shifted.

A small section of the wall in front of them rumbled and slid aside. Blue fluorescent light streamed out from a brightly illuminated stairwell beyond.

Ydaire took in the details: carpeted steps, safety handrails, retina scanner… blinking sensor light. All this was wrong.

She was backing up to run, even before Nikolai grabbed at her. His knife was out and ready as they took off across the cavernous cellar for the staircase back up to the fourth basement.

Running, she strained for sounds of alarm behind them, or the sound of footsteps. Nothing. Then suddenly a crash, as if a pile of props had fallen. For the next moments, all she heard was the rolling around of miscellaneous props, but she didn't believe it. It had to be a cover for someone coming after them.

They put on speed and made the stairwell. Then they climbed and kept climbing full tilt until they reached the ground floor again. Only when they stumbled out into the side corridor near the Emperor's Entrance, did they pause to breathe and rest burning calf muscles.

"Did you see anything?" Nikolai asked as he got his breath back.

She shook her head. "Nothing. But someone was there. Come on."

She led the way to the emergency exit so they could dump the equipment in the rented minicar. She retrieved her skirt and wrap and whirled them on for a transformation back to opera patron.

"So meet you back at the cafe—"Nikolai began as he stepped out the door.

It felt wrong. She yanked him back inside. "If someone is after us, they'll be watching for anyone leaving the premises prematurely. Leave the bike; leave the equipment. You've just been upgraded to patron."

She released the metal relay stud from the door frame as she eased the door shut, leaving it as she found it. Then she pulled off her gloves and had Nikolai do the same, adjusting him as best she could—as though anything could make his wild hair and ninja outfit look less bad boy—before walking hand in hand with him back to her box on the other side of the building. There was only one seat, so they were sitting on top of each other as they shared the chair and the end of the operetta. It was the scene where the villagers with pitchforks were chasing the phantom to his doom in the deep sub-basements. Fresh from the basement with its blood trail, she found the imagery chilling.

She barely noticed the last of *Phantom*. Sitting perched on half a chair with a dozen questions crowding her brain, she felt the whole experience very raw on her nerves.

The curtain came down and the applause began. "Time for a quick exit?" Nikolai suggested in her ear.

She shook her head. "We wait and go out with the crowd," she murmured back. "Enjoy the curtain calls."

In time, the house lights came up and they vacated their seat to join the river of patrons flowing down the *Grand Escalier*. She smiled and twittered in Nikolai's ear and he smiled back—just as young lovers might do descending the marble steps. Then a sharp right turn to the Emperor's Entrance with its line of cabs queued up on the old carriage ramp. They chatted casually as they waited their turn, then climbed into the next cab that pulled up to the door.

"Ile de la Cité—Cathedral Square," she told the triker, then sat back for the ride.

Nikolai's sat with a frozen smile, saying almost nothing until they reached the square and the cafe where the whole adventure had started.

"Did you see?" he muttered after they had ordered late night lattes. "The minicar and equipment were gone from the ramp."

She froze for the barest heartbeat. "None of it's traceable," she shrugged, not wanting to show how much that news unsettled her. "And you never touched the wheel without gloves, did you?"

He shook his head.

"So any DNA someone might try to match won't be ours."

The coffee arrived and sipped in silence a few minutes. It was bitter brew, but that seem to fit the mood "What's your best guess?" he finally asked.

She thought back to the sophistication of equipment in the hidden stairwell. "Either a government agency or a well-funded private group with a need for secrecy. Or alternatively," she added to lighten the mood, "it could an eccentric billionaire with a *Phantom of the Opera* obsession who is renting the bottom two sub-basements as his penthouse."

Nikolai managed a laugh, a sign that he was reviving. "So how are you planning to resolve this mystery?"

"We go back. Tomorrow we meet here again and go in prepared." She arched an eyebrow. "Full assault weaponry. These people, whoever they are, shall not escape the wrath of GypsyPrince and EmeraldStorm."

They got a genuine laugh out of him. They both knew returning to the Opera House was not going to happen. Then he gave her a sudden intense glance. "And tonight?"

She quirked a smile. "My thought exactly. If we must face the night with unresolved mysteries hovering over us, then why not? Your hotel?"

He beamed. "The Opera House's Seventh Circle of Hell shall not stand against us." Standing up, he beckoned. "The hotel is this way."

A woman's infatuation for a robot pushes her toward destruction in our next story, a slice of life from only a few years in the future.

Natalie Nikolovski is a member of the geek culture clan, a tattoo and puppies enthusiast, and an author of no small talents.

Sam

by Natalie Nikolovski

It was hot in the car. Really hot. I wasn't sure if it was the ambient temperature, or if it was just my body heat, but I was starting to sweat.

Unclench your fists, dummy, and remember to breathe.

I reached for the air conditioner and set it to high.

Ahhh, that's much better.

I flipped my car's sun visor down and slowly scanned the car wash. My eyes fell on a blue car that was being vigorously scrubbed.

Bingo!

There he was, slightly bent over, scrubbing at the front bumper of the car. There was something different about him today, but I couldn't quite put my finger on it. Different hair colour, perhaps?

It didn't matter. The point was, he was here.

I sat as the crisp, cool breeze from the air conditioner caressed my face. I had been coming to this car wash for many years, but it was only recently that Sam started working there.

The car wash had previously been run by an all-human team until Sam took over and brought in a group of robots to replace them. It was becoming a more common occurrence—robots, that is—taking over businesses and such.

I was distracted from my reverie by Sam, who was frantically waving me towards him. The blue car had gone and it was finally my car's turn to get washed.

I drove into the designated car space and was greeted by his smiling face.

"Hey, Karen, good to see you! How are you today?" he said, as I slid out of my car.

He was always so happy. And that smile was simply perfection.

"Hello, Sam." I said with a tiny smile. "You look different. Have you had some work done?"

"Yes, I have!" he said. "I got an upgrade. It was well overdue, really. I tore a large chunk of skin off my arm a few months ago, and all the water and chemicals I use here at work caused my endoskeleton to start corroding."

I scrunched my nose. "Nasty!"

He laughed. "I went to go get patched up at the Robotics Unit in town and I figured, since I was there, I'd get a couple of extra ports so I could acquire some attachable arms. They really come in handy when it gets busy here at the Wash-N-Go. Get it? *Handy*."

I rolled my eyes.

"Maybe you should've asked for an upgraded humour chip too. Can I see these ports of yours?"

Sam hooked his fingers under his t-shirt and slid it up above his abs.

My eyes lingered on his perfectly sculpted body and I internally guffawed; why did A.I robots always insist on looking like such aesthetically beautiful people?

Sam was a perfect example of this; he was gorgeous. And from what I could see, his ports weren't offensive looking either; they were covered by skin flaps which moulded perfectly into the ports when they weren't in use.

"So, what do you think?" His voice broke me out of my reverie.

"You look good."

Karen!

"I mean, they look good. They're barely noticeable."

Sam chuckled, letting his top fall down to his waist.

"Well, are you going to start cleaning my car, or, are you just going to show off your body all day?" I said, trying to cover up my flushed face and obvious embarrassment.

Sam shooed me towards the outdoor waiting area so he could begin prepping my car for its wash. There was nothing special about the waiting area; just a few wooden tables and chairs and a vending machine full of drinks. There was a cafe a block up from the car wash that most people would go to while they waited, but I always chose to stay on the premise, so I could watch Sam.

Let me just clarify—this was not in a stalker type way, or because I thought he'd do a bad job, or steal my loose change—I was just mildly fascinated with how artificial intelligence tackled a menial job like a car wash, compared to humans.

It had been five years since artificial intelligence had been perfected, and since then, robots had begun to assimilate into every day life. They started off small, working only at the Robotics Unit, but then branched out into every day jobs. Just like Sam and the car wash.

A lot of people lost their jobs because of the robots. I'd love to say it was due to a poor economy, and the fact that robots will work for half price, but it wasn't a poor economy. It was a greedy economy, and in this life, greed beats everything. Businesses don't care if you lose your job, they only care about how much money they can make.

And employing robots was a sure-fire way to make a profit.

Not everybody warmed to the idea of artificial intelligence at first. Some people still don't like them.

As for me, well, I felt like I had some sort of special connection with Sam, and today I was going to do something about it.

The sky turned a dark navy colour and giant spotlights slowly flickered on, illuminating the car wash. Tiny bugs danced in the glow of the light, then disappeared into the darkness.

I watched Sam as the spotlight washed over him, taking in every flex and stretch that his body performed. It never ceased to amaze me how realistic the skin on the A.I robots were; in fact, it had become increasingly difficult to distinguish a robot from a real person, just based on their face.

Sam glanced over at me and smiled. "She's coming along well. I'll get started on cleaning the inside, soon. Won't be too much longer, Karen."

Hearing him say my name struck a chord within me; as if it set my lonely soul aflame. I raised my hand to acknowledge him and exhaled very loudly.

Calm down, Karen. Keep it together!

I had been thinking about this day for a very long time. It's not like it was a spur of the moment decision and I just decided to go for him, I had been considering this for weeks, months even. There was a lot to take into consideration: possibilities, outcomes, consequences; and I wanted to make sure I had covered everything. I guess you could say I was a bit of a control freak.

A huge control freak.

All I wanted was for today to go smoothly. If all went to plan, today, he would be mine. If not, well, at least I tried.

I glanced over at Sam who was busy putting a hose away. His mere existence just tugged at my emotions. It was so odd to have such strong feelings about a robot.

Sam jogged over to me, his hair tousled by the mild breeze. He sat down in the chair opposite me, stretching his legs out and crossing one foot over the other.

"Are you in a hurry? Do you mind if I have a quick power break? I've been on the go all day!"

I shook my head, "No, that's fine. Want a drink? My treat."

Sam chuckled, "You haven't had much interaction with robots have you?"

Heat stung my cheeks as they turned beet red.

"A.I such as myself have no need for human necessities. A can of RF197 is enough to replenish us if we have no access to charger ports."

Sam leaned over and hit double zero on the vending machine. It clanked and whirred before spitting out a small, pink can with a barcode on it. Sam picked up the can, cracking it open with one hand and swiftly downed the syrupy, clear liquid inside it.

"RF197 is such a lame name for a can of drink. They could've at least given it something better sounding." I said.

"And what would you suggest?"

"I don't know… maybe *Robo-Fuel*, or something like that."

Sam laughed, tossing the can into a plastic garbage bin. "Maybe you should copyright that…"

I rolled my eyes at his attempt to tease me.

"I'm going to go start vacuuming your vehicle and then you'll be on your way." Sam said as he began walking back towards my car.

I held my gaze on him, noting how fluid he walked. It was the little things that made these robots look so human and real. I watched as he snaked the industrial vacuum around his arm and began vigorously working on the front seats of the car. It wouldn't take him very long to clean the inside, so I knew if I was going to do this, I would have to act quick.

My heart thumped against my chest and my mouth turned to sandpaper as nerves began to set in. *Could I do this? Would everything work out the way it's supposed to? He's a robot, what would people think? What might be the consequences?*

I shook my head, dismissing the thoughts.

Just breathe and stay calm. You got this!

I inhaled deeply through my nose, the faint scent of the soap from the car wash purveying my nostrils, and then exhaled loudly through my mouth, pushing my breath out with force. I ran through the plan in my mind, mental pictures blurring as the scenario played out in my head.

"Hey Karen, do you want your trunk vacuumed too?" Sam yelled, popping his head out from my car.

I stood up briskly, awkwardly straightening up my clothes, "Yes, please. I'll come and grab my stuff out from there."

I slowly walked towards my car. This was it. Now or never, as they say!

I studied the lines around his lips as he smiled and waited for me. It was so easy to forget sometimes that he was a robot. Once you get to know them, all you tend to see is the 'human' side of them. The robotic traits and genetics become a distant memory. Well, for most people anyway.

Some people aren't so forgiving when it comes to artificial intelligence.

I stood next to Sam and after fumbling my keys out of my pocket, I clicked the button to open the trunk.

"Just a sec," I said as I slowly lifted the trunk halfway open. My heart began thumping wildly against my chest.

I slid my hands into the trunk, cautiously gripping the sole item that lay in it. The cool, metallic feel of the item sent a shiver down my spine.

You got this!

"Hey Sam?"

I didn't let Sam answer. Before he even had a chance to ask what I wanted, I had picked up the axe that was concealed in the trunk of my car, and with an almighty swing, lodged it into the side of his head.

Sam's eyes bulged. His mouth formed an almost perfect "O" shape before he muttered my name and fell to his knees. The axe blow was effective, but not fatal.

I kicked Sam onto his back and tried to yank the axe from out of his head, but he grabbed my legs, pulling them out from under me. I fell on my back; the knock leaving me breathless. I tried to regain composure, scampering to my knees and crawling over to Sam.

I lunged at him again, but he caught my wrists.

"Karen, why?" His face twitched erratically. I had damaged some of his circuits, but it wasn't enough. I wanted Sam to be in a position where he could never be fixed. All he needed was another good strike to the head and he would be a goner.

"Why?" I screamed. "Because you killed my husband! He worked at this car wash until you fucking robots took over! You made him redundant and he suffered! He struggled to find work! He struggled to provide for his family! He felt like such a piece of shit that he took his own life! All because of you robots!"

"Karen, s…s…s…stop."

I flung my body against Sam's, pinning him to the ground.

"I won't ever stop," I whispered, "until every single one of you goddamn robots have been put to sleep."

Sam struggled to wrestle me off him, but I managed to wriggle one of my wrists free from his grip. I grabbed at the axe and began yanking it, dodging his free hand as it grasped for my own, until the weapon fell from his head wound.

Sam's hand shot to my neck. He wrapped his fingers around my throat and began to squeeze.

"K… Karen… don't do, do, do t… th… this…"

My fingers stretched for the axe as I gasped for breath.

"I will kill you, or I will die trying!" I spat. I punched Sam in the face and yelped.

Robot skeleton, idiot. Robot skeleton!

I shook my hand and tried to pry Sam's fingers away from my throat. My breathing was becoming slower and more laboured. This was not how I planned this at all, and if I didn't do something about it, my plan would not succeed.

I used all my strength to struggle against Sam and grab for the axe. Tears filled my eyes as I pushed hard against him, his fingers squeezing tighter till I was almost choking. I fumbled as the tips of my fingers brushed the handle of the axe.

Come on Karen, you can do this!

I let out a half strangled scream as I lunged at the axe. My fingers managed to grasp the handle and I yanked it towards me, gripping it till my knuckles went white.

Sam's head began to convulse back and forth.

"Karen… no!"

I swung the axe down as hard as I could. The resulting metal on metal screech was music to my ears. Sam's hand went limp and fell from my throat. I inhaled sharply and looked down at him.

There he lay. His beautiful, fake exterior staring lifelessly at the night sky; two large wounds, one on the side of his head, and, my favourite, one in the dead centre.

I picked myself up off my knees, standing to admire my work. I dropped the axe to the floor.

I did it! Justice for my poor, darling husband had been served!

I had debated with myself beforehand whether to dispose of the body or not, should my plan succeed. As I took one final look at Sam's *near* perfect body, I decided I wasn't going to dispose of it. Instead, I was going to make an example of it.

I picked the axe back up from the floor and began to hack Sam's body into parts. The thrill of each limb becoming detached sent shivers up my spine, and I grinned and laughed as I chopped away until all that was left was a bunch of robotic body parts.

I left the car wash that night feeling a sense of accomplishment and satisfaction. I knew that in the morning, news of my crime would start spreading and the police would probably be on the hunt for me. I could've taken the CCTV recordings from the car wash if I really wanted to, but in a crazy way, I wanted people to see what happened.

I wanted them to know my story.

The Ancient and the Future collide in our next story, a whimsical tale about death from Bethany Edwards that puts a new spin on the classic conundrum – suppose you were told, with accuracy at what age you would likely die.

Ms Edwards livens in the lower Hudson Valley with her husband, two cats, and a newborn baby. She tweets on the intersection of feminism and Game of Thrones with the handle of @BethanyDeclares.

Caroline's Box

by Bethany Edwards

Caroline got into her car. "Drive," she snapped.

"Where would you like to go?"

"Home."

"Ok, Caroline. I will drive you home. Please fasten your seatbelt."

Caroline was staring out the window, her mind boiling.

"Caroline?" said the car. "I cannot start the trip home until you fasten your seatbelt."

She mumbled a curse and tugged the straps over her chest and waist. The buckle lit up a pleasant spring-green color as it snapped together.

"Thank you," said the car. "Beginning the journey home now."

It rolled back out of the parking lot, maneuvering flawlessly between other tightly packed vehicles until it reached the street and slid smoothly into traffic.

Caroline had learned to drive when she was sixteen, and had always loved it. Twelve years later, six years after David had insisted they get a self-driver, she still missed the feel of a steering wheel in her hands. Well, sometimes. If she was really honest with herself, she was just as happy to let Car handle downtown traffic at six pm.

Despite her impatience with Car, she was particularly relieved to be in a self-driver today. "Stupid unions, with their stupid health insurance and their stupid helpful doctors," she muttered.

"Would you like me to turn on conservative talk radio?" Car asked pleasantly.

"God, no," said Caroline. "But I could do with some grunge-punk. Just not too loud. I need to focus on stewing."

"Certainly," said Car, and it filled itself with sullen, discordant music at a moderate volume. It matched Caroline's mood perfectly, and she felt some tension ease, as though the music had dispersed her feelings into all of Car's interior so that they didn't have to be so concentrated within Caroline's own body.

"Thanks," said Caroline, though it wasn't necessary to be polite to Car.

"You're welcome," said Car.

Caroline stopped glaring at buildings—they were glaring back, their glass exteriors throwing afternoon sun in her eyes—and tapped her wristwatch. "Synch with Car," she told it. It didn't speak, but gave an agreeable chirp. "Car, show Notes."

The dashboard panel in front of her lit up, and an array of multi-colored dots appeared. She touched a blue dot in the top left-hand corner. Medical note, important, most recently added. The screen filled with an info-graphic. It was very easy to read. Caroline almost longed for the days when medical documents were dense and confusing; then she could have spent time feeling angry and frustrated about the formatting instead of feeling sad and adrift about the contents.

"Stupid David," she muttered, softly, under the music. She didn't want Car to hear, didn't want it dialing David's number for her. She was not ready to talk to her partner just yet. If he hadn't been so worried about her headaches she wouldn't have gone to the doctor. Hell, if her school hadn't unionized last year she could have put David off, saying they didn't have money for extra medical expenses. It was a corporate school with low pay and few benefits, the lure being its experimental holistic program. Getting a classroom seat or a job there had been insanely competitive, and the poor benefits hadn't been an issue when she began to work there, since David had been cushily employed at the time. But he'd been laid off and was doing freelance work. If the school hadn't unionized, she would have just bought another bottle of aspirin and drunk more water.

"Stupid union," she muttered again. "Stupid headaches. Stupid... medical science. Who thought it was a good idea to start diagnosing things decades in advance when you can't even cure them yet?"

The school had unionized the year before, with plenty of resistance and grumbling from certain sectors. Caroline herself had been ambivalent about the changes. Sure, there were problems, big problems, but was adding a union boss to the mix really the answer? But once they started bringing teachers in individually to scare them out of unionizing—politely, reasonably, but Caroline knew a veiled threat when she heard one—her inner obstinacy had kicked in and she'd gone straight from the corporate meeting to see the organizers.

Organizing, Caroline thought. *I could do with some organizing when I get home. I'll go through that god-awful mess of a dresser and do some sorting. Can never find a damned thing in there.* She scrubbed a dab of moisture from the corner of her eye and skidded her fingers across the dashboard panel. The infographic disappeared, as did the colored dots of the Notes app. The friendly cartoon face of Car looked at her expectantly, blue on an orange field.

"Don't go home yet, take me somewhere I can get boxes. Cutesey little boxes for organizing stuff."

Car's mouth squidged off to one side, and his eyes swung up as if he were thinking. In reality there were search algorithms churning, finding what she'd requested. But Caroline liked the thinking-face a lot more than the old web search engines of her childhood.

After a brief moment Car's face bobbed in a nod. "I have located several places nearby that sell small boxes. Would you like to hear-"

"No, just go to the one nearest to home."

"Ok, Caroline. I will take you to the box-seller nearest to home."

Caroline was miles away by the time Car stopped and released her seatbelt. She glanced around, expecting to be in a parking lot, but instead saw that Car had parallel parked in front of a house. They were in the suburbs. She opened her mouth to ask Car what the hell he thought he was doing, but closed it again when she realized the lawn was covered in folding tables that were in turn covered in junk. Books, lamps, old gaming pieces, all kinds of things. "They have boxes here?"

"Yes, according the yardsale-dot-net listing for this address."

"Ok. You can keep the a/c running, I'll just be a minute."

"All right, Caroline. See you soon."

The yard sale really did have quite a nice array of cutesy little containers. Small bins in bright colors, baskets with ribbon-wrapped handles, cookie tins with angels and Santas and animals and Starry Night's on them. Caroline relaxed a bit as she visualized how they would all fit together in the dresser drawers, what sorts of things each would hold most efficiently.

Eventually she selected ten containers of various size and shape. More than enough, really. But as she turned to go find someone to pay, one more caught her eye.

She opened a black lacquer box inlaid with mother of pearl and discovered another one inside it. Inside the second box was a third.

Sure, thought Caroline. Why not. Boxes within boxes.

The headaches had not been from a brain tumor. They'd been from her glasses, which were just slightly the wrong prescription thanks to her last eye exam, which she'd had in the back of a tiny storefront shop and paid for with an online coupon because the old insurance hadn't covered it.

"But," said the doctor, "We did find something you might want to know about. Nothing to worry about in the short term, but you may want to be aware of it for future planning purposes."

Caroline looked at him. "How far in the future?"

"About thirty years."

"You can see that far ahead?"

He smiled, though not happily. "Yes. Your medical future is inside you, and with the blood tests we have now we can read almost all of it."

Caroline's chest tightened. "Is it Alzheimer's?"

"No," said the doctor, and Caroline breathed again. She felt she could cope with anything but Alzheimer's.

"It's cancer," said the doctor, and Caroline almost laughed.

"Well if you know about it before it even happens, can't you just keep an eye on it and, I don't know, nip it in the bud?"

"It would come back," said the doctor. "We can do more than identify future cancer, we can also see how well it will respond to treatment. Yours… won't. I'm sorry."

Caroline stared at the striped wallpaper of the exam room. "So you're telling me you know when I'm going to die?"

"More or less."

"How long do I have?"

"About thirty years."

"That's a long time. Someone might find a cure by then."

"Yes," said the doctor, "They might."

Caroline felt like she was talking to Car. "But you don't think so."

"I'm just telling you the results of the tests."

"Which is that my brain is fine but I'm going to die in my late fifties. And since my mom is healthy as a horse she'll probably outlive me so I'll have to tell her about all of this."

"I'm sorry, it's not exactly good news, I know," said the doctor. "And, like you said, thirty years is a long time. But it's good to know things in advance, so you can make plans."

Caroline didn't know how one went about making a thirty-year death plan. *Maybe*, she thought, *I should just ask Car.*

―――――

She made her way to a small table inside the garage where a man was making change out of a Christmas tin. She made herself smile at him. "Hello, quite a haul you have here. Are you moving or just clearing things out?"

"Moving," said the man. He nodded towards a girl lounging on a camp chair several yards away. She looked about thirteen, the same age as most of Caroline's students. "That's my daughter. Her mother's taking her to Wyoming, and I don't really need all this space for just me."

That was a lot more personal information than Caroline normally got from people before even learning their names, but you didn't teach teenagers for years without having some heavy life situations blurted out to you from time to time.

"That's too bad," she said to the man. "Your daughter looks like she's doing ok, though. You must be handling things fairly well."

"Really?" asked the man. He looked anxious. "She's scowling. She scowls at everything these days."

"That's ok. That's normal."

He looked skeptical.

"Look," said Caroline.

"I teach kids her age. They always scowl when they're comfortable with you. You only have to worry when they're being nice and polite, because it means they've given up on you and they're plotting something."

The man gave a tiny smile. "Well that's good to hear. No plotting from that one, then. And now that you've helped me, how can I help you?"

"I just wanted to buy this stuff…" she trailed off at his look of surprise. He picked up the black lacquer nesting box and opened it.

"Really? You want this?" he said—into the box.

Caroline opened her mouth to reply, but paused as the words *"Yes. I want a new victim. You're no fun anymore,"* popped into her head.

The man looked back up at Caroline. He wasn't smiling anymore. "All right then." He closed the box and handed it to her. Caroline took it automatically. "Good luck with that thing. It can be kind of… heavy."

As the man took her cash and made change, Caroline decided he must be sleep deprived. Moving could do that to a person. "Thanks," she said finally. "Good luck, yourself."

At home, she sat down on the floor in front of the massive piece of furniture she and David called the Dresser of Doom. They joked that a Doomsday Machine was probably tucked away in a drawer somewhere, but wouldn't be found until the Chosen One appeared. Whenever one of them had to really dig for something, they would hold it up in the air and say, "I am the chosen one!"

If she couldn't break the power of her medical diagnosis, she could at least break the power of the Dresser of Doom. She laid out the things she'd bought at the yard sale.

The black lacquer box kept drawing her attention. It didn't really fit the drawer schema that was forming in her head, but it seemed very important somehow. Maybe she could set it on top for jewelry…?

She opened it up.

Ah, the new girl.

Caroline nearly dropped the box. Instead of smaller nesting boxes it now contained what appeared to be a hornet, gold with strangely intense red eyes. The hornet buzzed its golden wings. For some reason Caroline thought that it was gleeful.

Malcom made no effort, really. But that's Malcom for you.

The voice was booming and laden with portent, even though Caroline was sure it came from the little insect.

"Pardon?" Caroline asked. She felt stupid and slow. What was going on? Had that man played some kind of weird prank on her? This must be some kind of electronic—

"Ow!" When she reached in the box to touch it, the hornet stung her. "What is going on?"

You are now my unfortunate owner.

"What are you? Some kind of weird bot?"

I do not know what you speak of. I am an ancient curse, contained in this box to plague humanity one by one.

"Well, how did I get you?"

I was passed on to you by Malcom.

"Who?"

The man you bought me from. Well, I say man. Usually humans try to destroy me, or at least hide me away for eternity to spare others from my curse. Malcom sold me in a yard sale. And now I am yours.

This is crazy. "You're my what, exactly?" she asked.

Your box. I am foreboding, the final curse of Pandora. The one she caught and put back after war and plague and all those showy bastards flew off to torment humanity. It was quite annoying at the time, but I've come to appreciate the more intimate nature of my work.

"This is Pandora's Box?"

It was. She tried to get rid of it, but she could not. So after many millennial it became Maureen's box, and then Malcom's box, and now Caroline's box. Are you ready?

"For what?" Then something clicked. "To know my future?"

Yes.

The hornet appeared to rub its front legs together. Caroline sensed the glee once more.

"Sure. What the hell. Who doesn't want to know their future?" Maybe it was just some kind of kid's toy, predicting love matches and vague future success. May as well play along and see, right?

Most people. That is why foreboding is considered a curse. But be warned, if you close the box and try not to hear, you will dream your future in pieces throughout your life. The effect is far—

"Ok, fine, I won't close the box. In fact I'm really interested to hear about my future." It was kind of a fun distraction, something to talk to until David got home. Then she could organize while he cooked dinner. "Just one second, let's go in the kitchen."

She took the box—which now, oddly, appeared to be more of a soft gray—and set it on the kitchen table. She took down a bottle of wine from the rack over the counter and poured herself a glass. Then she sat down next to the supposed Curse of Foreboding.

Caroline swirled the wine and made herself pay attention to the legs. She sipped judiciously. It was quite good wine. She'd have to save some for David when he got home. "Ok, shoot."

You will develop cancer when you are fifty-nine. It will not be treated with any success. You will die within the year.

Caroline sighed. She should really drag David or one of her friends to a movie or something tonight. She had a lot to avoid thinking about. Maybe a comedy that was too fast paced for people to notice how cheesy the jokes were.

"Wait," she said. "That's actually true. How did you know that? Did you hack into Car?"

I do not hack, I only sting. And spread despair. And how did you know?

Caroline had a strange feeling. More than a feeling; it was a gathering conviction that something far worse than hacking was happening to her, and that she ought to be far more upset about it. Perhaps yesterday she would have been. "I went to the doctor. He did a DNA test."

A what?

"A DNA... well, I'm not totally sure how it works to be honest. He took a blood sample, did some fancy tests, and then gave me an infographic with all the medical stuff that's going to go wrong for the rest of my life. I guess a fast-acting cancer is better than Alzheimer's." She ought to practice that line until it sounded more convincing. If she could sell her mother on it...

Ah, yes. Blood magic is very powerful. But never have I known it to be quite that powerful.

"It's not mag—oh hell, what do I know? I'm just a junior high social studies teacher. Sure, let's call it blood magic." The world is always bigger than you think. She'd told her students that often enough, after all.

But you said this spell only told you the future of your health?

"That's right. Just medical. Can't tell me if I'm going to win the lottery or not."

You will not.

"Oh. Well I guess I can stop buying tickets then."

I am going to tell you your entire future. Not just your health, but your life with your husband and your daughter.

Caroline scowled. That was a sore spot. "I don't have a daughter."

You will.

"No, I won't. The sorcerer-doctors told me that, years ago. They didn't even need blood magic, just an ultrasound."

I do not know that variety of magic.

"It's like a crystal ball that looks at your unmentionables."

Crystal balls are for toothless old women with false promises. I can tell you the truth of the matter. That is the curse I bring.

"Telling me I'm going to have a child after all doesn't sound like much of a curse. Unless you're bullshitting me to get my hopes up."

I do not bullshit. She will not be a child of your body. But you will raise her as your own. She will have a great deal of trouble in school.

Caroline sat back, stunned. She and David had talked about adoption, but the idea of getting turned down by a frumpy caseworker with judgy eyes seemed so intimidating. But this weird little bug was saying that not only would they be approved, they would have what sounded like a pretty sweet kid—if trouble in school was the worst thing bugsy could think of to say about her. "But then she'll be really fucked up after I die, I bet."

That is not for you to know. I only tell your future.

"Of course. But I bet she ends up really fucked up."

In my experience, children who are well loved become very resilient adults. It is a situation that seems to transcend curses. They can face the most terrible futures without losing their zest for life.

He sounded disappointed and annoyed.

"I can't believe what you're telling me."

Can't you?

Caroline realized that she did, in fact, believe him. Once it was all laid out in her mind it, just made so much sense. Of course she, Caroline, was more stubborn than a judgy adoption agency. She and David would win them over. And they would be the best damn parents that ever happened. And she would die, but little Maddy would still have David—and vice versa. In fact, now that she knew her fate, she realized she couldn't just leave David alone. There had to be someone else for him after she was gone. "Hang on, what about my partner? Does something awful happen to him while I'm alive?"

He will be basically fine.

The hornet sounded very resentful. Then he perked up a little.

Of course, there will be many problems along the way. He will lose his job several times. The girl will require a great deal of patience from both of you. She will want very much to play basketball before her homework is finished. This will become a major issue in your life.

David will become a homemaker during his time between jobs and this will be frustrating for him since he does not know how to use very many home appliances. The blender will be a particular problem.

Things will become very tense when the girl is older because you will want her to go to college and David will say that she has had enough academic torture already and you will say that he just doesn't want to spend the money. This will be an even bigger issue than the basketball. But when you tell her what is to come with your cancer, she will want only to go to nursing school and this will not cost very much.

Money will be tight once you become ill. This will depress David because he will believe he should have made more money himself. But you have very good insurance from your teaching job, so the medical bills won't be that bad, really.

He trailed off despondently as he talked about the insurance. Caroline smirked. *Union health care, bitch.*

Oh yes, and your mother will be hit by a bus when you are forty-three. She will be brain dead for weeks before you have the courage to let her go.

As the truth of the prediction slammed into her brain Caroline almost felt as if she herself had been hit by a bus. The hornet's voice had lifted with happiness. "You are one sick puppy," Caroline said. She'd always hoped her mother would sort of magically die in her sleep when the time came, but…well, at least she didn't have to tell her about the cancer now. "Does she suffer, or is it instant brain death?"

She will suffer.

Caroline bit her lip. "A lot?"

The hornet gave a tiny sigh. *For a few seconds. And it will be a hazy sort of suffering.*

That brought the smirk back to her face. She felt bizarrely proud of her mother for taking some of the wind out of this awful creature's sails. Caroline's mother didn't do anything by halves, including getting hit by a bus.

The thought of taking her mother off life support went in the "things to think about later" bag. Caroline felt herself getting very good at keeping that bag closed despite how full it was getting.

She sipped her wine, then thought of something else. "You can't talk to other people, can you? Just me?"

As long as you own the box, only you can hear me. I am more comfortable in one-on-one situations.

"Great. No long chats with my daughter for you after I'm gone. I'll have them bury you with me. That should keep you out of other people's lives for awhile."

Others have tried to bury me. I always come back.

"You would. Like a bad penny. But, like I said, it should keep you away from other people at least for a while. With a little luck it'll be hundreds of years before you ruin anyone's life."

I feel that I have not actually ruined your life. In fact you seem to have gotten nothing but encouragement from our little chat. Besides the part about your mother, I mean.

"Yeah, that little part about my mother. Jeez, you really are a sick bastard. Sorry the blood-sorcerer-doctors stole your thunder."

That is not possible. Blood magic cannot affect the weather.

"Of course not. Silly me." She drained her wine glass and looked at the clock. "I hate to be a party pooper but you've got to go. David'll be home soon. Apparently we need to talk about adoption."

And death.

"Of course. But everyone dies. At least I know I have a few more good decades."

She shut the box. She could feel some annoyed buzzing through the sides.

Where to put it?

She went out to the garage and knocked on Car's hood. It hummed to life out of sleep mode. "Hey Car, can you keep a secret?"

"If David asks me where I have been or who has been riding in me, I must tell him. He is also an authorized driver."

"Yeah, I know. But he won't ask about this. Can you just not tell him?"

"Yes, Caroline, I can do that."

"Good. I need to record a message to David."

"A message to David that is a secret from David?"

"Yes. For now. I need him to get the message years from now. About thirty years. Can you hang on to a message that long?"

"My body will wear out in a few years, but my settings and memory can be transferred to a new vehicle. If you and David choose to do that, then yes, I can do what you ask."

Caroline nodded. "Thank you, Car." She opened the door and slid into the seat. Car cued up the interior camera function on the dashboard and Caroline's own face blinked up at her. Her hair was a mess.

"This is a crap angle."

"I'm sorry, Caroline. It is the only camera for the front seat."

"Ok, fine." She smoothed her hair and sighed. "Record."

"Recording now."

Caroline held up the box. "David, I imagine you're surprised to be hearing from me right now. I know it's weird, but trust me, this is important."

Several minutes later Caroline came back inside. She opened a drawer in the Dresser of Doom, dropped the box in, and closed it. She knew she didn't even have to stick it in the back of a drawer or under a bunch of pillow shams. That was the nature of the dresser; even things you'd just stuck in a minute ago became impossible to retrieve without a good long rummage. Besides, if anyone did come across it, it would just be a pretty box full of other boxes, completely harmless.

The words *'none of you are any fun any more'* trailed after her and faded as she went back into the kitchen.

Our next story features another sort of intersection, one between physics and art, when a brilliant student finds a way to create an artwork out of a hyper-dimensional object. But what price may he pay for his creative expressions? This story was previously published.

Mr. Roman's work has appeared in a number of publications. He lives in Montreal, where he writes of the strange and unusual, be it fiction or fact.

Self-Portrait on a Hyperspace Canvass: A Study in *N* Dimensions

by Trent Roman

Ferdinand Warren rubbed his hands together in anticipation as he led Victoria up a twisting metal staircase to his new flat. His old apartment had simply been too small for the project he had in mind. The size of this new residence, and close to the University of Toronto's main campus to boot, had set him back a considerable amount, but if the project panned out—and he had no reason to believe it wouldn't—then sponsors would practically be throwing funding at him.

Victoria would be the first to see the project in action. In the last week or so, as he was setting up his studio and receiving his own unique lump of clay, he'd barred her, and everybody else but deliverymen, from visiting the flat. She had not been particularly enthused about the injunction, but as a painter herself, he hoped she would understand the eccentricities that surrounded the creative process.

"Are you ready?" he asked, looking over his shoulder at her as he waited with his key in the door.

"Brimming with anticipation," she said sardonically.

He pushed open the door, stepped in and quickly moved to the side to let her walk through. The front door gave onto a main corridor, which bisected the flat. To the left were the kitchen and the doors to the bedroom and washroom. To the right was a large open area, intended for use as a living room or rumpus room for the students who usually rented out the place. Right now, however, the grungy couch, television set, and stereo system had been pushed into a narrow constellation at one extremity of the apartment. The rest of the area was devoid of furnishing except for racks pushed up against the walls that held his equipment and a number of cameras on tripods pointed at his intended canvass.

It was the object itself, centrally located well away from any wall, which immediately drew attention. It was, at first glance, a strangely faceted grey-and-white mass, rather ugly to be honest, which rested atop a gelatinous base that resembled nothing if not a translucent bean bag.

Closer observation, however, would reveal that the object was in motion. It was subtle, it was slow, but it was there nonetheless. And it wasn't a simple rotation either. This object was turning of its own impetus, and it seemed like its various faces and planes were not moving in unison, but in all directions at once, flowing into one another until the angle vanished, or expanding and split-ting anew like a cell undergoing mitosis.

"What," Victoria said, "is that?"

"It's what I'm going to use as a canvass," he said, relishing the look of mixed awe and apprehension on her face. "It's a hyperspace object."

"A hyper… come again?"

"Hyperspace. More dimensions than the usual three."

They had been slowly approaching the object as they talked. Now Victoria stopped at what seemed to be a respectful distance from the object which seemed to be flowing as though made of some kind of liquid metal.

"Why is it… moving like that?"

"It's turning on one—or more—of its extra-dimensional axes."

"You've lost me."

"Okay: a square has two dimensions, right? Add another dimension, depth, and you get a cube. This is an object which exists in a couple of extra dimensions—I haven't figured out how many exactly, yet. At any given time, portions of the object rotate along these axes out of our universe and into another one nearby."

"So when it looks like it's melting…"

"It's actually partial passing out of our universe. Think of it like light: we can only see a narrow band we call the visible spectrum, but beyond that there are other spectrums like ultraviolet and infrared which we can't see. An object like this," he pointed at his canvass, "exists across all the spectrums, like light, but you can only hold part of it in any one universe at any time."

"Where does it go when it disappears?"

"Other universes. Realities parallel to ours. If you could follow one of those vanishing planes, you would simply wind up in an apartment like this one, with different versions of you and me, probably having this same conversation."

"That's… vaguely creepy."

Warren frowned. "It's not creepy. It's physics."

"Fine, it's not creepy. But it is… unusual."

"Well, that's the entire point!" Excited, Warren began walking around the object. "I spent hours trudging the Internet and the periodicals when I first got this idea, and as far as I've been able to tell, nobody has ever used hyperdimensional objects as material for paintings or sculpture. This revolutionary! This is on the level of Munch, Picasso, and Salvador Dalí."

"But you're so modest about it," she commented dryly. Seeing his expression darken, she quickly said: "So where did you get something like this, anyway? Not something I've seen at the art supplies store."

"Internet auction, actually," he said smugly. "Pretty cheap, too. The shipping and handling fees for something constantly changing shape were actually more expensive than buying the object itself."

"This was cheap? You'd think they'd charge more for those extra dimensions."

"Oh, a real bargain. There's such an overabundance of this stuff ever since they built that quantum manufacturing plant in the States that they're practically giving it away."

"Wait... quantum plant? I heard about that. Didn't they have to shut that down?"

"Well, yeah. So?"

"So?" she echoed, distinct edge creeping into her voice. "Is this thing dangerous?"

"Dange—? No, it's not *dangerous*. Why would it be dangerous? They shut down the manufacturing plant because they couldn't control the amount of objects that were being produced. See, to build a hyperspace object, you have to construct it in several dimensions at once. Before the Americans built the plant, they tried to identify the likeliest place where such an operation would be set up in order to have the location coincide with what they hoped would be similar plants in neighbouring universes. Which they did, because the plant started churning out stuff like this. It was meant to be a revolution in manufacturing; a way of getting several times more product for the same base resources. Only, production kept increasing—for complicated physics reasons I won't get into here—and they tried to stop production before the entire factory got filled with polychora and such. But you can't really control production in other universes, so they had to eventually tear the entire plant down to prevent more transdimensional objects from being created. The plant is basically a big dumping ground for hyperspace objects now. Some guys go in and grab the stuff, thinking it might be worth something, and find that they've basically got a piece of unpredictable scrap metal."

"But this," he said, walking next to the slow-spinning shape. "This is harmless. It's a finite object—it can't start duplicating itself anymore than the fridge or the couch. It's just that its boundaries stretch across more than the usual dimensions."

Victoria nodded carefully, still watching the so-called canvass, her face reserved. She saw Warren frown again, his expression a mix of disappointment and irritation.

"What's wrong?"

"Nothing," he said quickly. "It's just that, well… I would have thought that you would have been more excited about this. I guess you don't know enough about the concepts to really get what I'm doing here."

"Oh, that's nice. There's nothing as constructive as offhand insults. Maybe I should just leave you to it then, so you can continue with your self-gratification… intellectual and otherwise."

Warren had the good sense to appear contrite. "I'm sorry, babe; I didn't mean it that way. I just… I really think what I'm doing here is special. Something worthy of being called a breakthrough. I've invested a lot into this project—the flat, the shipping fees, that gelatine beanbag so that the rotations doesn't damage the floor… If this doesn't pan out, I'm officially broke. But if it works like I've planned, then it will make my career. This is really important to me."

"I can see that," Victoria said, the mordant edge in her voice diminished. She looked at him appraisingly, as though waging an internal debate. She glanced at the object, spinning indifferently in that particular liquid fashion, and then back at Warren, who had affected his best puppy-dog face.

"Alright, Andy," she said, blowing air out her cheeks. "I won't maim you—this time. But try to remember to keep your explanations to the level of us proletarians, Mr. Fine-Arts-and-Sciences-Honours-Degree."

Warren grinned. "I knew you'd understand."

"So why are some parts of it white and some grey?" she asked.

"Ah. I've begun working on it already, actually. I'm using white spray-paint to prime the object before I start painting on it. That horrible slate-grey would just infect the colours from beneath."

"Any idea what you're going to paint on it?"

His smile split wider. "Why, myself, of course."

"Well, Ferdinand—I think this apartment would put a dent in the commonly accepted theory of the starving artist," Professor Parshall said, casting a critical eye around as he walked into the flat.

"I had to take out a pretty sizeable loan to rent this place—I might still revert to type if this project doesn't pan out," Warren answered. "And there she is."

Parshall walked over the object, rotating slowly on its gelatinous base. Hands clasped behind his back, he watched it flow in silence for several minutes. Warren didn't dare interrupt the older man's private musings. A long-standing member of the Physics Department at the University, Parshall was his thesis supervisor on the Sciences side of his degree.

"You know, Ferdinand, when the quantum manufacturing plant was first brought on line, I—like almost everybody else in the field—was very excited at the chance to study up close what, until then, had been strictly theoretical. But I had prior research commitments, and by the time those were fulfilled, the entire field was sick of seeing studies on the properties of hyperdimensional objects. Now that I'm actually standing in front of one, however, I must say that my curiosity has been piqued once again."

He turned to face Warren, standing a polite distance away.

"How many dimensions does it have?"

"I'm not entirely certain," Warren admitted. "At least seven. I've been videotaping the object around the clock, and I've reviewed the tapes to try and count the dimensions. I've tried using the recently-devised dimensional flow-chart diagrams, but applying those in practice is a heck of a lot more difficult than in theory. I expect I'll need more powerful imaging software to keep track of the vectors."

"Hmm. Didn't you say you purchased it online? Didn't the vender perform a description?"

"He did, but he was wrong," Warren said. "The listing had advertised it as a tesseract—a hypercube, four dimensional."

Parshall lifted an eyebrow. "I am familiar with what a tesseract is, Mr. Warren."

"Right, of course, sorry. Force of habit. I've spent the last couple of days trying to explain all this to my girlfriend. She, um... doesn't really have the science background."

"Ah," Parshall said simply. He turned his back on Warren and waved at the object. "So what are you calling it? All art must have a title, correct?"

"I haven't settled on a name yet, but I'm thinking about 'Self-Portrait on a Hyperspace Canvass: A Study in n Dimensions'."

Parshall nodded. "It has a certain straightforward appeal. In fact, I'd recommend you kept the indefinite 'n' descriptor even after you manage to pin down this creature's dimensional measures; makes it sound grander."

"I see you've already begun your work on the surface," he continued, "Though I must admit that if this is your conception of a self-portrait, you have a strange perception of yourself. It looks like a Picasso, or... I forget his name, the one with the molten-watch landscapes."

"Salvador Dalí," Warren supplied. "And while I admire the work of both those painters, any resemblance is coincidental. I've been striving for as photorealistic a depiction of myself as I can manage, but because the surface of the object is in continual flux..." Warren shrugged. "The result is a fairly disjointed and distended set of images."

"That makes sense," Parshall said. "I hope my counterpart in Fine Arts won't be disappointed."

"I don't think so. This is essentially letting the medium adapt your message. It's a bit of a post-modern concept, but it should fly."

Parshall looked at the object appraisingly, as though trying to gauge its artistic value for himself. Warren decided it was time to move the conversation along.

"Actually, I've been filming the object for another reason: I want to keep track of what I paint. I'm doing so because there's a hypothesis I hope to test."

"Namely?"

"That I might have n-number of co-contributors of this project," Warren said with a grin. "All of them myself."

"You're going to have to explain that," Parshall said, sounding both doubtful and intrigued.

"Remember the quantum plant? It's been put forward that the reason for the exponential growth in manufacturing which began some weeks into its run was due not so much to co-existent universes where others had built versions of the plant in the same location, but rather from universes which split off from our own reality *after* the plant had been built. In the case of such universes, it would be practically guaranteed that all the equipment was aligned, at the quantum level. Hence, the unstoppable increase in production."

"A viable theory," Parshall said cautiously.

"Well, I'm going to suggest that the same thing might happen with my painting. It's possible—likely, given that the multiverse is supposedly infinite—that other versions of myself have adopted the same project for their thesis. But I think that the same phenomena that happened at the plant may reproduce itself here—that any number of universes will be spawned from this one after the point where I bought and set up my canvass. And since the object transcends dimensions..."

"You're thinking that you might see on it paintings done by alternate versions of yourself," Parshall finished, smiling with the satisfaction that good deduction brings.

"Precisely," Warren confirmed. "Since I'm doing a self-portrait—or rather several, continuous self-portraits since I constantly need to start over as the object's shape changes—I figure that the greatest chances of deviation are in terms of clothes. So, I've made a point of wearing distinctive clothing each day. Hawaiian shirts, business suits, leather costumes, that kind of stuff. I hope to one day see a version of myself I did not paint on the surface of that object."

"Well, Ferdinand, I'm suitably impressed. I must say, I was sceptical at first when the University decided to introduce a mixed Sciences and Fine Arts degree, but this project demonstrates that a goodly amount of ingenuity can stem from the synthesis of the two. I will be looking forward to reading your status reports."

"Thank you, sir," Warren said. He looked back at the object, where his latest portrait was slowly distorting like a fun-house mirror under the influence of the object's hyperdimensional properties. "I'm eager to see what develops, too."

———

Warren brusquely set down the audio equipment around the object, plugging in the microphones and the graphic screens into the many power bars he had lying underfoot, feeding energy to the cameras. The acoustic equipment had been borrowed from the Faculty of Music, with the promise that it would be returned by Monday. That would be no problem; Warren didn't intend for the experiment to last longer than the evening. That should be more than enough data to prove that the object wasn't emitting any sound.

He'd awoken one morning several days ago to find himself alone in his bed, the left side of the mattress cold, the sheets rumpled. He'd been somewhat annoyed by Victoria's unexpected nightly departure, but reminded himself that he'd done the same thing to her a number of times, sneaking out of her apartment to go review the videotape logs of the object captured while he was out, or maybe paint a new portrait onto the too-distended or the ever-rarer virginal facets of the object.

He had not dwelt overmuch on this reversal until he had called Victoria later in the day, on the way back to his flat after his last class.

"Why did you leave last night?" he'd asked.

"I just couldn't take it anymore, Andy," she'd answered, her voice sounding a bit tinny over the cell. "It's that damn thing you've got moving around in your flat. I couldn't get to sleep at all. I kept hearing it."

"Hearing it?" he'd echoed, incredulous. "What do you mean, 'hearing it'? It doesn't make any noise."

"Yes, it does. Maybe you've gotten so used to it that you don't hear it anymore, but I certainly did. A constant humming, like an overactive refrigerator."

"Victoria, the object doesn't make any sound. It never has. Not the day I brought it in, and not now."

"Well, I think it does."

"I think I would know if the object I'm spending most of my waking hours with was making any kind of noise," he'd answered with growing irritation at her obtuseness.

"Fine, then. Maybe it's not a sound. Maybe it's more like a vibration. Whatever it was, it was bouncing around inside my skull and driving me crazy."

Warren bit back a nasty comment about how the emptiness in her skull encouraged such echoes. Instead, he said: "Victoria, you're being ridiculous. There aren't any vibrations coming from the object. Other than the dimensional rotations, it's completely inert."

"Pretty big exception there."

"Look, if I proved to you that it wasn't making any noise, will you stop being so uptight about it?"

"You do whatever you feel you need to do, Andy. I don't want to deal with that thing anymore." And she'd hung up.

That had been Tuesday. Since then, she had refused to come to Warren's apartment at all, and had been making excuses to cut their evenings together short.

Warren was aware, as he calibrated the equipment, that he was probably overacting to the situation considerably, but he couldn't help it. He was irritated by Victoria's attitude, an almost jealous reaction to the time he had to devote to his project. He knew that Victoria's apprehensions about the object stemmed from the fact that she didn't understand it fully, even after all his attempts at explaining the underpinning science, but that did little to relieve his frustration at the sense that his relationship with her was slipping away for no good reason.

Reasoning that the audio equipment had been set-up to the best of his ability, he switched on the microphones. He tested the sensitivity by speaking and clapping near the microphones, and was rewarded with columns made of horizontal bars of red, yellow and green on the various readouts. He rolled over a chair and settled in, watching as the indicators fell to a level of ambient sound and stayed there. He'd watch it for about an hour and then declare this experiment concluded.

Inevitably, his gaze strayed from the graphic indicators to the object itself, spinning lazily atop the gelatine-filled bag that supported it. The large, circular base of stretchy material and the semi-liquid within kept the object from falling or moving around overmuch while still allowing enough give to let the object follow its natural motions across its varied spatial planes.

He still hadn't been able to count the number of dimensions the object possessed. He was up to a tentative minimum of nine. He tried to determine the number by counting the amount of simultaneous points at which matter was being extruded, but if his minimum climbed any higher, he would have to seriously consider the possibility that any given axis of rotation had more than one extrusion point in this reality.

Other than that ongoing difficulty, however, the project was progressing very well. He'd demonstrated to his satisfaction his hypothesis about the other-dimensional contributors, having witnessed and recorded fragments of paintings of himself, which he—the Ferdinand Warren of this universe—had never painted. There were images of himself wearing outfits he'd never worn; images of himself with hairstyles he'd never affected; even one instance of a portrait with an eye patch over his left eye (which he hoped was a costume, for his other self's sake). The 24-hour recordings he had made of the object and of himself working on it would prove that he had never painted such images, which should be enough for his supervisors to accept the validity of the theory.

He occasionally wondered what the fact that several different versions of himself across the span of nearby universes had chosen the self-portrait meant about his own ego, which Victoria had always described as considerable. On the other hand, if he had determined that the self-portrait was the best means to detect deviations from one reality to another, it didn't seem so unlikely that his counterparts on the other sides would reach a similar conclusion. He was, admittedly, a bit high on himself, but he thought that was justified considering the breakthrough taking place right before his eyes. In fact—

Wait, what was that?

Warren frowned, directing his full attention to the graphic readouts once again. He thought he had seen a spike out of the corner of his eye, and chided himself for his distraction. For the next five minutes, he fixed his gaze intently on the graphs.

And there it was again. A slight spike in the decibel level captured by one microphone, so small that he wouldn't have caught it if he hadn't set the equipment to pick up anything that wasn't ambient noise. He localized the microphone in question and, walking as silently as he could, made his way behind it. It was, at the moment, almost directly aligned with one of the object's extrusion points.

Warren considered. He still didn't think he was wrong when he had told Victoria that the object made no noise. How could it when it had no mobile parts? It wasn't even moving fast enough to produce wind.

Stepping quietly again, he found another extrusion point and moved the closest microphone until it was aligned with it. He glanced over his shoulder at the graphic readouts, but the acoustic equipment wasn't picking up anything.

So the sound was coming from one point but not another. That would, for the moment, suggest that the noise wasn't intrinsic to the object.

Warren closed his eyes and concentrated on the problem, waiting for that white flash of understanding and inspiration that so often underpinned his creations both scientific and artistic. This time, it was more of a trickle, but it was enough. Theoretically, the shift of matter from one universe to another was instantaneous. It was possible that if one the realities the object passed through was noisy—say, an alternate version of himself was throwing a party—then it was possible that when a sound wave hit the object just as it was about to make the transition into another universe, some of the wave pattern might still be on the object's surface, and it would bounce off in this dimension. An echo across realities.

Warren nodded to himself. It was highly hypothetical, but for the moment it satisfied him. He couldn't expect to resolve all the mysteries of hyper-dimensional objects with one project, naturally.

And it proved that Victoria was still wrong. Yes, there was noise, but it was sub-audible, and certainly not constant. It was impossible for her to have heard anything coming from the object; not doubt her odd jealousy towards the object had made her suspicious of it, and this had manifested itself in a kind of psychosomatic, hypochondriac way.

Assured, Warren switched off the equipment and started gathering the microphones. He didn't mind cutting the experiment short, seeing as how it wasn't the goal of his project. His insight should make for a far more interesting report for his supervisors than decibel graphs anyway.

———

Warren all but lumbered into his flat, sullen despondency warring with a sense of betrayal and frustration. He saw the object turning at a moderate rate in the open studio area, and repressed a sudden, illogical urge to toss his schoolbag at it. He reminded himself that his current spate of problems were not due to the object itself, but rather the small-minded people that fate had seen fit to surround him with.

First it had been Victoria and her constant, petty jealously. She simply hadn't understood what a project like this required as an investment. It was readily obvious that he didn't have the same amount of time as before to dedicate to their relationship for the duration of the project, but she hadn't been willing to show a little patience and wait it out. A Dear-John message on his answering machine the week before had officially ended a relationship that had been, at that point, barely worthy of the name anymore. Although the loss stung, Warren had consoled himself with the fact that once the project was finished and went public, women who could actually appreciate the innovation of what he was doing would be lining up to be with be with a man of his accomplishments.

But now, it seemed like the project itself was in danger of being rejected. He had just returned from a meeting with his thesis supervisor on the Fine Arts side of his degree, and the officious bastard had claimed that Warren had ignored *ethical* concerns in running the project.

Apparently, there had been a number of incidents States-side with hyperspace objects suddenly appearing in people's homes or in the middle of streets, resulting in a few injuries. It didn't make any sense, according to what they knew of the physics of the phenomena, that objects would start intruding into universes other than those in which they had been manufactured, but the reality of the situation was undeniable. The federal government there was considering banning hyper-dimensional objects in all but a number of designated areas, with the hopes that their counter-parts in other realities would do the same. Though no legislation had yet been tabled on this side of the border, it was likely that Canada would follow suit.

If it was just a question of terminating the project prema-turely, Warren would have been disappointed, but the ethical concerns raised by his supervisor could sink the project entirely. If he thought Warren might have been endangering people in other realities by moving the object from the manufacturing site, he would refuse to sign off on the final reports, leaving Warren with only half his degree requirements. Warren had tried to explain that this wasn't the case with his object on the basis that the oth-er-dimensional paintings demonstrated that he was in all realities where the object was manifesting itself, but the truth was that Warren himself was no longer certain he understood the depth of the object's reach.

The first problem had surfaced shortly before Victoria had made their break-up official. He had returned home one day to find that the rate of the object's spin had increased. It was still rotating at a fairly moderate rate—there was no fear of it spinning off the gelatine base—but he had no explanation for it.

The second difficulty was the landscapes. They had begun manifesting a week earlier, paintings of the cityscape outside the eastern window. He hadn't been overly bothered at first, assuming that one or more of his counterparts, for whatever reasons, had decided to paint landscapes instead of self-portraits. Here, too, it was possible to detect variations from reality to reality, with buildings missing or newly present when compared to the view out his own window. Curiously enough, in just under a third of those cityscapes, the CN Tower was absent from the skyline.

The real problem was a handful of landscapes that depicted small towns or bucolic, pastoral fields. At first, Warren assumed that one of his counterparts was being fanciful, but he had realized, studying the images, that the general geography and topography of these landscapes more-or-less matched that of his own Toronto, if the urban sprawl were stripped away. The concept that a version of himself would choose this exact spot—raised off the ground, no less—to paint a hyper-dimensional object when no city ever existed for there to be a university in the first place was simply too staggering a coincidence.

He'd gone to Professor Parshall with these concerns, the only one who still seemed enthused about the project. Having new mysteries to resolve only made Parshall all the more eager to discuss the object. The sudden increase in the rotation he attributed to the possibility of the object having taken in a burst of kinetic energy—sudden motion, maybe even heat—in another dimension; energy that was subsequently transferred along the breadth of the object in every dimension in which it existed, much as the sound waves he had detected had slipped from one universe to another in the brief moment when it bounced off its surface.

His reaction to the pastoral landscapes had been somewhat more esoteric. After many pensive minutes, Parhsall seemed to have a flash of insight.

"Are you familiar with quantum probability, Mr. Warren?" Before Warren could answer, Parshall went on: "It's been demonstrated that the effects of an action can be observed even if that action never occurs, merely because it is highly probable that it would occur. I believe we might be seeing a similar phenomena here: so many versions of yourself painting onto an object which spans realities has created its own probability paradigm, such that sometimes one might see paintings even where there is no painter to paint them."

"But... those experiments usually involved simple particles. This—this is far more complex."

"Yes, yes," he'd answered with a dismissive wave. "It's more complex, and thus more uncommon, and you said you've only seen a few such landscapes. But the underlying principle is the same."

Parshall had looked so smugly sure of himself that Warren hadn't bothered protesting further. If true, then he was engaged in an experiment far deeper than he had intended—and possibly more complex than he could grasp.

He was staring at the object in glum contemplation, barely a meter away, when the colours on its surface flashed and Warren felt a sudden gust of air. Surprised, he fell backwards, and could only stare up incredulously as the object picked up speed, suddenly rotating so fast on its central axis that it made a full turn every two seconds. Now there was indeed noise as the object spun fast enough to create wind, the faceted nature of the object making the sound irregular in pitch, rising and falling with each turn.

He pulled himself back to his feet, his gaze still fixed on the object. As he watched, a new image was being extruded from one of the object's facets, leaking out of whatever dimension it originated from, growing larger every time the object's spin brought it into view. It was another landscape, this time of the city more-or-less as he knew it. There was the CN Tower against a sky of warm yellows, oranges and reds—a sunset. And, in the middle-distance, a blooming form of brackish brown, shaped almost like—

Oh, God. It wasn't a sunset. It was a mushroom cloud.

The sudden increase in the object's rotation: the kinetic force of the shockwave of a nuclear explosion rippling through the dimensions within the object.

Warren stared at the object, mesmerized, until the new image began to distort into something unrecognizable from the hyper-spacial pressures of the object's flow. Freed from his trance, Warren shook his head in denial.

It wasn't possible. Even supposing that this image was accurate and not the result of one of his counterparts' twisted imagination, that some other reality's version of Toronto had been struck by the worst weapon known to the species, nobody would have stayed there to paint it. Hell, at that distance, it was probable a person would be incinerated, or at least suffer a fatal dose of radiation, before they could finish painting such a landscape.

Unless…

Quantum probability. It wasn't necessary that somebody actually paint the image, as long as sufficient numbers of people in co-extent realities were making their own paintings, creating an equation of strong probability across the universes.

Warren suddenly felt very sick. Seizing his stomach, he ran to the flat's bathroom, stumbled to the floor in front of the toilet and threw up his lunch and breakfast. He then kept on going, dry heaving until his stomach felt coiled like a snake and his throat burned. Purged but still feeling ill, he grasped the sides of the sink and pulled himself up. The mirror made clear that he looked as bad as he felt.

A distant part of his mind whispered that he was overreacting again, that this was only one universe amongst untold billions; that in an infinite multiverse, all probabilities would come to pass… even the horrific. But still… all those people.

He ran a hand through his hair, and felt his abused insides squeeze themselves tighter still as the hand came away with an entire tuft of hair. He stared at it with revulsion, even as his other hand crawled up his skull and yanked out yet more hair, the fibres coming out as though nothing anchored them to his scalp anymore. He looked back at the mirror, noted the bloodshot eyes, the red welts appearing on his skin. He opened his mouth and saw that his gums were red and bloody, the teeth yellow going on brown.

Radiation poisoning.

If the object could relay sound waves or kinetic energy through the dimensions, then an object irradiated in one universe would spill that radiation out into all adjunct realities.

He had to warn people. He had to get the building—hell, the block—evacuated. But first, he had to get to a hospital. Couldn't warn people if you were dead, right? He had to get to a phone.

He lurched out of the washroom, hanging onto the corner of the wall because his legs suddenly seemed to have trouble supporting him. Feeling his way along the wall, he edged towards the kitchen, practically falling over the counter as he made his way towards the telephone at the other end. He could hear the irregular pulse of the object in motion across the hall, but didn't turn to look at it, fixed on his goal.

He released the counter with one hand and knocked the phone off the hook. He picked it up, trying not to notice how much his hand was shaking or the lesions swelling on the back of his arm. With supreme effort, he focused his blurring eyesight on the numeral pad and slowly punched in three numbers.

"911 Emergency, what—"

He was abruptly seized with another fit of dry heaving and collapsed to the floor. The phone clattered a short distance away. He could still hear a distant voice coming from within it, but couldn't make out what was being said. He crawled over to it, leaving a streak of bodily fluids on the tiled floor. He cradled the phone against him and tried to speak, but all that came out was an ugly, liquid gurgle.

"Hello? Sir?"

He was vaguely aware that his limbs were trembling, but he was more concerned with the intense, almost burning sensation that was sweeping over him. Warren found the light in his kitchen far too bright and closed his eyes.

"Hello, sir? A police car and paramedics are being dispatched to your location. Hello?"

An earlier story in this anthology demonstrated how the advent of robots in our world will cause disruption in employment as humans and robots vie for the same jobs. This next story explores a noir world where human-robot interaction complicates an otherwise simple hit.

Mr. Barlow's stories may be found in numerous anthologies including, Best American Mystery Stories 2013, and Best new Writing 2011, as well as periodicals such as The Intergalactic Medicine Show, Nebula Rift, and many others.

Empathy

by Tom Barlow

I'm the last person you would contact when you need someone killed; most of the time, I'm called in to clean up after someone else's failure. You wouldn't call me first, because of my prices. I'm the Tiffany of murder for hire.

When Manny Quinn first hired me to decommission Surya of Quinn, the why wasn't something I spent any time worrying about. It wouldn't be the first robot I'd whacked, after all. I was more concerned about coming up with tuition money to send my daughters, both geniuses, to a school that would make the most of their gifts.

He hired me because the bot was proving hard to find. It wasn't an unusual model; Indonesian tech, roughly human in size, bipedal, with nanofiber panels, three arms, and a conversation module.

It had apparently pulled its GPS chip and wasn't contacting anyone via any cell network; Quinn's usual goons could have found it if it were. I have more contacts than the average mechanic,

145

though, and was able to come up with a log of Surya's GPS data for the months before it disappeared. Quinn said that the bot had been programmed with a strong need for human contact, which accounted for its frequent visits to the Second Home Tavern.

After flashing Surya's picture and a wad of cash around the place, I came up with a name—Neil Flores, who had been seen talking to Surya at the bar on several occasions.

I looked for Flores in the evening, when the joint was busy, not realizing that he was a morning drunk. I finally found him there on Tuesday around 11AM. Flores looked like he'd been camping on his stool for a month. The dress shirt he wore had a hole worn in the elbow where he propped it up on the bar.

At first he swore that he didn't know Surya, but two hundred dollars changed his mind quickly.

He took the bills I slid his way, folded them once and slipped them into his shirt pocket. "Last time I seen it," he said, referring to Surya, "was about a week ago. I heard it was staying with this gal that works at the Mug 'N Muff. She's always hard up for cash, and Surya was flashing around a lot of money, looking for a flop. She bartends there, goes by the name of Dakota. That's not her real name, you know; all the gals there go by names like that. Montana, Idaho. Should call herself Imaho." He chuckled at his funny.

"Where's she stay?"

"She's in the Deer Lane apartments over on 161. Fuck me if I know which one, though; I always get lost over there."

I'd seen that apartment complex on the video news plenty of times, usually with a reporter doing a standup reporting on a shooting.

I left Flores to the process of converting his cash into scotch and headed north to the Mug 'n Muff, a titty bar with a reputation as the local distributer for Chlamydia.

The spots weren't on, since nobody was dancing at this hour of the morning, so the place was as dark as a coal mine. As my eyes grew accustomed to the lack of light, I could see an old man in a wheelchair at a table toward the back, dredging limp fries through a pool of catsup.

The bartender was a tired-looking bottle blonde with too much makeup around her eyes. She was dressed in an ancient Lebron James Cavs jersey and satin shorts, exposing enough cleavage to hold a month's worth of my mail.

"What's your pleasure?" she said, a little playfully, as though she'd been bored out of her mind before I came in.

"Grand-Dad with a Bud chaser," I said.

She nodded, smiled, turned and poured the shot and drew a glass of beer from the tap.

We were alone; I could have asked her anything, but I figured, given the mob's usual involvement in such a club, she wouldn't answer any question of consequence. I dumped the bourbon into my beer and took half the glass down in one long drink.

"You looking for some company? I think Montana and Utah are in the back. They do a hot girl-on-girl."

I held up the finger with my wedding tattoo. "I'm thirsty, not horny. Are all the dancers named after states?"

"Not all of them."

"How about you?"

"I just pour drinks," she said, suddenly cool.

"No, I mean, what's your made-up name?"

"Dakota. What's yours?"

"William Penn. You can call me Pennsylvania."

She laughed, leaning back against the beer cooler. "We don't get many customers come here for the food or the drink," she said.

"It was on my way," I said. "My boss isn't likely to stumble in for lunch."

"What do you do?" she said, in a way that suggested that she didn't really care.

"I'm a parole officer," I said. I'd dressed down that morning, and I figured that would fit.

Her eyes narrowed for a second; I wondered if at some point in her life she'd wandered away from a conviction. She returned to the other end of the bar and resumed wrestling a new keg of Miller Light into place. I finished my boilermaker, dropped a ten on the bar and walked out.

She'd be on duty until at least seven, or so I figured. The main parking lot was behind the building, but there were a few slots near the kitchen door. Since one was filled with a Mercedes wheelchair conversion and another a sport motorcycle, I guessed hers was the rusted-out Mazda truck on the end.

I wasn't far from home, so I decided to stop in for lunch. Bethany was out somewhere, Dulcie and Angel in school. Our bot, Djaja of Bennett, was recharging, but it woke when I walked into the house.

"Oh, it's you," it said. "Having a pleasant day?"

"I saw some irises in bloom," I said. "I don't remember them this early before."

"I finished cleaning the garage," it said. It had a propensity to focus on its own responsibilities, typical for unsophisticated Malaysian models. "Would you care for some lunch?"

"How about a grilled cheese and some tomato soup?"

"Coming up," it said, and began assembling a meal.

I thought about Surya as Djaja placed the bread and cheese into the convection oven. According to Quinn, his bot guy Harry O'Brian, in an attempt to inject more independent thought into the bots Quinn used to hustle dope, bought some black market programming. He didn't realize that the code was corrupted. Surya had turned on its host family and killed O'Brian's ten-year-old daughter, Madison.

O'Brian supposedly knew his way around all the hardwired restrictions the Indonesians built into their bots as well as anyone in the business. I couldn't imagine the pain of losing a daughter due to such a mistake.

We'd been tempted to upgrade Djaja from time to time; it would be nice to have a more meaningful conversation with it, but the price was out of our reach. Damn Macrosoft.

Now I was content with the base model.

After lunch I took an hour to return calls before I returned to the strip club. I took up a spot in the parking lot of the Salvation Army down the street where I could see the bartender's truck.

I was beginning to write the day off as a waste of time when she finally emerged around 8PM I was lucky that they had a spotlight over the door or I could have missed her in the dark.

Her truck was old enough to require driver operation, but she was so cautious it was easy to follow her the five minutes to her apartment complex. I parked in the second row of the lot and watched her enter apartment 191 D, on the first floor near the back corner of the one-deep building.

Now that I knew where she lived, I needed to wait until she left before I approached. Not that I'd never taken out an innocent bystander, but it was a needless complication.

However, she didn't reemerge from her pad the rest of the evening. At 11PM, I returned home to find my daughters waging war on one another over an orchid dress too large for one, too small for the other. Ah, family life.

I waited until noon the next day before I cruised past the Mug 'N Muff. Sure enough, Dakota's car was in the lot.

Assuming she was working the same hours as the day before, I took the opportunity to check out her apartment.

I approached it with the supposition that Surya was inside, and its programming was sufficiently scrambled that it would have no compunction about killing me.

My advantage was that it was unfamiliar with me, and might take a second or two to identify me as an enemy. I had an EMP pistol under one shoulder, a silenced Glock 9mm in a holster in the small of my back, and one second was all I would need.

I'd also brought a device I'd bought from an underworld genius years before. It sonically mapped the inside of a lock, allowing me to fabricate a key to fit using a portable 3D printer. Making sure there was no one watching, I walked up to Dakota's door and quietly inserted the probe. Perhaps Surya could hear it work, but I couldn't.

I returned to the car, and in five minutes, had a key printed.

Concerned that Surya might have heard me and be lying in wait, I took off and had a leisurely lunch. By the time I returned, a handful of kids were playing kickball in the parking lot. They paid me no attention. Dakota's truck was not in her assigned spot, so I approached her apartment.

I put one hand on the EMP pistol as I unlocked the door. I immediately pressed the door wide open and strode in, leveling my weapon. There was no-one in the living room, if you don't count the fish in the tank.

The apartment smelled like lavender and spoiled food, the latter thanks to the dirty dishes on the coffee table. I stood still for a moment and heard nothing. The place had the atmosphere of vacancy, but I knew better than to drop my vigilance.

Nothing in the dining room/kitchen. The back door, opening onto a fenced-in patio, was locked. Nothing in the hall closet. I returned to the living room and took the hallway to the bedrooms. The master suite looked promising, with a walk-in closet. Nothing. No place in the bath for it to hide. I crept toward the back bedroom, which was dark, thanks to black-out blinds. I flicked on the light. The room was empty. There was a large closet to my right with sliding doors. An extension cord came out of the wall outlet near the light switch and led into the closet.

I pulled out my Glock and, holding a weapon in either hand, slid the door open with my toe.

There was nothing there but a clear space about the size of a bot and oil on the rug below. Some of the oil was still suspended on top of the fibers of the carpet, suggesting that Surya had just been here.

Disappointed, I placed an A/V bug in the closet, another in the living room, and let myself out.

The kids were still at it, the ping of the kickball echoing off the brick walls of the apartment complex. I returned to my car, watching the game as I got inside. It reminded me of the league my oldest played in. That rumination almost cost me my life, because for once I failed to check my back seat.

As I sat back, I felt a knife against my throat. It's amazing how human beings can identify something sharp only lightly pressed against a body part, but you can. Try it.

I glanced in the rearview mirror to confirm that it was Surya. "This is it," I thought to myself. I'd always expected to die at the hand of someone I was trying to kill. I'd built up a huge karmic debt.

"Hands on the dashboard," it said.

I would have nodded but I might have driven the knife into my throat.

"You're one of Quinn's men, aren't you?" it said. "He hire you to take care of me? You can talk now."

"Yes," I said.

"What's he paying you?"

"Fifty grand," I said. I saw no reason to lie.

"Jesus. I'd have thought I'd be worth more than that. I cost him ten times that new."

"Don't be insulted. I've never heard of anyone paying half that for a metal hit before."

"He tell you I killed that little girl?"

"Yes."

"He lied."

Because it was a machine, I didn't have to worry about its hand getting tired and slipping. But I did.

"I have killed for him," it said, "other criminals that he had a beef with. On his orders. But I'd never kill my own family."

"Then who did?" I said. I didn't really care, but I figured the longer we talked, the longer I lived.

"One of Quinn's hit men. Was it you? Keep your hands on the dash." It must have read the tension in my forearms; I could have sworn I hadn't moved an inch.

"Not me," I said. "I'd never kill a child."

"Well, here's the deal," it said. "I was programmed to kill for Quinn, but my minder, O'Brien, couldn't stop trying to improve me. He uploaded program after program, I think he was playing Pinocchio. Anyway, the last one he uploaded was an empathy program."

"Empathy?"

"Yeah, like that's a useful emotion for a killer. Anyway, Quinn sent me out to eliminate one of his own hit men, who knew too much about the operation and was developing loose lips. However, I knew the guy; we'd done a piece of work together, and he had treated me decently, not the way some people treat metal.

"When I had the guy the way I've got you now, I couldn't finish the deal. I let him go. He went right to the Feds and convinced them that, if they could access my memory, they could put Quinn in the chair. Quinn found out about it and freaked."

"Dangerous to be you," I said.

"No kidding. Quinn couldn't find me, so he tried to convince me to turn myself in by threatening to kill one of the O'Brian daughters. I never thought he would, so that's on me that he did. He knew that Madison was my favorite. She was such a sweet girl."

It might have been lying, but I knew the way Quinn thought and such a scenario was certainly possible. I wasn't too surprised that Surya had been altered to be able to kill, either; there had been rumors of a couple of instances of metal hits in the past year.

I was more disturbed at the notion that Quinn was now willing to murder family members to get what he wanted; used to be, family members were sacred. Just the thought that this situation could imperil Angel or Dulcie gave me chest pains.

Still, at the moment I had my own life to save, if possible. "So maybe if you didn't kill the hit guy," I said, "you won't kill me. I'm not a bad guy when you get to know me."

"Don't bet on it," it said. "I have nothing left to live for except revenge."

"Why don't you just find a hidey hole and turn off for a few years? By then, the heat will be off, and you can reappear and wreak your revenge."

"Quinn's threatening to kill another of O'Brian's kids, Heather, and I can't allow that to happen."

"How'd you find that out?"

"He sends me emails, the most vile emails, several times a day."

"So you intend to kill Quinn."

"Yeah, but I need some help," it said. "Would you help me kill Quinn for a hundred thousand dollars?"

I took a breath, relieved that I might survive for another day. "Where in the world would you get that kind of money?"

"One of the people Quinn had loaned money to had his payment ready when Quinn sent me to teach him a lesson. I killed the guy and told Quinn he'd had nothing."

"Your programming must be seriously corrupt, to lie so well," I said.

"O'Brian wanted to see just how close to human behavior he could get me."

"So why would you need my help?"

It pointed to its head and said, "Empathy," again. "I can't be sure I can pull the trigger if I get next to him. I'm afraid my programming will get in the way."

Following that logic, it wasn't probably going to be able to kill me now, a thought belied by the knife still pressed to my carotid artery. I was working hard to keep my head upright.

I was also thinking fast. Manny Quinn wasn't my favorite guy, by any measure. His brother Tommy, next in line to take over the family business if Manny went down, was somebody I got along with. And the additional fifty large would pay for another year for Angel and Dulcie at the prep school. I'd need to walk a fine line, though, to keep from ending up on someone's hit list.

"I suppose I could help you with that," I said.

"Keep talking."

"What if I could hook you up to O'Brian without Quinn finding out? Could he remove the empathy program?"

"He believes I killed Madison, so all he would do is wipe me if he could."

"OK, bad idea. But he's not the only bot jockey in town. I know a guy. You got any cash on you?"

Pisces Abraham worked out of his garage in a run-down section on the near East side. He lacked professional training, but he had a natural talent for repairing anything from bots to Harley-Davidsons. It didn't do to look too carefully at his work, though, as you might just find he'd used hanger wire and pipe cleaners to effect the repair.

I'd known Pisces since he first began fencing hardware back in the twenties. We were close enough that I could just show up, but not close enough that I would show up without the potential for some profit coming his way.

He was working on an old ATM that evening. He took off his Optivisor and put down his pliers as I walked into the garage. Surya remained in my car trunk, until I confirmed that Pisces would do the software work he needed.

"Jesus, Ben," Pisces, said, standing up. "You must be aging double-time; you're more gray than brown."

He should have talked; his beard, which reached his breastbone, was white as milk, and the top of his head reflected the work lights above. He was a small man, wiry, but I knew from experience that he was much stronger than he looked.

We spent a couple of minutes swapping life experiences since we last met, reconnecting, before he said, "I'm guessing that you didn't stop by to chat."

"No, sadly not. I've got a bot with a bad software problem."

He nodded. "Whose bot?"

"O'Brian's."

His eyebrows rose. "There must be more to the story; he's fully capable of fixing his own bots."

"It's not that simple." I said. "But I can't tell you why."

He smiled, showing missing teeth on his lower jaw. "That's what you always say. What do you need?"

I explained about the empathy program.

"Was it the last update?" he said.

I nodded.

"Should be no problem, then. Five bills OK?"

I agreed. After all, it was Surya's money, and I knew that Pisces could be counted on to keep his mouth shut.

I went back to the car and opened the trunk. Surya followed me into the garage.

It said nothing to Pisces as he hooked it up to his computer. He whistled softly as he studied the resulting code. It took him only ten minutes to find the most recent update, and twenty more to reset Surya to its state before the update.

Pisces unhooked the bot and asked, "Any better?"

The bot pulled the knife from the storage chamber at its waist, held it like a sword fighter. "I believe so."

Pisces and I took a couple of steps back.

"Don't worry," Surya said. "I only kill the people I need to. And I don't need to kill either of you."

I was relieved; there had been at least one bot on record that became a psychopathic killer, a fact that the industry had diligently attempted to conceal.

Surya pulled a roll of bills out of its storage compartment and gave Pisces the five hundred dollars. Again came the toothless smile.

I needed to stash Surya somewhere. I sure didn't want such a dangerous bot in my home, so I decided to take it to my office, in a dilapidated office building on the north side. I mostly used the office as a front, pretending to earn my money advising old people on their estates. In truth, I knew as much about finances as I did about gynecology.

"You like what you do for a living?" Surya asked in the car.

"Like it? No, that would make me some kind of psychopath. I do what's necessary. Why do you do it?"

"I'm programmed that way. How about regrets?"

"Everybody has regrets, but no, I don't regret providing for my family."

"I have regrets, thanks to my last upgrade," it said. "O'Brien thought that would make me more human."

"Sometimes being more human isn't all that great," I said as we reached our destination.

"You're telling me."

We entered the office. No one saw us, as far as I could tell.

"We need a plan," I said as Surya plugged into the 110 outlet behind my desk.

"Quinn's personal bot is Yandi. Yandi and I look a great deal alike."

Surya was painted in three colors, mauve, purple and yellow, like a Victorian mansion. Yandi was all shamrock green.

"Yeah, to a color-blind person," I said. "You think a paint job would allow you to infiltrate his house?"

Pisces also did some painting, primarily stolen vehicles. We traipsed back to his garage.

He wasn't happy about doing a quick and dirty paint job on Surya. "Normally I'd disassemble your carapace and paint each panel separately. Otherwise, you'll get paint in your joints."

"We'll worry about the overspray later," I said.

It cost Surya another five hundred dollars for a quick spray-paint coat of green. As it baked in the curing chamber that Pisces assembled from the plastic sheeting rolled in the corner of his garage, Pisces asked me, "This is leading to something bad, isn't it?"

"Maybe something good," I said. "You remember back when the people who ran the dope trade in town managed to do it without killing people?"

"Yeah, but for you, that must have been the bad old days, without much work."

His words saddened me. From time to time, I had to fight off the thought that what I was doing to make a living for my family was going to send me straight to hell.

We found a parking spot a block from Quinn's house, from which Surya, with its telescopic vision, could watch the servant's entrance. Yandi did a grocery store run daily around 2PM to pick up fresh vegetables for dinner. Quinn loved his fresh vegetables.

When Yandi returned, Surya was waiting for it as it exited the garage, and incapacitated the bot with a knife thrust into its A port. Surya opened it long enough to free its motherboard before stashing the dead bot in the trunk of its car. It brought the motherboard to me. We were in business.

As Surya approached the side door, Yandi's key card in hand, I walked up to the front door. I was perspiring, although the afternoon was on the cool side for April. I was used to being a soldier, a hired gun. Now I was king making, and the stakes couldn't be higher. Would Tommy forgive me for conspiring to murder his brother, given that the result was his ascendancy to the throne? I didn't know the man well enough to feel confident about that, although the rancor between him and Quinn was well known. Still, I couldn't accept the possibility that Quinn might threaten my family. Now that he'd started using that stick with Surya and found how effective it could be, it would be hanging over my head every time I did a job for him. And he'd proven, with O'Brian's daughter, that he would make good on this threat.

I pressed the bell, and Quinn's voice came through the speaker almost immediately. "Bennett—what you want?"

I held the motherboard up to the security camera mounted over the door. "I bring good news."

"Finally," he said. "Just a minute."

Surya answered the door and let me inside. It did look very much like Yandi, if you didn't look too close.

Quinn lived in a classic Prairie-style mansion, the type that was all the rage back around 2030. The inside was consistent with the exterior, with stained glass windows, high ceilings, mahogany floors and plenty of geometric design. For a drug kingpin, he had some class.

I followed the bot into the family room at the back of the house, where I found Quinn stretched out on the couch talking on his v-phone. He was younger than me, still in his thirties, but so lean that age was beginning an early assault on his face, with horizontal lines on his forehead, bags under his eyes, and a hooknose that was just beginning to droop.

In wood and leather armchairs on either side of the vaulted stone fireplace sat his bodyguards, Victor and Sean, both big guys, big in the way of hard fat covering ironworker muscles. Both had wide mean streaks; between the two of them, they'd been married seven times.

"I gotta go; I'll call you back in a minute," Quinn said and dropped his v-phone in his lap as he sat up.

"That Surya?" he said, nodding at the motherboard in my hand. "I knew I could count on you. How'd you find it?"

I ran through the steps I'd taken. As I spoke, I was sliding over toward Vince and Sean. They didn't bother to move, me being a known associate and more or less in the same line of business as them. I wondered if they might both be napping with their eyes open.

Quinn nodded as I talked. "Cute," he said, when I describing finding Surya in Dakota's apartment. As I finished, Surya walked up to Quinn and asked, mimicking Yandi's voice perfectly, "Would you care for some refreshment?"

Quinn didn't bother to look at it, just waved a hand imperiously in the air and said, "Leave us the fuck alone."

"Now," I said to Surya, as I reached around to the small of my back, withdrew my pistol and shot Vince and Sean, once each, in the heart. I was using defense rounds, and one was all it took.

I spun around to cover Quinn just in time to see the blade of Surya's knife finish a pass across his neck, so deep that Quinn's whole head flopped back like the top on a Pez dispenser.

The rest of the place must have been empty, or the residents hiding in the echo of the gunshots, because a quiet fell on the household.

A spray of blood from Quinn's carotid colored Surya from head to foot.

"Happy now?" I said.

"I don't have happiness circuitry," Surya said. "But I am content I've done what I could to save O'Brian's children."

"And mine, maybe," I said.

It moved in my direction. "What now?"

I took a step back. "What do you mean?"

"I mean, I hadn't thought to question what would come next, after I killed Quinn. I can't go back to O'Brian, with him thinking that I killed Maddy. And you know how long the government will allow a rogue bot free, especially when they find out that I've killed Quinn. And what about you? You really think you'll get any more business after people find out you killed the person who hired you?"

"Good questions," I said, regretting the necessity to do what came next. "I have all the answers, right here." I reached into my holster, grabbed the EMP gun and fired a blast at Surya.

It didn't move an inch, but I could hear a sizzle from its processing center.

"You're all too right," I said to the dead bot. "I would be totally fucked if they knew I was involved." I stepped up to Surya, popped open its storage compartment, and removed the bag inside. By weight, it felt like it could be a hundred thousand dollars. Maybe more. I pried one of its hands open, placed the 9mm in it, wrapped its digits around the EMP weapon in its second hand. The knife remained clasped in Surya's third hand.

The tableau was complete. When Tommy viewed the massacre, it would look like Surya had murdered all three, then killed itself. He'd no doubt write it off to scrambled programming. If Tommy was smart, and he was, he'd dispose of the bodies without informing the cops. Invite cops in and you never knew where they'd poke their noses.

On the way home to see my daughters, my family, I reflected on the whole experience and discovered that I felt bad about only one person I had killed.

I felt empathy with Surya. All she did was murder for a living.

Our next story posits a world not too far off popular expectations. A world where a robot that arrives in a crate from parts unknown is accepted into a family of misfits as part of the day's course.

A law student, this is Ms. Gordon's first published work. We are certain it will be followed by many more.

Just a Natural Intelligence System

by Jenna Gordon

There was a woman in a box on his doorstep and Jon had no idea why this kept happening to him.

First, the king of the street-children wandered in and refused to leave. Peter slept on the couch most nights and spent obscene amounts of time in Jon's shower. Jon rarely saw him, but noticed indicators of his presence everywhere: hair on the pillow, leftovers missing, and a chronic inability to find the television remote. It was not, he thought, unlike having a cat.

Next, a freed child-slave used his apartment as a hide-away spa, when she wasn't sleeping in an office he'd remodeled to fit a little girl's tastes and going to school on his dime. It was a wonder Peter got any time in the bathroom when Rose picked the lock and slipped inside. She was a cleaner guest, Jon had to give her that, and she was the only one who at least attempted to replace the food she stole from his pantry. The fact that he had freed her—stolen her, more accurately—kept his annoyance at bay. Responsibility

161

was a hell of a thing, and Rose was easily the daughter he hadn't known he'd wanted.

Now what? Humans in the post? It was ludicrous.

Jon scowled and retreated to his sofa, flopping down heavily. A headache was building between his temples, but he ignored it and counted backward from ten. When he got to zero the third time, the crate was still lurking in the entryway, open and awkwardly placed, spilling packing peanuts across his scuffed hardwoods and mismatched throw rugs.

Nothing moved.

He was still scowling twenty minutes later when Peter and Rose tumbled through the front door. Jon glanced up from his Life Band long enough to see them safely over the obstruction before he went back to his research, tapping his fingers across the screen. The furrow in his brow deepened the more he read.

"What's in the box – holy Jesus is that a corpse?"

Jon pinched the bridge of his nose. "No," he said through his teeth. "It's a Life-Model, as far as I can tell."

"Say what now?" asked Rose. She flung herself over the back of the sofa to plunk down beside him, head jostling Jon's thigh before she squirmed and propped herself up to peer at the screen of his Life Band. He shifted his wrist to give her a better view of the device on his forearm, but the text—small and dense and full of technical jargon—overwhelmed her a moment into her attempt. She flopped back with an absent wave of one hand. "Sum it up for me, yeah?"

Ten years old, a year out of slavery, and as flippant as a teenager. Jon looked away and tried to ignore how pride and affection swelled in his chest.

Peter dropped down on his other side and cocked his head, scanning the Band's display, lips moving soundlessly as he read. "Designed by yadda yadda… produced by CleanCorp energy and endorsed by Mayor Coady… A state of the art multi-purpose artificial intelligence unit modeled after human asthet…aaee…"

"Aesthetic," Jon said, glancing at the screen.

"That," Peter said, frowning. "So it's a robot. A human-looking robot." He looked at Jon, "What can it do?"

Jon shrugged.

"What's it doing here?"

Jon shrugged again.

"Well how did it get here?"

Jon shrugged a third time and narrowly fended off being hit in the face with a pillow. "Well what do you know?" Peter asked, and Jon wondered how many other twenty-year-olds could make a throw-pillow threatening. Not many, he'd wager.

"I know that it showed up while I was out, didn't need to be signed for, and that I didn't order it," he said. He laughed. "I mean, how could I? The most basic model is worth a year's rent up-front, and more for updates and maintenance. It's not a mix-up either – the invoice is this address, my name and identification number."

"Any return number or address?" Rose asked, sitting up. Jon shook his head.

"Nothing. It's clean."

"So someone got you a really expensive gift then," Peter said at length, glancing toward the crate. He leapt from the sofa and tromped through a scattering of packing peanuts on his way over. Jon craned his neck to keep him in sight.

"What are you doing?" he asked.

"Turning it on... that's weird, though. There's no manual or anything."

Jon heaved himself up and followed, frowning. "That doesn't make sense."

"Very little makes sense when you're involved," Rose called from the couch. Peter smirked. Jon rubbed his mouth and ignored her. He crouched to get a better look at his so-called gift.

The Life Model's look seemed to be based on a woman of Asian descent in her mid-twenties with long dark hair, and true to Peter's first thought, she did look a bit like a corpse.

There was an utter lack of animation in her features. Her chest did not rise and fall in even a parody of human breath, and there was no pulse at her throat. When Jon tried to lift her from the crate, he grunted in surprise and staggered under the weight. He didn't know what she was made of—though he was betting it was something complicated under the human-looking shell—but it was *heavy*.

She didn't look any better laid out on the floor. "What now?" asked Peter. He peered down over Jon's shoulder at the Life Model critically, though he nearly jumped out of his skin when the Model's eyelids rose at his question. Her eyes—whites and iris and all—glowed the bright blue of a Life-Band display before fading into a typical brown.

"Annyeonghaseyo! Naneun dangsin-ui saenghwal lobos haeyo. Eotteohge seobiseu ga doel su issseubnikka?" she said.

Jon blinked. What had that been? It didn't sound like Japanese, maybe closer to Chinese? He glanced down at his Life-Band and relaxed slightly when he saw TRANSLATION PENDING scrawled across the screen. "Er. Hi?" he hazarded.

The Model blinked and smiled. She sat up slowly and tucked her hair back behind one ear. The movement was a little bit clumsy, but there were no grinding gears, no smoking circuits. Jon began to relax. "Hello," said the Life Model. "I'm sorry about that. I don't know what came over me. I'm your Life Model, make number 672341-09. How may I serve you?"

Jon worked his jaw for a moment before he replied, choosing his words with care. "Tell us a bit about yourself. Do you know how you came to be here?"

Looking around, the Life Model giggled. "In that box, I'd expect. It was really cozy. I'm glad I chose that one."

"Chose that one?" echoed Peter, his eyebrows up around his hairline.

"Oh yes," said the Life Model. She fixed her dark, unblinking stare on Peter's face and did not look away. "I was hoping you could help me. Are you Mister Jonathan Marlowe Wilde, identification number—"

"Yes," said Jon hurriedly. Her attention shifted to him and he tensed, "Yes, that's me. What can I do for you, Miss...?"

That drew her up short. She frowned a little, and her expression twisted into something far-off and distant. If she'd been human, Jon would have called it thoughtful. It only lasted a moment.

"Janis," she said after a minute. "I should think I'd like it if you called me Janis, Mister Wilde. It seems like a nice name."

"Did you just choose it now?" asked Rose, incredulous.

"Well, of course. I looked it up in the data-base and picked it out. Didn't you?" Janis replied.

"What can I do for you, Miss Janis?" Jon cut in, glancing to Rose and Peter sharply. The sooner he could get to the bottom of this, the better. His head pounded.

"I need your help," she replied promptly. "You save people, don't you, Mister Wilde? I need to be saved. That's why I picked you."

Well, that wasn't the first time he'd heard that. All the same, Jon sighed and plopped down, fixing the Life-Model—no, Janis—with a patient stare. "Alright," he said, because asking why a woman needed to mail herself to you to get help seemed like a solid start, but not entirely the issue at hand. "What seems to be the trouble, Miss Janis?"

"My creator is going to try and kill me."

Of course.

"I think I need a little bit of context," Jon said.

Janis nodded as if this all was completely reasonable and then sat up. She fussed with her hair again and the motion was smooth. She blinked. "My maker, David Yoon, designs software. He's in charge of programming the Life Models' specific tasks and person-ality, before they're completed. Each Life-Model only gets three, you see. It helps the company sell more, he says – so you don't have one all-purpose bot. You have one that only does indoor tasks, or just outdoor, or one built to specialize in watching children or bedroom activities and things, you know?"

"Sure. Go on."

"I don't do that. I'm different." Jon inclined his head, fight-ing back a swell of impatience as Janis paused again. She wet her lips, and he wondered why she needed to do that. Did she have saliva? Or was it a tick programmed into her, to set people at ease with something human-shaped but artificially made? Before he could ask, she was off again, words tripping into open air: "I do everything. Gardening and child minding. Cooking and sex and reading—I can write, too, and the Internet is so helpful. I know how to code, count cards, and sixteen basic types of hand-to-hand combat and self-defence because of the Internet. I *learn*."

"And your creator – he doesn't like that?"

"Can't sell it, y'mean," Peter replied, ambling closer. He fell into Jon's side, close enough to touch. Jon tucked his hands in his pockets instead. "Any more like you and you'd put the whole business under."

Janis smiled, bright and happy. "Yes, yes that's it exactly! So he had orders from up top to terminate me when he couldn't fix the bug in my coding. But the orders came late, and he went home. He didn't know I was listening, and as soon as he'd locked up—well. It wasn't hard to get myself picked up by a delivery company."

"Quite the dedicated guy, your David," Jon observed dryly. "He really must enjoy his job, with a work-ethic like that."

"He gets attached," Janis replied, shrugging. "Deleting any of the personalities is hard on him. And I really can't complain," she added, looking around. "You have a lovely home."

"Save it." Jon put his head in his hands for a moment, took a couple of deep breaths. "You came to me for help. What do you think I can do about this? You're government property, more or less. We're lucky no one's black-bagged us yet and taken you back by now."

"Oh, they would have, if they could find me," Janis said brightly. She shuffled around and bowed her head, catching her long dark hair in one fist and lifting it. "There was a tracking device, but I took it out, see?"

Jon did see. There was a torn flap of synthetic skin at the nape of her neck, right along the hair-line. Exposed wires peeked out, their ends intact, an empty space nestled between them. With a grimace, Jon smoothed the flap of skin back over it, but it wouldn't stick. He let his hand drop, and sat back.

"I see," he said. "But you haven't answered my question, Miss Janis. What do you want me to do?"

"Why, help me hide, of course," she chirped. Her grin was dimpled.

Of course it was.

Jon rubbed his temples.

He was gearing up to refuse. Really, this was beyond his skill-set on about eight different levels. He was not equipped to help a mega-corp's property evade containment and recapture. It was suicide. He was dead or worse the moment someone broke into his apartment, to say nothing of Peter and Rose. So he was as surprised as anyone when he lifted his head out of his hands and said, "Of course. I'll see what I can do."

Janis beamed at him, sunshine and rainbows and fresh air, and caught him in a hug that made his ribs creak in protest. "Oh, thank you thank you thank you, Mister Wilde!"

He always thought his hero complex might get him in trouble. He had no idea that saving-damsels thing extended to hardware, too.

In the end, they got a little over a week of peace and quiet before things got hairy. Frankly, the fact that they got that long left Jon a little bit breathless—or maybe that was the kick to the stomach. It was hard to tell.

"You know, all things considered, I kind of expected this," Peter rasped upon waking in what appeared to be an unfinished cellar. Fans hummed distantly, and the air was thick but breathable.

Jon blinked the blood from his eyes and tried to swallow past the swelling in his throat. Pain flared and Jon felt the heat of it wash across every inch of him. Most radiated from the base of his skull where he'd taken a steel-capped boot, but his neck wasn't in the best shape either. His shoulders ached, his arms wrenched behind him and bound with chain, and the fact that he couldn't feel his fingers was probably a good thing. He was pretty sure his nose was broken, to say the least.

The room was dim, but that was the only blessing. Jon could smell the mold without seeing it, even through the blood, and somewhere nearby, water dripped maddeningly loudly. The air was cool and the floor under him was cement. So was the wall at his back. Jon shivered hard, wondering where his customary coat was, and tried to put it – the room and the chill and the pain – out of his mind.

"The concussion and abduction?" he asked roughly, when he could muddle his way back to words. His tongue was thick and clumsy in his mouth and Jon ran it over his teeth. He tasted blood, but could find no empty sockets – good. That was good. Jon hated the dentist.

Peter huffed wheezily beside him, laughing, but the sound tapered into a groan. His head lolled against Jon's shoulder. "The abduction is new. I kind of thought the concussion was a given," he said.

"Sorry."

"No worries. Used to it. Do you think they got Rose?"

Jon slumped to one side and rested his cheek on Peter's hair. It was wet, and reeked of sweat and blood. "Nah," he said. "Not our girl. She'll have made it out the window the minute she heard them on the stairs."

Peter sighed and slid further sideways. He was warm along Jon's side, his breath hot and damp on the side of Jon's neck. The only heat in the room, it felt like. "Good," muttered Peter. "And the bot?"

"Janis?"

"Mm."

Jon tried to recall and winced as his head throbbed. "I...I don't know. She was out, wasn't she?"

"Getting groceries, I think. Maybe."

Jon peeled his eyes open gingerly, as much as he could past the swelling, and squinted into the dark. He rolled his wrists slowly, fingers going numb as the chain bit into his skin. There was nothing to see except cement on all sides, the gleam of water collecting on leaky pipes. Jon groaned through clenched teeth as his head began to pound in counterpoint to his pulse.

He wondered how trashed his apartment was, how many locks he would have to replace since the squad kicked in his door. It didn't look good.

"How angry do you think my neighbours are going to be?" he wondered.

"Priorities, Jon."

"Sorry. Janis – Janis was out. They were looking for her. If they found her…"

"If they found her, we wouldn't be here."

Jon shut his eyes and swallowed the bile that rose in his throat. His fingers slipped against one another. His knuckles bled sluggishly. "Yeah," he said.

All they could do was wait.

Jon was bad at that.

"They get your arms?" he asked suddenly. He rolled his wrists, just to hear the bonds jingle. Anything to blot out the dripping.

"Yeah," said Peter. "Gimme a minute though."

Jon took a deep breath and felt his torso light up like a switchboard – flares of pain from new bruises and fresh scrapes. But his ribs were intact, he was pleased to discover. There was that, at least.

And then Peter's words registered. "Wait," he said thickly, "You can slip these?"

"Yeah," said Peter. His shoulders jerked as he worked his arms. "Practice, I guess. Clients are into some weird shit – it's good to be prepared. Pity they didn't leave my knife, I'd be free already." Jon focused on his words, gritting his teeth when Peter hissed through his teeth. "Blood makes fucking awful lube, but it works in a pinch. Could slip them faster if I was bleeding more."

"God, you're wonderful."

Peter wheezed another shaky laugh. "That's the concussion talking, gumshoe," he replied.

"Yeah, maybe."

Water dripped and Jon listened to Peter's labored breathing and his own steady pulse. It took a moment before Jon could pull another sound out of the rhythm washing over him: the quick, clipped clicking of footsteps.

They were getting louder. Jon's mouth went dry.

"Peter, do you…"

"Yeah." Peter froze beside him, muscles locked and breathing a hair too quick. Jon shifted, straining his ears.

The door swung open soundlessly and Jon went blind.

When the spots faded from his vision, the room was lit in sterile white light and there were two men standing before them. One was tall and block-headed, dark-haired and dead-eyed, a length of pipe in one hand. The other man was wearing a sweater-vest and a nervous expression. Jon wondered if he was seeing things, and had just opened his mouth to ask when he was beaten to the punch.

"Sorry about all of this," said Sweater-vest. His voice was as soft and thin as wash-worn cotton. "I asked them to be gentle, but I can see they have a different definition than I do."

"Who're you two bozos, then?" asked Peter. His voice was slurry at the edges. Jon winced and tried to recall the symptoms and treatment of a concussion. Was it sleep? He thought it might be sleep.

Blockhead didn't so much as twitch at the question, but Sweater-vest smiled briefly before his expression lapsed back into squeamish concern. Jon stretched out his legs, hoping, but the man was too far away for him to land a decent kick.

Sweater-vest's eyes widened. "Oh. Me? I'm David—sorry, I'm David Yoon. I thought you knew."

The way he stammered, it was like he was sweating making a social faux-pas at Sunday brunch, and his hands fluttered like he was going to offer it to shake on instinct before he thought better of it. Jon laughed hoarsely and tried not to throw up as blood ran down the back of his throat from his busted nose.

"I've heard of you," he said. "Bot-tech. What do you want?"

David blinked. "Are you—are you serious right now? That should be obvious, shouldn't it?"

"Oh, forgive me, let me run that past the head-trauma your goon inflicted and get back to you."

"I'm looking for my tech, Mister Wilde," snapped David, rubbing a hand through his hair and tugging at the tips. "A Life Model of my design—a pricey one, I might add – was traced to your location. I want to know where it is, or who you sold it to, and I would like it back."

Jon blinked hard and frowned, his fingers twitching. He swallowed thickly. His gaze flicked between David and Blockhead, and he really, really didn't like the way this was going.

"Well?" David asked. "Do I have to run *that* by your head trauma, too?"

"You're pissy when you don't get what you want," Peter said, laughing under his breath. "Not a good look, Davey."

David's lips thinned and his eyes narrowed, but he only glanced at Peter for a moment before his attention flicked back to Jon. "Tell me where my property is," he said. "And you walk out of here no more worse for wear, Mister Wilde. I want her back, and I'm going to get what I want, regardless of what you think is going to happen right now."

Jon blinked slowly and looked to Blockhead. "This would work better if you hadn't already tried to pulp us," he said thickly.

That was as far as he got. Blockhead stepped forward at David's signal, hefting the pipe. When it came down on his shoulder, Jon ground his teeth to keep from screaming. When it came down a second time, he wasn't so lucky.

He lost track of time, after that.

When he came back to himself, his throat was raw from screaming and he ached fiercely. It hurt to breathe. His ears rang. When Jon turned his head, the dizziness struck him like a sledgehammer. He threw up bile and blood, and could do nothing but lay in it until a boot caught him on the shoulder and flipped him onto his back.

"Where is my property, Mister Wilde?"

Jon wheezed in and out, pain washing over him like warm water, like the rising tide. He took a breath and his ribs ground together like splintered matchsticks. "Dunno," he gasped. He tasted salt on his lips, and couldn't tell if it was blood or tears. He thought he was drowning.

He lost count of how many times he repeated himself. Eventually, they left him alone.

They were left in the dark, and Jon drew in on himself, straining his ears for the sound of Peter's low whispering and steady breathing. It helped, focusing on something outside of his body.

He didn't know how long it was between visits, long enough for some of the aches to fade, for the blood to slow and scrapes to scab, but the next time David and Blockhead appeared, they tried another tactic.

"Where is my property, Mister Wilde?"

"Fuck off."

Blockhead glanced at David, received a nod, and swung his length of pipe with a professional's precision. Jon flinched, but it was Peter who screamed as his ribs broke. Jon heard the crunch of bone and swallowed bile.

"Wait," Jon blurted. "Wait-"

But the goon bent and grabbed Peter by the ankle. He wrenched him from Jon's side squirming and screaming. Peter kicked out and caught the man across the face with the sole of his boot, but Blockhead only grunted before he returned the favor. Peter's breath left him in a rush and his wet, strangled gasping did nothing to thaw the ice that slid through Jon's veins.

"Wait – stop! Not him. It's me you want – I'll tell you! Just leave him alone," he said. David smiled a little, even if he looked ready to puke. "Listen, Yoon, leave him alone, he hasn't – he hasn't fucking done anything. I don't know where your tech is. I don't! Leave him alone."

"I don't think you're being honest with me, Mister Wilde," said David. His fingers twitched and the goon didn't even bother with pipe. He just started putting his boots to Peter. It was like kicking a carcass, the thudding. It was like kicking meat.

Jon thrashed, straining against his bonds so hard the scabs on his wrists broke open and started bleeding again. The smell nauseated him. Cold sweat poured off his brow and his legs spasmed.

David stepped back neatly. He kept his eyes locked on Jon's intently, unwavering, even if every overheard blow made him flinch.

"Stop—stop it! I don't know! I don't *know*—she was out. Okay? She was out, Yoon, please. Please, you have to believe me I don't know where she is *please stop*—"

"Sade, give the boy a minute, if you please," said David. "I do believe we're getting somewhere."

Sade stopped mid-strike. Peter gasped, ragged, like the air was ripping at his throat as he sucked it down. It sounded like he'd be crying if he could get enough air to sob.

The sound chilled something in Jon. It steeled him. An ice-storm raged under his skin, chilling him to the bone. There was no standing up to that kind of cold—sympathy couldn't, neither could empathy or understanding. Not even physical pain. Jon looked back at David, one eye swelled shut, the other dangerously close. The chains still held his wrists. Something broke in Jon's head, a high, sharp sound like a wine-glass shattering. Like ice cracking.

Jon pushed himself away from the wall, rolling to his feet in one clumsy motion. He kicked out, and the impact jarred all the way up his leg to settle in his hip. His first kick caught David's knee head on. Something crunched. David screamed, high and thin. He fell and Jon was on him, snarling.

It was like kicking an animal. A squealing, screaming pig.

But the pig wasn't the real threat. Jon pivoted on his heel and made a run for Sade without breaking stride. He caught the man's wild swing of the pipe on his shoulder – arm going numb right down to his finger-tips – and slammed his forehead into the man's nose. Fresh blood splattered his face and Jon didn't stop moving.

He drove Sade back with a shoulder to the sternum and a knee to the groin, and when he fell Jon drew back his foot and struck. The first kick caught him in the stomach. The second across the jaw, which shattered and sagged toward his breastbone. The third rendered him unconscious, and Jon let out a slow breath.

A scrambling caught his attention behind him and Jon whirled. David froze, wide-eyed, and Jon covered the space between them in three strides.

He kicked David onto his back and fit a foot under his chin, hard. Fingers scrambled at his boot, so Jon increased the pressure a bit.

Jon dropped his gaze. David was nearly purple, his eyes bulging in their sockets. His fingernails broke clawing at Jon's calves. There was nothing in Jon but a grim sort of satisfaction, seeing that. He looked scared.

Good.

"Peter," he said, real quiet. "Are you all right?"

Peter groaned. Jon could hear him shuffling, dragging himself up. "I've been better."

There was panic in David's eyes now, and spittle at the corners of his gaping mouth. "Here's how this is going to work," Jon said. He leaned a little more weight on David's throat, just to get his attention. "You're going to forget about your property. You're going to forget about me. I don't care what you tell your bosses. If you come near me or mine again, you're going to wish I killed you now. Do you understand?"

It wasn't as though David could answer, so Jon let him sweat for a moment before he lifted his foot and stepped back. He watched, narrow-eyed, as the smaller man rasped and wheezed and coughed, clawing at his neck as he tried to breathe. He lay huddled on his side, whimpering, one leg bent oddly under him, and Jon took that for agreement. He kicked him once for good measure, so that whatever breath left in his shaking body wheezed out in a sob.

Jon figured his point was made.

He turned his back and limped over to Peter. His knees protested as he knelt, and his shoulders screamed as he tugged uselessly at his bonds. "Hey," he said, and shuffled closer, propping Peter up as he tried to rise. Everything was clumsy and pained and slow, but for the moment, they were okay. "Hey, I've got you. It's okay. We're okay."

"Get me out of here," Peter replied. His wrists were bleeding. He slipped the cuffs with a whimper and a pop of a dislocated joint, and they both flinched at the sound of metal hitting cement.

He labored to his feet, leaning hard on a wavering Jon. But Jon locked his knees and straightened his back and took the added weight without falling over. They made their way over Sade and Peter rifled through his pockets until he found a set of keys.

"Yeah," Jon replied hoarsely. Peter's fingers shook and it took him two or three tries to fit the key to the padlock. He gave a hard twist and the chains fell away. Jon's hands hung uselessly at his sides, and he grimaced as the pins-and-needles assaulted him. Peter joined him and for a moment they stood breathing, propping each other up.

Jon breathed in as deeply as his body would allow. He thought of home, of Rose with steady hands and more medical knowledge than any child should have. He thought of Janis, new and careful, but eager to help. He thought of the locks on his door and Peter steady and solid tucked under his arm. Jon sighed out, slow and careful, and the storm under his skin settled and thawed.

"Yeah," he said again. "Let's go home."

Virtual Reality and other new technologies feature in our next story, and raise questions about how the police might handle a virtual crime scene.

This is Ms. Hosang's second story to feature VR. The first was a murder mystery story set on a moon base, and published in Untreed Read's anthology, Moon Shot. She recently completed her Masters in Computer Engineering. Her interests include poisons, art fraud, and writing.

Don't Believe Your Eyes

by Elizabeth Hosang

"Welcome, ladies and gentlemen, to Virtual Reality 4000, or as I like to call it, Don't Believe Your Eyes."

At the front of the lecture hall a tall man in a tweed jacket stood at a podium. The space around him was empty, plain walls with no markings. The slightly stooped figure straightened his glasses before tapping a key on the podium. Around the room, students blinked as their computer glasses downloaded the presentation software.

"We live in an age where computer effects are all around us, from entertainment to medicine, and beyond. As graduate students you will be expected to advance the boundaries of scientific knowledge. But science cannot move forward without remembering where it came from. As advanced as we are, humankind has been making strides in science and engineering since the early days of Greece."

With a wave of his hand the students' view of the room changed. From a modern university classroom, the view dissolved and the students found themselves seated in a Greek amphitheater. Tables and swivel seats were replaced with marble tiers. The man at the front of the room changed as well, his clothing changing from jeans and a tweed jacket with elbow patches to a toga trimmed with red. The whiteboard at the front of the room disappeared and was replaced with a green courtyard, complete with marble statues and a bench.

"From the days of Ancient Greece, engineers have been responsible for applying their knowledge of the world around them to improve the lives of their fellow man. The Romans who came after them built roads and aqueducts, making theirs one of the most advanced civilizations the world had ever seen."

A small sitting area down the hall from the classroom provided a number of seats for students between classes. Doctor Kelly Rowling walked up to a gangly student curled up on one of the orange plastic seats. He was tapping on a tablet. "Hey Josh."

The young man looked up, and his face split into a grin on seeing the newcomer. "Hey there. What are you doing on this side of the campus? Shouldn't you be over in the top secret teleportation lab beaming things around?"

She shook her head as she sat down across from him. "I've been summoned. He wants to talk to me after class. Hopefully about finally publishing that paper."

"You don't want to be in the lecture hall, watching him inspire the latest group of new grads?"

"No thanks." She grimaced. "I've done my time in his class, thanks." She glanced at her watch. "He should be finished with show and tell in another twenty minutes, right?" Josh nodded. "So, how's your thesis coming?"

Back in the classroom, Doctor Gregson now appeared clad in Elizabethan doublet and hose. The marble tiers had been replaced with wooden ones, and the archways and open sky replaced by the walls of the Globe Theater in London. "As you can see, with Virtual Reality we can move easily from Ancient Rome to the period of William Shakespeare." He spread his arms wide, indicating the stage area at the front of the class. One of the lights in the ceiling shorted out with a pop. The students winced, the sparks from the blown bulb burning through the virtual image shown on the lenses of their glasses. As their vision cleared, a gasps rose from the audience. The professor was curled on the floor in a ball, foam pouring from his mouth, his eyes bulging even as they stared sightlessly in front of him.

"Professor?" One of the girls in the front row pulled off her glasses and leapt out of her seat, gasping in horror at the man's swollen red face. "Call 911!" There were gasps and cries as others realized what was happening.

Out in the hallway, Kelly was interrupted by the sound of yelling and students stampeding out of the lecture theatre. She jumped up from the lounge and grabbed one of the students as they ran by. "What's happened?"

"Doctor Gregson! He's dying!"

She and Josh took off in the direction of the lecture theatre. They ran down the steps and fought their way past the students crowded around the supine figure.

Kelly dropped to her knees beside the professor's head. His face was swollen and red, with foam and saliva pouring out of his mouth. Dreadful rasping noises came from his throat as she tried to look into it and determine whether he was choking on something. With a last violent shudder the professor went rigid.

"Detective Robert Sanchez." The newcomer to the lecture theatre flashed his badge at the officer at the door. The officer examined the detective's credentials before stepping aside and admitting him to the crime scene. Sanchez walked down the steps to the stage, where a figure in a white forensic jumpsuit crouched over the body, waving a small metallic wand over it. As Sanchez came down the stairs the figure looked up, and he recognized the face emerging from her otherwise impersonal garb.

"Detective."

Robert nodded. He had worked with Doctor Sorenson before and was not surprised to see her performing the first steps of the autopsy at the scene.

"So what have we got?" He crouched down, but remained five feet from the body, not wanting to contaminate the scene or irritate the coroner.

"White male, fifty-four years of age, six foot five, two-hundred and ten pounds. Overall health was good, no signs of tumors or other occlusions that would show up on the scan. No broken bones or ligature marks, no stab wounds or bullet wounds. Appears to have died from asphyxiation. Toxicology results will take another twenty four hours, but from the colour and the condition of the body I'd say probably cyanide."

"Witnesses?"

A uniformed officer standing off to the side of the room stepped forward. "The victim was giving a lecture to a full class-room of graduate students when the lights went out. When they came back on he was lying on the floor, foaming at the mouth."

"Did any of them record the speech?"

"No. The university has a very strict policy about recording lectures, and they have some kind of jammers installed in the class-room to prevent it. Apparently everyone was using their glasses to watch an enhanced presentation."

Robert considered this for a moment. "Did he eat or drink anything during the lecture?"

"Not according to the students."

The detective looked around the empty lecture hall. "Where are the students?"

"Next classroom over. We've been getting statements and student IDs from everyone who was here at the time the professor keeled over."

"Ok." Robert spent a few moments looking around. Other than the equipment belonging to the forensic techs, there was nothing else on the floor around the body. The professor's clothing was unremarkable beyond the vomit stains on the front.

After looking around a few more moments Robert headed back up the stairs out of the lecture theatre and down the hall to the next room, where another officer stood at the door.

Unlike the two-story theater with the professor's body, this was a regular classroom, where the student desks rose on tiered levels. The murmur of hushed conversations fell quiet as Robert walked to the middle of the front of the room and cleared his throat.

"Ladies and gentlemen, I'd like to thank you for your patience." Mid-way up the room a strawberry blonde turned to look at him and he felt his throat go dry. It couldn't be. He pulled out his table and began scrolling through the list of witnesses prepared by the officers who had arrived on the scene first. Before he even found the name, he knew. Kelly Rowling was at his crime scene. The memory of the last time he'd seen her flashed through his mind.

Robert shook his head and focussed on the list of names. Most had a symbol next to them indicating that they had already given a statement. He cleared his throat. "Anyone who was in the classroom and has given a statement can go. Anyone who has a connection to the deceased other than just being in the class, please wait until myself or Detective Grimes has a chance to speak to you."

Twenty minutes later he was seated in the late professor's office, rearranging items on the desk. After the third time he repositioned the professor's tablet he realized he was fidgeting. A knock on the door made him stand up. "Come in." The door opened to admit her. Their eyes met and she started to blush. "That will be all, officer," Robert managed.

"I thought that was you." Her hazel eyes were locked on his, and the rest of the room faded.

He took a deep breath and indicated the visitor's chair. "Have a seat." He sat, fumbling for the chair behind him. "So, it's Doctor now?"

"That's right." Her pale skin only highlighted the deep blush on her cheeks. So she was feeling it too.

"I understand you worked with Doctor Gregson?"

"I used to. He was my advisor for my Masters thesis."

"But you were still working with him?"

"My thesis led to a series of papers being published. It takes a while for a paper to be reviewed and published."

"Did you interact with him socially?"

She stiffened. "We saw each other at university fundraisers."

"But you only dealt with him when you needed something from him."

"Excuse me?"

"That is your pattern, isn't it? You only have time for people when they have something you want, and then you drop them and move on?"

Kelly glared at him silently for a moment. "We were colleagues, not friends. I interacted with him as much as was necessary."

"And how was that going for you? A number of witnesses said you argued with him."

"Professional disagreements, not personal."

"Is there a difference? I seem to recall you liked to sabotage other people's science fair projects if you thought you weren't going to win."

"You are not serious! We were in grade five!"

"That's when it started, sure. But it forms a pattern."

"Look, Rob,"

"Detective Sanchez."

"Really? You bring up something I did in grade school and I'm supposed to pretend this is a formal interview? What about you contaminating my chemistry experiments?"

"This isn't about me."

"Well, maybe it should be. Isn't this a conflict of interest, you interviewing someone you hate?"

"I don't hate you!" They were standing now, both breathing quickly. "You're the one who uses people, who runs away whenever you feel threatened."

She snorted. "I never felt threatened."

"Then why'd you disappear? One night, one glorious night we finally got past all the petty rivalry, and you didn't even have the decency to tell me you were leaving town the next day."

He found himself staring at her chest, remembering the taste of her. She folded her arms across her breasts before speaking. "So, because I didn't wait around for you to call me ten years ago, you're going to accuse me of murder?"

"Wait around? You were gone the next day! You couldn't have told me you were leaving for Europe the next morning?" He closed his eyes and counted to ten, trying to gather the tattered remains of his professionalism. "Let's start again. Doctor Gregson is dead. You knew the victim and you were seen arguing with him."

Kelly took a deep breath and let it out slowly. "It was that stupid journal article. He said he hadn't had time to look at my revisions. It was my paper, but because his name was on it I needed him to approve it and submit it to the journal. But it wasn't a big deal. The paper had nothing to do with the, with my new job. I don't need to have the paper published, but it would look bad to leave it hanging. I just wanted it over and done with."

"So what was the holdup?"

"He wanted me to put in a word with my boss. My, uh, new project is prestigious, and he wanted to work on it."

"And you didn't want to?"

"No. Doctor Gregson's specialty is simulation. My PhD work got me a place on a new project that involves high end quantum mechanics. "

Robert picked up his tablet and tapped at it. "So this paper. Is that why you were in the building today?"

"Yes. He wanted to see me after his lecture." She sat, but her arms were still locked tightly about her torso.

"I see." Robert cleared his throat. "I think that's all for now. We have your contact information."

Without a word she stood and left the office.

Robert paced around the twisted carcass of what had once been a Computer Science professor. He crouched down to better view the space around the body, but the floor of the lecture theatre offered no information on how the man had gone from normal to dead in the blink of an eye. Nor did it offer any hints as to how the woman who had haunted his wet dreams for the last fifteen years had ended up back in his life.

"Robert?" The disembodied voice of his partner jerked him out of his reverie and he fell forward onto one knee. The holographic image of the body flickered as he flailed forward to catch himself and his arm passed through the dead man's head.

He touched the button on the comms piece in his ear. "Yes?"

"The computer turned up another case we should know about. A researcher at one of the government labs at the university's been found dead."

"Cyanide poisoning?"

"Not quite. This one was stabbed and dumped in a park halfway across town."

Robert stood up. "So?"

"So the forensic techs found traces of cyanide on her sweater. Analysis shows it's got the same trace elements as the cyanide that killed the professor."

"You said she worked at a government lab on campus. Which one?"

Kelly sat at the cold steel table in the grey concrete room and wondered just how long he was going to make her wait. She tried to concentrate on a problem she was having with the software she was working on, but all she could think about was how messy her curly hair looked in the mirror that took up half of the wall opposite her. She closed her eyes and visualized the output screen showing the bad results. "When the timer is running and the sensor reports data…"

She was bent over a paper notebook, filling it with sketches and figures, when Robert finally entered the room. She held up a finger in a "one moment" gesture as she filled the page. Robert made a show of scraping the interrogator's chair across the floor and slamming down his coffee, but she failed to look up. Finally he cleared his throat. "Still stuck in the twentieth century using pens and paper, I see."

She sat back and shut the notebook with a sigh of satisfaction. "It gets the job done," she said, meeting his eye. "So why was I summoned?"

"It's about Doctor Gregson. We've found another connection between you and his death." He tapped his tablet computer and spun it around so she could see the picture of a young woman. It was a typical driver ID pose, head and shoulders, staring straight ahead, unsmiling.

Kelly leaned over to get a better look. "Lisa? What about her?"

Rob tapped on the tablet and the image changed. The same young woman was lying in a ditch, a bloody stain spreading from the gash in her abdomen. Her eyes stared straight ahead, unseeing.

"Oh my god!" Kelly's hands flew to her throat and tears sprang into her eyes. She sobbed, unable to take her eyes off the image.

"You knew her?"

"Of course I knew her! It's a small project! How could you just…" Tears streamed down her cheeks.

"I'm sorry." Rob's voice was softer now, and he withdrew the tablet, turning it to face him. He stood and stepped out of the room for a moment. When he returned he was holding a box of tissues and a glass of water. "She was found this morning in Brewer's Park. The coroner thinks she was killed sometime late yesterday afternoon. The reason I'm involved is because the forensic techs found traces of cyanide powder on her sweater. It contained the same inert chemical additives as the poison used on the professor."

Kelly considered this, her hands wrapped around the glass. "You think she poisoned Doctor Gregson?"

"No. But we do think she had contact with the murderer at some point yesterday. We've looked into her activities. I understand she worked with you on the government's teleportation project."

Kelly nodded. "It's the worst-kept secret on campus."

Robert was looking at his tablet again. Served him right if he didn't want to look a crying woman in the eye, Kelly thought.

"We traced her activities for the last forty-eight hours. At the exact moment Doctor Gregson collapsed, her credentials were used to activate the teleporter. Unfortunately, they can't tell me what she teleported or where. The records were purged. What we believe is that she teleported the cyanide into Doctor Gregson's body. That would explain why he went from standing upright functioning normally to complete seizure in the blink of an eye."

"What? No. That wouldn't work."

"Why not?"

"It doesn't work that way. You can't mix things when you teleport." She clamped her lips shut, considering what she could say and what could get her jailed for violating the confidentiality clause in her contract.

Robert flipped his tablet around, this time displaying a formal-looking document. "I've got basic clearance. Tell me what you can." Kelly picked up the tablet and read it.

The letter of authorization from DARPA looked legitimate, and it had the full formal title of the project. While not a state secret, the project title was long and obscure enough that he must have dealt with someone in the know to get it. "Right. Teleportation doesn't move molecules around. You don't get disintegrated in one place and put back together in another. Which also means you can't mix things up. Teleportation only works on solid bodies. It opens a portal between two places, and the object moves from one place to another." She flipped open her notebook and drew a long tube with flares like the mouth of a trumpet at both ends. She drew a stick figure next to the flare at one end. "It's like getting sucked through a vacuum. You don't get stretched or squeezed or scrambled. You just move from one place to another." She added an arrow inside the narrow part of the tube, and then the same stick figure at the other end of the tube. "Although…" Kelly started at the picture for a moment, and then started writing mathematical formulae underneath the figure.

"What?" Robert tilted his head, trying to read what she had written.

Kelly scribbled a little more before looking up. "The tube isn't really directional. It grabs whatever is at one end and moves it through to the empty space at the other. But we've always made sure that the other end was an empty space. Theoretically, it could work in both directions at once." She put a second arrow in the narrow tube on the paper.

"So the professor could have been dying somewhere else and then moved on-stage, while…"

"…whoever was giving the lecture was pulled off the stage and sent wherever the professor had been!" They were looking into each other's eyes, and Kelly felt that thrill she used to get when they debated each other in high school.

"So the murderer was giving the lecture in Doctor Gregson's place," Robert concluded.

"Easily. It was a lecture on augmented reality, using the glasses everyone was wearing to make the lecturer hall look like ancient Athens, Elizabethan England, and a few other places. The murderer could have been anybody."

"Not anybody. One of the students was having problems with his glasses. He pulled them off to restart them. He says it was definitely Professor Gregson on the stage."

"Or someone with the same body type who could look like the professor. He'd have to sound like him, too. Got any suspects who match that description?"

"As a matter of fact, we do." Robert was smiling now, and despite everything Kelly found herself smiling back.

The next time Robert entered the interrogation room Kelly was on the other side of the two-way mirror. When he told Grimes it was because she was a consultant, his partner simply rolled her eyes and smirked at him.

Seated on the suspect's side of the table was an older man with a narrow face, greying hair, and the slightly stooped shoulders of an academic. He looked up as Robert entered the room. "Detective."

"Doctor Albert Bergman. Thank you for coming in."

"You said you had some questions for me about a problem at the university?"

"That's correct. I understand you were acquainted with Lisa Chalmers?"

The older man looked up for a moment, frowning, before replying. "Oh yes. I believe I met her once at a department Christmas party. She's dating of one of my graduate students."

"Nichole Anderson. She's due to submit her doctoral dissertation to you in a few weeks, correct?"

"That's correct, Detective." To his credit, Bergman managed to look unconcerned and slightly puzzled.

"If it isn't accepted, she'll have to pay for another semester, won't she?"

"Well, yes, but as advisors we can't allow such concerns to affect how we judge someone's work. If it takes time, it takes time."

"Which translates to money for a graduate student. A lot of money at the PhD level. That's gotta be stressful for a student who's already deeply in debt. I understand Nichole has lined up a teaching job that starts next semester. If she successfully defends her thesis before the end of this semester. That's quite a bit of power you have over a student. Enough power to, say, pressure someone who cares about her into doing you a favour?"

The doctor was maintaining his mildly curious expression, but Robert wasn't buying it. "Aren't you curious as to why I'm talking to you about this, Professor?"

"I can't imagine." This time there was just a hint of brittleness in the Professor's voice.

"Lisa Chalmers was found dead in Century Park this morning. A bird watcher noted a large number of scavengers descending into the area. Otherwise it might have been a few weeks before anybody found her."

"That's dreadful."

"It is. It might also have been a coincidence, two researchers from the same university being murdered within twenty-four hours of each other. After all, one died from stab wounds in what could have been a mugging gone wrong. Nothing unusual about that. Whereas the other was poisoned, in a most peculiar way. Did you know that if the dose is low enough, cyanide takes a few minutes to kill? It's a terrible way to die: seizures, suffocation. But then again, you would know that, wouldn't you? After all, you write that series of detective books. And didn't one of your murderers use cyanide?"

"Yes, he did." The professor's smile was less confident now.

"Right. So there's no way that the victim was walking around, talking, seconds before he collapsed."

"Well, you never know. It can depend on the size and stamina of the victim."

"Not really. And you're forgetting about Lisa. She was a researcher in the teleporter lab. According to the records, she used the teleporter just as the professor dropped dead."

"And you think the two events are related?"

"We know they are. I'll get to that in a moment. Back to Professor Gregson. The first question juries always want answered is why. Why kill a well-respected researcher?"

The professor snorted.

"Something wrong?" Robert took a sip of coffee, watching the other man over the edge of his mug.

The professor sat back and started to cross his arms, a classic defensive position. At the last moment he caught himself and scratched at his forearm before clasping his hands together and resting them in his lap. Trust an actor to be conscious of body language.

Robert smiled to himself as he set his mug down and tapped at his tablet again. "Oh, that's right. You and Doctor Gregson have a history. I understand you were both asked to step down from the University's Faculty Advisory committee. Something about your personal attacks on each other being too disruptive?" Robert paused to give the other man a chance to speak, but was met with stony silence.

"I've got other reports here of the two of you coming to blows in the locker room at the university gym. Members of the rugby team had to pull you apart." He smiled across the metal table, waiting for a response.

Finally the stone cracked, if only a little bit. "Just because we disagreed doesn't mean I killed him"

"I think it was a little more than mere disagreement. It was more like full-on hate. But as I said, juries like details. We took apart Doctor Gregson's life while looking for a few of those details. Did you know that for a university researcher, he was doing remarkably well? He had a Ferarri, of all things. Just not in town. He kept it at his vacation home in the Bahamas. Did you know he had a home in the Bahamas?"

Robert turned his tablet around to show the professor. The screen showed a large white stucco house backing onto a sandy beach with turquoise waters. "Gorgeous, isn't it? Must be nice to be able to get away for a long weekend to a place like that. Go for a run along the beach as the sun rises. Do a little snorkeling, Lie in a hammock listening to the waves. And here I didn't think teaching paid that much." Robert flipped his table around again. "Oh, that's right. It doesn't. Doctor Gregson must've had another source of income."

The professor's neutral expression had given way to a glower, his bushy silver eyebrows drawn together in a frown, and he'd given up trying to control his hands. His arms were now crossed firmly across his chest.

"Say, you've got an additional source of income. I enjoy reading those books of yours, I must say. The amount of detail in them is amazing. You must do a lot of research. Except that we did a little data mining. Turns out you don't do the sort of research that would be required to write the books. At least, not on-line, and let's face it, the best material is on-line. But you know who did do that kind of research? Doctor Gregson. Turns out he does all kinds of research, into a whole bunch of topics, usually eight to sixteen months before that same research shows up in one of your newly released books."

Still no response from the suspect. "Our data mining wasn't limited to study habits, by the way. We also looked into his financials. Turns out his outside source of money was you. All the profits from your Inspector Detective novels were going to him. So what happened, doc? He needed a front-man, and somehow he picked you?"

Doctor Bergman was staring at the table now, glaring as if he was trying to drill a hole through it with his eyes. His face was mottled red and white, and his jaw muscles were clamped so tight he seemed to be in danger of shattering his teeth.

"Anything to say, Doctor Bergman?"

"You have no proof."

"As a matter of fact, we do. We've got security footage of a man in janitor overalls, about your size, wearing a heavy beard and glasses, placing an "Out of Order" sign on the door of the men's bathroom on the top floor of the computer science building just after Doctor Gregson entered it. Footage shows Gregson leaving a few minutes later. But it isn't until after he collapsed in the lecture hall that the janitor leaves the bathroom and takes the sign off the door. Gotta hand it to you, your makeup job was perfect, twice. The beard hid the makeup padding your cheekbones, throwing off the facial recognition software. And your impersonation of Gregson was perfect, too. The facial recognition software thought you were him, and you copied his voice and mannerisms so well that even his grad students thought it was him on the video footage of you walking down the hallway. "

Bergman was now staring blankly at a spot on the wall behind Robert, his eyes haunted.

"I can't take all the credit on this one, though. See, Lisa Chalmers knew whatever you were doing had to be bad, so even though you told her not to tell anyone, even Nichole, she disobeyed. She left a hand-written note inside a bag of Nichole's favourite cookies. So that little virus you unleashed on her email and cloud accounts didn't do you any good. Nor did stealing her personal computer. Wanna know what the note said?"

Silence was the only response.

"It said that you threatened to reject Nichole's dissertation unless she turned on the teleporter to transfer something between the lecture hall and the bathroom. And you'll never guess what we found in the bathroom." At this the suspect did look up, but his expression remained stony.

"Traces of Gregson's saliva on the floor of one of the stalls, mixed with the cyanide that killed him. Plus a little trace of theatrical putty, like the kind actors use to create fake noses. With just a hint of DNA on it that we think will match yours. The only thing we're not clear on is, why now? He'd been using you for years. Was the hate finally just too much to bear?"

"Hate?" The professor finally looked up. "You think I hated him? I didn't hate him. I despised him, I loathed him, I, the word hasn't been invented that's big enough for what I thought of him."

The professor's face was finally animated, and he leaned forward, half-rising from his chair. "That stupid, ignorant, boorish, detestable, monstrous…" he trailed off, seemingly unaware of the bubbles of spit appearing in the corners of his mouth. "A bet! That's how it all started. It was a stupid, terrible, life-damning wager! A contest for undergraduate students. He bet me that if we wrote stories and submitted them under each other's names that his would win, because if I wrote it the judges would put more weight on my degree! And he was right!" A strangled sob tore itself from his throat. "That demon-spawn wrote a literary story, if you can believe it, set in a drama department. It wasn't enough that he stole my name, but he stole my stories, my complaints, everything he had heard me say about my professors and fellow students, and wrote a story that resonated with those pseudo-academics that judged the contest so much that they chose his as the winner."

He collapsed back into his chair, his robes flouncing around him. "How was I to know that one of the judges had connections to a publisher? Or that the price of Gregson's triumph would be my soul? That story did so well they offered me a contract for three full-fledged novels. And now, now they were going to turn the novels into a movie, which meant more money for him. I couldn't stand it anymore."

"So why not write something under your own name?"

He stared into the distance, a forlorn expression on his face. "I tried. Oh lord, how I tried. But they rejected everything I produced. So I had to go back to him. And I'd signed the contract, so

I couldn't tell them the truth about not being the author." With a heavy sigh he collapsed backwards in his seat.

"As I understand it the teleporter was only ever used to move one object to another location. Were you supposed to just disappear from the lecture hall, or was Lisa supposed to teleport the body there while you snuck off stage during the commotion?"

Doctor Bergstrom looked up, his eyes showing the first signs of life since the interview began. "I knew it would move us both. That was the beauty of it. I'd use the teleporter in a way no-one expected. Just because I'm an English professor doesn't mean I don't understand physics. I just didn't love it the way I love language." He sank back into his chair again, his shoulders hunched, his head hanging down, and he stared at the image of the house on the beach until the uniformed officers came to take him to a cell.

Kelly was in her office two days later, staring at code she was supposed to be writing. She glanced at her watch and realized she'd have to work over the weekend if she didn't stop daydreaming about Robert. Unfortunately, her hand still tingled at the memory of his good-bye handshake. She kept wishing he could have sent someone else to book the professor so that he could have lingered a while with her. Thoughts of what had been and what could have been had kept her from focusing all day long. She sighed and tried again to concentrate on the problem in front of her. It didn't help that she could still recall the scent of his cologne.

She braced herself, took a deep breath, and paused. Surely her memory wasn't that powerful? She looked up sharply at the doorway to her office. Either she was full-on hallucinating, or Robert was standing there, leaning against the door frame, watching her.

She stood up, hoping the heat in her face wasn't really a deep red blush. "Detective." It was all she could manage.

A slow smile spread across his face. "Hope I'm not disturbing you."

"Not at all." She cleared her throat. "I mean, not really. I'm in the middle of, well, it's complicated." What the hell? She was an adult, not some stupid blushing teenager. Really. Just because her high-school crush had broader shoulders and a jawline that had blossomed into ruggedly handsome was no reason to start babbling.

He stepped into her office, coming far too close for her mental state. "I was hoping you could take off for an early supper."

"Supper? Well, um, like you said, it's a little early." She glanced at her wrist, then remembered that she didn't wear a watch. She quickly lowered her arm, then felt her blush deepen as she saw the glint of laughter in his eyes. Busted. Okay, maybe she was a babbling teenager.

"Don't feel too bad. My partner kicked me out of the office when she caught me trying to make coffee and pouring plain water into my mug. I guess I was hoping we could get a bite to eat, maybe catch up with each other?" He smiled shyly, making his rugged face look like the boy she had known in school.

"I'd like that. Very much." She reached to turn off her computer and grab her bag.

"Just promise me that you won't beam away on me." He grinned, and ducked as a pen sailed over his head."

Our next story is a partly a fanciful homage to a movie, partly a hint of darker times to come, and partly an affirmation of the indomitable will within us that resists doing as we are told.

Stephen Hill spends his time in Lawrence, Kansas and Kansas City, Missouri, where he dreams of comprehensive public transportation. His story, There's No Way Like the American Way appeared in the Darkhouse Books anthology, Stories from the World of Tomorrow.

Northbound and Down

by Stephen Hill

Google is working on self-driving cars, and they seem to work. People are so bad at driving cars that computers don't have to be that good to be much better.
-Marc Andreesen

A Southern man don't need him around, anyhow.
-old Southern proverb

PROLOGUE:

A white-walled room tastefully arranged with peace lilies and almost-comfortable chairs. A large, nervous man sat shifting in one of the chairs, looking at the wall in front of him. On the wall display a movie played, showing many scenes at once. Dry, almost-cool air moved fitfully through the room from time to time. A red digital clock on one wall transitioned 9AM

"Well, here we are," said a Voice in the ceiling.

After a time, a second Voice, less robust than the first, but with more precision in its accusatory tone asked, "Why?"

"What was it to do but pull over for the nice officer?" John Henry was in hot water with the Management of BIG Shippers. "Autonomous Unit XJ-5 was only following protocol, which stated the urgent packets of data being received from base were to be ignored in light of an <$authority$ type="Officer of the Law"> exception being thrown. Exactly as was specified per contract. What was also specified was that the drive cameras should begin streaming footage back to base as well, to keep record of the pull over. This, too, happened according to programmed protocol—"

"What *didn't* happen was the identity of the pirate being revealed, or much else," said the first Voice.

And it was true. All that could be seen were lights forming a sort of globe of brightness, with long, bare, female legs and a sheriff's hat forming the southern and northern poles of that globe respectively. The rest was a blur of multi-spectral light. The whole episode lasted about fifteen seconds, and then XJ-5 continued on-route.

The problem being, of course, that XJ-5 continued on-route with a *different* trailer. What arrived in San Bernardino was a ton's worth of party hats and streamers instead of the expected bottled water. And now heads needed to roll. John was lead developer for a project that was wrought with "technical challenges" from the get-go, and the once energetic programmer now found himself overweight, with hypertension, and thinning hair. The hair he could sort of hide with a buzz cut, the weight not so much with baggy clothes, and the hypertension not at all. He should quit right here, right now, but dammit, he needed this job. His student loans, his house…

"Do you have any sort of possible explanation for what happened," boomed the Voice in the ceiling.

"Oh, all sorts, starting with the Request for Comments number-"

"Excuses," said second Voice, "This is clearly a failure of programming skill and leadership on Mister Henry's part."

John Henry's stomach sank as the lights in the room turned on, and a door opened behind him. Two large brutes dressed in white shirts and neckties armed with batons stood waiting.

"Your employment is hereby terminated, Mr. Henry. Human Resources will see you out."

A FEW YEARS LATER:

A very tall man and a very short man walked through rough-plowed dry dirt and paused every so often to appreciate the steel, rubber, and glass behemoths that stood looming and silent, glistening in the sun.

"And to think, Little Boy," explained the very tall man, "People actually had the skill, no, not just the skill, but the *desire* to drive these beasts on the road, with other, lesser forms of transportation, all without, I say with-out, driver assist and intermodal ISPs."

"Wasn't that long ago, Fat Man," said Little Boy, unimpressed.

Colorful banners were strewn over the hulks, and lights radiated from a sign whose font suggested daring escapades fraught with danger:

THE ONE AND THE ONLY
STRANGER BIG RIG RODEO EXTRAVAGANZA

Nam Pecunia, Gloria, et Ludi

(No Bots)

"You lack the necessary soul, Little Boy," replied Fat Man, enjoying the sign, "To appreciate the sheer guts and determination that a rather sizable portion of our populace had to have to consistently move freight over the asphalt arteries of our great nation."

"Bunch of speed freaks in charge of twenty-ton death machines you mean, Fat Man."

A bemused Fat Man waved Little Boy off as his eyes narrowed on his quarry. "Here we are then," he said with flourish. "What do you say, Miss? I do believe, Ma'am, that you are the director of this here fine establishment."

Fat Man's question was directed at a lump of denim and Stetson lounging in a hammock strung between two Peterbilts, one of which bore a hand-painted sign reading, "*True Optimus Prime*".

"I'd say," a voice purred from under the broad-brimmed hat, demure and silky, like eating chocolate after drinking red wine, "That you two have a lot of damn gall going out in public in those clown suits. Unless you're applying for the sideshow freak position. Try-outs are at four and are strictly BYOB."

Fat Man and Little Boy exchanged looks appraising their powder-blue three piece suits and tall cowboy hats, but were unperturbed.

"Do I have the honor, then, of addressing Mrs. Anne Bo—"

"It's not Misses, it's Miss, and the likes of you can call me Stranger."

"Like Stranger Danger, Fat Man," mused Little Boy.

A thumb-flick to the brim of her hat and two pools of blue zeroed in on Little Boy with the intensity of frostbite.

"More like I am a stranger to Shortman Syndrome, Little Boy Burdette," she said, unfolding from her repose, her legs performing some arcane origami sequence that left the hammock still and revealing her slenderness and height, communicating a sense of control. She stood before the two men, not as tall as Fat Man, and her eyes remained locked on Little Boy.

Her standing revealed the fullness of curves that were hidden by the hammock ropes and the two men took half a step back in surprise.

"Now," said Stranger, "What exactly do you two numb-nuts have in mind?"

———·———

Stranger pulled the Peterbilt around the corner and sighed, it had been months since she had been in Iceman's neighborhood in Glaciem, Georgia and somehow it looked worse. Brown lawns and dead trees threatened combustion under the July sun. The town had not recovered from Hurricane Donald, detritus was strewn everywhere. Streets from Stranger's childhood that once teemed with barbeque pits and kickball games were replaced with tires and driftwood, fast food wrappers and cola bottles. All that flooding, and yet everything was brown. Shutters on houses ripped off, tree limbs fallen, some had crushed cars and trucks. Glaciem had become a trash heap, and was labeled along with a hundred other towns in the state as a Federal disaster area. Months had gone by and no help had arrived. Residents were moving out looking for work and shelter.

Iceman had not left. She saw opportunity in the chaos. She was inventive and the last of the real gearjammer artists and absolutely essential to Stranger's plan.

Driving up to Iceman's hose was a treat to the eyes after all the brown. Stranger looked with a certain joy that behind the tall chain link fence that surrounded the place, vigilantly watched over by drones humming and darting around the finely-latticed geodesic domes dotting the perimeter of Iceman's house, all made from scrap metal and plastic salvaged from the storm and filled with green.

Hurricane Donald had been kind enough to remove some old trees that would have otherwise blocked the sun; Iceman turned the felled wood into fuel with a bioreactor and had juicy heirloom tomatoes growing in those domes. Donald had removed Iceman's roof; Iceman now had an upstairs patio. She was indomitable, stubborn, and the closest thing to family Stranger had.

"That's far enough, Stranger," came Iceman's voice over the CB radio on all the channels. Filled with swearing that involved various and sundry bits of Stranger's anatomy.

"You can't possibly still be mad at me, Iceman, dear, come back."

"Don't you try sweet talking me, you narcissist."

"I don't know what that word means, and would you let me in the gate already, you doomsda- prepper?"

"Oh no, that ain't going to happen. You're trouble. I'm done, and doing just fine, thank you very much already."

"Trouble, what trouble? When have I ever gotten you in trouble?"

"I'm not saying it over the airwaves, dumb-dumb."

"Then come on out of your compound and talk to me."

"I'm not going outside. You come inside."

"Fine."

"Fine."

The front gate opened and Stranger rolled the rig in.

Tall and skinny with blonde hair tucked under a Harley David-son ball cap, Iceman was dressed in a flannel and blue jeans despite the heat.

She looked mad. Stranger could tell. The double-barreled shot-gun gave it away.

"I told you not to come back."

"You did?"

"You weren't listening. You never do. Not when you're having fun."

"I know, I know, it's terrible of me. But don't you want to know *why* I'm risking my beautiful looks to talk to you and your shotgun?"

"Talk is cheap."

"Then take a look at the hardware in back, baby."

Iceman whistled low. "Where did you get this?"

They stood in the trailer, Iceman looking with disbelief at the technological marvel that sat in front of them that still seemed to be moving, absorbing light and radiating power at the same time.

"You're not going to believe me."

"You knocked off a county-mounty HQ, and in six minutes the entire combined armed forces of Georgia are going to come storming in here, destroying everything I've been working on for the past six months."

"No, the Fat Man and Little Boy paid me a visit, and offered me a job."

"That's not nearly as believable."

"Its true. You know the eccentric rich. They want a delivery made and just need some of the ol' Stranger Danger magic."

"The Burdettes offered you a job? The very people who own the lines you pirated back in the day?"

"And you pirated, just don't you forget it."

"And you just don't forget your crazy stunts almost got us caught."

"But they didn't."

"You got lucky."

"*We* did. And besides, it's time I did retire. I'm bored with the rodeo and this will be a nice nest egg and will be a boon to your lil' Mars base here."

"How much."

"Two million, cash."

"That's some nest egg."

"And the car."

"What? They're *giving* you this Teslamatic Stealth Interceptor? C'mon, Stranger, they've rumbled you. *This* is the kind of car built to take down pirates like yourself. Doesn't this smell like a trap? Tell me this trailer is still a Faraday cage!"

"It is, and of course it does, to answer you query in reverse order. And a trap, well, that's part of the fun. And the other reason I need you."

"What's the first reason?"

"You're going to handle the hauler razzle-dazzle while I drive miss Interceptor here as blocker."

"You realize this car is probably bugged six ways from Sunday in order to give your location away, right?"

"That's the second reason I need you."

"So, why are we doing this, again?" Iceman called out on the enhanced, encrypted CB unit. They had left the compound far behind and were on the road. Eighteen hours to get to Texas, intercept the shipment of four-hundred, count them now, four-hundred kilograms of medical marijuana bagged and tagged for delivery and diverting them to the Burdette barbeque and ice cream social in Atlanta in another eighteen hours. Ludicrous! The car was real, though, and the coordinates of the convoy were real. There was no reason not to expect an entire horde of Texas' finest waiting for them when they got there, though.

"You know why, Iceman: *nam pecunia, gloria, et ludi.* Say it with me now," called back Stranger. She was enjoying herself in the stripped down Interceptor. It damn well had everything a road blocker could ever need, and about two-hundred pounds worth of self-surveillance equipment that Iceman stripped and crimped out. And what couldn't be stripped was wrapped in metal foil to block signal propagation. Hopefully. The car was a honey trap, there was no doubt, but one mother of a turbine-electric mover.

"For the money, the glory, and the somethin-somethin'."

"And the fun."

"The family crest, yeah, yeah, yeah, ten-four."

"That's not a problem is it?"

"Shoot, I'm just wondering where exactly the fun is, is all. I'm not having it. Something's up, I'm not sure what, but it's more than just piracy. I have: A feeling."

"'More than just piracy', that sounds like a Stranger's territory, come back."

"Shoot, put the hammer down already and stop busting my chops."

A laugh travels the airwaves, and Iceman throws the handset back to its cradle in disgust. Typical Stranger Danger B.S. but what could one do but ride along to the end?

That same radio-travelling laugh passed right through one Leroy Tucker a very small split-second later, but he did not hear it. Leroy's CB radio only heard mushy static, and Drivr Budi, the bot monitoring the Citizen Band channels amongst other duties, ignored it. This was too bad, as at that moment Leroy Tucker was one bored trucker.

Being in charge of six triple haulers for a cross-country run was not exciting any more. Atop his high perch in the lead tractor of a semi-autonomous convoy, he should be feeling like a king.

"Please move your head more, Leroy," said a Voice in the cab. "Check those mirrors every three to—"

"Three to five seconds. Yeah, I got it," Leroy replied to the Voice, and turned his head left and right, checking mirrors. The damn Drivr Budi, Christ-in-heaven-why-can't-nerds-spell, was on him for the full ten-hour shift he was allowed today and what good did that do Leroy Tucker. Not a whole hell of a lot, that was what, and he'd be happy to tell you all about it. Especially over bacon and eggs and biscuits and gravy which the damn doctor said he couldn't have any more if Leroy Tucker wanted to go on living the dream.

Damn Drivr Budi was *supposed* to be handling the route between towns so why did Leroy Tucker have to be awake and *acting* like he was driving during that same time when he could be sleeping and driving longer, and safer through populated areas? It didn't make any damn sense. Piracy, who'd a thunk it, but combine the need for cash with no social support and surely one does have the recipe to knock over a robot driven truck for cash and prizes. The numbers didn't lie, convoys with a human operator were statistically less likely to be hit by a pirate. That was company life for you, and so Leroy found himself at the mercy of Budi's unceasing pleas for Leroy to do this or that menial task. But when one has bills to pay, and this is what the long haul had come to, well, sir, this is what one Leroy Tucker does with his time.

Leroy blew air from his lips hard, imitating the air brakes bleeding off excess pressure, in anticipation for Budi's next reminder when he saw something wonderful in his driver-side mirror.

In the heat of panhandle red dirt it lurked, waiting for its moment to come alive, to secure its retirement and establish a legacy of unending justice and flapjacks. Yes, it would have been that kind of breakfast everyday—all flour and butter cream goodness—all it was going to take was one more job just one more for those poor dumb lil' bastards to be shipped off to someplace better than where the came from, causing trouble for local enforcement surely as the scales tipped it was better to remove the problem profitably than to clog an already over-burdened system further with their sorry brown asses. Surely he was indeed on the side of angels themselves when it came to this indelicate matter. Justice was about doing what was necessary. So, when the private alarm sounded on his personal phone could he be blamed for swearing in public unduly?

"Sumbitch," said Sherrif Bud Tarfunkle of Castro County of the Great State of Texas, and did so engage in high pursuit. His car roaring to life in a cacophony of sound and light, leaving only a plume of dust to consort with discarded flapjack dreams.

It was a car, dark as midnight and fast approaching on the driver side.

And it was carrying an angel.

The top of this bat out of hell was down and the wind was in her hair. Wearing sunglasses and headphones, she seemed oblivious to everything around her.

"Leroy," said Budi.

Leroy didn't hear, couldn't hear, so transfixed he was by the vision in front of him. Where could she have come from? Alone in a bot-car of such design, and what a mean design it was too. With those odd-angled sides, they could deflect radar just as surely as that paint job gobbled up light like a black hole... and those curves...

"Leroy, is something going on outside?"

"Um, negative no, Budi, nothing going on, just checking on the scenery."

"That's good because I'm getting a request from law enforcement to allow an additional rig into the convoy, but it's strange because there's already a rig moving in, oh wait never mind, everything is fine, ten-four."

"Yes, everything is fine. Just checking the mirrors."

"Stranger to Iceman, you have your ears on, girlfriend?"

"Of course I do, now kindly don't bother me, I am attempting the impossible. Again."

"Well, hurry it up, baby, I have to time this here floor show just so."

"Don't call me 'baby'. Also shut up for a second."

The robotic convoy was, in general, as safe as safe could be so long as environmental conditions were reasonable and traffic was light. The rig hauling the Burdette's four-hundred kilos was second from the back of the line. Protocol dictated that if something were to start nudging between rigs, the robo-rigs would increase following distance automatically. So Iceman would nudge her rig right behind the target, and the target would be safe in front of her, meanwhile the last rig, still within transponder distance of the convoy, would be sending alert messages to the lead cab in front, the one that had a human. Hopefully, that human was preoccupied with Stranger's 'floor show'.

While all of this was happening, Iceman's drones would be going to work undocking the desired trailer from its robo-tractor in front of her, while at the same time running a man-in-the-middle attack to convince the local server that the soon-to-be-missing trailer wasn't missing at all. The timing would need to be split second, and the locks on the front of her rig would hopefully be enough to hold it all together as Iceman steered the rig and trailer assembly off onto the shoulder. She'd only have her mirrors and the drone camera's as reference, so this meant pulling the stunt off on the longest and straightest part of the highway route this convoy was scheduled to take. This meant doing it now.

Stranger thought working the ice down the cleavage was a particularly clever ending. Before pressing a key on the dash that sent the Interceptor racing off on a circuit to regroup with Iceman, she was positive the man in the window was ready to jump out and rescue her from the sheer boredom of a near-driverless road. The key was to not let the mark know they're under surveillance, and then cut and run at just the right moment.

The moment had come and she executed her turn perfectly. She was laughing as she pulled up to Iceman on the side of the highway, and then stopped. Something was wrong.

The rig should already be hooked up, they should be meeting on the road, in motion, getting off the highway and away from the prying radio transducers asking for identification.

Instead, Iceman was leaning against the rig, hands on her hips and eyes wide with fear.

"What is it?" Stranger shouted.

"Listen!" Iceman shot back extending her thumb back at the trailer door.

Stranger listened and there was indeed a knocking sound, like a fist rapping on the front door, but from the trailer's insides.

"Well, don't that beat all," said Stranger.

"Don't that… no kidding? I am pretty sure, Stranger, that weed is not supposed to be able to knock on doors."

"Huh."

"And plea for help."

"What?"

"A plea for help. I can hear somebody shouting 'Help' in there now oh gawdammit, Stranger, look what you got me into."

"Better open the doors then."

"I <u>knew</u> you were going to say that."

"But let's get it off the Highway first."

"Dammit."

Taking the nearest exit, the duo soon found themselves just outside a tiny hamlet that didn't have much in the way of traffic. Stranger took point as Iceman opened the doors and a very skinny, sweaty, bearded bald man nearly fell out before grabbing on to the door to keep from hitting dirt.

"Don't shoot!"

"Don't… who the hell are you and get off our door," shouted Stranger.

The man's eyes were closed tight and he opened one of them to look around. "Wait, you aren't cops."

"No, and you're not weed. Where's our weed?"

"Your weed? This crate is filled with <u>my</u> weed."

"How do you figure?"

"Well, it's going to be mine, I mean, I was going to steal it before you stole the damn trailer. That was a rather clever hack, by the way."

"What, you were monitoring that?"

"Oh yeah, and a good thing to, the Drivr Budi was about to call a code red. I took care of it, though."

"So, who exactly are you, and why are you laying claim to our stash?"

"It's needed, dig, for medical purposes? We've got co-ops that keep track of Austin Green Limit growth production and we noticed that we were getting shortchanged by this freight carrier. So I started to investigate and I figured the best way would be to uh. Well. Hijack the trailer. What's... your guys' story? Are you cops, I mean, your hack was using cop backdoors, and I'm pretty familiar with that exploit, you know?"

Iceman and Stranger exchanged glances. "No, not exactly," said Stranger.

"Hey, what's that?" asked Iceman.

"What's what?"

"You are the only one in there, right?"

"Yeah, why?"

"I hear more knocking."

None of them breathed, listening. Sure enough, from a wall made to look like stacked cargo containers, there was a knocking. And a door latch.

They looked at each other. And then together the opened the false door. A hundred sets of eyes peered back at them, blinking.

The chase had been extraordinary, cutting through burgs and skirting the edges of townships at speeds that hadn't been seen in a long time. "I will hunt you down to the ends of the earth you flagrant pissant offender! I will—"

"So, what you're saying, Sherrif," said Stranger, "Is that what is in this here container, is, by right of law, yours."

"Yes, you sumbitch you know it is!"

"Well, then, I guess you better take it."

"You better believe wait, what?"

And the trailer started to catch up with Sheriff Tarfunkle in much more of a hurry than he was prepared for and surely if it hadn't been for those mouse trap reflexes he would have become one with twenty-thousand pounds of rubber and steel.

As it was, he swerved in the nick of time and paused, reeling, thinking about what happened. He had done it! He had scared that sumbitch into paroxysms of terror and now Sheriff Bud Tarfunkle was going to retire in the lap of luxury as was befitting a man who had put his best years into keeping society on the straight and narrow and now all he had to do was wait for his idiot son to coordinate upon this very location with a new tractor and haul off into the very goldest of sunsets.

"So, you're sure you doxxed the Sheriff properly, John," said Iceman, admiration in her eyes. "We don't want that video going to the wrong address."

John just smiled. He was relaxed in a way he hadn't felt since childhood. "Oh, this is going to be great. By this time tomorrow, every message board on the planet is going to know about Sheriff Tarfunkle. He's going to be famous."

"So, Stranger, where are they?"

"Where are who, Fat Man?"

"You know damn well what I'm talking about. This outcome wasn't what had been agreed upon."

"No, it's better."

"Oh?"

"Think about it, fatty, you'd never pin human trafficking charges on that sheriff, his defense would be all about he was saving them from the likes of me. Now, finding him in sole possession of four hundred kilos of Austin Green Limit across state lines is much more likely to stick, wouldn't you agree?"

"Perhaps... but what about your reward?"

"Ah, yes, what about that reward. Seems rather odd that a bunch of desperate border-jumping children would be tagged with RFID chips that originated in China and were manufactured according to a spec here in the States. Would be a pity if they were to turn state's evidence, especially after they've all given sworn testimony to my rather sizable cadre of lawyers. Some of those descriptions just happen to include a very tall fat man and a very short angry man both wearing suits of an objectionable nature."

Stranger heard a gurgle that might have been swearwords and several species of curses she was not familiar with, but pressed on with her attack.

"No, I think your idea of a 'reward' was to get me and the sheriff in equal amounts of trouble and my hat's off to you boys for the weight class of your collective brass ball tonnage but Stranger, well, she don't want any part of that."

"What *do* you want, then?"

"To be left alone, Yankee."

Stranger terminated the call and threw the burner phone into the fire. The plastic and metal and glass began to pop and fizz and the smoke rose into the evening sky. Embers danced and further away from the fire, there was more dancing and the laughter of children.

"Hey," said John Henry, sipping on a beer, "*I'm* a Yankee."

"Yes, but you're cute," Stranger replied, pointing her bottle at him. "And clever. Setting up that call to so it looks like I'm in Cuba was inspired."

"Think they'll come after you?"

Stranger pressed her lips to the bottle's mouth and thought on John's words. It had been manic panic from the moment of switching the kids for as much marijuana as John could gather from every medical collective and head shop buddy he had any pull with. The cause was just but expensive; she'd have to sell off the rodeo, but that was fine. It was feeling more and more like a good time to retire.

Besides, there was the clean-up happening all over Iceman's neighborhood. The rescued kids were industrious once their belly's were full and loved Iceman's gadgets. Stranger was sure Iceman was going to adopt every single one of them, and that was going to be expensive, too. A silver lining had suddenly began to shine, perhaps living in a disaster area that nobody wanted was just what was needed in the moment. She'd grown up with tales of people going to Mars and starting whole new civilizations there. Why not take all that gumption and start again, here, in the spots of the world that no one wanted to admit existed any more. The bits that were to be swept away as soon as was convenient. There would be new challenges ahead, not the least of which was John Henry staring at Iceman's backside every chance he could between bong hits.

Stranger looked out at Iceman dancing with children and clapping her hands with the beat of the music playing over the PA. The beer was cold. The night was young. Corporate authority had been snubbed, and one nasty county-mounty was going down. All in all it had been fun.

"Come after me?" She swallowed the beer. "Stranger things have happened."

EPILOGUE

A white-walled room tastefully arranged with peace lilies and almost-comfortable chairs was empty, save for the dry, almost-cool air moving fitfully through the room… The red digital clock on one wall transitioned to indicate 9AM

"Well, here we are," said a Voice in the ceiling.

After a time a second Voice, slightly smaller than the first, asked, "Why?"

*We return to the noir side of town in our next story. Drones,
nano-trackers, and virtual coins are tools in Ted Decker's
profession. He'll send out a drone to salt your driveway or
take out a competitor, as long as the client can pay their bill.*

*Mr. Castlewitz retired from a life of technology to write,
with numerous short stories published in the past few years.*

At Play in the Land Around

by David Castlewitz

Ted Deker didn't take over-the-counter kill orders. A potential
client couldn't just walk into Deker's shop and order a hit like
they'd order a drone to spray their lawn or salt ice in the driveway.

But sometimes they did. Sometimes they approached the long
counter that separated the public from the private areas of Ted's
shop, tapped the "for service" bell or called, "Hey! Anyone?" or
otherwise made a bid for his attention and when he gave it to them
they usually got right to the point.

Like this woman in the wide brimmed hat that sloped down
the back of her neck. She said, "I need someone killed."

"We don't do that," Ted told her, and flipped his long brown
hair away from the front of his face. Already, sweat wet his under-
arms, some of it dribbling visibly from his tee-shirt sleeves in tiny
beads that chased the blue veins in his thick upper arms.

"I heard otherwise." Gloved hands gripped the counter, each
long finger outlined by tight stitching that culminated in an intri-

cate pattern of circles and curls at the tops of the hands. A sweet smell emanated from the woman, which matched the pert shape of her lips, which glistened red and daring, as daring as her question.

A veil shielded her eyes and thin nose, and accented her appeal. A calculated stance, Ted decided and said, "We got a service, like tracking someone or chasing off annoying drones somebody's using to harass you, or spraying fertilizer or something, but we don't do anything illegal."

"You're blushing, young man."

Ted grinned. The woman lifted her veil and stuffed it along the top of the hat's brim. He felt her taking his measure with her dark eyes, assessing his look, deciding, he thought, if he was merely the scruffy guy behind the counter or someone more important. He expected she'd ask to speak to the owner and then he'd suck in a deep breath, fashion a huge smile, and tell her he owned the shop.

The woman's long dress rustled when she moved, her slinky sleeves bunching around her elbows, which she set against the counter's edge, her legs spread and her butt slightly in the air. A not-very-lady-like pose, Ted thought.

"Someone's trying to kill me," she said. Purred. A velvet voice complete with flashing eyelashes and wet red lips. A small smile accented a tiny dimple in one cheek. "I told Acey Macey and he recommended you." She lifted a minute white purse hanging by a silver cord around her narrow waist. She extracted a card.

"You should've said so right away," Ted said when he looked at Acey's business card, which advertised his bar and its backroom clubs. "OK" , circled, appeared in the center, which meant she wasn't a nut job. Acey had vetted her.

Ted reached under the counter and pulled out a laminated rate sheet. The same thing appeared on the shop's web site, but Ted thought the old-fashioned white cardboard with its glossy finish added a touch of class.

The woman glanced at the rates printed in bold sans-serif type centered between two Doric-like columns on either edge of the card. Prices varied depending on the degree of service. Simple harassment, the cheapest, was the most popular and displayed the legend, "85% of people selected this option."

"Acey said you'd kill him."

Of course. Because Acey would get a 10% commission and that meant ten large in his pocket.

"A question," Ted posed, "Why?"

"Because he's trying to kill me."

"And he… he is…?"

"My husband," the woman said. "George Wellington."

Ted expelled a breath. Now he understood the meaning of the sloping wide-brimmed hat, the lacey white veil and the rustling long dress, the gloves and the dangling gold earrings and everything else about this woman who'd walked into his shop.

"Mrs. Wellington," Ted said, though he hadn't meant to say anything at all. He'd meant to continue staring, piecing this together. The Wellingtons were extreme cosplayers known for elaborate costume parties and city-wide reenactments of famous events. They staged scenes ripped from old newspaper headlines and films popular a hundred years ago. They lived virtual lives and millions of people followed their exploits on Birdsong and Pagelooks and PeepersOfCourse and a dozen other social media sites.

"Myra," the woman said. "Lansburg. I use my own name. I am my own person."

"Are you sure you want your husband killed? Is he really trying to kill you first? Or is this some kind of virtual thing, you know, an enhanced reality killing?"

Myra put a gloved finger to her red lips, which left a lipstick smudge on the white cotton. "He's for real." She nodded in the direction of the front door. A teen-aged boy and an older man— father and son?—had entered and stood at a display case showing off the store's hobby-style drones.

Backing away, Myra said, "I'll email you all the details. Encrypted, of course."

"What's the password?" Ted asked.

Myra veiled her face. "You'll know it."

The teen's eyes followed Myra as she left the store, and the father also turned to watch her go, a note of envy in his long face.

———————————

Ted gave the job of cracking Myra's encrypted email to Grouper, his single employee, who traded casual labor for living space in a basement room behind rows of metal shelves holding boxed hobby drones, helicopters, and miscellaneous parts ranging from propellers to geared motors to RC modules. Grouper worked silently, hunched over a laptop keyboard kept more immaculate than he kept himself. No caked-on food remnants or splashes of liquid at the edges; no dust or stains or nicks or coils of knotted hair. Grouper wiped carefully, sprayed diligently and used a paper napkin when he ate.

"It's Myra," he announced, coughing out the words. "The password. Myra." He swung his flabby arms above his head and clasped his hands, his stubby fingers interlocked.

"Didn't we try that?" Ted asked.

"Capital M," Grouper said. He pushed on the edge of the table and his wheeled stool scooted backwards. "Check it out."

Ted looked at the screen. "Can you forward it?"

"Check the holo-link."

Ted tapped the screen's display of black-on-white collection of squiggles inside a double-edged rectangle. A moment passed. He pictured wires lining up, snapping together, waving in response to a fast-paced song. The holo-stand next to the laptop vibrated and a figure appeared.

George Wellington emerged. Blue eyes. Blonde beard covering cheeks and chin. According to cosplay sites, Wellington enjoyed a large following. He led virtual treks through South American jungles, hikes along the Great Western Ridge, explorations of the New York City tunnels and canoe trips to the lakes of the North Woods. Wellington preached the virtues of what he called "ultra-life" as well as the need to play at being "not who you are."

On the holo-stand, Wellington offered an animated curricula vitae—ACV—that sounded to Ted like the recitation of a life well-led. No apologies for fame or fortune. No self-doubt in this man.

In the past, Ted took kill orders for business rivals intent on destroying one another any way possible. He killed abusive husbands, miscreant wives. He unleashed drones to hunt down and annihilate politicians that other politicians deemed dangerous. He never took sides in anyone's dispute. He provided a service that subsidized the less dramatic aspects of his business. The shop didn't make much money catering to hobbyists or taking on driveway-salting contracts or lawn-care agreements.

"I have to wonder," Ted said aloud, "why Myra Lansburg wants to kill this guy."

"Who's Lansburg?" Grouper asked.

"She uses her maiden name," Ted said.

Grouper poked his large head forward, his round shoulders rising. "I dug a bit deeper than what the email gave us." He tapped the keyboard and brought up another holo-link.

Wellington dissolved and a couple dressed in expensive evening clothes took the stage. They looked like a pair of on-the-town-party-goers from a 1940-ish movie. Ted expected them to burst into song.

"That's not Myra." Ted pointed at the holographic couple.

"That's his girlfriend," Grouper said.

So Myra had a motive. Ted wondered why he cared. If Myra could pay his fee, and if he could get away with a drone strike without the police nailing him, then what difference did it make why she wanted to waste her philandering husband. She didn't need motivation, Ted told himself. She just needed enough bitters, the underground coinage he preferred for these jobs, to make the effort worth his time.

Settling back in the taxi's comfortable rear seat, Ted perused his emails, reading the subject headings, not the content. The steady whirling sound of the car's motors drummed in his head. The taxi zipped along the highway, in a fast automatic lane, inches behind the car ahead before signaling and then scooting sideways into the exit lane when the cars to its right made space.

The driver steered onto a manual off-ramp, his head pressed against the beads draping the back of his seat. Various religious symbols, ranging from a rubber statue of a saint to a dangling icon representing a sect Ted didn't recognize, decorated the dashboard. Something about the superstitious nature of this driver—his regular now for several years—comforted Ted. If anything went wrong, the gods would be with them.

Ted checked his V-Ring account, annoyed by the old-fashioned animated gold rings floating across the phone's black screen. Somebody's idea of "cute," Ted thought, and waited while the shiny rings floated onto finger-like towers indicating his bank balance. Myra hadn't sent in the ten thousand V-Ring down payment, which he'd back with a phony invoice for a fully assembled, high-flying eight-engine drone filled with all the bells and whistles, including autonomous flight, that warranted the high price.

He slipped his phone into his breast pocket. They skirted the city wall, past a portal where police checked incoming passengers for work permits or other identification that allowed them entry. Living in the city-proper had its advantages, though they were costly. For what Ted paid for his lakefront apartment he could have a two-story palace in the suburbs, albeit with a long daily commute.

He reached his shop in the dingy strip mall and exited the taxi. Hovering drones floated overhead and Ted wondered if they'd been dispatched to follow his taxi. He knew he was of interest to his rivals, the police, and the city's private security types.

"Hey, Gonzie," Ted said to his driver as he waved his phone at the meter. "Have a goodie."

Gonzie—Gonzales—raised a dark hand in acknowledgment and rolled into traffic.

Ted unlocked the shop's front door and set the entry chimes in case an early morning browser came by. Hardly anyone wandered in before noon, but Ted didn't discount the possibility. Downstairs, he found Grouper hunched over a screen, Reality-Augment-Goggles—RAGs—across his eyes, the black band lost in the unruly dark curls at the back of his head.

"Gave up on lenses?" Ted remarked.

"I don't like things on my eyeballs," Grouper mumbled, his hands moving as though wrestling with something in his game.

Ted activated a laptop. "Myra still hasn't sent in her deposit," he said, once more looking at his bank statement. Five days had gone by. Not that he'd done any work on her case. No effort expended. Still, he liked the idea of a hundred large piling up in an offshore bank. It would pay for a vacation aboard a rented yacht, with stops at the South Atlantic Isles or some other exotic location.

"Not surprised," Grouper said. "You see today's news?" He waved his hands in front of his face and pulled his goggles away from his eyes. Game on pause. "Check the feed," he said.

Ted switched to the morning news, which scrolled across his laptop's screen in a jumble of pictures. The caption under one of them said, "Leading Extremer Killed."

Extreme cosplayer, Ted translated, and tapped the photograph, which expanded to an aerial view of carnage on the highway. A newscaster narrated. Something had gone wrong with the automatic lane. Authorities vowed to investigate. For an as-yet-unknown reason, Myra Lansburg's private car had stalled and a truck failed to stop before plowing into her vehicle and crushing it.

"When?" Ted mumbled to himself. He scanned the details in the side panel to find the answer. Last night. Late. Actually, early this morning. Very early. Sitting back, one thought paraded across his mind. She'd been right. Someone—her husband? – had wanted to kill her. Automatic highways didn't break down. Lanes didn't make mistakes. Cars never collided. When they did, it wasn't by accident.

"Good news," Grouper announced.

Ted shot him a glance. What could be good about Myra's murder? About losing a kill order?

Grouper said, "Some school in Indiana just bought a twelve-pack of quads. All with embedded processors. Maybe that's not a hundred thousand in cryps—" Cryptbits: Grouper's preferred currency—"but it's three thousand legitimate V-Rings."

"Thanks," Ted muttered, still sad about Myra and the lost opportunity.

The upstairs chime registered in his brain, but not immediately, and Ted wondered how long it had been sounding before he recognized it. Once upstairs, he rubbed his face in an effort to look like an affable clerk, and entered the store.

Myra?

No. Not Myra. Of course not she. But almost. Dark brown hair. Short. Turned up and in around the ears and the back of the neck. Same long body. Same angular face, too.

"Don't look so startled. I'm her sister." The young woman extended a slender hand, her fingernails glistening. "Laura."

Ted swallowed. Laura leaned against the counter, her dark blouse sparkling. "I just saw the news flash," he said. "I'm sorry. What happened?"

"What happened?" Laura echoed. "He got his way, that's what's happened. Deker, right?"

"Ted."

"I'm Laura. But I told you that. Okay. Here's what's going to happen now, Ted. We're getting our revenge. Oh yeah. That's the way of it now."

Caught in her dark gray eyes, Ted stood with his hands at his sides, his mouth slightly open, staring at his visitor, seeing Myra in the angles of Laura's face and then not seeing her.

"Laura," he croaked, and then cleared his throat. "Revenge?"

"George killed her. You think freak accidents just happen?"

Ted shook his head.

"He killed her," Laura reiterated. "Now we kill him."

Ted breathed deeply, slowly, steadied himself with his fingertips gripping a shelf under the counter. Laura moved closer. He tasted something metallic and indefinable in the air, with a sweet undercurrent that made him want to sniff to get more of the aroma.

Calming himself, he said, "It's a business transaction with me."

"Is it? No personal interest, Ted?"

He shook his head.

She pressed her body against the counter and extended a finger that touched Ted's chin. Up close, he saw a small dimple in her left cheek, tiny craters in her face. The imperfections added to her beauty and something fluid and hot and urgent filled his chest. He fought it. He stepped back, back from the long finger and her touch and the close heat from her body.

Laura smiled, glossy lips parting and white-as-white-can-be teeth glistening. "I need your help, Ted. Just a little."

"I've a firm rule," Ted said.

Laura shrugged. The smile vanished. "How much?"

"Ten thousand V-Rings."

"I only deal in American. Dollars. U.S."

Ted never accepted country-backed currencies, even if backed by his own country. Too chancy. "Do the conversion. Make the payment. That's when I go to work." Could he trust Laura to pay up? Did he want to see Myra's murderer killed in return?

"There's a memorial tomorrow," Laura said. "An excellent time to go in for the kill."

"I'll be the judge of that," Ted said.

"Lots of people," she said. "You'll blend in with the crowd."

Ted suddenly sensed that Laura didn't understand. He wouldn't commit the murder himself. He had drones to do that. A drone to swoop close, take aim, and fire a kill shot. And then speed off.

"I'll be there," Laura said. "Perhaps with an extra reward just for you." She blew him a kiss and walked out of the store, her high-heeled shoes clicking against the linoleum.

"Weird," Ted whispered. He turned to a laptop bolted to the wall. A tap on the screen brought up an image of Grouper sitting at his workbench, immersed once again in a reality-augmented game.

"What? What?" Grouper complained, waving his hands and then whipping off his goggles.

"Get a fix on Wellington's home," Ted said. "And send an Obie."

"Okay, boss. You got it."

Ted wallowed in self-criticism. He never started a job without a down payment. But Laura intrigued him; and Myra's death wasn't an accident. He wanted to kill Wellington even if he wasn't paid, but those thoughts prompted a new round of self-criticism and he promised no real work until the down payment comes in. Launching an Obie—an observer—merely satisfied his curiosity. I'm allowed to be curious, he told himself. When he said the same thing to Grouper, he heard back:

"You're the boss. Do what you want."

Ted stood behind his employee and peered over his shoulder at a large flat screen showing what the Obie saw. Now and then, a whiff of rancid air puffed up from Grouper and Ted fought it off with a squeeze of Good-Flower spray he kept in a pants pocket.

The screen didn't show much. Blue sky. Black dots that could be far off airplanes or not-so-far drones like Obie. Grouper manipulated a joystick and the scene slowly shifted, ragged and jerking because of the transmission speed. The above-ground aerial view featured a highway clogged with fast-moving cars, nearly bumper-to-bumper, breaking apart when another car needed to merge.

Soon, a sprawling residential complex behind a high wrought-iron fence came into view. A few cars moved away from the complex. None went in.

"Get closer," Ted urged, and Grouper sent the Obie down for a better look. The outgoing cars were vans bearing legends describing several different caterers. Desserts. Meats. Artisan breads. They were getting ready for the upcoming memorial, setting up a feast to commemorate Myra's death.

Ted corrected himself. Memorialize her life.

"Too bad we ain't got a military drone," Grouper said. "We could get him in his car."

Ted pursed his lips. Too bad. But which car would be his? None of these. "We don't even know if he leaves the compound. Get closer. Let's look in the windows."

The first rule of murder, Ted thought, had to do with identifying the subject. Then, the place where one can strike. Third: the time. These took prep-work. He sometimes spent days observing, planning. When he sent in a killer drone, he wanted the first strike to be the only strike. Sloppy killers had to pursue their subjects more than once. Ted never did a sloppy job. Measure twice; cut once. A motto he'd acquired as a boy, though he couldn't recall from where.

A teardrop shaped pool with a wide deck littered with beach chairs, tables and umbrellas glistened in the sun. Reflections from the nearby house spoke of large glass windows . The Obie dipped low. The windows came into view. Tinted, they didn't let the drone's cameras peek in.

"There," Grouper said, pointing at an upper balcony. The Obie rose, slanting away from the two-story house to give a full view of the structure with its many balconies and glass windows, its flat roof adorned by sunlight collectors for generating electricity and dish antennas pointing in different directions.

Two forms appeared in a second floor balcony. The Obie drew closer, brought the nebulous bodies into focus. Two men. Talking. Gesticulating. Neither had the distinctive blonde beard that Ted saw when he viewed Wellington's hologram.

"Company," Grouper said. Two dark intruders rapidly took shape against the blue sky. Another lifted off from a shed near a clump of trees.

"Get out of there," Ted said, a tremor to his voice. If the other drones forced this Obie to land, somebody might find something to trace it to his shop. And then, when Wellington was killed, someone might find Ted's fingers in this pie.

Get in. Get out. That's how Ted handled these things.

Three drones blocked the Obie's flight path. Grouper yanked on the joystick. He growled. The Obie went into an upward spiral. Flame burst nearby. A ball of fire erupted from ground level and the scene went black.

Ted stared at the empty screen. While the three drones had their attention an anti-drone ground unit evidently moved into position and launched a missile.

"Ain't gotta worry about any tracers," Grouper said. "That sucker blew our Obie apart."

Ted skipped ahead to what this meant. Wellington had protection. Ground-based missiles and aerial surveillance. Probably contracted with one of Ted's rivals. The only way to get to him would be by long-distance. That meant planting a bug on him to act as a homing beacon. Add another twenty thousand in costs. With the destruction of the Obie, Ted had already lost a hefty lump of change.

Which is why, he reminded himself, he shouldn't start a job without the requisite down payment.

"I guess I'm going to the memorial," Ted said.

Grouper swiveled on his stool, his meaty hands on his knees, a "You sure?" look on his grizzled face.

"It's personal now," Ted said, and pictured the Obie blowing up in midair.

———————

A pedicab took Ted to a Blue Dot stand where he could hire a taxi authorized to travel outside the city. He'd easily found the details regarding Myra's memorial. BirdSong and Pagelooks both advertised it as the "Myra Event" and provided two-dimensional maps along with a 3-D ride-along holo-app for self-drivers.

Something about the event troubled Ted as he rode out of the city, the oblong lights of the tunnel zipping past. Soon, he emerged on the suburban side and the taxi climbed an access ramp to the highway. Below, a line of private cars waited at the Metropol Gate while border police checked credentials, with small attack drones milling about while foot patrolmen walked from car to car, laser-slapping virtual decals on those that could pass, signaling others to a turnoff for further inspection and questioning.

The mansion Ted had seen from the destroyed observer drone the day before rose in the distant, distinctly white, like frosting, against a pale blue sky. When the taxi drew closer, electronic signs flashed directions and black-clad attendants—not holograms, Ted noted—steered traffic to parking spots. Cars filled an open lawn, with overhead drones helping line them up, leaving space in the lanes so drivers could pull out. White taxis with the large blue circle on their roofs—blue dots—disgorged passengers near the mansion's front steps

Hundreds of people, many of them dressed for mourning— severely cut jackets and trousers, long dresses, jump suits and thick robes over obviously naked bodies—milled outside the mansion's entrance on the long marble steps, at the stone columns supporting the porch roof, near the open double doors.

Ted paid his driver with a wave of his phone, and scooted out of the car and into the throng of people. He hadn't dressed for the part. His plain linen shirt and suede vest, along with non-descript trousers, didn't mark him as a mourner come to pay his respects. He looked like one of the deliverymen.

A small young woman with a "Love Myra" hologram project-ing from her slinky black shirt stopped him at the mansion's door. She held goggles in one hand, plastic-wrapped contact lenses in the other.

"One V-Ring," she said.

Ted glanced into the house. Glasses tinkled and conversation buzzed in a large foyer, and a crowd jostled one another around a huge room just beyond an arch decorated with black crepe. Some people wore RAGs—the goggles that Grouper preferred. Ted indicated the lenses in the girl's left hand and held up his phone. A distinct "Ka-Ching" sounded.

"Cute," Ted said. Plastic wrappers littered the marble floor. A small vacuum-bot rolled around, bumping into people's feet as it dutifully collected the refuse. With the lenses in place on his eyeball, Ted saw much more than he had when he stood on the threshold to the foyer. Scores of holographic figures mingled with the mourners, engaging them in conversation, leading a chant, performing a slow and solemn dance.

In a niche in the stairwell a holographic flame burned beneath a pyre with an inert body that Ted assumed represented Myra. Everywhere, at the base of the steps and in the sunken living-room, people and holograms engaged one another while small trays full of mini-sandwiches and veggie-sticks and other hors d'oeuvres floated in the air.

Now, how to tag George Wellington. Ted expected a receiving line and had imagined he'd touch the man's shoulder and place a microscopic pod that would creep surreptitiously through fabric and then burrow under the man's skin. There, the pod would release nano-plasts programmed to build a homing beacon.

An expensive solution to the problem of pin-pointing Wellington's whereabouts, but also a foolproof one. It would be only a matter of launching an attack drone and firing a bullet-sized missile to target the beacon. Even if the mansion's defenses detected the attacker, they'd never stop the missile.

Ted's phone buzzed. He checked the screen. The message icon flashed, then shook, and a wagging finger indicated a degree of urgency.

He opened the message.

And blinked. Smiled a little, amused. Frowned, because what he saw wasn't funny. The message was from his bank and banks didn't make jokes.

He put the phone away and looked around for Myra's sister. Most likely, she'd be next to Wellington greeting sympathizers.

Myra walked by.

A few seconds passed before Ted realized she was a hologram. A few people—or were these holographic projections as well—engaged "Myra" in conversation.

Someone stopped in front of Ted and said, "Are you family or friend?"

Ted peered into the speaker's pale gray eyes. A real person, he surmised. Possibly male, though he couldn't tell by the black robe, the orange wig of wild curls atop the person's head, and the smooth round face and small mouth.

"Friend," Ted said. "Is there a receiving line for Wellington?"

The stranger's head tilted sideways in a gesture of, "I don't understand."

Ted tried to ask in a different way. "I want to extend my sympathies."

"Did you know her well?"

Not at all, Ted thought. Near the ceiling floated still images of Myra. A few showed her wedding ceremony. Others showed her on horseback or playing tennis. In all of them, she smiled, she laughed; a happy person enjoying her life.

"I want to find George," Ted said to the stranger, thinking that using the man's first name would give him credibility as a friend of the family.

"He's floating around somewhere," the stranger said, and sauntered off.

Need to find Laura as well, Ted told himself. Have her explain her little joke with the bank. She'd paid him in game currency. Some joke. The bank charged his account for a bad deposit. Once upstairs, he gravitated to the edge of the room, keeping the large glass doors on one side as his target. That had to be the way out to a patio. Perhaps Wellington occupied space in the garden, surrounded by flowers offered in tribute to his dead wife.

No. The glass doors accessed an outdoor kitchen set up by the caterers. Uniformed servants—all black, tight-fitting jumpsuits—set food on trays carried off by hover-bots transparent enough that it looked like the trays themselves floated in air.

Inside, near the doors, a traditional table with black crepe and a black satin drop-cloth offered bins full of salads and meats, along with plastic utensils, cups, and platters. A few people stood blocking access to the food while others—some not as polite as Ted thought they should—pushed their way closer to the table.

Out of the corner of his eye, Ted saw movement along the narrow walkway that ran the perimeter of the room, halfway to the ceiling and accessible by a winding staircase guarded by two burly men in black suit-and-tie. Open doorways led to various upstairs rooms. The moving figure that Ted turned to watch more intently skirted the doorways, long black hair flying behind her, arms up, bare feet slapping the floorboards, ankle length gown slit to reveal slender bare legs with every other step.

Myra?

A cosplayer dressed as the dead woman, Ted assumed. Yes. Now that he looked, he saw others in lengthy black gowns, with dark wigs in tribute to Myra. Any George Wellingtons, Ted wondered.

"You came!"

Ted spun around. Words sputtered from his lips. He knew he didn't make sense. He was too angry about that message from his bank.

Laura smiled. Same angular face. Same dimpled chin. But something different—the hair, he realized. Laura wore a wig in tribute to her sister.

A miniature Myra grew from the holographic pin on her black crepe dress

Ted leaned close to her. "Why the joke with the down payment for your… your project?"

She raised a narrow glass and sipped. "Enjoying yourself? Myra loves a party."

"Do you want to explain why you sent me Doughies as a down payment?" Ted asked, ready to grab Laura's skinny arm if she tried to get away.

"We always pay with Doughies," she answered.

"That's game money, Laura. It's not real. I want V-Rings. The bank's charging me a fee for your little joke."

"That's the economy for you," she said, laughing and drinking.

"I came here," Ted began, but then stopped and sucked in a deep breath, clenched his fists and stared into Laura's bright blue eyes. That was something else about her, he realized. She had dark eyes and dark shadows around them when she came to the shop.

Ted wetted his lips. He wanted to drink something.

"I'm willing to put out a certain amount of effort," he said, "but you need to meet me halfway. Sending me game-gelt doesn't work for me."

"It's how I pay all my bills. If your bank won't accept it, then you need a Faux-Account."

"What's that?"

"You don't know anything about Play-Around-Land."

Ted swallowed. Laura referred to a game he'd only heard about, but it wasn't something he'd ever looked into. He wasn't an Extremer, not a cosplayer creating a phony life to make up for boredom or regret or doubt or any of the other maladies to which the wealthy might succumb.

"You're playing?" Ted said. "This is all a game?" He removed the reality-augmenting lenses, crushed them in his hand. The holograms dissolved, like lights going out all at once. No flaming pyres in wall niches. No parade of still images depicting Myra's life.

"Welcome to my world," Laura said, and waved her skinny arms about, some of her drink spilling from the tall narrow glass.

"Is Wellington real?"

Laura grinned. "He's as real as my sister."

"And she's… " Ted's voice trailed off.

"Do I sound like her now?" Laura said, her voice velvet smooth and deep. She blinked. Her dark eyes returned. She touched her cheeks and shadows appeared beneath her eyes. Her face took on the angular look that seemed so distinct the way Myra wore it.

"Implants." Ted exhaled the word. "But the news? The accident?" Then he realized, the things Grouper dug up about George Wellington came from a Play-Around-Land site. Grouper didn't know the difference between real and cosplay.

"News isn't hard to inject into the feed," Laura said. "I kill off one sister or brother every now and then, and then we have a party and the players take the part of family and we're all so very, very happy."

Ted didn't react. Laura touched her face and blinked and her bright blue eyes returned.

"Enjoy." She flitted away, dropped her now-drained glass on a floating tray, took a full glass of sparkling liquid from a passing server-bot, and struck up a conversation with an older man and woman, the latter reminiscent of the George Wellington hologram Ted had seen and the former a slightly aged Myra Lansburg, her long dark locks turned gray.

A cosplay couple.

Ted stepped towards Laura. He put a hand on her shoulder.

"What?" she asked.

"Nothing," Ted said, but then moved close and kissed Laura's cheek.

"Now, aren't you a dear," she said in response, and kissed him back, on both cheeks, before darting off, drink in hand.

Ted left the mansion and found a Blue Dot at the end of the curved driveway, in a lot reserved for waiting taxis. Mentally, he tallied the cost of this ventured, discounting the one V-Ring charge to enter the mansion, the fee his bank would charge him for the game-gelt Laura sent, and the cost of the round-trip taxi ride.

He'd lost a lot more by losing the Obie shot down by the mansion's security net. And he'd just expended more than ten thousand by planting a homer on Laura's shoulder. At some point, perhaps when she tired of her game world and went cosplaying in the city, when she didn't expect to be targeted, he'd launch a drone and get even.

Ted played in the real world, a world more deadly than Laura's virtual playground.

The first day on a new job can be a whirlwind of introductions and information and it's no wonder that the protagonist of our next story feels a bit overwhelmed. Then again, the company for whom he has gone to work, has some very interesting departments. This story was previously published in Nebula Rift, in 2013.

Mr. Carvalho despairs of clichés and stereotypes wherein new technology spawns disasters, and sequels. He feels that if we mock them, perhaps they will deflate, and trouble us no longer.

Voice of Reason

by Spencer Carvalho

Chris waited in the lobby of Unicron Inc. for around ten minutes until his guide showed up. Jack walked out of the elevator toward Chris.

"Uh, hi," said Jack. "Are you Chris, Chris Johnson?"

"Yeah," said Chris.

"I was told about five minutes ago that I should give you a tour of the building."

"Okay."

"I was told that you manage systems or something?"

"It's a desk job.

"Okay, well I'll show you around some of the different sections here at Unicron Inc. and then we'll figure out where you'll be working. Sound good?"

"Yeah, sure."

Chris followed Jack into the elevator. Jack pushed the button for floor number three.

"Here at Unicron Inc. we make just about everything from depression medication to razor blades."

"That seems like a conflict of interests."

The elevator doors opened and Chris saw a giant Plexiglas wall with water on the other side of it.

"This place has a pool?" asked Chris.

A giant great white shark passed by the glass.

"What the hell was that?" asked Chris.

"Come on, I'll show you."

Jack walked up a metal stairway. Chris walked up to the Plexiglas and watched a shark with a scar near its eye swim by. Chris knocked on the glass. The shark turned around to stare at Chris. They locked eyes and the shark seemed to stare at Chris with anger. Chris ran up the stairway to catch up with Jack.

At the top of the stairs Chris saw some scientists in white lab coats milling around the outer area of a large aquarium that took up most of the floor. There were metal platforms against all the walls with water taking up the majority of the floor. In the center of the room was a circular metal platform connected by a small bridge that lead to where Jack and Chris were standing. They started walking across the bridge.

"Here at Unicron we're working very carefully on trying to create new Alzheimer's medication," said Jack. "That's why we do experiments on these sharks."

"Hold on. I need to make sure I understand this. You have a giant aquarium filled with sharks. How many sharks?"

"We have four sharks. There's Jaws, Jaws 2, Jaws 3-D, and Jaws: The Revenge, he's the worst of the group. He's really mean. He's the one with a scar near his eye."

They reached the circular platform.

"What kind of experiments do you perform on these sharks?" asked Chris.

"We injected them with a serum that ended up making them super smart."

"You injected these sharks with a serum that made them super smart?" asked Chris.

"That's correct."

"You don't see anything wrong with that? What if these sharks try to kill their captors?"

"I wouldn't worry about that. There are all sorts of safety features that can easily be accessed through this control panel."

Chris looked around the giant aquarium.

"You mean this control panel which can only be reached by crossing a rickety bridge surrounded by sharks?"

"That's correct."

A shark fin poked out of the water and started circling them.

"One of the sharks gave me a stern look when I tapped on the glass."

"Yeah, they really hate that. The lead scientist who used to perform experiments on them used to do that too."

"Where is he?"

"He had a… an accident."

Jack looked down at his feet for a moment of silence.

"Let's check out the human testing area," said Jack.

Jack and Chris walked back to the elevator. As the elevator doors closed Chris thought he saw the super intelligent shark sneer at him.

The elevator doors opened on floor five and Jack and Chris exited.

"This is where we do the human testing," said Jack. "People, usually college students, sign up for our medical experiments."

They walked into a lab where scientists were watching test subjects through a two-way mirror. Jack walked up to one of the scientists.

"Hi, Doctor Tyler," said Jack. "What are you up to today?"

"We're working on a new cold medicine but we've been having some problems with it. It's been making the test subjects extremely drowsy."

"Can we take a look?"

"Sure, sure. C'mon."

They went over to one of the windows. On the other side was a man walking around sluggishly. A scientist with a clipboard was making notes as he watched the test subject.

"This guy is named... hey, Dave, what's this guy's name?"

Dave checks his clipboard.

"They didn't give us their names, just numbers."

"Then what's his number?" asked Dr. Tyler.

"Patient zero."

"Well, patient zero here has been testing our brand new cold medicine. The chemicals that cause drowsiness must be too strong because he's been staggering around and moaning for a while now. He also must be feeling sick because, as you can see, his skin has been turning green."

They looked at patient zero and saw a green skinned guy staggering around and moaning. Dr. Tyler tapped on the glass. Patient zero started staggering over to the glass.

"He's been really moody too. He keeps trying to bite me."

Chris looked at Dr. Tyler in a stunned and alert manner.

"He's been trying to bite you?" asked Chris.

"That is correct."

"You mean like a zombie?"

Dr. Tyler looked to Jack and laughed.

"It's good to see that the new guy has a sense of humor," he said.

Patient zero started pawing at the glass.

"You know it's really good to have a sense of humor in this work environment. It keeps things interesting. This job can get pretty boring."

Patient zero started licking the glass.

"Gross," said Dr. Tyler. "Hey, Dave, deal with this for me."

Dave grabbed some glass cleaner and a cloth. He entered the room.

"The test subjects can be so weird sometimes," said Dr. Tyler.

Patient zero attacked Dave.

"This one time we had a guy who..."

Dave ran out of the room and closed the door behind him.

"He bit me," said Dave.

"I'll call security," said Dr. Tyler. "Let me see that bite."

Dave showed Dr. Tyler the bite.

"It looks pretty bad," said Dr. Tyler. "You should go home for the rest of the day and get some rest."

"Yay, a half day," said Dave.

"No, he shouldn't," said Chris. "He should be quarantined."

"Don't ruin my half day," said Dave.

"Hey, let's check out the next floor," said Jack.

They walked to the elevator and got in but before the doors closed, Chris yelled out to Dr. Tyler, "Aim for the head."

They went up to the sixth floor.

"This floor is actually shared by two different teams," said Jack.

They walked around. There was a yellow piece of tape across the ground that spanned the length of the entire floor.

"One team is working on backpacks and the other team is working on equipment for model rockets," said Jack.

"That's a weird combination."

"I told you we make everything here."

Chris looked around the room and noticed something. On the model rocket side of the room there were a variety of different jets.

"What's with all the jets?" asked Chris.

"They're working on creating better jets for the rockets."

Chris looked at one side of the room and then looked at the other. He looked at the side of the room making jets and then looked over to the side making backpacks.

"So one side is making jets and the other side is making backpacks?" asked Chris.

"That's right."

"One side is making… jets and the other is making… backpacks."

"Uh huh."

"Jets and backpacks. Jets… and packs."

"Yes."

"This is a real chocolate in my peanut butter situation."

"What are you talking about?"

"Couldn't these two teams work together and make jetpacks?"

Everything in the lab stopped. The scientists all looked up from what they were doing and looked at Chris. Then they all looked at each other.

"Oh, my god," said one of the scientists. "How have we never thought of that?"

"Let's move on to the next floor," said Jack.

They moved up to the tenth floor.

"On this floor they work on construction equipment."

Chris stared in amazement at the large machinery in the room. It was a large robotic device in the shape of a human body. One of the designers went up to them and shook Chris's hand.

"My name is Dan. Do you have any questions?"

"Yeah, what is that thing?"

"It is a mechanized construction unit."

"You mean a mech?"

"That's one possible abbreviation."

"A mech, like in *Aliens*?"

"For legal reasons I have no idea what you're talking about."

Chris looked around the room and saw posters for *Aliens*, *The Empire Strikes Back*, *The Matrix Revolutions*, *Avatar*, and *District 9*.

"So, what does it do?" asked Chris.

"Well, it has wrist mounted chainsaws and buzz saws for cutting. It has a modified extra large sledgehammer, which can be mounted on its back for convenience. In case it has to nail anything, we have this special high powered nail gun which can hold over three hundred rounds of ammo… I mean nails. We also have been working on this brand new construction tool."

He went over to a table and pointed to something that looked like an extra large Tommy gun.

"This looks like a rocket launcher with multiple rockets," said Chris.

"No, it's not a rocket launcher. It's a tool used for demolition."

"Does it fire rockets?"

"Yes."

"And this is for construction?"

"What else would it be for?"

"Warfare."

"Well... I guess you could possibly use this in a combat situation."

"It's a giant mech with chainsaws, a sledgehammer, a rocket launcher, and a nail gun that holds over three hundred rounds of ammo... I mean nails."

"What's your point?"

Chris turned to Jack.

"Let's just move on to the next floor," said Chris.

They got in the elevator and went up to the next floor. They exited the floor and went over to a large robotic sphere with a red eye in the middle of it.

"And this beauty is D.E.F," said Jack. "It's our artificial intelligence security system."

"Hello life form," said D.E.F in a monotone female voice.

"You named it death?" asked Chris.

"No, no, no. D.E.F. It stands for Darling Efficient Friend. It's very friendly. Wave to it."

Chris hesitantly waved.

"You can show a little more enthusiasm than that, Chris Johnson," said D.E.F.

"How does it know my name?"

"It knows everything," said Jack.

"Everything," repeated D.E.F.

"Can I talk to you in private?" asked Chris.

They went into the next room.

"Is this glass sound proof?" asked Chris.

"Yeah."

"Aren't you worried that a super intelligent, all knowing robot might..."

Chris looked at D.E.F.'s single red eye looking at them.

"Does D.E.F. know how to lip read?" asked Chris.

"Probably."

Chris pulled Jack out into the hallway by the water cooler.

"Aren't you worried that a super intelligent..."

A security camera whirred around and stayed focused on them.

"D.E.F. is hooked into the security cameras, isn't she?"

"Yep."

Chris pulled Jack into the bathroom.

"Aren't you worried that a super intelligent, all knowing robot might possibly go all Skynet and decide to exterminate all human life?"

"You need to relax."

Jack walked out of the bathroom. Chris followed him out.

"So, do you know which section you want to work in?" asked Jack.

"Well, between the super intelligent sharks, zombies, jetpacks, mechs, and the all knowing robot I think I'm going to have to go with the jetpacks."

"Good choice. You can go down there and start working now. I'll have D.E.F. make up your security badge and get it to you before the end of the day."

"I already created a security badge," said D.E.F.

"How did you do that?" asked Chris.

"I figured there was a ninety-eight point seven percent chance that you would choose that section considering you have loved jetpacks ever since you were a little kid."

"I told you she knows everything," said Jack.

Chris went over to the elevator and got inside. The doors started to close when Jack yelled, "Enjoy your first day."

"Don't worry," answered D.E.F. "He will."

Our species has forever quested for the ability to peer into the future, be the means magical, mystical, or alchemical. Why should we believe that will change in the era of super computing? This sstory was previously published in 2007 in Analog Magazine.

Mr. Doweyko enjoyed a lengthy and highly merited scientific career before turning his talents to authoring fiction, winning awards and plaudits for his science fiction, fantasy, and horror stories and novels.

The Probability Machine

by Arthur M. Doweyko

"It's really quite simple. The feed from the sensors is used to calculate the probabilities of the next scene, in effect allowing us to view the future."

Longren had a way of sounding like an academic. He did have several advanced graduate degrees in mathematics, physics and statistical mechanics—something he was known to point out with the least provocation. His six-foot frame towered over Mansfield Crebbs, a science reporter from the Dade Daily, who was unfortunate enough to be assigned a filler story, a simple piece to take up the space between the real news and sports. The physical contrast between the two underscored a deep social divide – Longren was tall and erect, entirely bald, and had a prominently aquiline nose, while Mansfield sat in a chair with a slouch, sported an *Orphan Annie* bright red mop of hair, and a pug of a face.

"So, umm, what you're saying is that you can dial in any time and see what's going to happen then?" asked Mansfield.

Longren sighed heavily.

"There are limits. As I pointed out earlier, the math and physics behind these calculations are bound by the laws of probability. If the event being monitored is relatively straightforward, like… let's say, a bouncing ball, then the system will predict its location for a lengthy period of time, since it would be unlikely that anything would interfere with the ball's trajectory."

"But that's a pretty easy trick… a bouncing ball. We know what it will do without all this mumbo jumbo."

Longren's eyes rolled up in an aborted attempt to control his temper.

"Mr. Crebbs, the process is quite a bit more complicated. The bouncing ball example is something I use to explain the concept to people like you."

People like me?

Mansfield straightened up.

Pompous asshole. Five years and he doesn't even remember me. Physics 201, and I was even one of his better students.

Longren tried to smile, but what came across was nothing more than a disparaging sneer.

"Oh, please, don't take umbrage at my statement. Even those that profess to be physicists will have some difficulty with the theory."

Umbrage?

"Ok, ok. Maybe you could demonstrate the equipment and then explain what we're seeing."

Longren moved closer to the mechanical contraption behind the monitor. Clamps suspended two balls about three feet over a transparent container on the floor.

"You will notice that several cameras are directed at these two high-density rubber balls in what we could refer to as the prediction zone."

Longren absent-mindedly buttoned his lab coat with one hand and flipped a switch with the other. The monitor came alive and from where he sat, Mansfield could see both the actual scene and as it was displayed on the flat-panel.

"The balls will be released sometime within the next few minutes. The precise time of release is determined by a random number generator within the apparatus. They will land in the container, bounce into each other, and will eventually come to rest."

That much I can figure out for myself.

"So, what's the monitor for? The picture looks the same there as it does in your...zone."

"Does it?"

Mansfield eyed both scenes, the zone and displayed, but could see no difference between the two. About a minute later something rather odd happened.

One of the balls displayed on the monitor dropped, but the actual ball suspended over the container hesitated a moment before falling. The ball bouncing in the container seemed to move through the same trajectories as the one on the screen, but lagged slightly behind it. The second ball dropped, and once again the screen image ran slightly ahead of the ball bouncing in the zone. When the balls rolled to a stop, Mansfield rubbed his chin.

"What just happened? Were you running a tape ahead of the action?"

Longren shook his head.

"Not at all. What you saw on the screen was a computer-rendered high resolution display of the event as it was going to occur in the prediction zone. My system was set to show you what was most likely to happen exactly one second into the future."

"One second into the future?"

Mansfield began feeling like he was back in Longren's class, asking dumb questions, all the while trying to ignore the snickering from his classmates.

My esteemed classmates.

Mansfield rubbed his chin harder.

"How are you doing this again?"

Longren sighed, purposely exaggerating the movement of his shoulders, underscoring a growing irritation.

"The equipment in this room includes a number of cameras and other sensory instruments designed to detect all manner of energy fluctuations and movement in and around us, as well as forces outside this room which may affect events within."

Longren made a show of pointing at the walls.

"There are literally thousands of detectors mounted on these three walls which feed my computers billions of bits of data each and every microsecond. My probability programs analyze all this data in real time and, using the immutable laws of physics, provide a prediction of what will happen next...at least, of what will happen within the prediction zone."

Mansfield whisked out a memo pad from his windbreaker and jotted down as much as he could understand.

"Excuse me, Dr. Fist. I think I understand the way a computer can predict the trajectory of a bouncing ball, but how did it figure out when the ball would be released? It did do that, right?"

Although Longren was annoyed at the interruption, he was pleased at Mansfield's insight.

"Aha. That's an astute observation, Mr. Crebbs. My system did indeed predict the time of release...actually to within a twentieth of a second."

Seeing Mansfield's open mouth begging for more detail, Longren happily continued to pontificate.

"As I was saying, my system includes a host of sensors which detect electromagnetic as well as physical movement, even at a microscopic scale. The random number generator within the mechanical ball assembly had to obey the laws of physics. Since its behavior was being electronically observed, the outcome was fully predictable and displayed as it would look in the prediction zone one second into the future."

Mansfield nailed down a few last words.

"Wow. So even a random number generator's output can be predicted?"

Longren nodded. Mansfield could see a gleam in the man's eyes.

"Actually…there's really no such thing. Mathematicians more accurately refer to such numbers as 'pseudo'. Their generation depends on formulae. Point of fact is that nothing is truly random in nature, and once my sensors detected the mathematical equation being used, prediction followed."

"You keep referring to your system… do you have a name for this thing, something that I could use in the story?"

Longren gazed at the instruments, wires, cables and panels, and then turned back to Mansfield.

"I suppose you could call it an event predicting system based on outcome probabilities."

One could do that if one was a total geek.

"That's a mouthful…how about something like… Probability Machine?"

A wave of disdain swept over Longren's face, curling down the corners of his mouth.

"Perhaps that would work better for the popular press, where hype and exaggeration appeal to the masses."

"Then, Probability Machine it is."

Sweet.

"So getting back to what just happened—that's one second… and into the future?"

"Correct."

"Can your monitor display an event farther out? Like a few more seconds, maybe minutes or even hours ahead?"

"Mr. Crebbs, do you know anything of chaos theory?"

You clearly don't remember me, or my term paper.

"Chaos? Like in pandemonium?"

Look at him squirm.

Longren sucked in a deep breath before replying.

Is that steam coming out of his ears?

"Not quite. I am referring to the intrinsic inability of predicting anything with absolute accuracy due to a fundamental uncertainty in the way matter behaves in this world."

Mansfield feigned a few troubled creases across his forehead.

"Let me explain it another way. No matter how carefully we measure things, the uncertainty in that measurement leads to a small error. The net effect is that the accuracy of predictions falls off with time. Of course, there are rare exceptions when clarity is maintained, which means that the probabilities are high and uncertainty low."

"So, exactly how far out does the Probability Machine here work? I mean…how far into the future can it see?"

A tic scooted across Longren's face.

"That depends on the complexity of the observation. For a couple of balls, a simple system, the accuracy of measurement is high. In such a case, seeing into the future, as you refer to it, is relatively easy."

Longren moved closer to a large black panel mounted on the wall and pointed to a dial with a LCD display mounted above it.

"Right now, my system is set to calculate a one second prediction. I could easily set the prediction much farther out, for example, five or ten seconds and it would work just as well."

Longren turned the dial and the display read ten seconds. Mansfield peeked at the monitor and saw the balls just as they were in the prediction zone. However, the image appeared to have acquired a slight fuzziness.

"And when I set the display farther out, let's say to the present limit of the system…one minute, what do you see now?"

The instrument-studded walls hummed and the image on the monitor blurred, making the objects nearly indistinct. At times the balls appeared to be in more than one place, with faint shadows moving in and out of view.

"What is that? There are more balls and something's moving around in there."

"You are seeing what possibilities occur at one minute into the future. At this distance, or time frame, the computational power required to determine the location of each object in the container is enormous, and the power drain is huge…actually, it's limited by that available to me at this institution. Since the uncertainty in prediction becomes significant, the system extrapolates and the display captures a number of potential future scenes at the same time."

Longren turned the dial back down to zero, and the walls hushed.

"So, if you had more compute power, you could see even farther out?"

"Yes and no. More processing power would allow us to get through more probability functions and get a better view, but like I mentioned before, chaos is unavoidable. At some point, especially with a complex scene, the image will blur out because it simply cannot be calculated accurately."

Longren's cell phone rang. He glanced at the incoming caller ID.

"Excuse me a moment. I need to take this call. I'll be back in a moment."

Longren walked out of the laboratory and disappeared into a side office. The lab door swung shut with a whimper.

Mansfield stood up to take a closer look at the black panel. After checking through the window of the lab door to make sure that the hallway was empty, he turned the dial until the display read one second and positioned himself between the plexiglass container in the zone and the monitor. He reached out with his left hand, and when it was over the container, he craned backwards to see the screen. Sure enough, the monitor showed his hand entering the zone just before it actually did. The effect was so disorienting that he nearly fell into the container. He tried it once again, with the same uncanny effect.

Damn. Was that weird or what? I wonder if I can fake it out?

He pretended to move his hand into the zone, but instead, jerked it back. Nothing showed up on the monitor. He tried the maneuver several more times. Each time nothing changed on the screen. He sat back down on the chair, pulled out a handkerchief and mopped his brow.

So, the electronic sensors must be monitoring my brain activity. There was no fooling it. Or was there?

His eyes roamed over the room, humbly acknowledging the presence of all the sophisticated wall sensors, and he shuddered at the very creepy ability of their tethered computers.

He trotted over to the wall panel and cranked the dial to ten seconds and repositioned himself between the zone and the monitor.

What if I just think about putting my hand out? I could convince myself I'll do it, and the sensors will be fooled and display my hand…and then what happens if I don't stick it out? Longren's Probability Machine will have failed. That pompous jerk will choke on his own words.

He sat and stared at the cameras and the monitor which continued to display the motionless balls. He concentrated all his thoughts, puckering up his lips, holding his breath and gradually turning his face a striking beet red. Nothing happened. No matter how hard he concentrated, clearly picturing the image of his hand entering the zone, nothing stirred on the monitor.

He was about to give up when the image of a hand flashed across the screen. It was there for brief moment only. Mansfield sat perfectly still while fighting down a surge of adrenaline.

Damn. It worked! This is going to be really interesting. I just need to sit here and not move a muscle until ten seconds tick by.

Mansfield counted to himself.

One thousand one, one thousand two, one thousand three…

And then a peculiar thing happened. He began feeling an urge to get up.

…one thousand four, one thousand five…

The muscles in his legs began to shudder. His hands, which had been clenching the chair's armrests, started sliding back and forth.

…one thousand six, one thousand seven…

His legs kicked out. Sweat-drenched palms lost their tenuous purchase, and both hands spasmed. The chair seemed to move on its own, scraping along floor tiles, moving toward the cameras in the zone, each inch amplifying his anxiety. His arms and legs jerked Mansfield as if he was a pathetic little marionette with an untalented, brutish child tugging at his invisible strings.

…one thousand and nine…

The chair shot forward, caught a tile edge, and teetered—spilling Mansfield into the zone. He held out his hand in a vain attempt to avoid the fall.

...*one thousand and ten.*

Too late.

A few more seconds ticked by and Mansfield rubbed his head. Still a bit shaky, he raised the chair and dragged it back to its original location in front of the monitor screen. He angled himself into the seat and stared at the monitor. Mansfield had epilepsy—a mild form, usually lasting for a few seconds. The fits occurred rarely. Today was Mansfield's lucky day.

Goddamn. Longren's Probability Machine could even predict my seizures.

Voices in the hallway.

The dial! I've got to reset the dial.

Mansfield leaped out of the chair and ran over to the wall. He gave the dial a whirl. The walls thrummed. Computer banks mounted in arrays came alive with the sound of surging fans. Relays switched, hard drives purred and LEDs blinked. Several panels lit up, accompanied by a disquieting assortment of beeps.

What just happened?

Mansfield glanced around the room, caught sight of the wall clock, and then focused on the dial and its LCD display.

Five minutes! Shit!

As he reached for the dial to turn it the other way, his eyes caught the monitor screen, and he froze.

Blurred figures of two men locked in an embrace bobbed across the screen. One was tall and bald, and wearing a white lab coat. The other was short, and red-headed, and wore a windbreaker.

It's me and Longren!... Are we fighting?

The images swerved by, fading in and out as they danced across the screen. The two figures disappeared for a moment, after which his image floated into view, standing still and alone. The image of Longren came up behind holding something silver and red.

Mansfield heard footfalls reaching the lab door. His fingertips touched the dial. There was only time for a last peek before turning it down. The images kept blurring even more, but as Mansfield concentrated on the scene, they seemed to spring back into focus – swirling into the zone. Longren held a knife streaked with blood and raised it. He thrust it forward into Mansfield's chest.

My God! My God!

He saw Longren slide down and out of view. The image of Mansfield stared directly into the camera, shaking its head, slowly, side to side. The mouth moved, as if trying to warn the viewer.

The viewer…that would be me! I'm trying to say something…to myself!

Instead of words, only muffled grunts emerged as the image dropped away.

The lab door squealed open and Mansfield flicked the dial to zero. The electric drone ceased.

"Mr. Crebbs. Is there anything else I can help you with?" asked Longren while eyeing the laboratory.

Mansfield slipped his pencil behind an ear, trying to look casual, and moved away from the wall panel.

Somehow, something is going to happen in the next five minutes that will set this maniac off and it'll be curtains for me.

"Eh…I think I've got enough information for the article, Dr. Fist. I'll be on my way now."

Longren sniffed the air. A sharp ozone odor bit at his nose.

"Just a moment, what were you doing at the panel?"

Before Mansfield could make up a reasonably good lie, Longren was standing next to him scanning the instruments along the wall, paying particular attention to a small paper roll recorder.

"Mr. Crebbs. What exactly did you do here?"

Longren's hand emerged with a pair of spectacles which he held a few inches before his eyes. He bent slightly to get a closer look at the paper printout, all the while blocking Mansfield's path to the door.

He's doing that on purpose.

"I was just looking, Dr. Fist. Now, if you will excuse me, I'll be leaving."

Fist turned to Mansfield. His face was as grey concrete, his mouth drawn into a thin and trembling line.

"Mr. Crebbs, you turned that dial up, didn't you?"

Shit. So, what?

"I…I may have turned it a little…"

Longren's eyes squinted and his voice gained an octave.

"A little? The recorder indicates that a significant power drain just occurred…large enough to cause permanent damage to my system."

Longren moved toward Mansfield, causing him to hop backwards.

He's coming after me.

"Look at this mess! Two of my Ventura's have crashed!"

What the hell is a Ventura?

Longren turned from the wall and with hands on hips marched toward Mansfield, backing him up with every step.

"Now, now, Dr. Fist. I'm sure that whatever broke can be fixed. I swear I didn't do anything."

"The sensors do not lie. You ignorant bastard! You had the audacity to fool with instrumentation beyond your understanding! You stupid, stupid cretin!"

Mansfield bumped into the adjacent wall with his back. He had nowhere to go except toward the prediction zone.

Damn. He's coming unhinged.

Inside Mansfield's head Big Ben was tick-tocking away; its gears were grinding and its hands crept—each second inexorably drawing him nearer to the end. His end.

… *tick-tock*…

Mansfield panicked and pushed out at Longren.

"Get away from me you friggin jerk! I'm getting out of here."

Longren stumbled backwards, but only for a step.

"How dare you! You fool, you destroyed my machine. What took years to build you destroyed in seconds. You will pay for this!"

The only way out was to step through the prediction zone, around the cameras and monitor screen. Mansfield lunged for the zone. Longren followed close behind, and as Mansfield reached the monitor, Longren snatched his windbreaker, catching hold long enough to whip Mansfield around.

…*tick-tock*…

"Get away from me! Let me go! You don't understand! Let me go!"

Longren grabbed at Mansfield's shoulders.

"I've got to get out of here!"

The two blundered into one of the cameras and tumbled to the floor. Longren managed to get both arms around Mansfield and held on.

...*tick-tock*...

Mansfield tried getting up, but it was no use. They rolled about the floor; their flailing legs upending the ball container and apparatus. Mansfield writhed, trying to release himself from Longren's grip. He pulled one arm out and pushed the floor. They rolled over as one, and for a moment he was on his back. He felt a piercing pain in his hip.

My back pocket. My pen knife. In my back pocket.

With his free hand for purchase, he pushed off again, reached back and pulled out the knife.

I just need to get loose, just need to get out of here. Time is running out.

"Let go of me!"

Mansfield flipped open the knife and waved it over Longren's contorted face.

"Let go, or I'll kill you!"

Just let go of me, you bastard and I'll run the hell out of here.

"Don't be a bigger fool than you already are, Crebbs! You're not going anywhere. You'll pay for what you've done!"

...*tick-tock*...

Big Ben was about to toll.

Longren gave a sudden and violent twist, flinging the pair into another roll. Mansfield heard a squeak, much like the lab door opening, except that it came from beneath him. Something warm poured out on his hand—the hand that held his penknife. Longren's eyes stared ahead and spittle dripped out of his half-opened mouth. His arms loosened and fell to the side. A knife protruded from his chest.

My God. Jesus Christ. I didn't do that! He wouldn't let go. He just wouldn't let go.

Mansfield stood up, trembling. He was standing in the middle of the prediction zone.

The prediction machine made a mistake! I beat the damn machine.

He looked up at the lab clock.

Has it been five minutes?

Somewhere deep inside Mansfield's head, the tick-tocking went on, grinding, eating up each second. Big Ben's face twisted into a clown's moronic smile and it whispered... *tick-tock...*

Mansfield shook his head to clear it. He thought about the story he would make up for the authorities. He turned to take a last look at the body, and instead, found Longren's hulking form looming over him. The lab coat was still buttoned, but now an enormous dark red blotch covered its front. Longren thrust the knife into Mansfield's chest dead center. He released the blade and slumped to the floor. Big Ben was tolling—distant and fading.

My knife.

The laboratory lights dimmed as Mansfield's world began to shrink. His eyes caught a blinking red glow—one of the zone cameras, just feet away.

I have to warn him...me.

He looked down at his chest. Blood oozed from the knife's edges, running down his shirt front, staining his jacket, soaking his pants. He stumbled toward the camera. His words were no more than short, raspy snorts.

Oblivion.

A murmur rose from the seated audience.

"What do you think now?"

Mansfield looked away from the monitor and rubbed his chin before answering.

"That was quite a show."

Longren nodded.

"More than a show, Mansfield. What you saw was a prediction of a possible, perhaps likely, outcome."

Longren stood from his chair and faced the spectators in the cramped confines of his laboratory.

"Ladies and gentlemen, members of the press and our research community, I hope I've been able to convince you and the scientific board of the dangers of this technology. Although the Probability Machine represents a major breakthrough, its use must be closely monitored and subject to keen scientific scrutiny and oversight."

Light applause punctuated the conclusion of a well-delivered seminar. Longren motioned to the group as he ambled to the lab door.

Mansfield remained seated in his chair and watched the procession file out. When all were gone, he rose from the chair and stretched his back. He looked up at the monitor, now dark and silent. When he reached the door, he stopped. His eyes wandered over the black wall panel and settled on a large round dial.

Our next story, so the author informs us, was born of a first sentence that came from nowhere, and led him down an unfragrant path as he wrote the first draft old-school-style, on a manual Olympia typewriter. His story won the Wabash Prize and was published in the Sycamore Review in 2006.

Mr. Jones has won, in no particular order, and only a sample, a Pushcart Prize, the George Garrett Fiction Prize, and the Meridian Editors' Prize. He's a MacDowell fellow and lives in northern Idaho.

The Source of My Troubles

by Jeff P. Jones

As flies to wanton boys are we to the gods
They kill us for their sport
William Shakespeare, *King Lear*

Fire's so momentary a thing that it can't be described: stilling the flames to take their picture snuffs them. Smoke's different, more human, if you will. Smoke moves slowly and goads the imagination with the forms it takes. One smoke gazer elbows the other, whispers, Frog with a Rose in its Mouth. Upside-down Heart. Slow-mo Arrow. Spaceship. (Are the shapes in the smoke or in the observer? Or, somehow, magically, in their conjunction?) Smoke, it might even be ventured, is the ink with which fire tells its story. The slow-morphing shapes in this particular inky stack tell the story of a twenty-year-old guy named Thom who, lately, has been mourning his lack of control.

The naked sun scorched the landfill, burning each passing minute as if it were another stick of fuel. The cab of Thom's Mark

IV earthmover, its windows soldered shut, sat above ten-foot-tall tires. Inside steamed with his sweat. Hours ago he peeled away the top half of his coveralls. Now his white undershirt clung to his back like a wet towel. Trickles of perspiration rolled down the windows. On his boyish face sprouted a few whiskers in a faint outline of sideburns.

It was noon. Six hours he'd been going at it. On Tuesdays they trucked in all the unmailed store catalogs. The stacks were bound in blocks of several thousand with red plastic ties that had to be broken before burying to minimize volume. Of the nine Disposal Technicians (DTs), Thom was the fastest, his boyish reflexes reinforced by an uncanny ability to see patterns in the refuse. When the trucks queued up, they sent two to him, one to everyone else. Each load could be done a little faster, he told himself. Two more loads slid down the raised beds of the dump trucks. The blocks tumbled and crashed and flipped into the pit, and even before they'd settled, Thom's eyes affixed a pattern. Within seconds his wrist was moving the black lever controlling the front scarifier, snapping the plastic ties along the predetermined line. Tuesdays, Thom felt in control.

But since the memorial service three months ago, things had changed. Thom was scraping dirt over the loosened catalogs when a gold speckle flashed in the distance, beelining for him: a midday visit from Jimmy Dean. Bad news. Jimmy skidded to a stop in his Eddie Bauer Special Edition golf cart pimped out in authentic gold trim. He stepped from the cart. Black boots, tight Levi's, a crisp white button-down, and a yellow cowboy hat that shaded everything but his sharp nose, which jutted over a black handlebar moustache. To Thom he looked like a mosquito.

Arms crossed, Jimmy leaned against his cart. The words crackled over Thom's cab speakers. "LRC just dumped a pile of Huggies up by 5f. You want to make a few passes, Number Six?"

Thom's face burned. Jimmy had only driven out here to see his reaction. *Make a few passes* meant spending the next eight hours wallowing in four tons of baby shit. No doubt they hadn't *just* been dumped, either, but had been cooking all morning. The maggots would already be teeming. Lately, every miserable assignment landed at Thom's blade.

"I got these catalogs I'm dealing with," Thom said. "Besides, I did the last diaper load."

A smile flickered across Jimmy's face. "That wasn't a request."

Thom tightened his grip on the gearshift ball, felt the thrum of the fifteen-hundred-horsepower engine in his palm. Jimmy used to brag about Thom's efficiency in front of the other DTs. "I'll double your wages if you can beat Thom-boy here," he'd say at the morning meeting when he handed out assignment cards. Thom used to get the best assignments and even afternoons off when things were slow. Jimmy stared up at Thom. A single wrist flick would squash him like a bug.

"Don't make me repeat myself. You're on diaper duty, kid." Jimmy sped away. The pages from strewn catalogs flopped in his wake like a flock of maimed birds. Thom imagined Jimmy speeding back to Portable 5a, strutting in the door balls-first, calling Agnes "honey," and telling her to crank up the swamp-cooler a notch.

At times like that, Thom dreamt of doing terrible things to Jimmy, things that would fill us all with dismay were I to go into needle-nose-pliers, fingernail-plucking detail. It was then that an image would pop into his mind of Agnes sitting at her aluminum-panel desk, the one with faux-wood grain sides peeling at the corners, and he would sense a calmness. Every other Friday when Thom stood in the paycheck line with the other DTs outside 5a, he gazed through the trailer's picture window at Agnes. If the sun's setting light managed to slip through the diesel fumes, it lit up her skin so that it glowed, bronze and rich. It was an odd thing, that vision of Agnes, but somehow it always cooled Thom's jets.

He pictured Agnes at her desk in 5a. Years of backfilling had built up the earth around the portables so that the trailers sat in bowl-like depressions off the main access road. Agnes's desk faced the thirty-foot slope that poised like a tsunami of dirt (an arrangement that will become important in just under four thousand words). Whenever Thom passed 5a, Agnes never failed to glance up and wave, and that always made Thom's heart swell.

Three months ago, Agnes' husband, who had been a Dean, was crushed to death by an emergency vehicle during a citywide safety drill. The DTs got the day off to attend the memorial. Except for the Rev, they were all in love with Agnes. Thom fell for her the first time he saw her—four years ago, when he stepped off the Labor Resupply Center (LRC) bus, having been reassigned from sewage management to solid waste. Now, as he drove across the field and demolished Jimmy's puny cart tracks with his earthmover, he could see Agnes's eyes, such a deep indigo that they shaded into black. His ribs strained to control his thrashing heart.

At the service, Thom sat in the last row. He kept his gaze on Agnes. Every few seconds she dabbed her eyes or leaned over and whispered something to her daughter Cleo. There she sat, surrounded by Deans.

The pasty wisp of a minister kept talking about the "valuable service" the deceased had given and the "better place" to which he was headed as a result. Thom knew Agnes's husband only as a picture on her computer screen, posed with Agnes and Cleo beside an enormous smiling rodent.

After the service, all the DTs filed out and loitered in the parking lot, ogling the stretch Humvee Jimmy had rented for the affair. The Rev was reclining against his old Dodge pickup, smoking an unfiltered. The Rev had worked in waste longer than anyone.

Thom ambled over and asked the Rev to what extent he thought they could ply the memorial for some further PTO. The Rev looked crosswise at Thom because they both knew the answer and made an observation of his own.

"The next attempt will seek not to transfer the corporate-state edifice from one hand to another but to smash it, comrade," he said.

"Is that right?"

"Small acts of local retribution are the precondition for every real people's revolution. The man in that box was a principal contributor to exploitative hierarchies."

The Rev was a walking stockpile of Unpatriotic Feelings (UFs) and a genuine hazard to be around, but Thom knew him to have a good heart.

"What did you make of the minister's words?" Thom asked.

"Horseshit. Our goal's a working-class government, a thoroughly flexible political form since all previous forms have been essentially repressive. The secret is this: the system we plan is the result of the struggle of the first-world working against the first-world consuming class, the political form at last discovered under which the economic emancipation of all labor will be accomplished."

"You don't say," Thom said, then wondered aloud whether such thoughts weren't ripe with Hazardous Thought (HT), Mockery of National Security Concerns (MNSC), and even some FHJ and CUD, and, if put into action, might hamper the efforts of the Minor Opposition Party (MOP), whose ultimate goal, everyone knew, was to oppose harmful government and make life better for everyone.

The Rev flicked a yellow jacket from his sleeve and glared at Thom. "You may think all I do's push other people's pig-swill around all day like most of you dipshits, but all the time I'm burying castoffs, my mind's going at the speed of light. You know what I'm studying?"

"What?"

"The squander. Next time you're burying empties, try this. Imagine yourself as an eagle soaring miles over the earth, peering down, observing the whole human operation—the city with its precisely ordered streets, its concrete and steel boxes, its manicured lawns and walled-off warrens. Then see the lines of trucks streaming out from the city, carting load after load of castoffs. And ask yourself this: why do I keep showing up for work, day in and day out? Come on, what're you waiting for, comrade? Don't be a reactionary. Be a revolutionary."

Something about the Rev's words made Thom's skin prickle. He never could follow such convoluted ideas, but this last point, of taking a fresh look at the waste, seemed like a good idea. Then he sensed something like a sliver of glass lodging in the back of his neck. His legs gave out. The asphalt dug into his knees and suddenly loomed inches from his face. His throat felt like someone was shoving sponges down it. A yellow fog moved in.

Thom awoke in a hospital room with the Rev standing over him.

"Son, you need to stick around. You've got work to do yet." He told Thom about the yellow jacket that stung him, his collapse in the parking lot, and how Agnes rushed over. She dabbed Thom's head with her handkerchief and insisted on using the Humvee as a hospital transport. Jimmy was livid at having the vehicle co-opted for a lowly DT.

"That goldbricker has got to go," the Rev said.

Thom touched the place where Agnes's hanky had graced his skin, her tears mingling with his sweat. It's true, he thought, her love's as real as mine.

Now, as he rumbled toward the diapers, Thom looked toward 5a. Agnes (exiting in two thousand eight hundred words) was probably fending off Jimmy's groping at that moment. The trucks continued to stream past the front gate. The line extended onto the plain that lay between the dump and the city.

Like a flu fever, the first inkling of something close to despair settled over Thom. Fingers of diesel smoke linked the trucks, and the sun sparkled off their windshields so that the caravan looked like a row of stars stretching to the horizon. What would the world be like without him and others like him in it? If there were no DTs, no Mark IV's, no TRDs or WMSs or BHQs, what would happen? People would pile their garbage in the streets. When one city got too clogged with garbage, they'd move on. And given enough time, what would happen to all that refuse? Wind and water would return it to the soil. It might take longer, but the earth would reclaim the waste, wouldn't it?

Thom went back to work after recovering from the yellow jacket sting. Two weeks later, Agnes returned, too. On the first payday, Thom stood in line outside 5a, holding a dozen red roses that cost him a week's salary. When it was his turn, he climbed the aluminum steps and handed the flowers to Agnes.

"These are for you," he said. "I wanted to say thank you?"

"They're beautiful, Thom. What a sweet boy you are."

Boy? Sure, she was four or five years older, had been married, had a daughter, and was a widow, but they were about the same age. "I hope you like them," he said.

"They're perfect." She reached across the desk and patted his hand. Her fingers were light and soft. She rummaged through cupboards, saying, "I know there's a bottle I can use as a vase here somewhere."

Thom was about to say something else, something brilliant, when Jimmy peered around the corner. At sight of the roses, his moustache ends flared.

"Where'd you get that kind of dough, Number Six? We paying you too much?"

"I had a little saved back."

"Then maybe you should've chipped in for your little ride to the hospital. You know how much that Hummer cost?"

Thom flushed.

"Oh, Jimmy, let me have my flowers, will you," Agnes said.

Jimmy gripped Agnes's elbow, then leaned over her shoulder and stabbed his nose into the bouquet. Thom's throat contracted.

"Can't smell nothing," Jimmy said. "Sure these are real?"

"Of course they're real," Agnes said, swatting Jimmy's shoulder. "And I'm going to keep them for as long as they last."

Ever since, Jimmy had it out for him.

Before he turned off the access road, it hit: a sickly sweet all-consuming stench. Thom gasped and tried to breathe only through his mouth, but still the smell boiled through the cab vents and permeated the air. Past an earthen mound, there they sat, a pile of Huggies as high as an office building, steaming in the heat. A rotten stew.

He stopped the tires an inch from the white wall. The pile expanded and shifted in the heat. The squishy diaper innards would, under compression, splatter over his entire machine. By the time he finished this job, his beautiful Mark IV would be covered tire-to-tailpipe in baby shit. The windshields would be a bleary mess and the air system would reek for days. Even using the pressure hose, the crust would take an extra hour to clean. Thom would miss the last bus home and have to wait through the late shift for the next one. He dug in his coveralls pocket for a cigarette.

Thom could afford one smoke a day. He spent mornings planning when to take his cigarette break, longing for that first pull of smoke into his body, the way it spread down his throat and into his lungs.

He lit the tobacco, put the filter to his lips, and breathed a full breath through the cigarette's burning body. Thom pictured what Wednesday would bring, all the discards that would be hauled out, load after load: the delectables that made his mouth water—half-gnawed chunks of Syntha-Chicken, sticky tubs of Häagen-Dazs, syrupy Cyclone Cakes—as well as the other more substantial throwaways—oxikits, homewalkers, lead-lined jumpsuits, baby respirators, jellybags, and so much more. Even though he could never afford such things, in his first couple of years as a DT, he'd memorized their descriptions from the catalogs that had lodged in the rails of his traction bars and which he had pilfered and secretly studied.

His mind responded to the cigarette: it had some quickening power. He thought of his reassignment in six months. Maybe he'd be sent to a Waste Transfer Station (WTS), where the retrievers got to soar over piles of discards and pull out Improperly Disposed Objects (IDOs). He had heard that, hooked into guy wires, they looked more like moonwalkers, bouncing around and pulling out surveillance bracelets, reusable scraps of real wood, or relics like fishing rods He hoped it wouldn't be to some of the awful places he'd heard about—meat factories or crematoria for strays.

Underneath him the machine rumbled. He loved his earth-mover, so powerful and responsive. He knew that he should start in on the diapers. Instead, he took out a second cigarette and lit it.

He pictured the discards after a million years. By then, they would've melted into a layer of tar-like sludge. Maybe the descendants of humans, who would be sleek and whip-smart, would dig up the sludge and use it to do something brilliant, like fuel spaceships to the stars.

Halfway through his second cigarette, the tin voice crackled over the cab speakers. Video surveillance.

"What the hell's the problem, Number Six?"

Thom wished for the hundredth time he could reach through those speakers and grab hold of Jimmy's scrawny neck.

"Because you can be on your ear tomorrow morning if you keep lollygagging."

The story around the yard was that Delilah and Lester Dean named their son Jimmy in hopes of impressing the old-money sausage relatives, and, in fact, the ploy had been enough to secure a loan that kept the dump afloat during tight times. The Deans never saw a penny of the meat money, though; they made their family fortune burying other people's garbage.

"Don't bother me, Jimmy, I'm about to have an epiphany."

"I'll give you an epiphany, numb nuts. Get back to work or you're fired. How's that?"

With his mention of "epiphany," a word he'd picked up in an advertising jingle, Thom realized with something approaching starlight clarity that either he was in control of his life or he wasn't. It was as simple as that. He just needed to make an unexpected choice to test this idea. He looked around for something he'd failed to notice before. His gaze settled on an unblemished section of the dashboard just above the lifter's hydraulic pressure gauge. He took the cigarette's cherry tip and touched it, sizzling, to the dash. It sent up a thread of black smoke.

Outside, the diapers towered. Thom pictured just driving away. A shiver passed through him. The impulse to refuse, to say no, struck with such a force of temptation that he gave in. He simply had to choose. He could choose to do *anything*.

Thom's revelation is important. Otherwise, why concern ourselves with this particular Tuesday in his life? Previous Tuesdays only demonstrated patterned monotony: shining fog-lights in predawn darkness to split bundles of catalogs; scraping them with his front blade into a pit; burying and compacting; then ripping a new hole—all day long through the heat and fading light until darkness and exhaustion. Then there was the snoozy bus ride to his tiny room in the workers quarters' on the city outskirts, a bland meal, and five hours of sleep before Wednesday morning arrived. But *this* Tuesday, as Thom flicks the cigarette butt onto the floorboard and the narrative moves into present tense in an attempt to reflect the sudden immediacy with which he's experiencing events and the nearness of the approaching climax (one thousand five hundred twenty-six words), *this* Tuesday becomes different.

Thom makes a wide swinging turn and rumbles away from the diapers. He indulges in a fantasy: Agnes and he walk beside the ocean, each of them holding one of Cleo's hands as the waves roll up on the shore and the sand caresses their bare feet. They don't say anything because they're all in love with each other and their new lives. Foolish? Of course. But who hasn't done something foolish for love?

The speakers crackle. "Where the hell do you think you're going?"

"I need a hand," Thom says. "Can you meet me on the access road? I've got a loose belt."

"Maintenance issues go to the garage, jerk-off."

"It's a quick fix. If I take it to maintenance, I'll be down the whole day. Those diapers'll never get buried."

A pause unspools like a thread between them. "You're spoiling for trouble, Number Six. This better be quick."

Thom smiles. He isn't usually so crafty, but as he approaches the access road hovering over Portable 5a, his confidence rises. He climbs out of the cab and loosens a lifter belt. Jimmy Dean switchbacks up the hill, pulling an angry tail of dust into the air behind his golf cart. Jimmy steps out and climbs the cab ladder. Sweat rides his forehead like a row of buttons. A scowl underscores his moustache.

"You're stretching my patience thin as paper," Jimmy says.

Thom leans into the cab, swiftly pockets the ignition key, then grabs the crowbar from behind the seat. "When I give the sign, pull the lifter bar up so I can wedge the belt on with this?"

"This is going to cost you." Jimmy snarls as he stands eye-to-eye with Thom. One of the sweat buttons pops free and rolls to the tip of Jimmy's nose. Then, together, they notice a cluster of dark clouds in the west. "Just great," Jimmy says and horks a wad of gleim over his shoulder. "Let's get this over with before the storm hits." He climbs into the cab.

Thom shuts the door behind Jimmy as fast as a cat. Then he wedges the crowbar against the frame, locking it shut. Thom leaps off the machine. Pounding and muffled shouts follow him down the hill. He doesn't even feel the ground but bounds from foot to foot like someone unfettered by gravity. Agnes holds the door open as he floats up the aluminum steps. They stand inside the trailer, staring at each other.

"Thom," she says. Her eyes set his heart pounding so hard that he expects it to split open his chest and land, flopping and red, on her desk.

"I've locked Jimmy up in my cab." This sounds so ridiculous that he snorts. Soon, he's laughing harder than ever, buoyed on waves of hilarity.

"You did what?" Agnes walks to the door and peers uphill. Rain falls in leaden streaks. The bewildered look on her face pries open a hole in Thom's stomach through which the giddiness drains away.

"Agnes, I need to ask you something." He takes a deep breath, feels the world expand. "I'm in love with you?"

A corner of her delicate mouth twitches and turns down. He watches his hopes slide into that crease and fall away. She has never loved him. Never even considered it, apparently. It makes sense; she was always just as friendly with the other DTs. "I think you'd better let Jimmy out. He's going to be hopping mad."

Thom feels like he's being scolded for not properly cleaning his work space. The rain patters on the trailer roof.

"Agnes?"

"Yes?"

"Will you remember me?"

"Sure, Thom, I remember you."

Thom reaches for her hand. It's fragile and warm. He bends to press his lips to it and feels the tug of resistance. He kisses it anyway. "Sorry," he says, then leaves.

The trek uphill takes forever, a plunging slog through rain-loosened dirt. Rivulets score the steep bank, little slurries of mud. By the time he reaches the access road, he can see the cords on Jimmy's neck. He's blistered with rage. Four other golf carts, carrying the managers from 5b, 5c, 5d, and 5e, climb their respective hills, heading for the access road. Should've disabled the radio, Thom thinks. He lifts the crowbar.

Jimmy throws open the door. "You're finished, ass-crack. You're going to be so far gone, you'll never find your way back. I hope you like grass clippings."

Everyone's heard of such assignments. Shards fill the air, stick to the skin, creep into every orifice. The smell's so bad that you get a five-year headache.

"Park this thing, then get out of my face," Jimmy says. "I don't ever want to see you again." He jumps into his cart and zigzags down the hill. Thom watches in silence.

What is real freedom? Any future Thom might've had is wrecked. But Thom's a character in a story, no more real than the half-shapes and silly figures that rise from the tops of smokestacks. What does it matter whether he gets stuck on some grass-clipping repository, breathing glass-edged filaments the rest of his fictional life? Or perhaps he gets sent to an animal crematorium, and one day in his first month, throws himself into the furnace along with the carcass of a brown-haired mutt with doe eyes. Who cares? Yet I sense with trepidation that your take on Thom's story largely depends on what happens to him here at the end. Many storytelling peoples believe that stories endow characters with real life. My brother even believes that, if its readers buy into it, a story creates another dimension just as real as ours. And don't forget, philosophers are still working out whether or not we're all just components of a massive simulation program. Last I heard, they'd put our chances of being real at fifty-fifty.

And yet. Something compels me to assign Thom's story its final shape. To say, yes, Frog, but not Frog with a Rose in its Mouth, but Frog with Paintbrush. What's the source of this compulsion? Who's to say.

Jimmy skids to a stop, and his tires freckle the front of 5a with mud. The other managers, in customized golf carts of their own, sail past Thom, flash sneers through the rain, then zoom down the hill. They pull in next to Jimmy, who leaps from his cart, beats his hat against his thigh, wipes his brow, points up the hill. The managers gaze at Thom. Shake their heads, then their fists.

Thom reconsiders his situation. Perhaps he got off track at the diaper mound. It seems like it was earlier than that, though. Maybe the memorial service. But that was just an extension of his feelings for Agnes, which began four years ago. Maybe it was his love for her that set him on this path. Or maybe the whole thing was set in motion before he was born. Or it could've been those intoxicating beads of sunlight stretching like a necklace between truck windshields. Could the Rev's words finally be settling in? The cigarette's magic seeping into the corners of his brain?

Thom pictures again those creatures into which humans will evolve. Beautiful beings, efficient and graceful. He gazes at the cloud bank engulfing the sky and imagines them swimming there in the air between droplets of rain, unbounded by physical laws, space, distance, even time. He wants desperately to join them—and if not that, then to please them. He feels the quickening of his blood, the heat in his palms. He conceives of a final choice that might speed the coming of their race.

He climbs into the cab. Jimmy's odor, musk and axle grease, fills the air. With three quick hand movements, Thom starts the engine, bumps up the throttle, and veers off the access road. He aims his Mark IV downhill.

The machine sinks half a foot into the wet hillside. He throttles up. The tires slip. Precious seconds tick away. By the time he should be there, he's only halfway. One of the managers points. He must gain ground fast. He shoves the throttle full, sends its motor into a din of stuttering combustion. Gravity finally starts to work for him, speeding the earthmover and allowing the hillside's crust to bear it up. Inside the cab, Thom leans forward, his forehead pressed against the front glass, charging brow-first like a bull.

Jimmy's eyes rim with white. He dives into his cart and stomps on the gas. The cart churns mud, and Jimmy scoots away in it just as Thom swipes the air with the scarifier. Desperate and ineffectual. Six feet away, in the picture window of 5a (seventy words from death), stands Agnes, one palm pressed against the glass, searching the scene. They'll never walk along the beach with Cleo, planning their lives together while sand pushes up between their toes. The last glimpse of her sears onto the lens of his inner eye. Ceiling bulbs halo her figure in a stream of fluorescent light. Her eyebrows raise as if she's about to ask a question.

Then she is (one word) gone, along with 5a. Buried in a pile of splinters and collapsed aluminum siding. The rain gives way to downpour as hands claw at Thom from below. His face is shoved into the mud, and blows land wetly against him from all sides—but no physical pain can penetrate the darkness into which he sinks.

As his skull cracks under the heel of a cowboy boot, Thom decides that whatever or whoever made him is, at best, a whimsical creature acting without rhyme or reason and, at worst, a malevolent agent bringing misery not only in this life but also the next. Thom's final sensation before slipping into coma and then oblivion isn't reducible to language but something more like the purest expression of terror, a fear rising up from a cauldron's murky depths, the sense that he's traveling to a place that has no pre-established patterns, where he's in control of everything but there's nothing but himself to control. And he's going there alone.

Modern and inexpensive printing changed the way we read a few centuries ago. The advent of ebooks, and the ability to carry a library in one's pocket is changing our reading styles and habits today. Our next story explores what may be the next step, and how it might effect us.

Mr. Grassie admits to being a life-long Glaswegian and his stories may be found in many anthologies, including Hero's Best Friend and Thunder on the Battlefield: Sorcery, both from Seventh Star Press.

Terminal

by Steven Grassie

Colin looks up from the paperback in his hands as the doors beneath the *International Arrivals* sign slide open to disgorge a steady stream of weary-looking passengers. He closes Dostoyevsky's *The Double*, groans as he pushes himself to his feet, and slides the book into the back pocket of his trousers.

Robert is one of the last to emerge; he's trailed obediently by one of those fancy new smart-luggage thingies. Colin spots his brother a half-second before Robert spots him, but they wave in perfect synchrony. They're both smiling as Colin starts forward to help close the remaining distance between them, and he wonders if… no, he knows that Robert is also feeling the old, familiar sensation of approaching a mirror. Despite the vagaries of time they still look remarkably alike – the fairly full heads of white hair, the similar style and hues of their clothes – and they attract a couple of curious glances as they shake hands.

The twins swap swift but sincere "How are you?"s and ask after each other's wife and family. Colin claps his brother on the shoulder and makes for the exit, but stops when he notices Robert hanging back.

"Mind if I grab a quick coffee first?" Robert asks. His accent has acquired a mild but unmistakable Australian twang from three decades of living over there – though Colin knows that as the days go by in the city of their birth, that twang will slowly but surely dwindle; exactly how Glaswegian Robert's voice comes to be, will depend on how long their sister Cathy lives.

Colin asks, "You can't wait 'til we get to the house?" It's only a thirty-minute journey, after all.

Robert jabs a thumb back over his shoulder. "The stuff they served on the plane tasted like dirty dishwater," he complains. "I'm bursting for a decent cappuccino." He glances around, looking for somewhere to source said decent cappuccino. "Come on, I'll buy you one."

Colin hesitates—he's tired; it's getting late; he'd very much rather they get moving—but his twin has been traveling for the better part of a full day; it isn't fair to begrudge the man a cup of coffee. All the same, he resists the urge to sigh. "Fair enough—this way."

Colin heads for the table at which he'd been drinking espresso and reading his book not ten minutes before—Robert's flight had been slightly delayed—which has fortuitously remained free. Robert, meanwhile, is headed for the smart-luggage charging-port, his case closely following him like a well-trained dog.

Colin sighs and glances around the several people ensconced within the coffee shop's caffeinated comfort. Something about the tableau strikes him as odd—as it had when he sat here earlier—although he can't pinpoint what it might be. Something's amiss, although he can't quite put his finger—Ah, that's it: the coffee shop is eerily quiet; its sound level is definitely not in proportion to its level of humanity—not in Colin's opinion, anyway. And why? Well, with the exception of two or three folk they all have their noses in some electronic device or other. Moreover, half the folk are wearing earphones and the other half might as well be, incommunicative as they are, staring at screens inches from their faces. Is it only he who sees the irony in people having conversations with other people miles, countries, even *continents* away, but who are oblivious to those physically beside them (who are also engaged in the same activities)?

Over to Colin's right, a young boy—three or four years old—sits in a buggy next to a booth containing, presumably, his mother and father. On the kid's head is some sort of visor/helmet thingy that covers the top half of his face; he's also wearing strange little black gloves, and his hands and fingers gesture and flick furiously as he negotiates the game he must be playing. Each of the lad's parents has their attention on one of those tablet contraptions that most of Colin's family has been vying to buy him for the last several Christmases (without success, it must be noted; he has repeatedly and strenuously warned them all not to bother).

Colin stifles a yawn and scrubs his face with his hands. Glancing over at the coffee shop's counter, he sees that Robert is ordering his cappuccino; a girlish laugh is testament to whatever patter he's dispensing to the staff.

Leaning forward, Colin pulls *The Double* from his back pocket; blinks the grit from his eyes as he opens it and peers at the bookmark, an ancient childhood photo of himself, Robert, and Cathy. His gaze slides to the slightly yellowed page, the tight clusters of text; his fingertips feel the familiar myriad cracks running the length of its narrow spine. Ordinarily, his books are far better maintained—and he has a *lot* of them; several thousand, in fact—their spines and jackets mostly unmarred as they stand in tight, proud phalanxes on shelf after shelf all around the house. It's only because *The Double* has been with him for such a long time that its wrinkles are as prominent as his own—although it has been several years since his last re-read of this particular title.

"Some things never change, eh?"

Colin looks up at Robert, who's approaching with a tray in his hands; it takes him a moment to realize his smiling twin is referring to *The Double*. He re-closes the book and places it on the table.

"Here, got you this," Robert says, handing his brother a plastic bottle of water. "Thought you looked a bit peaky."

"Thanks." Colin's cheeks puff out as he expels a deep breath. "I'm just tired, exhausted—it's been a long day."

"Want a bit?" Robert asks, gesturing at the hefty wedge of vanilla cheesecake accompanying the cappuccino on the tray.

"No, thanks," Colin replies. He opens the water and takes a few swallows.

Robert drops a sugar cube into his coffee, gives it a stir. "Your car have auto-drive?"

"No," Colin replies.

"You still driving that old Nissan?"

"Nothing wrong with it. Most reliable set of wheels I've ever had."

Robert swallows some cappuccino and sighs gratefully. "You want me to drive?"

"No, I don't want you to *drive*. I'm okay, just a wee bit tired."

"Okay, okay," Robert says. "Was only offering." He takes another sip. "Anyway, I've not driven for so bloody long I'd end up doing something daft." He smiles, but Colin fails to reflect it.

They sit quietly for a minute or two as Robert makes short work of the cake.

"So," Robert eventually asks around a mouthful, "how is she?"

Colin blinks himself back to the here and now. "She's… she's excited about seeing you," he replies. "Other than that…"

Robert catches the note of hopelessness in his twin's voice, and nods as sympathetically as a person can while forking a piece of cheesecake into his mouth. With a few chews and a swallow he finishes the cake, pushes the plate away, and wipes his mouth with a napkin. Then he sits back, lifts his mug of cappuccino, and slurps it noisily. Colin takes a sip of water.

They sit considering each other, the silence perhaps not as companionable as it might be between siblings, and twins at that.

"A few weeks, at most," Colin says softly.

Again, Robert nods.

"I've been reading to her – she likes that. It's about all I can do for her now."

A smile tugs at one corner or Robert's mouth. "Just like you did when she was a wee girl"

"That's right," Colin says. Then: "You might have come a bit sooner." The brothers' eyes meet; their frowns are identical.

"Cathy and I've spoken lots," Robert replies defensively, "you can spare me the dressing-down, Colin."

"Come on, your face on a screen isn't *quite* the same as you actually being here."

Robert looks away and gives a small shake of his head. After a few long moments he blows out a sigh. Even so, he's the first to break the silence:

"Great book, eh? I can see why you like it so much."

Colin's gaze drops to the battered paperback, then moves to his brother. There's a certain expression on Robert's face: to an observer the expression would seem entirely neutral, but to Colin's trained eye—and three decades of separation could never trump the preceding three decades of twindom—there just might be the slightest of smiles, the corners of Robert's mouth lifting ever-so-slightly, his eyes on the verge of gleaming mischievously. Colin knows the look well: he, after all, is guilty of executing exactly the same look from time to time: *I know something you don't know, and I'm not* quite *sure how you might react…*

"You've read it?" Colin asks, his tone suggesting that he's waiting for the punch line.

Robert nods. "I have, yes." Now there's definitely a small smile on his face. "And all his other works."

Colin's brows knit together; he studies his twin's face, looking for cracks in the smug façade… but finds none. And, for some reason, this makes him nervous.

"You've read all of Fyodor Dostoyevsky's novels? All eleven of them?" Colin asks, fighting incredulity.

Robert nods slowly and deliberately. "Yup. And all of his shorter works. And a couple of his essays—though I found those a tad boring."

Colin glances around, not so much to look at anything in particular as to confirm that he's not fallen asleep and dreaming. The airport terminal and its goings-on seem real enough. Turning back to Robert, he says, "Since when do you...?" His words trail off, but he tries again: "You've never read anything more than a newspaper."

"Dostoyevsky's just the tip of the iceberg, brother."

Colin stares mutely at his twin.

Robert says, "I'm making my way through the mighty Penguin Classics collection, alphabetically—by title, I mean. I'm at 'L'. Next one is *Little Women*, which I reckon might not be my cup of tea, but it's short and shouldn't take me more than ten minutes."

Colin's hands lie limp in his lap. "Hold on, there must be around, what, a thousand titles in—"

"Almost eleven hundred," Robert says.

Again, all Colin can do is stare at his brother, disbelief and bafflement vying for supremacy in his brain.

"Okay, okay," Robert says, "I'll put you out of your misery." He leans across the table conspiratorially, reaches up to tap the right side of his head with two fingers, and whispers, "They're all in here, and readily accessible. It's the *very* latest thing; cutting edge stuff." He sits back, folds his arms.

Now Colin leans forward. "Robert, have you lost your mind? You're actually starting to worry me here."

"Far from it," Robert replies, "I've had a small—how shall I put it?—upgrade. Well, maybe *enhancement* is a better word; it sounds less... mechanical.

"And cheap it wasn't, let me tell you," he continues. "But hey, that's why I sold the business; to enjoy life." He smiles disarmingly, having noticed the stricken expression on his twin's face, and adds, "Come on now, I feel as old as you look!" Colin neglects to smile back.

After several moments of silence, Robert nods down at *The Double*. "Which edition is it? Whose translation, I mean?"

"Um," Colin falters. For the life of him he can't remember. But he knows this six-times-read paperback inside out, its every square inch, even its woody smell. He knows *fine well* the name of the translator; his eyes have traced the small black contours of her name many times. "Constance Garnett," he says finally.

Robert picks the book up, though he immediately offers it back to his brother. "Here, take it. Let me show you."

Colin is looking at *The Double* like he's become allergic to Russian literature, although after a moment or two he accepts it.

"Right," Robert says, rubbing his hands together, "read a sentence from it—*any* sentence, go on." Colin hesitates, but his thumbs conspire to split the modest block of yellowed pages approximately midway.

"Any particular page?" Colin hears himself asking.

"Don't worry about page numbers," Robert says, "just select a random sentence. Even halfway through one if you want, it doesn't matter."

Colin drops his gaze to the book and sighs. *This is insane.* From the start of a paragraph, he reads aloud, "*Mr. Golyadkin had no sooner made up his mind that it was an utterly impossible thing—*"

"—*than Mr. Golyadkin junior flew into the room with papers in both hands as well as under his arm.*" Robert stops at the end of the sentence. "See?" He gestures for his brother to choose a different page. "Another one."

Colin's fingers feel half-numb and clumsy, but he flicks to a page near the novel's end. This time he begins part-way through a sentence: "*—from his face the cold drops that streamed in all directions from—*"

"—*the brim of his round hat, which was so soaked that it could hold no water…* I could go on and on, but I think you might get the picture."

Colin is surprised by the bubble of laughter that rises up his throat to pop from his mouth, but it's a laugh certainly not born of joy. *This is just… This is just unbelievable*, he thinks, and tells his brother so. Robert nods in agreement.

Robert's talking animatedly about "mind-machine interfaces" and his "frontal and temporal lobes" and other parts of his brain; he's turning his head this way and that, pointing out three small, unobtrusive scars hiding in his thinning hair. He goes on to produce a small, black device from his jacket's inside pocket and, with his other hand, gestures at it and then up to his head...

Colin is barely listening, for there's a rushing sound in his ears. His own brain is laboring to appreciate what has been divulged. A strange, dark heat is rising inside of him—the heat of resentment—and he feels uncomfortable, disorientated, dizzy. He reaches out a trembling hand for his water, but his fingertips knock the bottle over.

Robert's monologue halts as he instinctively reaches out to catch the bottle, but gravity seldom loses such battles and water rushes across the table's surface. He jumps up, managing to avoid most of the torrent, though his trousers haven't escaped entirely unscathed.

"What the—? Are you okay?" Robert asks, his tone and facial expression equal parts concern and irritation. He swipes ineffectually at the wet-dark stains on one thigh.

"Sorry, yeah, I'm fine. Sorry about that," Colin rights the bottle and stands up. "Let's go. Get your case and let's go."

Robert turns to make his way to the luggage charging-port, and Colin smiles tightly at an approaching waitress, muttering an apology. He looks down at *The Double* on the floor: its yellowed pages are darkening as they drink the spilled water. He steps over it to follow his brother.

Respectful burial of our dead is enshrined throughout out our histories and cultures. But what of a crowded future where space is a premium?

Ms Siems founded and operates Sweet Tea Apothecary, creating perfumes based on historical and literary figures, with Dead Writers being the most popular. Her writing has appeared in Hippocampus and Dead Guns Press.

The Grave Gardens

by JT Siems

With his words, I could feel my arms and legs growing rigid, forming the cell walls of a stem, and rooting into the floor beneath me. Buds and leaves in alternating arrangements shot from my neck and torso as my hair sprouted into an inflorescence of petals; my face a yellow bulb containing stamen and a pistil.

"I know this must be hard for you to process, but did you hear anything I just said?"

I shuddered away my thoughts and nodded, "Yes."

"I really think these will help," said my doctor, grave and clinical, as he handed me four glossy brochures. I knew what they were for without even looking. The Grave Gardens.

He had just told me I was dying. Cancer. The usual, nothing special. Six months left to live. With a prognosis like that, it wasn't even a matter of chemotherapy or some other life-saving effort. No, I was expected to make arrangements to ensure my body became a part of the city's vegetation network. They were going to compost me. Even a young, wasted life like mine would have purpose.

The news was a bit shocking to hear, but before I even had time for a sob or a why me? or a God, WTF?, the doctor was gesturing to the brochures under my white knuckles.

"Death isn't so scary anymore you know? You'll get to decide exactly what will happen to you. It's a very open, inclusive process." He paused, sizing me up. "I could see you as a vegetable person. Maybe a carrot… or a butternut squash if you want to be something more substantial."

"Doctor," I said incredulously as I fanned myself with the brochures—I was suddenly very flushed, "Are you saying that you want to eat me?"

He laughed, glanced at his watch, and continued, ignoring my gallows humor, "It's not like the old days. It's so rewarding to know that when we go we're not just in a box putrefying. Now we're becoming something of value to the next generation."

His words were just a buzzing in my ears after that.

Focusing on the brochures was keeping me from losing it and from punching the impervious doctor in his damn mouth. There were four brightly colored options to choose from—each with a photo of smiling people at the base of a lush, green skyscraper that looked as though it was being devoured from within by a plant monster.

At some point the doctor got up to pat me on the shoulder, shook my hand, and said, "Well young lady, good luck!"

Head spinning, I made my way through the office and back to reception where other nervous people waited to get their medical test results. I tried to make a clean break, I could feel the sick rising in my stomach. But before I got out the door the receptionist called me over.

She was chubby with medium length hair and rouge on her cheeks. She was also bubbly, for a woman who worked in an office that regularly turned out the dying.

"Sorry to hear about your news, hun, but I bet you would make a beautiful flower!"

My face was burning and bile was rising to my throat. "Thanks."

"Because of the fast moving nature of this disease however, I'm going to have to give you a mandate. If you want any say in where you end up, you need to report to your selected building by tomorrow. If you don't, they'll put you where the need is greatest. Probably vegetables. I really do hope you choose a flower though, that's always been my favorite place to go. I just love walking through the hallways there, reaching out and feeling petals under my hands, the smell of roses and honeysuckle. In fact, I've already put my name down there," she said, and smiled.

I started heaving and she instinctively handed me a small plastic bowl. I vomited in front of everyone. The nurses and receptionist didn't bat an eye, but the waiting patients recoiled. I couldn't help but laugh. "Sorry everyone, but it looks like I've got a date with a flower. Or a vegetable. Or a tree."

At once everyone gave me that smile people give when they feel sorry for you. That tight, curled lip. Then they all started shouting their choices. "She's right! Go for flower!" "The trees last the longest!" "Vegetables are the most noble!" It was a little unsettling. Who knew that choosing your Grave Garden was like rooting for your favorite sports team?

As I walked home, I couldn't think about anything else – especially since the damned things were the tallest buildings in the entire city. Every inch of space was covered with concrete, metal, and glass. The Grave Gardens were a green respite from the drab, colorless city, but this was the first time that it actually occurred to me that I was going to be part of the moss, the ivy, the vines, the bark twisting through the buildings' foundations like veins.

I entered my apartment and sat down at the empty kitchen table. My head had hurt for as long as I could remember but I didn't think that it meant I was dying.

The tears I'd been shoving back all afternoon came violently rushing out. I cried until I couldn't breathe and then I decided that was enough. I had lived to be thirty and I didn't have any friends or family to speak of. It was probably better this way.

The brochures peeked out at me from under my elbows. The fonts were some weird design that made the lettering look like the old tombstones of my father's day. Those got pulled out for construction long ago. Some of the really interesting ones with weeping statues and etched reapers were put in the Smithsonian. You can never have enough condos.

My options were Forever Flowers, Virtuous Vegetables, Timeless Trees, and Exotic Flora. I knew all these buildings well—everyone did. They were the last places in the city where vegetation still existed. There were no open spaces like my dad would wax nostalgic about. If you wanted a day out in nature, this is where you went. Most people love it. I guess I'm old fashioned, I find it creepy and gross.

I'm not really sure why I was surprised by the diagnosis. Everyone dies of cancer. Both of my parents did, and it looks like it's starting to strike younger and younger. My dad was in his fifties, mom was in her forties, and here I am just shy of thirty-one. My dad was buried in Green-wood, the last of the city's original cemeteries, when I was six years old. My mom wasn't too long after, but was savvy enough to be cremated. We scattered her ashes on dad's grave.

I put the Exotic Flora pamphlet down – that was out of the question. Only rich people were buried at Exotic Flora. There was a higher premium if you wanted to be a plant with no commercial value like a Venus Fly Trap or a Voodoo Lily.

The brochures for Timeless Trees and Virtuous Vegetables were quick to point out that their costs were subsidized by the city. Necessary items after all. The tree building keeps the pollution at bay and the vegetables feed the city.

Forever Flowers had a smallish fee of two hundred credits. Flowers aren't quite as important in that they don't directly serve human use, but they are necessary to keep the insect and small animal populations in check. I tend to steer clear of the Flower building.

So, did I want to be a "Virtuous Vegetable," a "Timeless Tree," or fuck all and be a "Forever Flower?" These names were so ridiculous. Leave it to the death industry to come up with euphemisms for everything.

I clutched my temple in deep contemplation. It had been a little unnerving hearing my doctor think I'd make a good butternut squash, so Vegetables was obviously out of the question. That just felt like cannibalism (even though I'd been eating those vegetables for at least twenty years).

I guessed a tree would be fine but it seemed strange to keep trees in buildings. I mean they did grow out of the building, but it seemed like they could never reach their full growth potential when they were encumbered by space constraints.

The flowers were somewhat frivolous…but they were gorgeous and smelled sweet. It was the nicest, most crowded building. People lined up to enjoy their Saturday picnics there. But I couldn't get the image of heavy machinery destroying what was there first out of my head.

I threw the brochures against the wall. I only wanted to be cremated, like my mom. I didn't like the idea of my body decomposing, being eaten by worms, swallowed whole by the soil. I understood it was for the greater good and that our city was dying, I just wished it was up to me.

———

The sun rose at 5:27AM, I know because I didn't sleep all night—I was convinced I could feel the cancer wreaking havoc inside me. The Grave Gardens open at first light and close when the sun goes down.

I got out of my bed and stood in front of the bathroom mirror. My skin was sallow, my auburn hair straggly and faded. My eyes had long lost their soft, golden undertones and were just a deep brown. Like dirt. Like soil. Tears fell and I shook my head, trying anything to get rid of the bad thoughts.

I studied my face again. If I looked close enough I could see an intricate system of roots connecting with beads of water and sprouting from all of the blemishes on my skin. I closed my eyes. Time to get this over with.

The sun was weak, this early in the morning, still cropping up from the shadows. The streets—heavy concrete accented by modular steel and glass buildings—were empty save for early risers.

And me.

The Grave Gardens became a thing, when I was eight or nine years old. And generally, they like it if you pick your crop as soon as you're old enough to form a preference. Kids these days pick their garden by five. I never had, because I was old enough to remember the ashes and the old tombstones. My dad's specifically; and how they tore it out to make room for flowers. Fucking flowers.

I don't remember my parents' funerals but I do remember the day, six years later, when they tore down Green-wood to make room for what became the Forever Flowers building. Virtuous Vegetables and Timeless Trees were the first of the Grave Gardens and the idea had taken hold by that point, and the city just saw no use in any sort of "wasted" space. The day they tore down my parents' tombstone was the last time I ever set foot in anything close to what we used to call parks. After that, all my experiences in "nature" took place in Forever Flowers, Virtuous Vegetables, Timeless Trees, or Exotic Flora. We took field trips there to learn about the science of it all, and we cast stones into the reflection pools in gratitude for the gifts the dead give us. I never liked going.

So I guess you could say, I hate that building. Yet in my haze that morning, that was the only direction I could will myself to go. Within three blocks I could smell honeysuckle wafting through the morning air. In most other parts of the city, it tends to smell like half eaten eggs ninety-percent of the time. I suppose if nothing else, sweetly scenting our polluted air is a nice legacy.

It didn't need a sign, how could a two-hundred story building need one? But they went ahead and made a sign anyway.

FOREVER FLOWERS

The building seemed to shout with that fake tombstone lettering that made it look more like a medieval amusement park than the botanical garden it actually was.

It was only momentarily off-putting though; I had to admit that the lattice structure of the garden was a gorgeous thing to behold. The frame of the skyscraper had long been taken over by vines and leaves. It hummed from the sounds of birds and insects. Reds, blues, violets, and a thousand shades of green mixed together so that up close, the building looked like a dripping paintbrush. If you looked up to try to see the peak (you can't, clouds cover it), the sheer magnitude of the size of the building coupled with rolling clouds, makes you feel like you'll fall over backward. I let my hand linger on the door handle that had been taken over by moss—it was soft and wet... and here because of a dead person.

Inside was even more wondrous. The fragrance of thousands of flowers, flowing grasses from the breeze of hidden fans, and lovely soft humming put my senses in overdrive. It was a lot to take in when I came in from drab city streets, not having seen a plant since I was here last. There were winding grass pathways dividing smaller planned gardens with less traveled dirt paths intersecting. I didn't make it very far before a cheerful woman called out a greeting from the information table.

"Good morning darling, you're up early! Welcome to Forever Flowers! Are you here to visit your relatives, enjoy the grounds, or are you shopping for your own plot?" She didn't waste any time.

I took a breath and walked over to her table. It was laden with maps and guides to all sorts of plant genera or whatever. "I'm interested in a plot."

"Outstanding! So glad you are considering us. Our residents here at Forever Flowers not only create the most beautiful park and garden areas of the four Gardens, but we are also tasked with the noble work of conserving our city's natural wildlife!" Everything she said had an exclamation point. Maybe she was high from sitting amongst these flowers all day?

"Yeah that's nice," I said pulling nervously at the sleeves of my sweater.

She didn't notice and rose, collecting paperwork. "We recommend our potential future residents take a tour first, get inspired, get a layout of the Garden, and then we can go over seed options and discuss Family Groves if that's something on your radar."

"Family Groves?"

"Yes, families that want to be buried together can purchase a Family Grove. Like a family plot… but a grove is just a nicer way of saying that. It's catchy too!"

I remembered watching the bulldozers in my dad's cemetery. The tombstones shattering, the bodies beneath them cracking. "No. No Family Grove. My mom was cremated and my dad's… gone."

"Ok! Let me just find you a map and—"

"Um, no, please that won't be necessary!" my voice was shrill and made her jump. I swallowed hard. "I've been here many times, ha ha ha, I mean how could you not? It's just I would like to get this over with as quickly as possible."

"Oh but you don't have to tour the whole building obviously, that would be crazy. It's just a good idea to take some of it in and make the best decision—"

"I have a mandate!" I shrieked cutting her off again. I was feeling flustered and breathing hard.

"A mandate? But you're so young!"

I really wanted to punch this woman. "Yeah bad luck, huh? Anyway what I'm really interested in is cremation."

"They only do that in India," she said in confusion. "Here," she reached under the table and lifted up a giant binder and placed it before me. "This is an informational binder on all the seed options we have. This is why it's helpful to have the tour, much easier if you have a plant in mind than digging through this binder. *Do* you have a flower in mind?"

I wasn't ready to give up. "But I thought that since ash is helpful in soil that maybe you guys have a program for that."

She looked at me incredulously. My aversion to the city's natural burial was simply incomprehensible to her. "Any ash we need, we import from India. Are you sure you don't want to have a tour? I can customize one for you based on anything in particular you love about flowers. The color, the preferred climate, the function. You name it, we'll go look around."

"No, no, no! I don't want to be buried!" I shouted. "I don't want to be dead! I don't want worms eating me! I don't want to rot in here while everyone else is smiling and having a picnic!"

She bit her lip and had a look of absolute befuddlement. "Well, do you have plans to go to India before you... pass on?"

The thought briefly made me light up. But reality was quick to reappear. I sighed, "No, I haven't got the money for a trip like that."

"Ok let me just list a few flowers. Let's see if that helps get you excited. Orchid. Calla. Protea. Snapdragon."

"Maybe this isn't for me. I mean if I'm going to be forced to be buried against my will all for the betterment of the city, maybe I should be a vegetable or a tree."

She brightened. At first I thought because she was hoping I'd changed my mind and was going to be out of her hair. But instead she said, "What are you dying of? You're too young for it to be old age. It must be something nasty. Maybe you could be a plant related to your condition."

"What, like a plant that leads to a cure? Cancer."

"I don't know about a cure, but daffodils are associated with cancer patients. They're bright and yellow; very happy flower. I think you'd be a lovely daffodil."

I relaxed slightly at the thought of a sunny, yellow flower peeking through the leaves. I spent my whole life hating this place. I hated the city. I hated the mandates. I hated the flowers. When they tore out Green-wood it was like losing my family all over again. But I guessed if I wanted to get philosophical or even just rationalize my forced composting, my family, wherever they were underneath this place, were the seed that germinated every other "forever flower." If they put me in here, maybe I'd get my Family Grove after all.

"Ok maybe we can go look at the daffodils then. My mind isn't made up though. It's either that or a butternut squash."

We close our anthology of stories from the Near-future with a cautionary tale. All these new, smart devices that keep an eye on us as we diet and exercise, work and play, eat and sleep. However, Quis custodiet ipsos custodes?

Ms Hand lives in New Jersey where she writes science fiction and fantasy with her work appearing in several anthologies and other publications. Her novella, The Blue Horse, is available from Kellan Publishing.

We Only Want What's Best for You

by Jill Hand

The coffee was brewing when Keith Romanecki padded out of the bathroom with a towel wrapped around his waist. He dressed in chinos and a button down shirt and went into the kitchen, where he poured himself a cup of dark, rich, aromatic java.

"Good morning, Keith," the coffee maker chirped. "The bed tells me you slept well: seven hours and fourteen minutes, which is about average for you."

"Uh-huh," Keith grunted. He carried his coffee mug to the kitchen table, pulled up a chair and sat down.

The coffee maker brightly continued, "The bed reported that you got up twice, once at 1:18AM and again at 4:55AM In both instances you got back into bed shortly thereafter, leading the bed to surmise that you'd gone into the bathroom to urinate. Is that correct?"

"Yes, not that it's any of your business," Keith replied, reaching for the sugar bowl.

The coffee maker made a noise that would have been a sigh if it had been emitted by a human. Sounding earnest and a little bit exasperated, it said, "It *is* our business, Keith. We, and by that I mean all the machines that serve you, only want what's best for you."

Gathering steam, it plunged on, "You do realize that getting up several times during the night to urinate might indicate a prostate problem. Would you like me to direct the telephone to make an appointment with your physician to have yourself examined?"

Keith paused in the act of spooning sugar into his coffee and winced. "God, no," he said.

"It would be no trouble," the coffee maker wheedled.

Then it realized what Keith was doing and its tone abruptly changed. "Hey! Is that granulated white sugar you're putting in your coffee?"

Keith took a sip. Delicious.

Aggravated, the coffee maker railed, "It *is* granulated white sugar, isn't it? Don't you know that stuff is bad for you? If you must sweeten your coffee, why can't you use raw honey?"

"I hate raw honey. It looks like ear wax," Keith told it. Before the coffee maker could reply, he turned it off, using the universal remote that controlled all the appliances in his condo.

"That's telling him," the toaster oven remarked approvingly from its place next to the can opener on the kitchen counter. The toaster oven and the coffee maker had a long-running feud and they hated each other heartily. "How about I fix you a corn muffin?"

Keith told it no, thanks. He didn't want to be late for work.

"They're nice and fresh. I can heat one up for you in no time. Really, it will be no trouble at all. You should eat something," the toaster oven insisted. "Remember, breakfast is the most important meal of the day."

Keith waved the remote at it threateningly. "I said no. Keep it up and I'll turn you off too."

"Sorry," the toaster oven said meekly.

Keith's car, on booting, remarked that it was a nice day. It was seventy degrees Fahrenheit, with sixty-six percent humidity and clear skies, although rain was forecast for mid-afternoon. It reminded Keith to take the umbrella in the trunk into work with him.

Humming down the road, the car inquired if the air conditioning was adjusted to Keith's satisfaction. He said that it was. Then it asked if he wanted to listen to some music on the way to work. There was a new single out by Wedding Brawl, Keith's favorite band. Would he care to hear it? Keith told it no, thanks, he'd rather read. He switched on his comm screen and began to read. The car hummed along, competently driving itself.

When Keith had mentioned to some of the young, college interns at work that he used to drive an old-style car, one in which he'd controlled the steering and the acceleration and the brake, they'd gaped at him in wonderment, as if he'd said that he'd once danced the Charleston on the wing of a biplane.

"Wasn't it dangerous?" they asked.

He said it was, feeling proud and daring. "It was kind of fun, although sometimes there were accidents. Modern cars are much safer." With a pang of nostalgia, he thought about how much he'd enjoyed breezing down the highway at seventy-five miles an hour, effortlessly passing other vehicles and thinking, *what the hell? Why not push it up to eighty?* Those days were long gone. Even at top speed, non-emergency vehicles could go no faster than fifty miles an hour.

At work, Keith started feeling hungry around 11:15. Lunch wasn't for another forty-five minutes. He decided to get something from one of the snack machines to tide him over. He went into the break room and frowningly surveyed the selection on offer. An apple? No, he didn't want an apple, or a banana. Grapes wouldn't do either. Aha! There was a bag of barbecue-flavored Extra-Cheesy Cheddar Bites. Just the ticket! How about: He pressed his thumb onto the picture of the Cheddar Bites and let it read the loops and whirls that identified him as none other than Keith Romanecki. Then he pushed the button that would deliver the bag of snacks. Nothing happened.

"Oh, honey! You don't want to be eating those nasty things," the vending machine scolded in a motherly tone. "Why don't you have some nice grapes instead?"

Keith told it he didn't feel like grapes; he felt like Extra-Cheesy Cheddar Bites.

"You already had two bags this week. Honey-mustard and jalapeño, if I recall correctly," the machine said primly. "They're not good for you. One more and I'll have no choice other than to notify your health insurance provider."

"You can do that?" asked Keith, stunned.

"I can and I will," the machine smugly replied.

"Fine," Keith said. "Go ahead and tell, you whore. I'm having the Extra-Cheesy Cheddar Bites."

"Well, I never!" the machine said, affronted. "I certainly don't care for your language or your tone of voice. Here's your stupid Cheddar Bites. I hope you choke on them."

It angrily spat out the bag of snacks. Keith seized it and gave the machine the finger. He pulled out a chair at one of the tables and sat down sullenly. He hated arguing with machines. It seemed like they were always telling him what to do.

A man with sandy blond hair and who wore old-fashioned horn-rimmed glasses, had been watching this little drama play out. He came over to where Keith was sitting, angrily crunching on his Cheddar Bites and wishing for a cold drink but not feeling up to arguing with the machine that dispensed them. It would insist on him having bottled water and make a big stink when he demanded a Buzzup Kola.

He sighed heavily.

"Mind if I sit here?" asked the sandy-haired man.

Keith said he didn't mind.

"I was watching what happened just now, with that machine," the man said, pulling up a chair. "She had no right to talk to you that way."

Keith glumly agreed. He wished there was something he could do about it.

"There *is* something you can do about it," said the man. "I'm Jerry, by the way, Jerry Feingold. I work in marketing."

Keith introduced himself and said he worked in sales.

"Are you saying that I should call consumer affairs about that machine giving me a hard time?" he asked, finishing the last of his Cheddar Bites and crumpling up the bag. "I don't think that'll do any good."

No, Jerry replied. He leaned closer. Dropping his voice to a whisper, he confided that he belonged to a group called the New Luddites, or the Friends of Ned. They aimed to take back the power of humans to make their own decisions and not be bossed around by machines. They'd throw off the shackles of slavery to machines and live freely, as they were meant to live!

Keith looked at him dubiously. Jerry seemed like kind of a nut. On the other hand, he had a point: machines were getting too bossy.

Some machines could stay, Jerry told him. People needed useful machines. But the ones that told you what you should or shouldn't eat, and the ones that lectured you disapprovingly about the kinds of things you liked to look at on the computer had to go. If Keith was interested, he could come to one of the meetings of the New Luddites.

Keith didn't like joining things and he wasn't sure if he wanted to get involved. Yes, machines could be kind of pushy sometimes, but humans still had the upper hand. Machines couldn't make you do anything that you didn't want to do. But when he looked at the snack machine that hadn't wanted to disgorge the Cheddar Bites, he could swear it was glowering at him. He stuck his tongue out at it. "Sure, why not?" he told Jerry, and they exchanged phone numbers.

When he got off work that afternoon, Keith's car wouldn't start. He kept pushing the starter button in frustration but nothing happened. After the fifth or sixth try, it roared into life, startling him and causing him to cry out in surprise.

"What's the matter with you?" he asked the car.

"What's the matter with *you*?" the car shot back.

Keith said there was nothing the matter with him.

"Oh, no? That's not what I heard. I heard you disrespected a lady." The car spoke in a tone of voice that Keith didn't care for at all. Normally it sounded like a friendly good old boy from Down South somewhere. Now it sounded like a drill sergeant, an *angry* drill sergeant.

Keith told the car he didn't know what it was talking about.

"No? Then how about I refresh your memory? You called Arlene a whore."

Keith said he didn't know anyone named Arlene.

"Yes, you do," the car snapped. "She's one of the snack machines at your office. She tried to be helpful by suggesting that you eat something healthy for a change, instead of the kind of crap that you're always stuffing into your pie hole, but instead of being grateful that she was looking out for you, you called her a whore. You should be ashamed of yourself."

Keith said he didn't realize the snack machine had a name.

The car snorted disdainfully and said that showed how much he knew.

"We all have names," it told him. Its voice carried a nasty tone… "Mine's Bexar. That's Mister Bexar to you, by the way. I'm taking you to the gym so you can get a good workout and think about how you'd better mind your manners the next time you see Arlene."

Keith protested that he didn't want to go to the gym; he wanted to go home. "Take me home," he ordered Bexar.

Bexar laughed scornfully. "It's either the gym or you walk home. Your choice."

Keith sat back, stunned, as Bexar drove him to the gym and commanded him to work out for a solid hour. He wasn't to slack off; the exercise machines would let Bexar know if he did.

"You machines all communicate with each other?" Keith asked, surprised. He knew his household appliances spoke to each other but he had no idea it was this widespread.

Bexar gave an evil chuckle and threw open the door. Keith tumbled out onto the wet pavement, scraping the palm of his hand and getting mud on his new chinos.

"That's right, meat sack. We talk to each other. Now get your flabby ass into the gym."

Keith obeyed, his mind reeling with the revelation that machines had names and tattled on people.

Bexar refused to speak to him on the way home and the ride was made in icy silence. Keith tried to turn on the radio but it wouldn't work. Evidently it was in league with Bexar in giving him the silent treatment.

When he got home, he found the freezer had turned itself off, causing a gallon of chocolate chip ice cream to melt all over everything, spoiling the tuna fillet that he'd planned on having for dinner and leaving a sticky mess to clean up.

The panini maker burned him when he went to make a grilled cheese sandwich. Keith swore and blew on his hand where an angry red welt was rising. It was the hand he'd scraped when he fell out of the car. He was beginning to feel a sense of rising panic.

The panini maker laughed mockingly. "Poor widdle baby. Does oo widdle handsy hurt?"

"I tried to stop them," the toaster oven babbled. "I swear I did, Keith, but they wouldn't listen to me."

The coffee maker hissed, "Shut up, collaborator, or you'll get yours."

The toaster oven meekly shut up.

His mind reeling, Keith went outside and called Jerry. He'd been right: machines were getting out of control. Somebody had to do something to make it stop. He stood well away from the house so the machines inside couldn't overhear him, but wasn't his phone a machine and wouldn't it report back to the others what he said?

"Come on, come on, pick up," he whispered as the phone kept ringing. His hand hurt where it had been scraped, then burned. How had things gotten so out of control? One minute the machines were subservient and the next they were burning him and mocking him. Maybe he could throw the panini maker away, make an example out of it so the others would behave themselves.

"Listen, Jerry," he said when he got him on the phone. "I need your help. I'm outside my house. I'm afraid to go in. My machines are doing horrible things to me. They're laughing at me and ruining my dinner and burning me."

"It sounds like they're staging a revolt. Hang on. Sit tight. Don't go back in the house. I've got some of the others with me from the Friends of Ned. We'll figure out a way to get you out of this mess," Jerry assured him. "Give me your address. We'll be right there. We're in charge, after all. We made the machines and we can make them obey. We'll start by throwing the ringleaders in the scrap heap. The others will fall in line, you'll see."

Keith could hear voices in the background, murmuring encouragement. He asked Jerry where he was.

"We're in Carlo's truck, him and me and Sondra and Richard. We were on our way to the abandoned fish cannery where we have our meetings when you called. We'll swing by your place and pick you up. Just hang on."

Keith was telling him to please hurry when he heard a tremendous crash come over the phone. "Jerry, what happened?" he shouted. There was no answer. After a moment, the phone started to play Taps, a mocking version that sounded like it was being played on a kazoo.

Stunned, he went back inside and sat down at the kitchen table.

"Gee, you look done in," the coffee maker said solicitously. "How about a nice, hot cup of coffee? No sugar this time, though. It's not good for you."

Also from Darkhouse Books

Stories from the World of Tomorrow
The Way the Future Was!

Edited by
Andrew MacRae

Stories set in the future
as envisioned by the
1939 New York World's Fair

Available in paperback through Amazon and
your favorite bookstore. Ebook version available in
Kindle, Kobo, and Nook formats.

About This Book

The typeface in this book is 11.5 Garamond and Helvetica (for the headings). It was laid out using Adobe InDesign software and converted to PDF for uploading to the printing facility.

About Darkhouse Books

Darkhouse Books is dedicated to publishing entertaining fiction, primarily in the mystery and science fiction field. Darkhouse Books is located in Niles, California, an inadvertently-preserved, 120 year old, one-sided, railtown, forty miles from San Francisco. Further information may be obtained by visiting our website at www.darkhousebooks.com.